THE FABER BOOK OF DIARIES

Edited by Simon Brett

THE FABER BOOK OF USEFUL VERSE
THE FABER BOOK OF PARODIES

The Faber Book of
DIARIES

Edited by
Simon Brett

faber and faber
LONDON · BOSTON

First published in 1987 by
Faber and Faber Limited
3 Queen Square London WC1N 3AU

Photoset by Wilmaset Birkenhead Wirral
Printed in Great Britain by
Mackays of Chatham Ltd Kent
All rights reserved

British Library Cataloguing in Publication Data

Brett, Simon, 1945–
The Faber book of diaries
1. English diaries
I. Title
828'.03'08   PR1330

ISBN 0–571–13806–3

Contents

Introduction

There are so many diaries, and their content is so rich, that it is almost impossible to produce a definitive anthology. The best one can hope for is to present an entertaining selection and, since the anthologist's ultimate criterion for inclusion must be that he himself likes the item, this collection will inevitably reflect my own interests. Private life is more attractive to me than public life and, though great events are mentioned in these pages, the emphasis is on the diarist's reaction to them rather than on the events themselves. There are comments on the universal human experiences – birth, death, love, illness, hypochondria, wealth, poverty, joy, depression – the great sweeping changes of mood familiar to all of us.

My particular interest is in the creative process, the excitement of a new idea, the pain when it doesn't work, and the huge feeling of relief which attends completion, so charmingly expressed by George Eliot on 16 November 1858:

> Wrote the last word of *Adam Bede* and sent it to Mr Langford. *Jubilate*.

With regard to politics, I'm afraid I share the view expressed by Henry Edward Fox in his journal entry for 23 July 1820:

> Every day I am more and more persuaded not to meddle in politicks; they separate the best friends, they destroy all social intercourse. And why? Is it for power? Is it for popularity? How unenviable they are separately! How seldom you see them combined; and most politicians have neither.

So, though there are extracts from political diaries, they all concern the personal rather than the professional lives of their writers. This is partly because of my lack of interest in the subject, but also because politicians and the issues which preoccupy them are so quickly forgotten that most political extracts would have to be supported by vast scaffoldings of explanations and footnotes.

Which brings me to the way I have compiled this book.

One of my beliefs about anthologies is that they should be easy to read. And, though notes and footnotes are essential and fascinating in an academic work, I don't think they have any place in this sort of book. I therefore decided to restrict myself to entries that were self-explanatory. Basic information about the diarists quoted is contained in the notes at the end, and I have only included other explanatory details (in square brackets) where I feel they are essential to the reader's understanding of the entry in question. In other instances, the relationship of the diarist to the supporting cast of spouses, lovers, children and friends is either evident from the context or irrelevant to the appreciation of the entry.

Having taken that decision, I had drastically limited the choice of entries available. Even so, I soon realized that I had to impose further limitations on my selection if I was going to produce a manageable volume. All the research I did served to confirm the huge amount of material available; the more I read, the more I became aware of other diaries that I wanted to read.

I then decided to restrict my selection to the works of English diarists writing in the British Isles, and to exclude travel diaries, military diaries and purely topographical reporting. This rule obviously led to some strange omissions; it excluded the travels of William Dyott's early life, Nicholas Cresswell's accounts of his time in America, the Reverend William Cole's Paris journal and many others. At least I had an intention from which to deviate, and, as with all the best rules, it was no sooner made than broken.

I found, for example, that some of the liveliest introspections from Byron's journal were written in Italy, but there was no way I was going to leave those out! I included extracts from Katherine Mansfield, although I knew she was a New Zealander. And I couldn't resist the wartime London diaries of Charles Ritchie, even though he is Canadian.

The next question was how I defined a diary. For me, it has to be a daily record, written on the day of the events it describes, or very soon after. It must have the immediate appeal that Charles Ritchie identified when, as a boy, he wrote: 'I prefer diaries to memoirs. They are less made up afterwards.'

A diary rarely has the polish of professional writing, although some diarists clearly wrote with enormous care and with a view to publication. But the occasional roughness is part of the charm. A diary entry should glow with the immediacy of reaction (even if the diarist subsequently revises his opinion of what he has written).

I should also mention that I have excluded fictional diaries. Much as I admire Mr Pooter, I'm afraid this isn't the book for him. Nor would I allow in the thinly disguised Barbellion. Lovers of Adrian Mole will, I'm afraid, also be disappointed – though they may feel adequately compensated by entries like this from the adolescent diaries of Sydney Moseley:

JUNE 30th, 1905 – The chemist said that the pimples on my face have come because I am growing into manhood. Whilst others tell me to go with a woman! Many people hold such views and I feel ashamed.

I seem to inspire Loretta as she inspires me. She has left off wearing corsets because I convinced her it is bad for a girl's health.

Having formulated my fragile ground-rules for the selection of entries, I was faced with the problem of organizing the material. Anthologies are not books to be read from beginning to end; they are books to be dipped into, to be savoured at leisure, and it is the anthologist's duty to come up with a format that makes this kind of reading both possible and enjoyable.

As my collection of suitable entries grew, I experimented with various methods of layout. I quickly rejected the dire predictability of year-by-year chronology. I tried categorizing the material by subject matter, filing entries under 'Spiritual Life', 'Weather Reports', 'Illness', 'Sex', and so on. But I found that almost every entry deserved its own heading and, rather than helping the reader, the expanding categorization would only serve to confuse. I toyed with breaking the material down by the professions of diarists – 'Clergymen', 'Writers', 'Courtiers', 'Politicians', but I soon ran into the same problem.

Then I had the idea of laying out the anthology like a diary. The more I thought about it, the more attractive the idea became. First, it was apposite. Second, it gave the book a finite shape and size. Given such a massive field for research, the latter point was particularly important. I now had a structure into which I could fit what eventually turned out to be about fourteen hundred entries.

Finally, the diary format offered a pleasingly random element. It was likely to throw up what for me are the greatest joys of anthologies – serendipitous juxtapositions of material.

So I gave it a try, and reorganized the entries I had already selected into this new day-by-day scheme. Suddenly, the book made sense. The unlikely juxtapositions I had hoped for started to appear. Some entries stood up on their own; others (like James Boswell's affair and painful disillusionment with Louisa in January 1763 or the continuing saga of Elias Ashmole's health in August 1684) could be followed through as a serial from day to day.

I bought a large desk calendar and marked rings round the dates as each day's entries were completed. Very slowly the anthology's year filled. January, March and December fleshed out quickly; July and August remained thin at first. My excitement grew as the blanks became fewer and fewer, until, at last, I circled the final date, which, as it happens, was 8 December.

My selection of material completed, I was left with two strong impressions. The first of the amazing versatility of a diary, the variety of roles it can fulfil. It can serve as confessional or as apologia. It can be used to colour reality or to vent spleen. It can be a bald record of facts or a Gothic monument of prose. It can chart the conquests of a libertine or the seesawing emotions of a depressive. It can chronicle the aspirations of youth and the disillusionments of age. For a painter it can be a detailed notebook, for a writer an experimental canvas.

There is also great variety in the tones of voice used by the diarists and the images of themselves that they wished to project. Very few seem to be completely unselfconscious; all have the thought of a reader somewhere at the back of their minds. Even Pepys, whose diary was concealed in shorthand, demonstrated this by his coy lapses into foreign languages for his sexual escapades.

Like all writers, diarists are selective. They choose what they think is worth recording, and so this choice is obviously an indication of their character. For Colonel Peter Hawker the number of wildfowl he had shot was important; for B. R. Haydon, the number of hours he had worked; for Arnold Bennett, his word-count and the amount of money it had made for him.

Omissions are also significant. For some, emotional traumas are too painful to record. Writing about it can increase stress, particularly when yesterday's assessment stares up from the diary page as the writer tries to analyse today. It is significant, for example, that no diary survives of the breakdown of Evelyn Waugh's first marriage and his conversion to Catholicism.

For other diarists, formal recording of painful events was a necessary therapy. Queen Victoria's unflinching description of Prince Albert's death on 14 December 1861 is an example of this, as is John Evelyn's apparently dispassionate but moving description of his dead son's accomplishments on 27 January 1658. And there can be few bleaker sentences in literature than Mary Shelley's entry for 6 March 1815: 'Find my baby dead.'

The diary also has an identity – even a personality – of its own, and is frequently addressed by the writer. This can be seen at its most coy in Fanny Burney's commencement of her juvenile journal on 27 March 1768, but the 'Dear Diary' approach occurs in many other forms.

Another use of a diary is for reference, assessment of the diarist's progress or even, as in this entry by Evelyn Waugh, of the progress of his children:

FEBRUARY 13th, 1956 – In the hope of understanding Bron better I read the diaries I kept at his age. I was appalled at the vulgarity and priggishness.

A diary can also be a conscience, as Rev W. J. Temple observed on 29 February 1796:

> Strange that I have not begun my Papers. A Journal is certainly of use: at least it lets us see how little we do, and how difficult it is to carry good resolutions into effect. Every week, for some time past, I have intended to begin upon these Papers, yet have not.

For a writer, of course, a diary can be a wonderful medium of experiment, a place to try out phrases and descriptions, possibly a source for future writing. In this anthology there are many entries from writers who seem incapable of writing badly, notably Virginia Woolf, Denton Welch and J. R. Ackerley. Yet writing in a diary is more relaxed than the discipline of writing fiction. As Denton Welch wrote on 27 February, 1948:

> In Gide's Journal I have just read again how he does not wish to write its pages slowly as he would the pages of a novel. He wants to train himself to rapid writing in it. It is just what I have always felt about this journal of mine. Don't ponder, don't grope – just plunge something down, and perhaps more clearness and quickness will come with practice.

Virginia Woolf recorded a similar benefit on 1 November, 1924:

> As I think, this diary writing has greatly helped my style; loosened the ligatures.

One thing all diary writers have in common is that for them the diary is essential. The discipline of daily recording is considerable, and no one would do it if they didn't feel they had to. I write as someone who has kept a more or less continuous diary for over three decades, and, having immersed myself in so many great examples of the genre over the last few years, I realize what a dull document mine is. But that realization doesn't stop me from keeping up the daily record. I share the compulsion of all the writers quoted in this book. The motivation varies enormously, but the urge is the same. Maybe, at its simplest, diary-writing is a personal way of imposing some kind of order on the chaos of the world around us.

I'm sure all diarists would echo what Lord Byron wrote on 6 December, 1813:

This journal is a relief. When I am tired – as I generally am – out comes this, and down goes everything.

The second impression I received from my researches was a strong sense of the identities of the individual diarists. Though the voices they use are frequently disguised, I can always recognize the people behind them.

In almost every case, after reading two or three entries, I found that I had formed an impression of the writer. I could feel the bluff, harmless conceit of Colonel Peter Hawker, the warm good nature of Elizabeth Fremantle, the paralysing self-doubt of William Windham. I knew that I wouldn't get on with the constant whingeing of George Gissing; I was surprised to find that I would enjoy the company of William Dyott; I could sense that the Reverend John Skinner had no common touch and was an object of derision amongst his parishioners. Each diary I read gave me a very personal introduction to another person, opened a casement on to another life. I hope that this selection, like a huge Advent calendar, opens many such casements for its readers.

I would like to thank the many people who shared their enthusiasms for particular diarists with me, especially Frank Muir, Benjamin Whitrow and Alex Auswaks. I am grateful to the staffs of the London Library and the British Library, to Mary Holtby for her research assistance, and to Rosamund Connelly for her help with the biographical notes on the diarists. And anyone dealing with diaries must also owe a great debt of gratitude to the late Arthur Ponsonby's studies of the subject.

I must pay tribute to the diarists themselves for their infinitely rich legacy. But most of all, my thanks go to the enormous army of editors, past and present, whose painstaking research and dedication means that that legacy is available to the common reader. And I hope that this anthology, as all anthologies should, will give a taste of the riches available, and send its readers back to the full texts of the works quoted.

SIMON BRETT
July, 1986

1 January

1785 Whether this be the last or no, may it be the best year of my life!

John Wesley

1832 Sunday. I suppose I must go on here with my diary – as I cant get another book.

This is the first day of a new year; and I am not in the humour for being wished a happy one. Into thy hands oh God of all consolation, into thy merciful hands which chastise not willingly I commit the remains of my earthly happiness; and Thou mayest will that from these few barley loaves & small fishes, twelve basketfuls may be gathered.

My heart sinks within me – but not when I think of Thee! – Lord gracious & merciful, teach me to think of thee more often, & with more love –

Elizabeth Barrett

1841 A fresh year has opened, with its work. Was introduced to E. Seccombe's first born now four days old. No reason was *visible* for placing it higher than that which it most resembled, raw beef, with one exception, viz. that it was *dressed*. It is difficult to look on such little animals and honestly believe that there are souls inside of them.

Barclay Fox

1850 Cold, & foggy, & dismal the New Year opens. I pray most earnestly that I may never see the commencement of another. May I soon, very soon, lie in that grave where lie my Joys & Recollections! I am heart sick of everything, & long only for that peace which is nowhere but in the grave.

Edward Leeves

1915 What a vile little diary! But I am determined to keep it this year.

Katherine Mansfield

1980 'Another year ... another deadly blow' – so Wordsworth, but not so me. I enjoyed 1979 and expect to enjoy 1980 – my 70th on earth and my fourth as President of the Royal Academy (RA Presidential elections for the next year are held every December, and I have been about two weeks in office).

Resolutions? Two. First, to keep up this diary. My last attempt – a failure – was when, aged 11, I exchanged Charles Letts' School Boys'/Girls' Diaries for Christmas with my cousin Angela. After I had completed the personal particulars – size of collar ... size of boots ... hobbies – I gave up. Angela persisted for one day. Her entry remains vividly in my memory. 'Shoped in morning', it read. 'Sick in afternoon'. Second resolution? To try not to cheat. Even in the Charles Letts days I had not been totally honest: my size in boots was accurate (it was written inside them), but my hobby was not in fact 'carpentry'. I hated it. But on the page it looked boyish. At the time I was sensitive about my small size, my tendency to faint before breakfast, and my timidity, and I was guilty, I fear as always, of a wish to please. So I resolve to stick to what happens and not to drag in more interesting events of previous years to make for better reading. Dull or enjoyably uneventful days exist and will be noted.

Hugh Casson

2 January

1710 My Dear Daughter Bettey refus'd to speak French with Mrs Keen; & I taking it unkindly from her, she fell into Tears, & continued grieving in that way even after she came home, so long that I was doubtful of her hurting her Constitution: & upon her being sorry for Refusing what was desir'd from her & promising it should be otherwise another time, I forgave her & she was extremely pleas'd with the reconciliation.

Dr Claver Morris

1931 This is the turn of the tide. The days are lengthening. Today was fine from start to finish – the first we have had, I think, since we came. And for the first time I walked my Northease walk & saw the moon ride at 3, pale, very thin, in a pure blue sky above wide misty flattened fields, as if it were early on a June morning.

Here are my resolutions for the next 3 months; the next lap of the year.

First, to have none. Not to be tied.

Second, to be free & kindly with myself, not goading it to parties: to sit rather privately reading in the studio.

To make a good job of *The Waves*.

To care nothing for making money.

As for Nelly [cook-housekeeper], to stop irritation by the assurance that nothing is worth irritation: if it comes back, she must go. Then not to slip this time into the easiness of letting her stay.

Then – well the chief resolution is the most important – not to make resolutions. Sometimes to read, sometimes not to read. To go out yes – but stay at home in spite of being asked. As for clothes, I think to buy good ones.

Virginia Woolf

1978 [Barlinnie Prison] 3.14 a.m. I've been wakened for over an hour, am irritable and restless. The Radio Clyde disc jockey is speaking to people in their homes via telephone. I get the atmosphere of home parties from it. Pop music is blasting in my ears and I marvel at radio and how it must comfort lonely people. It's almost as though it's reassuring me I'm not alone. 3.55 a.m. One of these days I won't be 'still here'. It's amazing how difficult I find it to think of myself being anywhere else.

Jimmy Boyle

3 January

1645 A most tedious snowy day: the greatest snow in my memory all wayes made even impassable, God good to mee at night in the society of divers loving freinds abroad.

The Reverend Ralph Josselin

1899 As I approach the grand climacteric of 35 there is the usual, perhaps inevitable feeling that more ought to have been done, much more. But I am getting to feel . . . that it is my function to read more than to write, to judge more than to do, to enjoy rather than to create. And if I believe, as I certainly do, that the existence of a class of cultivated, intelligent people is of vital importance to a country, I may surely accept this as my part and not wish for a more ambitious or more obviously useful one . . . If one thinks what a difference in the tone of English Society would be produced if one could multiply by a hundred the people who have seriously cultivated a turn for literature and art, one cannot but realize that one has a useful part to play.

John Bailey

1949 Burgo and I have begun acting *Henry VI Part I* on the model theatre. He has become a stickler for detail: dead soldiers (lead) lay before the walls of Orleans, while the plasticine corpse of Henry V was draped in a white shroud. Sometimes I see the miniature world with such infatuated eyes that the delusion takes over and becomes real.

Ralph is up in the library writing something about human credulity, a subject that has always fascinated him – and me too. At dinner we talked of various irrational beliefs: in ghosts, Father Christmas, etc. Burgo thought that when people believed they had seen a ghost, it was really a symbol of fear, and that fear was the worst thing one could be afraid of, so it was really better they should believe in ghosts – rather good, I thought.

Frances Partridge

4 January

1831 A base gloomy day and dispiriting in proportion. I walk out with Swanston for about an hour, everything gloomy as the back of the chimney when there is no fire in it. My walk was a melancholy one, feeling myself weaker at every step and not very able to speak. This surely cannot be fancy yet it looks some thing like it. If I knew but the extent at which my inability was like to stop, but every day is worse than another. I have trifled much time, too much. I must try to get afloat tomorrow; perhaps getting an amanuensis might spur me on for one half is nerves. It is a sad business though.

Walter Scott

1837　A mild, calm day. Off at sea from morning till the afternoon, and then in the creeks with my new punt, which answers beautifully. Brought home 19 wigeon and 4 geese; 15 the first shot, 4 the second shot; and the geese with the shoulder gun from a creek, where I had to launch and then crawl for an hour. I never had such a filthy, laborious job, and never in my life made so long a shot with a shoulder gun. There were five punts and boats innumerable off in the mirror calm, but not a bird did any of them get, except, I believe, 'nabbing' a few of my cripples.

Colonel Peter Hawker

1944　John Betjeman lunched with me at Brooks's, the first time since the war. He seemed to enjoy himself, jumping up and down in his chair and snapping his fingers, in laughter. He is sweeter and funnier than anyone on earth. He never changes, is totally unselfconscious, eccentric, untidy and green-faced. He works at the Ministry of Information and simply hates it, returning every Saturday till Monday to Uffington. In his *Daily Herald* articles he surreptitiously damns the war and progress, and the left wing. Talked about the slave state in which we are already living. Said he loved Ireland but not the Irish middle class. Only liked the country eccentrics like Penelope's distant relations, the Chetwode-Aitkens. When they claimed to be cousins Penelope retorted, 'No, you can't be. Your branch was extinct fifty years ago.' When the Betjemans left Ireland de Valera sent for them. Penelope said to him, 'My husband knows nothing of politics; or of journalism. He knows nothing at all.' She offered to plan an equestrian tour for de Valera, and her last words to him were, 'I hope you won't let the Irish roads deteriorate. I mean I hope you won't have them metalled and tarmacked.'

James Lees-Milne

5 January

1821   Rose late – dull and drooping – the weather dripping and dense. Snow on the ground, and sirocco above in the sky, like yesterday. Roads up to the horse's belly, so that riding (at least for pleasure) is not very feasible. Read the conclusion, for the fiftieth time (I have read all W. Scott's novels at least fifty times), of the third series of *Tales of my Landlord* – grand work – Scotch.

Fielding, as well as great English poet – wonderful man! I long to get drunk with him . . .

Clock strikes – going out to make love. Somewhat perilous, but not disagreeable . . .

Lord Byron

1829   On the 5th dined and stayed all night at Lord Harrowby's. Lord Harrowby mentioned a curious circumstance respecting the age of wine. He told us he had in his cellar in London some bottles of wine considerably more than one hundred years old. They had been in possession of him and his father for very many years. The bottles were marked 1680. He had never tasted the liquor but once, and that was when the foreign ambassadors dined with him a few years ago. He described the liquor as perfectly sound, a white wine, but unlike any wine he had ever tasted. Lord Harrowby said he believed it was the oldest wine in the world. Very possibly, I should think.

William Dyott

1884   Resolved to conduct the first performance of the new Opera *Princess Ida* at night, but from the state I was in it seemed hopeless. At 7 p.m. had another strong hypodermic injection to ease the pain, and a strong cup of black coffee to keep me awake. Managed to get up and dress, and drove to the theatre more dead than alive – went into the Orchestra at 8.10. Tremendous house – usual reception. Very fine performance – not a hitch. Brilliant success. After the performance I turned very faint and could not stand.

Arthur Sullivan

6 January

1821 What is the reason that I have been, all my lifetime, more or less *ennuyé*? and that, if anything, I am rather less so now than I was at twenty, as far as my recollection serves? I do not know how to answer this, but presume that it is constitutional – as well as the waking in low spirits, which I have invariably done for many years. Temperance and exercise, which I have practised at times, and for a long time together vigorously and violently, made little or no difference. Violent passions did; when under their immediate influence – it is odd, but – I was in agitated, but *not* in depressed spirits.

A dose of salts has the effect of a temporary inebriation, like light champagne, upon me. But wine and spirits make me sullen and savage to ferocity – silent, however, and retiring, and not quarrelsome, if not spoken to. Swimming also raises my spirits – but in general they are low, and get daily lower. That is *hopeless*; for I do not think I am so much *ennuyé* as I was at nineteen. The proof is, that then I must game, or drink, or be in motion of some kind, or I was miserable. At present, I can mope in quietness; and like being alone better than any company – except the lady's whom I serve. But I feel a something, which makes me think that, if I ever reach near to old age, like Swift, 'I shall die at top' first. Only I do not dread idiotism or madness so much as he did. On the contrary, I think some quieter stages of both must be preferable to much of what men think the possession of their senses.

Lord Byron

1915 I wrote all the morning, with infinite pleasure, which is queer, because I know all the time that there is no reason to be pleased with what I write, & that in 6 weeks or even days, I shall hate it.

Virginia Woolf

1942 Day spent doing scenes over and over again to try and eliminate Noël Coward mannerisms. Saw yesterday's rushes and for the first time was pleased with my performance and my appearance. Ronnie has at last discovered what to do about my face, which is to photograph it from above rather than below.

Noël Coward

1946   An explanation is now called for. Why do I resume this diary which three months ago I brought to an end? There is no explanation. I merely missed it like an old friend. It has never intentionally been a confessor, to whom I suppose a good Catholic tells all. And being a bad Catholic I used, when I went to confession, to skate lightly over sins I had a mind to while emphasizing those I was less inclined to, and fancied I might with an effort abandon altogether. So too, being cowardly, I treated, and shall continue treating, my diary like an intimate friend who mustn't know everything. If a man has no constant lover who shares his soul as well as his body he must have a diary – a poor substitute, but better than nothing. That is all there is to it in my case.

James Lees-Milne

7 January

1907   Down-grade. Night-school – no prospects. Shall I leave Waterlow's? Am now resigned. If all turns well shortly – Good! If not – Blow it!

Sydney Moseley

1920   The studio dance at the Dixons' was fancy dress but we went in mufti and it was quite delightful. The floor was just right – quite smooth but with the essential grip. Our host was a wizened, pleasant little oik who makes the delightful brooches the Jacobs' deal so extensively in and perpetrates the most nerve-shattering pseudo-Pre-Raphaelite pictures. The band was only a piano but it was quite enough for so small a floor. There were fifteen couples which just fitted nicely. The supper was sufficient. One Dulcie Buchanan, the belle of Berkhamsted, was there. I could only get one dance with her as she was eternally compassed about by a great cloud of admirers. It is said that at the club the best tennis player plays croquet with her because she doesn't like tennis. She was a beautiful dancer. At the end they had a cotillion with 'Favour' 'Flirtation' and 'Fanfare'. All very jolly.

Evelyn Waugh

1936 Brian Lunn took me to lunch in the Inner Temple. It was like being back at Cambridge. I found him in a little wooden room, reading old divorce briefs. They were pencilled over with comment. The language was not at all bowdlerized. One contained a verbatim report of a telephone conversation a husband had overheard between his wife and her lover. He claimed that it proved adultery because, in this conversation, she used the same pet name for penis as with him.

Malcolm Muggeridge

1969 Dashed home to change hurriedly for the Buckingham Palace reception for the Commonwealth Prime Ministers. It was an awful nuisance having to dress but the only way I could see of meeting my old friends during my frantic week. It was nice to see Indira Gandhi again: I warm to her. She is a pleasant, rather shy and unassuming woman and we exchanged notes about the fun of being at the top in politics. When I asked her whether it was hell being Prime Minister she smiled and said, 'It is a challenge.' Oddly enough, I always feel protective towards her.

Every group I spoke to greeted me as the first woman Prime Minister to be. I hate this talk. First, I'm never going to be PM and, secondly, I don't think I'm clever enough. Only *I* know the depth of my limitations: it takes all I've got to survive my present job.

Barbara Castle

8 January

1788 Then he [Mr Bryant] told us a great number of comic slip-slops, of the first Lord Baltimore, who made a constant misuse of one word for another: for instance, 'I have been,' says he, 'upon a little excoriation to see a ship lanced; and there's not a finer going vessel upon the face of God's yearth: you've no idiom how well it sailed.'

Having given us this elegant specimen of the language of one lord, he proceeded to give us one equally forcible of the understanding of another: – The late Lord Plymouth, meeting in a country town with a puppet-show, was induced to see it; and, from the high entertainment he received through Punch, he determined to buy him, and accordingly asked his price, and paid it, and carried the puppet to his country-house, that he might be diverted with him at any odd hour! Mr Bryant protests he met the same troop just as the purchase had been made, and went himself to the puppet-show, which was exhibited *senza* Punch!

Next he spoke upon the Mysteries, or origin of our theatrical entertainments, and repeated the plan and conduct of several of these strange compositions, in particular one he remembered which was called *Noah's Ark*, and in which that patriarch and his sons, just previous to the Deluge, made it all their delight to speed themselves into the ark without Mrs Noah, whom they wished to escape; but she surprised them just as they had embarked, and made so prodigious a racket against the door that, after a long and violent contention, she forced them to open it, and gained admission, having first contented them by being kept out till she was thoroughly wet to the skin.

These most eccentric and unaccountable dramas filled up the chief of our conversation: and whether to consider them most with laughter, as ludicrous, or with horror, as blasphemous, remains a doubt I cannot well solve.

Fanny Burney

1934   At Marks and Spencer's I bought a peach coloured vest and trollies to match with insertions of lace. Disgraceful I know but I can't help choosing my underwear with a view to it being seen!

Barbara Pym

1954   Intense cold. Mass. Ordered central heating and donned woollen underclothes.

Evelyn Waugh

9 January

1832   Commenced schooling today by myself in the new school-room and made an address to it in 6 Latin verses. I knocked out a pane of glass with my whipping top. A very wet day. I have begun to go to bed at 9 instead of 10.

Barclay Fox

1907   Thoughts ... thoughts ... thoughts! Oh! *when* will all be settled? The top of my head aches ... face blotchy. Oh! I don't care a brass button. Blow it, hang it! etc., etc.

Sydney Moseley

1915   We had a very good walk. The purplish fields outside Kingston somehow reminded me of Saragossa. There is a foreign look about a town which stands up against the sunset, & is approached by a much trodden footpath across a field. I wonder why one instinctively feels that one is complimenting Kingston absurdly in saying that it is like a foreign town. On the towpath we met & had to pass a long line of imbeciles. The first was a very tall young man, just queer enough to look twice at, but no more; the second shuffled, & looked aside; & then one realized that every one in that long line was a miserable ineffective shuffling idiotic creature, with no forehead, or no chin, & an imbecile grin, or a wild suspicious stare. It was perfectly horrible. They should certainly be killed.

Virginia Woolf

1967   'Like a nice afternoon, gents,' a tout outside a strip club said as we passed. 'Naked ladies. All alive.' 'You look very pretty in that fur coat you're wearing,' Oscar Lewenstein said, as we stood on the corner before going our separate ways. I said, 'Peggy Ramsay bought it me. It was thirteen pounds fifteen.' 'Very cheap,' Michael White said. 'Yes, I've discovered I look better in cheap clothes.' 'I wonder what the significance of that is?' Oscar said. 'I'm from the gutter,' I said. 'And don't you ever forget it because I won't.'

Joe Orton

10 January

1775 Not having slept quite well, I got up somewhat gloomy. Knowing that I would be immediately relieved when I got to town, I indulged hypochondria, which I had not felt of a long time. I called up into my fancy ideas of being confined all winter to an old house in the north of Scotland, and being burthened with tedium and gnawed with fretfulness. It is humiliating for me to consider that my mind is such that I can at any time be made thus wretched, merely by being placed in such a situation. But let me comfort myself that I can keep out of it. My body would be tormented were it put into a fire, as my mind would be tormented in such a situation. But as the one thought gives me no uneasiness, neither should the other. As I would not wish to have my body of stone, so I would not wish to have my mind insensible.

James Boswell

1785 The last eight days were far from being among the portions of my life that I have spent with least advantage. Nor is that necessarily conveyed in the account given, but this fact is clearly deducible from it, that time so passed affords but little opportunity for the use of books, and will admit of but little advancement in studies requiring continued application. A man may be a poet, an essayist, and a philosopher, who lives in that way, but he cannot be an historian, a philologer, nor a mathematician.

William Windham

1826 Bodily Health, the mainspring of the microcosm, seems quite restored. No more flinching or nervous fits but the sound mind in the sound body. What poor things does a fever fit or an overflowing of the bile make of the master of creation.

The snow begins to fall thick this morning.

> *The Landlord then aloud did say*
> *As how he wishd they would go away.*

To have our friends shut up here would be rather too much of a good thing.

Walter Scott

1827 Enter Rheumatism and takes me by the knee. So much for playing the peace-maker in a shower of rain. Nothing for it but patience, cataplasm of camomile; and labour in my own Room the whole day till dinner time – then company and reading in the evening.

Walter Scott

11 January

1767 Greatest Snow, & severest Weather I ever remember. Only one Woman at Church, Gammar Kenney, who I asked to Dinner, with Gaffar Scot, Will Turpin, John Seare of Eaton & Sam Pollard, the only poor Men there: Tansley also dined in the Kitchin with them. I told the Clark to give Notice that there would be no Service in the Afternoon, it snowing all Day in the largest Flakes I ever saw.

The Reverend William Cole

1826 All idea of study is dissipated; the boys took their gun and their skaites immediately after our breakfast and went to the basin at Bengrove, but as the snow had fallen in the night were obliged to employ sweepers. I went to see whether it was hard enough to bear them with safety. They did not arrive at Camerton till nearly dinner time, having spent the morning in shooting. I regret the gun was purchased, as it has been a sad obstacle to reading; indeed, it seems now considered that nothing more is to be done in the way of study this vacation. When once the bow is unloosed it is difficult to new string it again.

The Reverend John Skinner

1981 Read [George] Herbert's long poem 'The Sacrifice'. No one can ever have expressed more poetically what it means to share the suffering of Christ on the Cross. Afterwards went over as usual at twelve o'clock to our little Catholic church which is locked up between services. As often before, I prayed before the figure of Jesus Christ set on the wall of the tower. If only I could feel a hundredth part of what Herbert felt.

Though I accept the death of Christ on our behalf without intellectual difficulty, it is only on rare occasions, most obviously on Good Friday, that I share a little of Herbert's feeling.

Lord Longford

12 January

1763 I came softly into the room, and in a sweet delirium slipped into bed and was immediately clasped in her snowy arms and pressed to her milk-white bosom. Good heavens, what a loose did we give to amorous dalliance! The friendly curtain of darkness concealed our blushes. In a moment I felt myself animated with the strongest powers of love, and, from my dearest creature's kindness, had a most luscious feast. Proud of my godlike vigour, I soon resumed the noble game. I was in full glow of health. Sobriety had preserved me from effeminacy and weakness, and my bounding blood beat quick and high alarms. A more voluptuous night I never enjoyed. Five times was I fairly lost in supreme rapture. Louisa was madly fond of me; she declared I was a prodigy, and asked me if this was not extraordinary for human nature. I said twice as much might be, but this was not, although in my own mind I was somewhat proud of my performance. She said it was what there was no just reason to be proud of. But I told her I could not help it. She said it was what we had in common with the beasts. I said no. For we had it highly improved by the pleasures of sentiment. I asked her what she thought enough. She gently chid me for asking such questions, but said two times. I mentioned the Sunday's assignation, when I was in such bad spirits, told her in what agony of mind I was, and asked her if she would not have despised me for my imbecility. She declared she would not, as it was what people had not in their own power.

She often insisted that we should compose ourselves to sleep before I would consent to it. At last I sunk to rest in her arms and she in mine. I found the negus, which had a fine flavour, very refreshing to me. Louisa had an exquisite mixture of delicacy and wantonness that made me enjoy her with more relish. Indeed I could not help roving in fancy to the embraces of some other ladies which my lively imagination strongly pictured. I don't know if that was altogether fair. However, Louisa had all the advantage. She said she was quite fatigued and could neither stir leg nor arm. She begged I would not despise her, and hoped my love would not be altogether transient. I have painted this night as well as I could. The description is faint; but I surely may be styled a Man of Pleasure.

James Boswell

1941 Reading Gide — the best antidote possible to the triumphant commonplace of an English Sunday. Not even the Blitzkrieg has been able to break the spell which the Sabbath casts over the land. One could not fail by just putting one's head out of the window and smelling and looking and listening for two minutes to recognize that this is Sunday. In my mind's eye I can see the weary wastes of the Cromwell Road beneath a sullen sky where a few depressed pedestrians straggle as though lost in an endless desert. One's soul shrinks from the spectacle.

Charles Ritchie

13 January

1668 Thence homeward by coach and stopped at Martins my bookseller, where I saw the French book which I did think to have had for my wife to translate, called *L'escholle de Filles*, but when I came to look into it, it is the most bawdy, lewd book that ever I saw, rather worse then *putana errante* — so that I was ashamed of reading in it; and so away home, and there to the Change to discourse with Sir H. Cholmly and so home to dinner.

Samuel Pepys

1800 Assisted at the first distribution of Soup to the Poor, in this hard season: — a mode of relief, which, however exposed to obloquy, seems eagerly and gratefully accepted. It was gratifying to observe Churchmen, Presbyterians, Independents, Unitarians, Quakers, all actively united in the same benevolent design; and warmed, from this circumstance, into complacency and kindness to each other. If no other good arises from the undertaking, this is a great one.

Thomas Green

1921 Rainy weather. Does the weather matter in a journal? Lunched alone; does *that* matter? (Grilled turbot and apple-pudding, if you want full details.)

Siegfried Sassoon

1946 Allington Castle and the river all cold and grey and swelling – something evil about its ancientness and turning inward – the windows like eyes that have turned into slots for money – nothing moving along the battlements, only the flag blowing glumly. It should not have been a Union Jack. It should have been something much less nationalistic and more narrow and family. It should have been as greedy and glowering as the rough walls and the businessman's-belly round towers.

Over everything brooded the greed and the joylessness. But it had its own beauty, which was a beauty of mournfulness and lack of understanding. One was not tempted to scrutinize it, to separate the restorations from the ruin, one took it as it was and dumped it down into one's mind as Gloom Castle, Castle Wet, Misery along the river.

We climbed up the steep bank above the river and looked down on its mass, and then we walked back to the huge lock gates where the water bulged through like wet bullocks tumbling with their buttocks in the air, all glistening.

We looked back, standing above the bellowing, roaring water, and saw far away a bonfire on the river bank. Something tindery had just been put on to it and it was climbing wildly up like a vibrating pinnacle.

Denton Welch

14 January

1743 I visited the condemned malefactors in Newgate, and was locked in by the turnkey, not with them, but in the yard. However, I stood upon a bench, and they climbed up to the windows of their cells; so that all could hear my exhortation and prayer.

Charles Wesley

1774 Had a new Wigg brought home this morning, which I put on before I went to dinner, it is a more fashionable one than my old ones are, a one curled wigg with two curls of the sides. I like it, and it was liked by most People at dinner. I gave the Barber's man, Jonathan o. 1. o. At Back-Gammon this evening with Milton only one gammon, and I lost to him by bad luck o. 10. 6. I supped in the Chequer and went to bed soon after.

The Reverend James Woodforde

1833 This day I had marked down as one of active employment; began the morning with late rising and lost what was left of it between indolent indecision, perplexity at the little progress made in accumulating surplus, and considerations of means to economize more effectually in our general expenses. I look at my own age, the uncertainty of my professional income, my dear children, and I come to the resolution that, for my own continued happiness, it is essential money should be put by to insure a provision for them. May the blessing of God confirm my good intentions, and prosper my endeavours.

William Macready

1920 We went to the Zoo of all places. It was really most amusing. I hadn't been for ages and thoroughly enjoyed it. The bears and monkeys were divine. In the evening Phil and I went to an awfully good dance at the town hall. It was one of the Private Subscription ones that Mrs MacFadden and Mrs Kendall are running. The people were all right and the supper most excellent with ices and claret cup and éclairs. The band was large but none too good. On the whole, however, it was one of the best I've been to this holidays.

Evelyn Waugh

---

15 January

1830   I felt uncomfortably irritated today by the behaviour of the people.

During the Evening Service I had to notice the bad behaviour of the schoolgirls, and also of my foot-boy, George, who was laughing; when I spoke to him on the subject he denied it: he is a bad boy. I have often said if the patient Job had been Rector of Camerton he might not have had much celebrity on account of that virtue.

I know my infirmity, which is too great irritability, yet I endeavour to correct it; of one thing I am certain, I never retain the unwelcome guest beyond the impulse of the moment, and every hour of my existence at this place is so exposed to insult that one must be a stock or a stone not to feel it.

The Reverend John Skinner

1917   A few hours in the pre-war surroundings . . . Pleasant enough; but what a decayed society, hanging blindly on to the shreds of its traditions. The wet, watery-green meadows and straggling bare hedges and grey winding lanes; the cry of hounds, and thud of hoofs, and people galloping bravely along all around me; and the ride home with the hounds in the chilly dusk — these are *real* things. But comfort and respectable squiredom and the futile chatter of women, and their man-hunting glances, and the pomposity of port-wine-drinking buffers — what's all that but emptiness? These people don't reason. They echo one another and their dead relations, and what they read in papers and dull books. And they only *see* what they want to see — which is very little beyond the tips of their red noses. Debrett is on every table; and heaven a sexless peerage, with a suitable array of dependants and equipages . . .

Siegfried Sassoon

1980 Young mother breast-feeding her baby while eating smoked trout at next table in RA restaurant. Nobody but baby pursing lips. Hooray! Could you do this at the Tate?

Hugh Casson

---

16 January

1763 I then went to Louisa and was permitted the rites of love with great complacency; yet I felt my passion for Louisa much more gone. I felt a degree of coldness for her and I observed an affectation about her which disgusted me. I had a strong proof of my own inconstancy of disposition, and I considered that any woman who married me must be miserable. Here I argued wrong. For as a licentious love is merely the child of passion, it has no sure ground to hope for a long continuance, as passion may be extinguished with the most sudden and trifling breath of wind; but rational esteem founded on just motives must in all probability endure, especially when the opinion of the world and many other considerations contribute to strengthen and preserve it. Louisa and I began this day to read French. Our book was a little light piece of French gallantry entitled *Journal Amoureux*. She pronounced best and I translated best. Between us we did very well.

James Boswell

1797 Rattle Snake I went to see in Bond St. It was caught 8th May last in South Carolina. A maid servant with a child in her arms heard it rattle in her master's gardens. It was caught alive by a noose being thrown over its head. It is about 9 feet long, and can *Coil* itself up so as to be a foot in thickness round the Body. Its eyes are always open it having no eyelids. The Rattle at the end of the tale is always erect. This Rattle is not *formed* so as to sound till the animal is 3 years old. The Bones which form the Rattle are a continuation of the Vertebra, and it is not by *shaking* but by a *thrilling irritation* that the sound is caused. I thought the sound something like the chirping of a bird, but the man better observed that it resembled the *running down of a clock*. The Rattle Snake has upper teeth *only* formed in a Curve which when the mouth is closed are recd. into sockets. The teeth of *this* snake are one Inch long. Sometime since a Rabbit was put into the Cage, which beginning to leap abt the Snake darted a bite at it, and the Rabbit falling died in a minute. The wounds were very small resembling such as would be made by large needles. Near the orifices of the wounds the flesh immediately smoked & fermented as if it were boiling. Some gentlemen wishing to dissect the Rabbit found when they attempted to clear away the Skin that the Flesh came away in pieces. The man told me that the bites of a Rattle Snake will produce their effect 10 or 11 times, after which the poison is exhausted. Sometimes when enraged the animal will bite *itself*, which proves mortal. It appeared evident to me, as the man asserted, that this Snake had sagacity to know him, and to be sensible when *required to rattle*. This Snake is known by the number of his *rattles* to be abt 11 years old. They have been proved to have lived 50 years. The Colour is dark & dusky with black spots. The Rattle Snake only takes food once or twice a year. This Snake has not taken any food since it was caught in May last. A bason of water was placed in the cage which it drinks occasionally. Food has been offered it. It has no evacuations but by perspiration. The Scales on the belly are *hard*, those on the back softer.

Joseph Farington

17 January

1720 Miss Nancey Dawe having continued all the night (with very short, & at last with no Intermissions) in the most violent and universal Convulsions (her left Leg & Arm being towards the Morning motionless but by being continued by the Convuls'd Body) died about 7 . . . She had been with me at Wells 9 week last Friday, she coming Nov. 13. And was the most obliging, Flexible, Good-Natur'd, Ingenious, & Civil Pretty Girl of little more than 11 Years old that ever I knew.

Dr Claver Morris

1763 Louisa and I continued our study of French, which was useful as it gave us some employment and prevented us from tiring on account of conversation becoming insipid from a sameness that must necessarily happen when only two people are much together. I this day again had full fruition of her charms. I still, though, found that the warm enthusiasm of love was over.

James Boswell

1922   Chekhov made a mistake in thinking that if he had had more time he would have written more fully, described the rain, and the midwife and the doctor having tea. The truth is one can get only *so much* into a story; there is always a sacrifice. One has to leave out what one knows and longs to use. Why? I haven't any idea, but there it is. It's always a kind of race to get in as much as one can before it *disappears*.

But time is not really in it. Yet wait. I do not understand even now. I am pursued by time myself. The only occasion when I ever felt at leisure was while writing *The Daughters of the Late Colonel*. And then at the end I was so terribly unhappy that I wrote as fast as possible for fear of dying before the story was sent. I should like to prove this, to work at *real leisure*. Only thus can it be done.

Katherine Mansfield

18 January

1845   Charles Johns, the Botanist, spent the morning with us. The earliest botanical fact concerning him is, that a biscuit was given him over which caraway seeds were sprinkled; he picked out the seeds, planted them, and waited, alas! vainly, for a crop of biscuits!

Caroline Fox

1946   Today we went towards Tunbridge Wells to shop, and first we stopped half-way up the narrow country road to Southborough Common to eat our picnic. As we were biting into the egg sandwiches, a thick-set dark youth passed us carrying a broad-bladed hay-cutter. His face was shy and a little glowering, but he had eyes that were remarkable for their up-pointing slant and length – rather unreal eyes, like long almonds. It was a strange face for England, and afterwards when we'd got out of the car I saw him cutting silage for cows. We talked, and he told me that he didn't smoke because he didn't think it too good for people; then he jumped up and down, thrusting the blade deep into the tobacco-smelling, flattened stack. Some of it had a whitish bloom and dust. 'This at the top's bad,' he said. 'It gets better down below. But we just put the bad stuff back on the land, so it's not really wasted.'

There was a broad avenue cut through the copses on the hills for a long way, to clear the bases of the electricity pylons. They reminded me of skeleton guardian giants on the ceremonial way to a great tomb. The air was so freezing that I had to look up at the pressing low sky and say, 'Do you think it's going to snow?'

'I shouldn't wonder,' he said, staring up. When he grinned and looked straight at me, I saw that his face was even rarer than it had seemed at first. It was a picture gypsy's face with glowing cheeks, and the slanting eyes and quirky eyebrows made it innocent instead of wicked. I saw that he wore strange little leggings round his trouser ends.

'Goodbye,' I said, walking away and wishing that his face and body need never be spoilt.

Denton Welch

1967   I heard a most fascinating conversation between an old man and a woman. 'What a thing, though,' the old woman said. 'You'd hardly credit it.' 'She's always made a fuss of the whole family, but never me,' the old man said. 'Does she have a fire when the young people come to see her?' 'Fire? She won't get people seeing her without warmth.' 'I know why she's doing it. Don't think I don't,' the old man said. 'My sister she said to me, "I wish I had your easy life". Now that upset me. I was upset by the way she phrased herself. "Don't talk to me like that," I said, "I've only got to get on the phone and ring a certain number," I said, "To have you stopped".' 'Yes,' the old woman said, 'and you can, can't you?' 'Were they always the same?' she said, 'when you was a child? Can you throw yourself back? How was they years ago?' 'The same,' the old man said. 'Wicked, isn't it,' the old woman said. 'Take care ,' she said as the old man left. He didn't say a word to her but got off the bus looking disgruntled.

Joe Orton

19 January

1778   This being the day for the Queen's Birth Day to be kept Bill fired my Blunderbuss 3 Times, each charge three Caps of Powder with a good deal of Paper and Tow on it. I fired him of in the evening with 3 Caps of Powder also.

The Reverend James Woodforde

1838   The cold increases, the snow is getting deep, and I hear the Thames is frozen over very nearly, which has not happened since 1814.

Queen Victoria

1882   Fancy Dress Ball to open the entertaining room at Barnwood. I was dressed as Mahomet Bel Hadgi, the father and Emily as the mother of Lindaraja. We were not recognized at first. After an hour Emily dropped the Moorish sheets and came out a full-bloomed Harmony in Yellow Liberty Silk with scores of sunflowers. Emily's waist on rising in a morning is 25 inches. When in corset, $22\frac{1}{2}$ inches.

Dearman Birchall

1940   My old schoolfriend Thetis came to dinner, and we talked about art and men till quite late and I told her about Gerhardt. I was pleased to find someone else who frequently wishes they were dead. Her trouble is that she says she can't co-ordinate religion, art, and life into a sane and purposed whole, and she worries herself sick because she can't put order into this chaos. Like me, she's still a virgin. Her family are very intellectual and give poetry readings in their drawing-room, which Thetis says are very embarrassing.

Joan Wyndham

20 **January**

1763   I rose very disconsolate, having rested very ill by the poisonous infection raging in my veins and anxiety and vexation boiling in my breast. I could scarcely credit my own senses. What! thought I. Can this beautiful, this sensible, and this agreeable woman be so sadly defiled? Can corruption lodge beneath so fair a form? Can she who professed delicacy of sentiment and sincere regard for me, use me so very basely and so very cruelly? No, it is impossible. I have just got a gleet by irritating the parts too much with excessive venery. And yet these damned twinges, that scalding heat, and that deep-tinged loathsome matter are the strongest proofs of an infection. But she certainly must think that I would soon discover her falsehood. But perhaps she was ignorant of her being ill. A pretty conjecture indeed! No, she could not be ignorant. Yes, yes, she intended to make the most of me. And now I recollect that the day we went to Hayward's, she showed me a bill of thirty shillings about which she was in some uneasiness, and no doubt expected that I would pay it. But I was too cautious, and she had not effrontery enough to try my generosity in direct terms so soon after my letting her have two guineas. And am I then taken in? Am I, who have had safe and elegant intrigues with fine women, become the dupe of a strumpet? Am I now to be laid up for many weeks to suffer extreme pain and full confinement, and to be debarred all the comforts and pleasures of life? And then must I have my poor pocket drained by the unavoidable expense of it? And shall I no more (for a long time at least) take my walk, healthful and spirited, round the Park before breakfast, view the brilliant Guards on the Parade, and enjoy all my pleasing amusements? And then am I prevented from making love to Lady Mirabel, or any other woman of fashion? O dear, O dear! What a cursed thing this is! What a miserable creature am I!

    In this woeful manner did I melancholy ruminate. I thought of applying to a quack who would cure me quickly and cheaply. But then the horrors of being imperfectly cured and having the distemper thrown into my blood terrified me exceedingly. I therefore pursued my resolution of last night to go to my friend Douglas, whom I knew to be skillful and careful; and although it should cost me more, yet to get sound health was a matter of great importance, and I might save upon other articles. I accordingly went and breakfasted with him . . .

After breakfast Mrs Douglas withdrew, and I opened my sad case to Douglas, who upon examining the parts, declared I had got an evident infection and that the woman who gave it me could not but know of it . . .

Thus ended my intrigue with the fair Louisa, which I flattered myself so much with, and from which I expected at least a winter's safe copulation. It is indeed very hard. I cannot say, like young fellows who get themselves clapped in a bawdy-house, that I will take better care again. For I really did take care. However, since I am fairly trapped, let me make the best of it. I have not got it from imprudence. It is merely the chance of war.

James Boswell

21 January

1671　This yeare the weather was so wet, stormy, and unseasonable, as had not ben knowne in many yeares.

John Evelyn

1821　Tomorrow is my birth-day — that is to say, at twelve o' the clock, midnight, *i.e.* in twelve minutes, I shall have completed thirty and three years of age!!! — and I go to my bed with a heaviness of heart at having lived so long, and to so little purpose.

It is three minutes past twelve. ''Tis the middle of the night by the castle clock', and I am now thirty-three!

> *Eheu, fugaces, Posthume, Posthume,*
> *Labuntur anni;*

but I don't regret them so much for what I have done, as for what I *might* have done.

> *Through life's road, so dim and dirty,*
> *I have dragged to three-and-thirty,*

> *What have these years left to me?*
> *Nothing — except thirty-three.*

Lord Byron

1888   Not quite 6 pages. Bought some bottled ale, thinking it might help me to sleep if I drank some before going to bed.

George Gissing

1908   The effects of disturbed nights cannot be too strongly stressed. Utter helplessness, loss of dignity . . . When I think how hard I've striven to keep moral — and its effects on me — I am sorry sometimes I did not go straight away and — be natural.

Sydney Moseley

1937   News that Miss West is dying of pneumonia. A melancholy walk with L. in the rain. The usual thoughts: & this too; that I was too aloof, & never friendly eno', & never asked her to dine. I must conquer this aloofness if I possibly can. So little one can do; but at least do it if possible. Such a mute relationship. I pass her room, & think I might have gone in; & now never shall.

Virginia Woolf

22 January

1737   I called upon Mrs Pendarvis, while she was reading a letter of my being dead. Happy for me, had the news been true! What a world of misery would it save me!

Charles Wesley

1821

Here lies
interred in the Eternity
of the Past,
from whence there is no
Resurrection
for the Days — Whatever there may be

for the Dust –
the Thirty-Third Year
of an ill-spent Life,
Which, after
a lingering disease many months
sunk into a lethargy,
and expired,
January 22nd, 1821, A.D.
Leaving a successor
Inconsolable
for the very loss which
occasioned its
Existence.

Lord Byron

1841 Found at home notes from Ransom, and one from Dickens
with an onward number of 'Master Humphrey's Clock'. I
saw one print in it of the dear dead child that gave a cold
chill through my blood. I dread to read it, but I must get it
over.

I have read the two numbers; I never have read printed
words that gave me so much pain. I could not weep for some
time. Sensation, sufferings have returned to me, that are terrible to awaken: it is real to me; I cannot criticize it.

William Macready

1888 Bottled ale has given me a headache. Clearly I can't use it.
Shall try a glass of hot water at bedtime.

George Gissing

23 January

1669 So to my wife's chamber, and there supped and got her cut
my hair and look my shirt, for I have itched mightily these
six or seven days; and when all came to all, she finds that I
am louzy, having found in my head and body above 20 lice,
little and great; which I wonder at, being more then I have
had I believe almost these 20 years. I did think I might have

got them from the little boy, but they did presently look him, and found none – so how they came, I know not; but presently did shift myself, and so shall be rid of them, and cut my hayre close to my head. And so, with much content to bed.

Samuel Pepys

1841 Having proclaimed that I would give soup to any persons on the Lizard who would think it worthwhile to walk seven or eight miles in deep snow, I found today thirty-three persons assembled at the door, to whom I gave from six to eight pints each, and I suppose (DV) to boil forty pounds of beef into soup weekly during the winter which together with about a peck of peas, a bundle of leeks and three or four papers of groats, boiled for ten hours, will afford nourishing food for upwards of forty families. One woman brought two boilers. I inquired the name of her neighbour she came for. She replied there was fifteen on the ticket and she thought it meant fifteen pints. I told her it was the day of the month on which she was to come. Poor things, they must be needy to walk so far for soup!

The Reverend W. W. Andrew

1875 When I went to bed last night I fancied that something ran in at my bedroom door after me from the gallery. It seemed to be a skeleton. It ran with a dancing step and I thought it aimed a blow at me from behind. This was shortly before midnight.

The Reverend Francis Kilvert

1940 This war that isn't like a real war still drags on. Poor Laura has left the first-aid post – the conditions there have apparently brought back her TB and she may have to go to a sanatorium. I miss her terribly.

We still do part-time work at the post, but it's very boring. Even Mummy and Sid are getting fed up with endlessly bandaging healthy limbs!

Joan Wyndham

24 January

1684   The frost continuing more and more severe, the Thames before London was still planted with boothes in formal streetes, all sorts of trades and shops furnish'd and full of commodities, even to a printing presse, where the people and ladyes tooke a fancy to have their names printed, and the day and yeare set down when printed on the Thames; this humour tooke so universally, that 'twas estimated the printer gain'd £5 a day, for printing a line onely, at sixpence a name, besides what he got by ballads, &c. Coaches plied from Westminster to the Temple, and from several other staires to and fro, as in the streetes, sleds, sliding with skeetes, a bull-baiting, horse and coach races, puppet plays and interludes, cookes, tipling, and other lewd places, so that it seem'd to be a bacchanalian triumph, or carnival on the water, whilst it was a severe judgment on the land, the trees not onely splitting as if by lightning-struck, but men and cattle perishing in divers places; and the very seas so lock'd up with ice, that no vessells could stir out or come in. The fowles, fish, and birds, and all our exotiq plants and greenes universally perishing. Many parkes of deer were destroied, and all sorts of fuell so deare that there were greate contributions to preserve the poore alive. Nor was this severe weather much lesse intense in most parts of Europe, even as far as Spaine and the most Southern tracts. London, by reason of the excessive coldnesse of the aire hindering the ascent of the smoke, was so fill'd with the fuliginous steame of the sea-coale, that hardly could one see crosse the streetes, and this filling the lungs with its grosse particles, exceedingly obstructed the breast, so as one could scarely breathe. Here was no water to be had from the pipes and engines, nor could the brewers and divers other trades-men worke, and every moment was full of disastrous accidents.

John Evelyn

1899   Last night I finished my sensational novel, *The Curse of Love*, 50,000 words in exactly three months, with all my other work. The writing of it has enormously increased my facility, and I believe that now I could do a similar novel in a month. It is, of the kind, good stuff, well written and well contrived, and some of the later chapters are really imagined and, in a way, lyrical. I found the business, after I had got fairly into it, easy enough, and I rather enjoyed it. I could comfortably write 2,500 words in half a day. It has only been written once, and on revision I have scarcely touched the original draft. Now I want to do two short sensational stories – and then to my big novel.

Arnold Bennett

25 January

1683 A sad cruel murther comitted by a boy about eighteen or nineteen years of age, nere Ferryhill, nere Durham, being Thursday, at night. The maner is, by report: – When the parents were out of dores a young man, being sone to the house, and two daughters was kil'd by this boy with an axe, having knockt them in the head, afterwards cut ther throts: one of them being asleep in the bed, about ten or eleven yeares of age: the other daughter was to be married at Candlemas. After he had kil'd the sone and the eldest daughter, being above twenty yeares of age, a little lass, her sister, about the age of eleven yeares being in bed alone, he drag'd her out in bed and killed her alsoe.

Jacob Bee

1846 My birth day – 60 years old!
O God, continue my eyes & faculties to the last hour of my existence. Bless me through my ensuing year, grant I may live to accomplish my 6 great works, & leave my family in competence. Accept my gratitude for thy mercies up to this moment, & grant I may so exercise the gifts which thou hast blest me with, that I may merit eternal life, & thy approbation, through Christ, my Lord & Saviour. Amen.
Burns was born the same day.

B. R. Haydon

1927 Beginning to feel that I ought not to be long with the BBC, but it is extremely difficult to find what the next job is to be. So few good jobs or ones that I would like at all. What a curse it is to have outstanding comprehensive ability and intelligence, combined with a desire to use them to maximum purpose.

John Reith

1979 Limousined to Toronto airport, and then off to New York. Peter Shaffer's *Salieri*, now called *Amadeus*, was waiting for me at the hotel. I think it's potentially one of the most remarkable new plays I have ever read.

Salieri on his deathbed confesses to, and through the play enacts, a consuming hatred of Mozart who is drawn as wilful, immoral, bewilderingly talented. Salieri is the decent man, the classical man of music without dissonance, without chromaticism. Though able to give Mozart opportunities he withholds them, destroys him, and is himself destroyed by Mozart's genius.

Peter's script is tougher, more precise, and more personal than anything he has done before. In one way, he is writing about how he sees himself and his uncertainties compared to, say, Sam Beckett. The *nature* of talent, of art, comes winging through.

Peter's usual obsession is there: to prove the existence of God and the nature of God. Here He is shown as selfish and uncaring, following His own needs, indifferent to the suffering of man.

The question in *Amadeus* is why does God bestow talent so indiscriminately? I had an absolute child's lust to direct it. John Dexter, though, has given Shaffer his greatest successes, and I want Dexter to stage *Amadeus* at the National. But he doesn't like the place – the new building, I mean. He's spent the last four years saying he will never work there. So it's going to be difficult.

I mustn't lose that play for our theatre whatever happens.

Peter Hall

26 January

1833 They have hired a French cook for the Carlton Club from Paris, who lived formerly with the Duc d'Escars, *premier maître d'hôtel* of Louis XVIII, and who probably made that famous *pâté de saucissons* which killed his master. It was served at breakfast at the Tuileries to the king, who with the duke partook so voraciously of it, that the former was attacked with a dangerous fit of indigestion, from which he with difficulty recovered, and the latter absolutely died from the excess on the following day. One of the French journals, remarkable for its *facéties*, announced the event in the following terms: '*Hier sa Majesté tres Chrétienne, a été attaquée d'une indigestion, dont M. le Duc d'Escars est mort le lendemain.*'

Louis XVIII was not only a great epicure as to the *recherche* of his dinners, but had also a surprising appetite; he has been known at table, in the interval between the first and second courses, of which he always partook largely, to have a *plat* of little pork cutlets, dressed in a particular manner, handed to him by one of the pages; and he would take them up one by one in his fingers, and before the second service was arranged the contents of his little *plat* had disappeared.

The poor duke emulated his royal master in this respect fatally for himself. In consequence of his office he presided always at a large table served for him in the palace, the menu of which was precisely the same as that served to the king. I remember once to have seen him in that time with his old duchess, and sundry other emigrants returned with the Restoration, who still retained their powdered heads and their *ailes de pigeon*, and who would eat almost to suffocation. When the coffee was announced, here and there one of the old pursy gourmands would sputter out to the lady, '*Madame la Duchesse, veut elle bien me permettre de prendre un instant de sieste*;' and then he would recline in his armchair, and throw his napkin over his head and slumber for a few minutes, till nature was a little relieved.

Thomas Raikes

1842   The mysterious influence under which I always begin a great work, is hardly to be credited, under all circumstances of necessity. Here was I with hardly money for the week – with commissions deferred – with a boy at Cambridge, in want of money I could not send him, & a boy on board the *Vindictive* still owed three pounds of the quarter (£10) – seized at daybreak with an irresistible impulse – a whisper audible, loud, startling, – to begin a great work. The Canvas was lying at the Colorman's to be kept till paid for. I could not pay. I wrote him & offered a bill at 6 months. He consented; the Canvas comes home, & after prayer, ardent & Sincere, I fly at it, & get the whole in, capitally arranged, in two days, about 12 hours' work, owing to the Time of year. Good & merciful God, am I not reserved for great things? Surely I am. Surely at 56 to be more active than at 26 is extraordinary! Continue Thy blessings, & grant I may finish both Alexander & the Curtius, & raise my Country's name. Amen.

B. R. Haydon

27 January

1658　After six fits of a quartan ague with which it pleased God to visite him, died my deare son Richard, to our inexpressible griefe and affliction, 5 yeares and 3 days old onely, but at that tender age a prodigy for witt and understanding; for beauty of body a very angel; for endowment of mind of incredible and rare hopes. To give onely a little taste of some of them, and thereby glory to God, who out of the mouths of babes and infants does sometimes perfect his praises: at 2 yeares and halfe old he could perfectly reade any of the English, Latine, French, or Gothic letters, pronouncing the three first languages exactly. He had before the 5th yeare, or in that yeare, not onely skill to reade most written hands, but to decline all the nouns, conjugate the verbs regular, and most of the irregular; learn'd out Puerilis, got by heart almost the entire vocabularie of Latine and French primitives and words, could make congruous syntax, turne English into Latine, and vice versa, construe and prove what he read, and did the government and use of relatives, verbs, substantives, elipses, and many figures and tropes, and made a considerable progress in Comenius's *Janua*; began himselfe to write legibly, and had a strong passion for Greeke.

John Evelyn

1776 It grows colder and colder and verifies the old saw – As the day lengthens, the cold strengthens. This is indeed the coldest day I have ever known since the hard frost 1739–40; everything freezes. When I sat down in my chair (indeed a wooden bottom) I started up surprized, thinking I had sat down on a pool of cold water, when it was only the coldness of the weather, and this evening my tongs and fire-shovel, which have been all day by the fireside, are chilling cold. Our people washed today, having deferred it for a fortnight or 3 weeks, looking for the weather to soften, and now wash'd, the coldest day we have had yet. The girls did not come to read tonight – so cold and have been washing.

John Baker

1846 I fear nothing on Earth but my Banker, when I have not 5/- on acct. & have a bill coming due & want help! The awful & steady look of his searching eyes; the quiet & investigating point of his simple questions; the 'hums' as he holds down his head, as if he had Atlas on his Shoulders, and the solemn tone when he declares it is against the rules of the House; the reprieve one feels as the tones of his voice begin to melt & give symptoms of an opening to let in light to the heart, are not to be described, & can only be understood by those who have been in such predicaments. Majoribanks is always kind at last. The Clerks seem to be wonder struck at the charm I seem to possess among the Partners.

The fact is, Coutts have had a great deal to do always with Men of Genius, & they have a feeling for them, & seem to think it is a credit to the House to have one or two to scold, assist, blow up, & then forgive. This is the way I have gone on with them 29 years.

B. R. Haydon

28 January

1661 At the office all the morning. Dined at home. And after dinner to Mr Crews and thence to the Theatre, where I saw again *The Lost Lady*, which doth now please me better then before.

And here, I sitting behind in a dark place, a lady spat backward upon me by a mistake, not seeing me. But after seeing her to be a very pretty lady, I was not troubled at it at all.

Samuel Pepys

1821 Why, at the very height of desire and human pleasure – worldly, social, amorous, ambitious, or even avaricious – does there mingle a certain sense of doubt and sorrow – a fear of what is to come – a doubt of what *is* – a retrospect to the past, leading to a prognostication of the future? (The best of Prophets of the future is the Past.) Why is this, or these? – I know not, except that on a pinnacle we are most susceptible of giddiness, and that we never fear falling except from a precipice – the higher, the more awful, and the more sublime; and, therefore, I am not sure that Fear is not a pleasurable sensation; at least, *Hope* is; and *what Hope* is there without a deep leaven of Fear? and what sensation is so delightful as Hope? and, if it were not for Hope, where would the Future be? – in hell. It is useless to say *where* the Present is, for most of us know; and as for the Past, *what* predominates in memory? – *Hope baffled*. Ergo, in all human affairs, it is Hope – Hope – Hope. I allow sixteen minutes, though I never counted them, to any given or supposed possession. From whatever place we commence, we know where it all must end. And yet, what good is there in knowing it? It does not make men better or wiser. During the greatest horrors of the greatest plagues, (Athens and Florence, for example – see Thucydides and Machiavelli,) men were more cruel and profligate than ever. It is all a mystery. I feel most things, but I know nothing except

Lord Byron

1943 On Monday – to meet someone who just takes you as you are – charming! – no fuss! We just walked on and on through the rain, down the muddy cow-smelling lane. The elms swayed and speared the misty wetness with their scarecrow fingers. We linked arms, walking tightly and neatly together. It was comfort and pleasure to walk in that tidy rhythm and to talk loudly and gaily about the blitz days . . .

We walked on, cosily talking of these horrors. It was so warming. We railed against the war and the blood spilt out. The rain came down thicker.

'Do you think there's any shelter here?' the soldier said.

'There might be a cattle byre or whatever you call it. Let's go on a little further and look.'

But there was nothing, so we sat on a fence under some trees and told each other our ages and what we could remember as small children. A car passed, a bicycle, and then another bicycle – why can't we do this with strangers more often? Why can't we just talk and amuse each other a little? Without any necessity for intricate or lasting understanding. Why can't we just go for walks in the rain and come back pleased?

Denton Welch

29 January

1718   Tho' this Winter was very mild 'till Christmass, yet since Christmass it hath been very severe, and it was observed that on Tuesday night, the 21st instant, the Cold was more violent than in any one night of the great Frost in 1683, and that it froze five Inches and a Quarter of solid Ice, between eight of the clock that Evening and seven a Clock on Wednesday Morning. It continues Freezing still, tho' there hath been an Intermission for a day or two since the 21st. This Frost hath very bad Effects upon human Bodies, so that it increases the numbers of the Dead much more than before.

Thomas Hearne

1763   The frost began to thaw today, after having continued very severe for five weeks; the ice was seven inches thick.

Thomas Turner

1776   These 2 nights past I could not be warm all night. I thought it was only poor Mrs Martin and I from age that were so, but speaking to Charles of it this morning, he said he was shivering with cold the whole night and his feet like ice, and could not sleep for the cold, the cook still worse – she was forced to get up in the night and put on stockings and petticoat. I have lain abed these 2 mornings till 10; my ink froze in the glass on the standish – yesterday two bottles of water, which I keep in my study, frozen and burst the bottles, one of which I gently knocked the glass of the bottle from, and the ice in the bottle, neck and all; one mass of ice, just the shape of the bottle.

John Baker

1935 Came back after dinner to meet Winston Churchill, who was very pleasant and seemed to appreciate my staying to meet him. His talk on India was awfully disappointing – a string of bombastic phrases with little sincerity at the back of it. Finished up by borrowing 5/- from me.

John Reith

30 January

1802 A cold dark morning. William chopped wood – I brought it in a basket. A cold wind. Wm slept better, but he thinks he looks ill – he is shaving now. He asks me to set down the story of Barbara Wilkinson's turtle dove. Barbara is an old maid. She had two turtle doves. One of them died, the first year I think. The other bird continued to live alone in its cage for 9 years, but for one whole year it had a companion and daily visitor – a little mouse, that used to come and feed with it; and the dove would caress it, and cower over it with its wings, and make a loving noise to it. The mouse, though it did not testify equal delight in the dove's company, yet it was at perfect ease. The poor mouse disappeared, and the dove was left solitary till its death. It died of a short sickness, and was buried under a tree with funeral ceremony by Barbara and her maidens, and one or two others.

On *Saturday, 30th*, Wm worked at *The Pedlar* all the morning. He kept the dinner waiting till four o'clock. He was much tired. We were preparing to walk when a heavy rain came on.

Dorothy Wordsworth

1832 The great Italian fiddler, Paganini, performed at Birmingham after filching John Bull's pocket in London, Liverpool, etc.

William Dyott

1907 I'm jiggered if I know how it's going to end . . . Will I be a 30s a week clerk, an ordinary fellow with a wife and children to keep – or (as I hope) a brilliant speaker, writer, singer?

Sydney Moseley

1953 Full days at *Punch*. Alternate between despondency and confidence. Probably on the whole, in the end it will suit, and I'll make something of it. Concerned now, nearly fifty, to evolve a routine, continuing work instead of sport and collapse. I must do much, much more.

Malcolm Muggeridge

---

31 January

1561 The xxxj day of January the sam man was sett on the pelere and ij grett peses of the measly bacun hangying over ys hed, and a wrytyng put up that a ij yere a-goo he was ponyssed for the sam offense for the lyke thyng.

Henry Machyn

1823 A wet day, and as no jackanapes could get his gun off in the rain it was my only chance; I therefore sallied out for one huge swan that had been the target of the coast, and had become so wild that he could scarcely be looked at: on my way out I fired a long shot and got 4 geese; soon after, as I expected, we saw this huge bird, floating about in a rough sea, and in a pour of rain; I had two punts to manœuvre on one side of him, while Reade and I drifted down on the other; he sprung at about four hundred yards, came luckily across my punt at about 75 yards, and down I fetched him, like a cock pheasant, with the swivel gun. His fall was more like the parachute of an air balloon than a bird; he was shot quite dead; he weighed 21 lb, and measured 7 feet 8 inches from wing to wing, being the largest, by far, of any I had killed; therefore my misfortune of last night was balanced by getting another wild swan.

Colonel Peter Hawker

1907 The thing which has tended to terminate my women-friendships is that at a certain juncture they begin to disapprove and to criticize my course, and to feel a responsibility to say disagreeable things. One ought to take it smilingly and courteously; and one would, if one liked the sex – but I *don't* like the sex. Their mental processes are obscure to me; I don't like their superficial ways, their mixture of emotion with reason ... Women, I think, when they get interested in one, have a deadly desire to improve one. They think that the privilege of friendship is to criticize; they want deference, they don't want frankness.

A. C. Benson

1 February

1667 Up, and to the office, where I was all the morning doing business. At noon home to dinner, and after dinner down by water, though it was a thick misty and raining day, and walked to Deptford from Redriffe and there to Bagwells by appointment – where the moher erat within expecting mi venida. And did sensa alguna difficulty monter los degres and lie, comme jo desired it, upon to lectum; and there I did la cosa con much voluptas. By and by su marido came in, and there, without any notice taken by him, we discoursed of our business of getting him the new ship building by Mr Deane, which I shall do for him.

Samuel Pepys

1828 I am, I find, in serious danger of losing the habit of my journal and having carried it on so long that would be pity. But I am now on the 1st february fishing for the lost recollections of the days since the 21 January. Luckily there is not very much to remember or forget and perhaps the best way would be to skip and go on.

Walter Scott

1829 On the 1st February I arrived at home and found snow and sharp frost. The weather had been mild and pleasant during the former week. Did not observe snow until I passed Lutterworth. During my absence a gang of poachers had attacked the Pool Tail and Swinfen wood, and one night (seven in number) shot many pheasants. Such daring lengths the poachers have arrived at, this season, that the gang came a second time and began soon after nine o'clock. If gangs of armed men are to commit depredations close to your door, and from their numbers to intimidate resistance, it is full time that the government of the country took some means to put a stop to these lawless proceedings, prejudicial alike to individuals as well as social order.

William Dyott

2 February

1751 Having received a full answer from Mr P—, I was clearly convinced that I ought to marry. For many years I remained single because I believed I could be more useful in a single, than in a married state. And I praise God, who enabled me so to do. I now as fully believed, that in my present circumstances, I might be more useful in a married state; into which, upon this clear conviction, and by the advice of my friends, I entered a few days after.

John Wesley

1751 My brother, returned from Oxford, sent for and told me *he was resolved to marry!* I was thunderstruck, and could only answer, he had given me the first blow, and his marriage would come like the *coup de grâce*. Trusty Ned Perronet followed, and told me, the person was Mrs Vazeille! one of whom I had never had the least suspicion. I refused his company to the chapel, and retired to mourn with my faithful Sally. I groaned all the day, and several following ones, under my own and the people's burden. I could eat no pleasant food, nor preach, nor rest, either by night or by day.

Charles Wesley

1767 *Purification of our Lady.* Fine Warm Day, like Summer. The Knats were out in my Bedchamber & my Blackbird sung out so as to be heard up Stairs before I was up.

William Cole

1821 I have been considering what can be the reason why I always wake, at a certain hour in the morning, and always in very bad spirits – I may say, in actual despair and despondency, in all respects – even of that which pleased me over night. In about an hour or two, this goes off, and I compose either to sleep again, or, at least, to quiet. In England, five years ago, I had the same kind of hypochondria, but accompanied with so violent a thirst that I have drank as many as fifteen bottles of soda-water in one night, after going to bed, and been still thirsty – calculating, however, some lost from the bursting out and effervescence and overflowing of the soda-water, in drawing the corks, or striking off the necks of the bottles from mere thirsty impatience. At present, I have *not* the thirst; but the depression of spirits is no less violent.

Lord Byron

1843 My other dear daughter was this day married at Christchurch, St Marylebone, to the Rev. Lewis Playters Hird. I never felt anything more acutely than parting from this dear child, and may God be a Father to her wherever she goes. My family are now all disposed of, and I remain as the mere scaffold on which has for more than twenty years been building, as it were, the edifice of their education.

Colonel Peter Hawker

3 February

1781 Had but an indifferent night of Sleep, Mrs Davie and Nancy made me up an Apple Pye Bed last night.

The Reverend James Woodforde

1815 I heard the other day of Jekyll the following pun. He said, 'Erskine used to hesitate very much, and could not speak well after dinner. I dined with him once at the Fishmongers' Company. He made such sad work of speechifying, that I asked him whether it was in honour of the Company that he *floundered* so.'

Henry Crabb Robinson

1826 From the 19 January to the 2d february inclusive is exactly fifteen days during which time (with the intervention of some days' idleness to let imagination brood on the task a little) I have written a volume. I think for a bett I could have done it in ten days. Then I must have had no court of Session to take me up two or three hours every morning and dissipate my attention and powers of working for the rest of the day. A volume at cheapest is worth £1,000. This is working at the rate of £24,000 a year, but then we must not bake bunns faster than people have appetite to eat them. They are not essential to the market like potatoes.

Walter Scott

1950 I forgot to say that when waiting for my train at Waterloo the other day I ran into one of the French correspondents in London. He asked me where I was off to. I said I was going down to Windsor to study the archives. He asked whether he might enquire what was the subject of my new book. '*Une biographie*,' I answered, '*de Georges V.*' He expressed surprise that there should be any documents at Windsor about any such person. Rather puzzled, I replied that there was a whole room full of papers. '*Quelle étrange personne*,' he said, '*avec cette passion presque nymphomane pour les hommes.*' I was much startled by this and then found he thought I had said George Sand.

Harold Nicolson

4 February

1663 Roger Naylor and Richard Twisse came, and would have me to goe with them to Alehouse. I went, and very mery we ware. I must not spend a 1d, but yet I did.

Roger Lowe

1830 Parliament met on this day; a more *slip-slop* composition I never read than the speech delivered for his Majesty. I verily believe the country (that is, all classes of the middle and lower rank of the community) never suffered greater distress than at the time I am writing. Agriculture woefully depressed, and trade and manufactures equally suffering, and which is greatly aggravated and increased from the severity of the season. Agricultural labourers, gardeners, and bricklayers' labourers in the most wretched state of misery.

William Dyott

1931 Today Ethel [Smyth] comes. On Monday I went to hear her rehearse. A vast Portland Place house with the cold wedding cake Adams plaster: shabby red carpets; flat surfaces washed with dull greens. The rehearsal was in a long room with a bow window looking on, in fact in, to other houses – iron staircases, chimneys, roofs – a barren brick outlook. There was a roaring fire in the Adams grate. Lady L. a now shapeless sausage, and Mrs Hunter, a swathed satin sausage, sat side by side on a sofa. Ethel stood at the piano in the window, in her battered felt, in her jersey and short skirt conducting with a pencil. There was a drop at the end of her nose. Miss Suddaby was singing the Soul, and I observed that she went through precisely the same attitudes of ecstasy and inspiration in the room as in a hall: there were two young or youngish men. Ethel's *pince-nez* rode nearer and nearer the tip of her nose. She sang now and then; and once, taking the bass, made a cat squalling sound – but everything she does with such forthrightness, directness, that there is nothing ridiculous. She loses self-consciousness completely. She seems all vitalized; all energized. She knocks her hat from side to side. Strides rhythmically down the room to signify to Elizabeth that this is the Greek melody; strides back. Now the furniture moving begins, she said, referring to some supernatural gambols connected with the prisoner's escape, or defiance or death. I suspect the music is too literary – too stressed – too didactic for my taste. But I am always impressed by the fact that it is music – I mean that she has spun these coherent chords, harmonies, melodies out of her so practical vigorous student mind. What if she should be a great composer? This fantastic idea is to her the merest commonplace: it is the fabric of her being. As she conducts, she hears music like Beethoven's. As she strides and turns and wheels about to us perched mute on chairs she thinks this is about the most important event now taking place in London. And perhaps it is.

Virginia Woolf

---

5 February

1840 Met Leigh Hunt after years, looking hearty, grey, & a Veteran.

We hailed each other. 'Haydon,' said Hunt, 'when I see you hosts of household remembrances crowd my fancy.'

'Take care,' said I, 'I have got an exquisite female hand.'

'Worthy of your own,' said he.

'Hunt,' (said I), 'I am going to write my Life & I'll do *you* justice. You would have been burnt at the Stake for a principle, & would have feared to put your foot in the mud.' Hunt was affected.

H.: Will you come & see my play?

Hay. I will – when?

H. Friday.

Hay. I'll applaud you to the Skies.

H. I'll put your names down. Bring your wife.

Hay. I will.

'God bless ye.' 'Good Bye.' We parted.

B. R. Haydon

1850 Fine. My weariness grows more oppressive, & I long for that repose, which yet I have not the courage to seek by my own hands. How gladly would I know that tomorrow should be the 'be all & end all' of my existence! My sole wish now, if I must live on, is to find myself again in my own apartmt at Venice. Twenty-five weeks since we went to Sheerness; 22 since he wrote me his last lines! Wet night, & storm of wind. Oh! how unlike everything is to him! How every fresh trial proves to me more & more that He was a thing apart. Alas! alas!

Edward Leeves

1975 The papers are full of Margaret Thatcher. She has lent herself with grace and charm to every piece of photographer's gimmickry, but don't we all when the prize is big enough? What interests me now is how blooming she looks – she has never been prettier. I am interested because I understand this phenomenon. She may have been up late on the Finance Bill Committee; she is beset by enemies and has to watch every gesture and word. But she sails through it all looking her best. I understand why. She is in love: in love with power, success – and with herself. She looks as I looked when Harold made me

Minister of Transport. If we have to have Tories, good luck to her!

Barbara Castle

---

6 February

1907 The Crisis of Youth! What is the solution? There are articles in the *Daily Mail* on 'The Age to Marry'. I believe it should be 18 for the girl and 20 for the man. That would do away with the question of Free Love, prostitutes, brothels, etc. The need for love presents a terrible Crisis in Youth. Unless he is guided it may be the cause of his undoing. But nobody ever guides him. He is left to grope alone and so – he falls. Will I be an exception?

Other fellows associate with girls. But I have kept myself aloof. Perhaps later I will score.

Sydney Moseley

1944 When we got to the opening which led into the wood, we pushed our bicycles up over the brambles and leaves; we came out at the charming clearing that I knew, and we laid my coat on the ground and spread out the lunch. Hard-boiled eggs, toast, coffee, beer for Eric, biscuits, apple tart, blackcurrant purée.

The world was slightly hazy and in a whirl. The weak sun shone. We were warm from the pub and the drink. We lay back against the tree trunk, close together because the wind was cold.

It seems unbearably sad now to think of that picnic, so unsuitable for the time of year, so lost in the wood and in time and with only two tiny points of humanity to remember it. It strikes at me and bites for some reason whenever I think of it.

We ate happily. I realized that I had been feeling quite drunk when it began to wear off.

Eric knelt up beside me and tried to put his coat right round me, for he saw that I was getting cold.

There we sat and knelt, smoking our pipes. I knew I would remember it afterwards and always. It was too sad to forget.

And there was a lovely quality too, because of the drink and the wood and our hunger for the nice food.

Eric saw how sad I was and he kissed me and lay down on the ground and shut his eyes. We both felt then, I think, how doomed we were, how doomed everyone was. We saw very clearly the plain tragedy of our lives and of everybody's. A year after a year after a year passes, and then you look back and your sadness pierces you. We were very sad from the drink, and clear-sighted.

I told Eric that he couldn't go to sleep there on the ground, as the sun was disappearing behind clouds and it was getting colder and colder. We got up to go, leaving the egg-shells on the ground. I think of those terribly sad egg-shells lying in the wood now. I feel that I shall go back to visit them.

Denton Welch

7 February

1602   Turner and Dun, two famous fencers, playd their prizes this day at the Banke side, but Turner at last run Dun soe far in the brayne at the eye, that he fell downe presently stone deade; a goodly sport in a Christian state, to see on man kill an other!

John Manningham

1827   Wrote six leaves today and am tired – that's all –

Walter Scott

1844   Eliza Dunstan died today. It was such a child's deathbed, so innocent, so unpretending. She loved to hold her father's hand, he, poor fellow, kneeling by her in silent agony. She thought none could nurse her so well as father. Her spirit was most tenderly released. It is a wonderful thought, that sudden total change of hers. Has Heaven its Infant Schools? Who can tell?

Caroline Fox

1888   Two days of blank misery; incapable of work; feeling almost ready for suicide. This evening a little light comes to me. Will it be credited, that I must begin a new novel? I am wholly dissatisfied with the plan of what I have been writing. This terrible waste of time. I dare not tell anyone the truth; shall merely say that I am getting on very slowly.

George Gissing

1947   Loelia dined with me. I took her to *Lady Frederick*, the Somerset Maugham play. Not good. L. told me that the Duke, her husband, was married again this morning. I believe she was feeling rather sad for she said she did not care whether she lived or died. I expect she feels like a dethroned sovereign. She should not seek happiness through pleasure. She is too clever.

James Lees-Milne

8 February

1754   As I by experience find how much more conducive it is to my health, as well as pleasantness and serenity to my mind, to live in a low, moderate rate of diet, and as I know I shall never be able to comply therewith in so strickt a manner as I should chuse, by the unstable and over-easyness of my temper, I think it therefore fit to draw up Rules of proper Regimen, which I do in the manner and form following, which I hope I shall always have the strictest regard to follow, as I think they are not inconsistent with either religion or morality . . .

If I am at home, or in company abroad, I will never drink more than four glasses of strong beer: one to toast the King's health, the second to the Royal Family, the third to all friends, and the fourth to the pleasure of the company. If there is either wine or punch, never upon any terms or perswasion to drink more than eight glasses, each glass to hold no more than half a quarter of a pint.

Thomas Turner

1766   It pleased Almighty God of his great goodness to take unto himself my dear good Mother this morning, about 9 o'clock, out of this sinful world, and to deliver her out of her miseries.

She went out of this world as easy as it was possible for anyone. I hope she is now eternally happy in everlasting glory . . .

O Lord God Almighty send help from Thy Holy Place to my dear Father, and to all my dear Mother's relations, to withstand so great a shock, and to live and dye so easy as she did.

The Reverend James Woodforde

1784 From the commencement of this account, January 1, to the present day, February 8, a space of five weeks and four days, it appears that, excepting one morning, viz. 2nd, and that for about an hour, not an attempt made to resume mathematics; no Latin written, little read; no Greek even looked into, no translation; no progress made in any author; nothing but a little odd information collected, of history, physiology, and biography.

Debated whether I should go out; at last resolved in the affirmative, intending to call at Lord Townshend's, and thence to proceed to Dr Johnson. The determination against my present liking, particularly in the first article; let this instance show the advantage of acting now and then against the present impression. I called on Lord T.; let in; stayed there till eleven o'clock, much pleased at what I had done, and enjoying myself more than I had done for a long while.

William Windham

9 February

1668 *Lords day.* Up, and at my chamber all the morning and the office, doing business and also reading a little of *L'escolle des Filles*, which is a mighty lewd book, but yet not amiss for a sober man once to read over to inform himself in the villainy of the world.

Samuel Pepys

1763 I got up excellently well. My present life is most curious, and very fortunately is become agreeable. My affairs are conducted with the greatest regularity and exactness. I move like very clock-work. At eight in the morning Molly lights the fire, sweeps and dresses my dining-room. Then she calls me up and lets me know what o'clock it is. I lie some time in bed indulging indolence, which in that way, when the mind is easy and cheerful, is most pleasing. I then slip on my clothes loosely, easily, and quickly, and come into my dining-room. I pull my bell. The maid lays a milk-white napkin upon the table and sets the things for breakfast. I then take some light amusing book and breakfast and read for an hour or more, gently pleasing both my palate and my mental taste. Breakfast over, I feel myself gay and lively. I go to the window, and am entertained with the people passing by, all intent on different schemes. To go regularly through the day would be too formal for this my journal. Besides, every day cannot be passed exactly the same way in every particular. My day is in general diversified with reading of different kinds, playing on the violin, writing, chatting with my friends. Even the taking of medicines serves to make time go on with less heaviness. I have a sort of genius for physic and always had great entertainment in observing the changes of the human body and the effects produced by diet, labour, rest, and physical operations.

James Boswell

1802   Wm. had slept better. He fell to work, and made himself unwell. We did not walk. A funeral came by of a poor woman who had drowned herself, some say because she was hardly treated by her husband; others that he was a very decent respectable man, and *she* but an indifferent wife. However this was, she had only been married to him last Whitsuntide and had had very indifferent health ever since. She had got up in the night, and drowned herself in the pond. She had requested to be buried beside her mother, and so she was brought in a hearse. She was followed by several decent-looking men on horseback, her sister, Thomas Fleming's wife, in a chaise, and some others with her, and a cart full of women. Molly says folks thinks o' their mothers. Poor body, *she* has been little thought of by any body else. We did a little of Lessing. I attempted a fable, but my head ached; my bones were sore with the cold of the day before, and I was downright stupid. We went to bed, but not till Wm. had tired himself.

Dorothy Wordsworth

1879 The first snowdrops appeared in the Churchyard.

The Reverend Francis Kilvert

10 February

1840 The Ceremony was very imposing, and fine and simple, and I think *ought* to make an everlasting impression on every one who promises at the altar to *keep* what he or she promises. Dearest Albert repeated everything very distinctly. I felt so happy when the ring was put on, and by Albert. As soon as the Service was over, the procession returned as it came, with the exception that my beloved Albert led me out. The applause was very great, in the Colour Court as we came through; Lord Melbourne, good man, was very much affected during the Ceremony and at the applause. We all returned to the Throne-room, where the Signing of the Register took place; it was first signed by the Archbishop, then by Albert and me, and all the Royal Family, and by: the Lord Chancellor, the Lord President, the Lord Privy Seal, the Duke of Norfolk (as Earl Marshal), the Archbishop of York, and Lord Melbourne. We then went into the Closet, and the Royal Family waited with me there till the ladies had got into their carriages. I gave all the Train-bearers as a brooch a small eagle of turquoise. I then returned to Buckingham Palace alone with Albert; they cheered us really most warmly and heartily; the crowd was immense; and the Hall at Buckingham Palace was full of people; they cheered us again and again. The great Drawing-room and Throne-room were full of people of rank, and numbers of children were there. Lord Melbourne and Lord Clarendon, who had arrived, stood at the door of the Throne-room as we came in. I went and sat on the sofa in my dressing-room with Albert; and we talked together there from 10 m. to 2 till 20 m. p. 2. Then we went downstairs where all the Company was assembled and went into the dining-room – dearest Albert leading me in, and my Train being borne by 3 Pages, Cowell, little Wemyss, and dear little Byng. I sat between dearest Albert and the Duke of Sussex. My health and dearest Albert's were drunk. The Duke was very kind and civil. Albert and I drank a glass of wine with Lord Melbourne, who seemed much affected by the whole. I talked to all after the breakfast, and to Lord Melbourne, whose fine coat I praised. Little Mary behaved so well both at the Marriage and the breakfast. I went upstairs and undressed and put on a white silk gown trimmed with swansdown, and a bonnet with orange flowers. Albert went downstairs and undressed. At 20 m. to 4 Lord Melbourne came to me and stayed with me till 10 m. to 4. I shook hands with him and he kissed my hand. Talked of how well everything went off. 'Nothing could have gone off better,' he said, and of the people being in such good humour and having also received him well; of my receiving the Addresses from the House of Lords and Commons; of his coming down to Windsor in time for dinner, begged him not to go to the party; he was a little tired; I would let him know when we arrived; pressed his hand once more, and he said, 'God Bless you, Ma'am,' most kindly, and with such a kind look. Dearest Albert came up and fetched me downstairs where we took leave of Mamma and drove off at near 4; I and Albert alone.

Queen Victoria

11 February

1840   When day dawned (for we did not sleep much) and I beheld that beautiful angelic face by my side, it was more than I can express! He does look so beautiful in his shirt only, with his beautiful throat seen. We got up at $\frac{1}{4}$ p. 8. When I had laced I went to dearest Albert's room, and we breakfasted together. He had a black velvet jacket on, without any neckcloth on, and looked more beautiful than it is possible for me to say . . . At 12 I walked out with my precious Angel, all alone – so delightful, on the Terrace and new Walk, arm in arm! Eos our only companion. We talked a great deal together. We came home at one, and had luncheon soon after. Poor dear Albert felt sick and uncomfortable, and lay down in my room . . . He looked so dear, lying there and dozing.

Queen Victoria

1881 I came upon Browning on the bridge by the Bishop's Road Station. A boisterous wind was blowing and he said he had had his umbrella turned inside out and his hat blown off.

Carlyle had been buried at Ecclefechan the day before. Browning said he had called at his house about three weeks ago; had seen him lying on a sofa 'in a comatose state'; so would not let him be disturbed but came away. Carlyle he said 'was anxious to die'.

Alfred Domett

1975 Everyone agog at the news that Margaret Thatcher has been elected Tory leader with a huge majority. Surely no working man or woman north of the Wash is ever going to vote for her? I fear a lurch to the right by the Tories and a corresponding lurch to the left by Labour.

To Buckingham Palace for the Queen's reception for the media, at least I suppose that's what we were. Newspaper editors; television controllers; journalists and commentators; Heath looking like a tanned waxwork; Wilson; Macmillan a revered side show, an undoubted star; a few actors (Guinness, Ustinov, Finney); and all the chaps like me – John Tooley, George Christie, Trevor Nunn. And Morecambe and Wise.

It was two and a half hours of tramping round the great reception rooms, eating bits of Lyons pâté, drinking oversweet warm white wine, everyone looking at everyone else, and that atmosphere of jocular ruthlessness which characterizes the Establishment on its nights out. Wonderful paintings, of course, and I was shown the bullet that killed Nelson.

As we were presented, the Queen asked me when the National Theatre would open. I said I didn't know. The Duke asked me when the National Theatre would open. I said I didn't know. The Queen Mother asked me when the National Theatre would open. I said I didn't know. The

Prince of Wales asked me when the National Theatre would open. I said I didn't know. At least they all knew I was running the National Theatre.

Home by 2 a.m. with very aching feet. Who'd be a courtier?

Peter Hall

---

12 February

1662   Alas I must endeavour to walke closer with God or I cannot keepe cart on wheeles.

The Reverend Henry Newcombe

1802   In the afternoon a poor woman came, *she said*, to beg some rags for her husband's leg, which had been wounded by a slate from the roof in the great wind – but she has been used to go a-begging, for she has often come here. Her father lived to the age of 105. She is a woman of strong bones, with a complexion that has been beautiful, and remained very fresh last year, but now she looks broken, and her little boy – a pretty little fellow, and whom I have loved for the sake of Basil – looks thin and pale. I observed this to her. 'Ay,' says she, 'we have all been ill. Our house was unroofed in the storm nearly, and so we lived in it so for more than a week.' The child wears a ragged drab coat and a fur cap, poor little fellow, I think he seems scarcely at all grown since the first time I saw him. William was with me; we met him in a lane going to Skelwith Bridge. He looked very pretty.

He was walking lazily, in the deep narrow lane, overshadowed with the hedgerows, his meal poke hung over his shoulder. He said he 'was going a-laiting'. Poor creatures! He now wears the same coat he had on at that time. When the woman was gone, I could not help thinking that we are not half thankful enough that we are placed in that condition of life in which we are. We do not so often bless God for this, as we wish for this £50, that £100, etc., etc. We have not, however, to reproach ourselves with ever breathing a murmur. This woman's was but a *common* case. The snow still lies upon the ground.

Dorothy Wordsworth

1840   Already the 2nd day since our marriage; his love and gentleness is beyond everything, and to kiss that dear soft cheek, to press my lips to his, is heavenly bliss. I feel a purer more unearthly feel than I ever did. Oh! was ever woman so blessed as I am.

Queen Victoria

1961   A great pleasure resulting from being rid of servants — one can throw away all the presents they have ever given one.

Evelyn Waugh

13 February

1840   My dearest Albert put on my stockings for me. I went in and saw him shave; a great delight for me.

Queen Victoria

1870   *Septuagesima Sunday, St Valentine's Eve*
Preached at Clyro in the morning (Matthew xiv, 30). Very few people in Church, the weather fearful, violent deadly E. wind and the hardest frost we have had yet. Went to Bettws in the afternoon wrapped in two waistcoats, two coats, a muffler and a mackintosh, and was not at all too warm. Heard the Chapel bell pealing strongly for the second time since I have been here and when I got to the Chapel my beard moustaches and whiskers were so stiff with ice that I could hardly open my mouth and my beard was frozen on to my mackintosh. There was a large christening party from Llwyn Gwilym. The baby was baptized in ice which was broken and swimming about in the Font.

The Reverend Francis Kilvert

1924   In bed all day (as usual). Haddock and baked apple at 5.30 p.m. Soup, omelette, and stewed prunes at the Monico 10.45. Since then, reading Wycherley's *Plain Dealer*, and very dreary stuff it seemed. It is now 4 a.m. and I've just had some tea and bolted three sponge cakes. I now take my pen and wonder inkily what I've got to *show* for my nocturnities of tea and toil since October 1. *Then* I said 'No hunting; no sociability; five months of seclusion – if I can achieve it – and we'll see what happens.' No more was demanded of the lustrum of dark months than that I should add 350 lines of *Recreations* stuff.

As regards the *Recreations* part of the programme (sponge cakes are causing abdominal pains – a three-cornered fight, I suppose) I have added 132 lines to the previous 628, but only 69 lines are *new* (the remainder being the revised poems on Hyde Park and Blenheim). A few of the little elegies may be added, in which case I have a book of sixty pages to publish. But I am already jibbing from the idea of the reviewers and their shoddy patronage, and I dread being left 'cleared out' and empty-desked. I suppose I've added to my awareness of the English language, through looking up thousands of words in Webster, and wearing out the binding of Roget's *Thesaurus*. And I've read a lot more than in any previous winter of my life. *What? Seven Pillars* (350,000 words) for a start. That was worth doing, and needed concentrated effort.

Siegfried Sassoon

1956 In the hope of understanding Bron better I read the diaries I kept at his age. I was appalled at the vulgarity and priggishness.

Evelyn Waugh

14 February

1602 I heard that about this last Christmas the Lady Effingham, as shee was playing at shuttlecocke, upon a sudden felt hir selfe somewhatt, and presently retiring hir selfe into a chamber was brought to bed of a child without a midwife, shee never suspecting that shee had bin with child.

The play at shuttlecocke is become soe muche in request at Court, that the making shuttlecockes is almost growne a trade in London.

John Manningham

1661 Up earely and to Sir W. Battens. But would not go in till I asked whether they that opened the doore was a man or a woman. And Mingo, who was there, answered 'a Woman'; which, with his tone, made me laugh. So up I went and took Mrs Martha for my Valentine (which I do only for complacency), and Sir W. Batten, he goes in the same manner to my wife. And so we were very merry.

Samuel Pepys

1662 I did this day purposely shun to be seen at Sir W. Battens – because I would not have his daughter to be my Valentine, as she was the last year, there being no great friendship between us now as formerly. This morning in comes W. Bowyer, who was my wife's Valentine, she having (at which I made good sport to myself) held her hands all the morning, that she might not see the paynters that were at work in gilding my chimny-piece and pictures in my dining-room.

Samuel Pepys

1752 This being Valentine Day gave to 52 Children of this Parish, as usual 1 penny each 0. 4. 4. Gave Nancy this morning 1. 1. 0.

The Reverend James Woodforde

1858 This is what I wrote in F. Sharpe's album, which filled the little page, the left side being uniformly left to be filled up by the owner: – 'Were this my last hour (and that of an octogenarian cannot be far off), I would thank God for permitting me to behold so much of the excellence conferred on individuals. Of woman, I saw the type of her heroic greatness in the person of Mrs Siddons; of her fascinations, in Mrs Jordan and Mdlle Mars; I listened with rapture to the dreamy monologues of Coleridge – "that old man eloquent"; I travelled with Wordsworth, the greatest of our lyrico-philosophical poets; I relished the wit and pathos of Charles Lamb; I conversed freely with Goethe at his own table, beyond all competition the supreme genius of his age and country. He acknowledged his obligations only to Shakespeare, Spinoza, and Linnæus, as Wordsworth, when he resolved to be a poet, feared competition only with Chaucer, Spenser, Shakespeare, and Milton. Compared with Goethe, the memory of Schiller, Wieland, Herder, Tieck, the Schlegels, and Schelling has become faint.'

Henry Crabb Robinson

15 February

1911   I got as far as the death of Mrs Lessways in *Hilda Lessways* on Sunday afternoon, and sent off the stuff as a specimen to Pinker yesterday. 33,000 words. During this time I haven't had sufficient courage to keep a journal. I suspect that I have been working too hard for 5 weeks regularly. I feel it like an uncomfortable physical sensation all over the top of my head. A very quick sweating walk of half an hour will clear it off, but this may lead, and does lead, to the neuralgia of fatigue and insomnia and so on, and I have to build myself up again with foods.

Arnold Bennett

1915   We both went up to London this afternoon; L. to the Library, & I to ramble about the West End, picking up clothes. I am really in rags. It is very amusing. With age too one's less afraid of the superb shop women. These great shops are like fairies' palaces now. I swept about in Debenham's & Marshalls & so on, buying, as I thought with great discretion. The shop women are often very charming, in spite of their serpentine coils of black hair . . .

Then I had tea, & rambled down to Charing Cross in the dark, making up phrases & incidents to write about. Which is, I expect, the way one gets killed . . .

I bought a ten & elevenpenny blue dress, in which I sit at this moment.

Virginia Woolf

1952   The King's funeral day; the problem was how to get across the path of the procession so as to lunch with Burgo in Kensington. My bus decanted me at Selfridges, and all at once

– like a bucket emptying its contents on me – I saw a horde of human beings advancing towards me. The procession must just have passed as their faces distinctly showed traces of a cathartic experience, like blackboards after a teacher had wiped them. I slipped between two files of soldiers and there I was across the frontier, in the milky sunlight of the park. The ponds shone like pale tea, and equally pale was the gold on the Albert Memorial.

Frances Partridge

16 February

1830   Last night the English Opera House was burnt down – a magnificent fire. I was playing at whist at the 'Travellers' with Lord Granville, Lord Auckland, and Ross, when we saw the whole sky illuminated and a volume of fire rising in the air. We thought it was Covent Garden, and set off to the spot. We found the Opera House and several houses in Catherine Street on fire (sixteen houses), and though it was three in the morning, the streets filled with an immense multitude. Nothing could be more picturesque than the scene, for the flames made it as light as day and threw a glare upon the strange and motley figures moving about. All the gentility of London was there from Princess Esterhazy's ball and all the clubs; gentlemen in their fur cloaks, pumps, and velvet waistcoats mixed with objects like the *sans-culottes* in the French Revolution – men and women half dressed, covered with rags and dirt, some with nightcaps of handkerchiefs round their heads – then the soldiers, the firemen, and the engines, and the new police running and bustling, and clearing the way, and clattering along, and all with that intense interest and restless curiosity produced by the event, and which received fresh stimulus at every renewed burst of flames as they rose in a shower of sparks like gold dust. Poor Arnold lost everything and was not insured. I trust the paraphernalia of the Beefsteak Club perished with the rest, for the enmity I bear that society for the dinner they gave me last year.

Charles Greville

1898 As I opened the front door this morning to leave for the office, the postman put a parcel in my hand. It was from John Lane, and it contained the first copy of my first book. I untied it hastily, and after glancing at the cover, gave it to Tertia to read. Tonight I looked through the tale, picking out my favourite bits. The style seemed better than I had hoped for.

Arnold Bennett

1944 News has come of the bombing of Monte Cassino monastery. This is comparable with the German shelling of Rheims cathedral in the last war. No war-mindedness can possibly justify it.

James Lees-Milne

17 February

1784 Did not get up till ten minutes past ten. The first effect of what is here stated is, that I have two hours less in the day, at least that my day begins two hours later. Are there not also other losses? Are not the two hours which I should so gain, better than any other? Would not every other hour be improved by additional health and spirits? And might not the advantage gained in the application of my time be more than in proportion to the time added? There is great reason to think that all this difference would be found, and if so, the conduct is very unwise that sacrifices the hopes of such advantages, either from the pleasure of continuing an hour or two in bed between sleeping and waking, or from the uneasiness of shaking off sleep before it has left me of its own accord. I will continue this conduct no longer, but tomorrow morning revert to the practice of rising as soon as I wake.

William Windham

1830 I feel very unwell, and think it is the bile which hangs about me. I strive to amuse myself by reading novels, and have finished that of *The Black Dwarf* by Sir Walter Scott. I must be reduced to a sad state when I feel obliged to such nonsense for a pastime.

The Reverend John Skinner

1926   More lunches lately – now include several with BBC executives. Interesting – useful – but *always I want to get out into the fresh air*. Smoky, foul atmosphere tires me. I am never at my best unless I am in the open air.

So, worth while or not, politic or not, I shall have to forgo them once the sun begins to shine again.

I wonder whether my diaries can trace the source and time of youth's gradual process of disillusion. When did I discover, as one ultimately must, that intelligence, good-will and common sense alone are not enough to ensure sensible and friendly human relations? Reasoning cannot offset bile, bigotry and boorishness.

Sydney Moseley

18 February

1796   Still dissatisfied with myself. Must get into a better method. Alas! what have I done today. Looked into Boswell's *Life of Johnson*; rode with Anne. Wrote one letter and read a little in Xenophon, Denina and Cicero. But what is this? Here is no progress, no exertion! Must dedicate the morning to labour, to composition: begin on Monday.

The Reverend W. J. Temple

1814   Redde a little – wrote notes and letters, and am alone, which Locke says is bad company. 'Be not solitary, be not idle.' Um! – the idleness is troublesome; but I can't see so much to regret in the solitude. The more I see of men, the less I like them. If I could but say so of women too, all would be well. Why can't I? I am not six-and-twenty; my passions have had enough to cool them; my affections more than enough to wither them – and yet – always *yet* and *but* – 'Excellent well, you are a fishmonger – get thee to a nunnery.' They fool me to the top of my bent.

Lord Byron

1841 Worked & advanced well. How people can complain of Life
who have health & a pursuit, I do not know.

B. R. Haydon

1980 Brief ceremony at which Unilever present us with the famous
Millais *Bubbles* on indefinite loan. A tiny child model called
Christina – white socks and a fringe – patiently pirouettes
before press men for half an hour and then for the
photographers sits briefly on my knee while I make stilted
conversation about Ribena. Nice to have the picture but the
PR circus takes the edge off the occasion, forcing everybody
into artificial behaviour. Obediently we point, grin, shake
hands, gravely consider, look thoughtful, point again . . . 'just
one more, please' . . . until Christina, wise girl, shows signs of
restlessness.

Evening at National Theatre (*Death of a Salesman*).
Excellent, unsentimental, but dispiriting. As usual get lost in
the foyer, where the staircases follow you about in a funny
way.

Hugh Casson

19 February

1662 I had an occasion y^t might have sadded mee this eveninge. My
son D: in his passion spoke very irreverently & sinfully to mee.
I did desire to deale wth him as well as I could to make him
sensible of his sin, & I prayed to God to forgive him poore
childe.

I meditated of Mr Kenyon his sermon & it was very
nourishinge to my soule.

The Reverend Henry Newcombe

1716 This hath been such a severe Winter that the like hath not
been known since the Year 1683. In some respects it exceeded
that. For tho' the Frost did not last so long as it did at that
time, yet there was a much greater and deeper Snow. Indeed,
it was the biggest Snow that ever I knew: as it was also the
severest Frost that ever I had been sensible of. It began on

Monday, Dec. 5th, and continued 'till Friday, Febr. 10th following, which is almost ten weeks, before there was an intire Thaw. Indeed, it began to thaw two or three times, but then the Frost soon began again with more violence, and there was withall a very sharp and cold and high Wind for some Days. When it first began to thaw and afterwards to Freeze again, it made the ways extreme slippery and dangerous, and divers bad accidents happened thereupon.

Thomas Hearne

1967   Watched an old film on television called *My Favourite Blonde* with Bob Hope. This had sentimental overtones for me. It was at the companion picture, *My Favourite Brunette* (also with Bob Hope) some time in the early forties that I was interfered with. A man took me into the lavatory of the Odeon and gave me a wank. I relived those happy moments as I sat watching the picture today. I remember coming down his mac. I must've been about fourteen.

Joe Orton

1981   In the evening I distributed the prizes at the Prendergast School at Lewisham. The school, with nearly six hundred girls, is in process of changing from grammar to comprehensive and has a high academic reputation, which the young, vital and very pretty headmistress has no intention of allowing to decline . . .

I distributed a number of prizes to black girls and asked the headmistress why they seemed to be specially applauded. Did the other girls feel sorry for them? No, I was told, it's because they are such good athletes. I am not an observant person, but I had noticed their long, graceful limbs. 'The athletes and the naughty ones are always cheered the loudest.'

Lord Longford

20 February

1814   There is something to me very softening in the presence of a woman — some strange influence, even if one is not in love with them – which I cannot at all account for, having no very high opinion of the sex. But yet – I always feel in better humour with myself and everything else, if there is a woman within ken. Even Mrs Mule, my firelighter – the most ancient and withered of her kind – and (except to myself) not the best-tempered – always makes me laugh – no difficult task when I am 'i' the vein'.

Heigho! I would I were in mine island! – I am not well; and yet I look in good health. At times I fear, 'I am not in my perfect mind'; – and yet my heart and head have stood many a crash, and what should ail them now? They prey upon themselves, and I am sick – sick – 'Prithee, undo this button – why should a cat, a rat, a dog have life – and *thou* no life at all?' Six-and-twenty years, as they call them, why, I might and should have been a Pasha by this time. 'I 'gin to be a-weary of the sun.'

Lord Byron

1924   Was up 'very early' (lunched at 1.30). Feeling moderate, so went to have hair cut before the concert for which Berners had sent me a ticket. Got there later than I intended, and missed all but the last movement of Schoenberg's Quartet (Op. 10), which sounded exquisite. (Last time I heard it, in 1914, I thought it excruciatingly ugly.)

Siegfried Sassoon

1944   By the evening I was very tired for I slept badly last night. On returning home was obliged to shelter in South Kensington tube during another severe and noisy raid. A lot more fires and a bomb dropped on the Treasury buildings. The Carmelite church in Kensington destroyed.

James Lees-Milne

21 February

1850   Was called up at about two o'clock by dearest Letitia in manifest fear that my blessed child was dying: threw on some clothes and went down to her; found her in an alarming state,

Letitia and Mrs Wagstaffe watching her in evident belief that the dear creature's hour was come: stood long beside her in the same agonizing apprehension. What thoughts passed through my brain; what a horrid mixture of recurrences of grave and trifling things, that passed like malicious antics through my brain, like those various faces that seem in savage fiendishness to pass before the eyes at night and will not be shut out! The sweet scenes of her birth, her infancy, her girlhood, and spring of youth came to my heart, softening and soothing it. My prayer to God, to the all-good, all-bountiful God, is for peace, peace and tranquillity, in this world. In the next, I cannot doubt her acceptance and her home with the spirits of the pure and good. But, oh! for remission from pain to her dear wasted frame here, I pray oh God!

William Macready

1887 Visited the prison and found Admiral Fenwick the Government inspector there. He comes once a fortnight. He was investigating a charge of drink brought in surreptitiously for Berry the executioner. It seems that functionary demands a pint of champagne the morning of his employment.

Dearman Birchall

1949 I kissed her, and took her hand. I kissed that and her arm, which also looked fat and strong, as did her hand and fingers too. She had some papers on her lap – *Woman* and *Picture Post* – and was reading one of them upside down. She seemed to forget me as soon as I was beside her; but as the nurse left, she said, in a thick, trembling voice, and with a smile, 'What a lot of locking of doors.'

'How are you?' I asked.

'All right.'

'Nice food?'

'Not very.'

We had that kind of conversation, and every now and then I kissed her, or smiled at her, or made some little laughing remark. Whereat she smiled or gave a little laugh back. But she volunteered nothing herself, except suddenly to say laughing, when someone I had not noticed begun to sing in a distant ward, 'I can do better than that.'

'Why don't you?' I said. 'Do.'

But she went dead again . . .

For long periods we sat in silence. I wondered whether to say anything to her about the past, but could not bring myself to. How awful if tears came into her eyes.

And so we sat in silence, every now and then I would kiss her or take her hand, and she would play with mine for a moment, before going back to her game with the papers, lifting them slowly, wanderingly up in the air and she would begin to fall sideways in her bed towards me, as though her head were too heavy to carry. This was my sister, the beautiful Nancy Ackerley, who had come into the world with every advantage of looks and money and position, this was what she had come to at the age of fifty.

J. R. Ackerley

22 February

1796   Prevented this morning.

Drove Anne to Milor and called on Miss Penrose and Mr and Mrs Gould.

How difficult it is to follow a plan!

Xenophon, Denina, and Cicero as usual. Wrote to Miss Hannah More at Bath in answer to her letter concerning the Cheap Repository, or little Pieces to counteract Paine's and other such Trash, undertaken by her and her friends. Shall I never be satisfied with myself? Robert grows very troublesome. Yet alas! what is he fit for? Yet to keep him at home – what a trial and perpetual vexation: restless, yet capable of nothing. Octavius rude from too much indulgence. Anne petted from the same cause. Laura all the disagreeable qualities of a girl just come from school. Poor me!

The Reverend W. J. Temple

1827   Was at court till two – then lounged till Will. Murray came to speak about a dinner for the theatrical fund in order to make some arrangements. There are 300 tickets given out. I fear it will be uncomfortable and whatever the stoics may say a bad dinner thows cold water on the charity. I have agreed to preside, a situation in which I have been rather felicitous not by much superiority of wit or wisdom far less of eloquence. But by two or three simple rules which I put down here for the benefit of posterity.

1st. Always hurry the bottle round for five or six rounds without pressing yourself or permitting others to propose. A slight fillip of wine inclines people to be pleased and removes the nervousness which prevents men from speaking – disposes them in short to be amusing and to be amused.

2d. Push on, keep moving, as punch says – Do not think of saying fine things – nobody cares for them any more than for fine music, which is often too liberally bestowd on such occasions. Speak at all ventures and attempt the *mot pour rire*. You will find people satisfied with wonderfully indifferent jokes if you can but hit the taste of the company, which depends much on its character. Even a very high party primd with all the cold irony and *non est tanti* feelings or no feelings of fashionable folks may be stormed by a jovial rough round and ready praeses. Choose your texts with discretion, the sermon may be as you like.

If a drunkard or an ass breaks in with anything out of joint, if you can parry it with a jest, good and well; if not, do not exert your serious authority unless it is something very bad. The authority even of a chairman ought to be very cautiously exercized. With patience you will have the support of every one.

When you have drunk a few glasses to play the good fellow and banish modesty if you are unlucky enough to have such a troublesome companion, then beware of the cup too much. Nothing is so ridiculous as a drunken praeses.

Lastly always speak short and *Skeoch doch na skial* – cut a tale with a drink.

> *This is the purpose and intent*
> *Of gude Schir Walter's testament.*

Walter Scott

23 February

1662   *Lords day.* My cold being increased, I stayed at home all day, pleasing myself with my dining-room, now graced with pictures, and reading of Dr Fullers *worthys*. So I spent the day; and at night comes Sir W. Pen and supped and talked with me. This day, by God's mercy I am 29 years of age, and in very good health and like to live and get an estate; and if I have a heart to be contented, I think I may reckon myself as happy a man as any is in the world — for which God be praised. So to prayers and bed.

Samuel Pepys

1669   Up, and to the office, where all the morning. And then home and put a mouthful of victuals in my mouth; and by a hackney coach fallowed my wife and girls, who are gone by 11 a-clock, thinking to have seen a new play at the Duke of York's House; but I do find them staying at my tailor's, the play not being today, and therefore I now took them to Westminster Abbey and there did show them all the tombs very finely, having one with us alone (there being other company this day to see the tombs, it being Shrove Tuesday); and here we did see, by perticular favour, the body of Queen Katherine of Valois, and had her upper part of her body in my hands. And I did kiss her mouth, reflecting upon it that I did kiss a Queen, and that this was my birthday, 36 years old, that I did first kiss a Queen. Thence to the Duke of York's playhouse, and there finding the play begun, we homeward to the glass-house and there showed my cousins the making of glass, and had several things made with great content; and among others, I had one or two singing-glasses made, which make an echo to the voice, the first that ever I saw; but so thin that the very breath broke one or two of them. So home, and thence to Mr Batelier's, where we supped, and had a good supper; and here was Mr Gumbleton, and after supper some fiddles and so to dance; but my eyes were so out of order that I had little pleasure this night at all, though I was glad to see the rest merry. And so about midnight home and to bed.

Samuel Pepys

1801 This day completes the 12th month since I lost my dear and lamented wife, from which time sorrow has been my portion. Well might I say 'that the blessing of my life was gone' – experience has proved it. My interests in life are deadened, my view of this world no longer captivating – for Scarcely an hour passes without something occurring to remind me of the value of her I have lost – or to some defficiency on my part. But trying as my situation is I hoped my heart and my Manners have been amended, & that at last I have endeavoured to make her my pattern, who was my blessing.

Joseph Farington

24 February

1738 At six in the evening, an hour after I had taken my electuary, the tooth-ache returned more violently than ever. I smoked tobacco; which set me a vomiting, and took away my senses and pain together. At eleven I waked in extreme pain, which I thought would quickly separate soul and body. Soon after Peter Böhler came to my bedside. I asked him to pray for me. He seemed unwilling at first, but, beginning very faintly, he raised his voice by degrees, and prayed for my recovery with strange confidence. Then he took me by the hand, and calmly said, 'You will not die now.' I thought within myself, 'I cannot hold out in this pain till morning. If it abates before, I believe I may recover.' He asked me, 'Do you hope to be saved?' 'Because I have used my best endeavours to serve God.' He shook his head, and said no more. I thought him very uncharitable, saying in my heart, 'What, are not my endeavours a sufficient ground of hope? Would he rob me of my endeavours? I have nothing else to trust to.'

By the morning my pain was moderated.

Charles Wesley

1832 The news of the cholera being in London, has been received abroad. According to the feelings of the different nations towards England, France, who wishes to court us, has ordered a quarantine in her ports of three days; Holland, who feels aggrieved by our conduct at the Conference, one of forty days. The fog so thick in London, that the illuminations for the Queen's birthday were not visible.

Thomas Raikes

1947   Today is the coldest day of all; frost feathers, flowers, ferns all over the windows, giving a dim clouded light inside; my pen frozen, so that I could not write with it or fill it.

Then broadest sunlight pouring on to me in bed, warm, melting the frost flowers so that a steam goes up, waving, wreathing its shadow across this page as I write. I have a lot to do.

Denton Welch

25 February

1806   Ly Mary Fleudyer came this morg. but could not be prevail'd upon to stay for our performance – We began it at 10 o'Clock this evening and it went off with *great* éclat and much applause: the parts were fill'd up as follows –

Lovel – Ld Pollington
Freeman – Justina
Duke's Servant – Henry Bankes
Sir Harry – Dr John Willis
Philip – Caroline
Robert – Charles Fane
Kitty – Myself
Lady Charlotte's Maid – Anne
L^y Babs – Mary Lowther

The best characters were Ld Pollington, Henry and Charles Fane – Henry was extremely well dress'd – I performed like a true novice and was often tempted to laugh – Justina was a strange figure in man's cloathes – Our audience however was very indulgent and we certainly succeeded in making them laugh – all the House was assembled, great and small, Steward's room, Hall, and Stables: the latter seem'd much the most entertained and were by far the most entertaining to us, by the efforts with which they endeavour'd to restrain their laughter – Mr Finch and the Miss Breartons were the only Strangers admitted to our Theatricals – I ought to praise *the prompter* Edward Fane, who did his part in perfection.

Eugenia Wynne

1821   Came home – my head aches – plenty of news, but too tiresome to set down. I have neither read not written, nor thought, but led a purely animal life all day. I mean to try to write a page or two before I go to bed. But, as Squire Sullen says, 'My head aches consumedly: Scrub, bring me a dram!' Drank some Imola wine, and some punch!

Lord Byron

1831   A drawing-room yesterday, at which the Princess Victoria made her first appearance, a short vulgar-looking child.

Charles Greville

26 February

1844   A day of intense interest. The morning was spent in plodding through the snow, shopping, & calling on the 3 Miss Broadbents, young lady acquaintances of William's. After dinner we went to a Mr Hall's to meet Spencer Hall, the phreno-mesmerist & 2 or 3 other gentlemen. S. Hall struck me as a highly intelligent & sincere person. I saw no indication of humbug whatever. After tea we had in a remarkable mesmeric patient, a boy of 12 belonging to Bradford, who possessed in the state of 'Coma' the marvellous faculty of clairvoyance. His organ of vision seemed to be the tip of his thumb, with which he was able to see a person who rang the front door bell & could describe his dress & appearance. He was struck by the waistcoat & described it by drawing lines on his hand crossing one another at right angles & saying it was black & white & red; it proved to be a plaid answering the description. But the most remarkable of his gifts, tho' not so easy to test, was that of seeing your interior organization & prescribing the remedy for what he saw amiss. His mode of doing it was to put one thumb in the patient's mouth & one on the pit of his stomach. On looking into our host he became quite sick & would not look at him again. His stomach had been out of order, as he confessed after the examination. On looking into Miller (a young German) he described the lungs as out of order & the quick breathing which caused him a good deal of pain. He prescribed linseed, spanish juice & sugar candy. Miller fully confirmed the boy's account of his affliction, which had been produced by over-exertion. At the lecture 3 young men were brought forward, two of Bradford & one from the neighbourhood. They showed the most marvellous effects on touching various phrenological organs, after being first mesmerized. The greatest fun of all was to see them with their philo-progenitiveness excited, nursing 3 great coats which we gave them with the greatest solemnity. One of them, having had his language & tune previously excited, was singing with deep feeling.

> *Hush, my dear, lie still & slumber,*
> *Holy angels guard thy bed &c.*

Another was kissing his babe extravagantly & clasping it to his breast. After these experiments, the youths were completely locked to the floor by a single motion of the operator. No temptations could move them, tho' each of them was offered £5 if he would stir one yard. Similar experiments were made with them separately, & finally the clairvoyant, being once more mesmerized, examined 2 patients & described their diseases. He told one gentleman that one of his lungs was much diseased & all the medicine in the world would not cure him. His doctor told me afterwards that he had frequent fits of haemoptyses. On the whole I never saw anything so closely resembling the preternatural before, & can only suppose that under certain peculiar physical conditions another sense becomes developed which informs the mind thro' some unknown channel. The night was bitter cold. The frozen snow in Bradford streets was like the ruggedness of an iceberg. We did not get home till ½ past 12.

Barclay Fox

27 February

1821 I have been a day without continuing the log, because I could not find a blank book. At length I recollected this.

Rode, etc. – wrote down an additional stanza for the 5th canto of Don Juan which I had composed in bed this morning. Visited *l'Amica* . . .

Last night I suffered horribly – from an indigestion, I believe . . . At last I fell into a dreary sleep. Woke, and was ill all day, till I had galloped a few miles. Query – was it the cockles, or what I took to correct them, that caused the commotion? I think both. I remarked in my illness the complete inertion, inaction, and destruction of my chief mental facilities. I tried to rouse them, and yet could not – and this is the *Soul*!!! I should believe that it was married to the body, if they did not sympathize so much with each other. If the one rose, when the other fell, it would be a sign that they longed for the natural state of divorce. But as it is, they seem to draw together like post-horses.

Let us hope the best – it is the grand possession.

Lord Byron

1833 Whatever may be in store for this country, whether it work for ultimate good or ill, none can foretell; but that a great revolution in the state is advancing none can deny. The democratic power is raising its fearful head, and, as *The Times* paper says this morning, let the present Government resign or not, the march of affairs will continue, and defy all opposition; no sooner is one innovation accomplished than a fresh inroad is proposed, as if increase of appetite had grown by what it fed on. The aristocracy are hourly going down in the scale; royalty is become a mere cipher. I was walking the other day round the Royal Exchange, the *enceinte* of which is adorned with the statues of all our kings. Only two niches now remain vacant; one is destined to our present ruler, and that reserved for his successor is the *last*. Some people might say it was ominous.

Thomas Raikes

1948 In Gide's *Journal* I have just read again how he does not wish to write its pages slowly as he would the pages of a novel. He wants to train himself to rapid writing in it. It is just what I have always felt about this journal of mine. Don't ponder, don't grope – just plunge something down, and perhaps more clearness and quickness will come with practice.

Denton Welch

---

28 February

1782 Was rather uneasy to-day on Account of being afraid that I have got the Piles coming or something else – unless it is owing to my eating a good deal of Peas Pudding two or three days ago with a Leg of Pork.

The Reverend James Woodforde

1785 The Frost severer than ever in the night as it even froze the Chamber Pots under the Beds. Wind very rough and tho' the Sun shone all the morning very bright yet it continued freezing every minute. Most bitter cold to day indeed, and likely to continue.

The Reverend James Woodforde

1850 A heavy fog, so that I can scarce see to read at midday.

Edward Leeves

1920 Very little happened. In the afternoon there was a long fives match v. Olds. It was successful for the House but most tiresome for the spectators. The most exciting event was the simultaneous outbreak of pinkeye, flu, german measles and scarlet fever, and tantalizing rumours of being sent home.

Evelyn Waugh

1951 I feel rather like a bat hanging upside down in the dark, and even when devoured by fleas putting out small hook-like claws and clutching surrounding objects – such things as a wonderful little group of yellow dwarf irises spotted with black that has sprung up outside the dining-room window in a miraculous fashion. True I planted them there, but I never expect what I plant to grow, nor does it generally. And there is the frenzied early morning singing of the birds.

Frances Partridge

29 February

1796   Strange that I have not begun my Papers. A Journal is certainly of use: at least it lets us see how little we do, and how difficult it is to carry good resolutions into effect. Every week, for some time past, I have intended to begin upon these Papers, yet have not.

The Reverend W. J. Temple

1920   Oh, to be a *writer*, a real writer given up to it and to it alone! Oh, I failed today; I turned back, looked over my shoulder, and immediately it happened, I felt as though I too were struck down. The day turned cold and dark on the instant. It seemed to belong to summer twilight in London, to the clang of the gates as they close the garden, to the deep light painting the high houses, to the smell of leaves and dust, to the lamp-light, to that stirring of the senses, to the languor of twilight, the breath of it on one's cheek, to all those things which (I feel today) are gone from me for ever . . . I feel today that I shall die soon and suddenly: but not of my lungs.

Katherine Mansfield

1952   The Brenans are back from America; Gerald came to dinner last night. He looked like someone who had just been shot off a machine in a fun-fair, still whirling and dazed and unaware where he was. His eyes were nearly closed with the violence of his emotions and the number of impressions needing to be got off his chest, which spurted forth in an inchoate stream of talk . . .

There were also some good Geraldisms – e.g. 'Parents have to learn that they are to their children what a lamp-post is to a dog.'

'Why have them then?' asked Ralph.

'Because in spite of all it is an experience not to be missed, and one gets some sort of animal pleasure in their company.'

Of girls, he said he couldn't resist any who made themselves agreeable to him, in spite of his age. 'I'm just a Sir Walter Raleigh tearing about putting my cloak down in puddles.'

Frances Partridge

1674

My berthe day

O Let that day which gaue me breth,
  Be spent in prase to thy great name,
Let it a new, and joyfull berthe
  Become, of grace, of Loue, of fame.
A berth of all that's good and just,
  Of all, that may make me thy owne,
And make me on thy mercis trust,
  That I hencforthe may joy, in none
But thee,
  Thee, who alone can'st make me, what I ought
  to bee.

Amen

Viscountess Mordaunt

1788 I considered, what difference do I find by an increase of years?
I find, 1. Less activity; I walk slower, particularly uphill: 2.
My memory is not so quick: 3. I cannot read so quick by
candle-light. But I bless God, that all my other powers of body
and mind remain just as they were.

John Wesley

1940 I couldn't sleep for excitement – at last something new is
going to happen to me!

Got to Jo's café soon after ten, and found he had been up
early, scraping down an old canvas, and hadn't even had time
to wash or shave. Luckily he didn't seem to expect me to pose
in the nude, as he'd got a beautiful, off-the-shoulder pale-blue
evening dress for me to wear, which he says will be the very
devil to paint! His room at the back was small and rather dark
– no wonder he wants to use my studio!

The pose was quite an easy one, seated in an armchair in
front of the open stove, with Jo's two rather smelly dogs
asleep at my feet, Jo, silhouetted against the window like a
shadow-play, was the inspired artist incarnate, slashing away
with his palette knife, with occasional cries of 'bugger' or

'Christ, that's good!' Soon my arms got cramped and I began to droop visibly, owing to lack of sleep. Before I knew what was happening, Jo had put down his palette and was bearing down upon me.

'You're tired my lovely, my precious petling! Wouldn't you like to take a rest?'

What happened after that was so quick and unexpected that I had no time to protest. My neck and shoulders were bare, and Jo was covering them with kisses. I could feel the unshaven bristles rasping against my skin. To my amazement, I felt a great shiver of pure delight run through me, rather like the way I felt in church when I was thinking about Gerhardt.

Well, I thought, I'm not going to be so stupid the second time round, so this time when I saw Jo's face looming over me, blue stubbly chin and rather thick sensuous lips pouting for a kiss, I decided to shut my eyes and bear it. Actually it wasn't as bad as I had expected. In fact I even found myself responding a little, kissing him back. A pity he smelt of garlic.

Just as things were beginning to get hectic the doorbell rang furiously. It was the dustman. Jo said, 'This pisshole is just one damn thing after another,' and went to the back door. By the time he had disposed of the dustman the atmosphere of passion had somewhat evaporated and so we resumed the sitting.

Joan Wyndham

---

2 March

1815   A bustle of moving. Read *Corinne*. I and my baby go about 3. Shelley and Clara do not come till 6. Hogg comes in the evening.

Mary Shelley

1896   A black day in memory, though weather fine. Went to town, to get measured for clothes etc. Bought some seeds for garden. Had dinner with Tinckam. Got home by 11 o'clock, and to my horror found all the front windows of house standing open. During my absence, man was to test the gas pipes; this he had done with a candle, and there resulted a bad explosion. Ceiling of drawing-room completely blown down, and a patch in the dining-room. In front bedroom a chair burnt up, bed-clothes damaged by fire, carpet drenched with water. All this happened at 3 in afternoon and on my return, E. with Walter and baby and two servants were sitting all together in the kitchen. Drawing-room a hideous wilderness of plaster. With difficulty made ourselves beds for the night.

George Gissing

1949   The evening was immensely enjoyable. We talked without stopping, drank just enough to stimulate the mind without fuddling, and that was quite a lot, laughed a great deal and carried on some quite dense arguments. Very shortly after this Philip [Toynbee] suddenly melted like a candle in the fire, his features softened, and he gently draped himself round the neck of Julia Mount. When he tried to stand up he nearly fell down again, and when he began a melancholy monologue about his loneliness and how lucky we all were to have mates, we saw it was time to go. He is a touching figure, and he was hospitable and sweet to us all. His new lady doctor friend, Ruth, comes down at weekends, meanwhile there he is alone with an absurd white poodle, shaven all over except for a mushroom of curls on top of its head. This creature somehow symbolizes and external-izes the clown element in Philip, and I feel that by laughing at it and guying it he is able to laugh at that part of himself.

During dinner he told us about his schooldays: how he was expelled from the Dragon School for a start.

'What for?' asked someone.

'Collecting money for Dr Barnardo's and keeping it myself.'

His bewildered parents took him to Dr Crichton Miller, who sent him to work on a farm for nine months, though he was only ten or eleven. The farmer was a slave-driver and worked him desperately hard, and at length he could bear it no longer and persuaded the bailiff's son Jesse to run away with him. They covered some eighty miles, when they were stopped by the police who sent for the farmer.

'Now you've always been a truthful boy,' he said, 'tell me the truth – you and Jesse did something dirty behind a hedge, didn't you?'

Thinking he wouldn't be believed if he said, 'No' (which was the truth) Philip said, 'Yes, we did,' and of course Jesse said, 'No.' All this must have made a deep impression, for he told us he went back to the farm a few weeks ago to look at it.

Frances Partridge

---

3 March

1815   Nurse my baby; talk, and read *Corinne*. Hogg comes in the evening.

Mary Shelley

1833   I am forty years of age! Need I add one word to the solemn reproof conveyed in these, when I reflect on what I am and what I have done? What has my life been? – a betrayal of a great trust, an abuse of great abilities! This morning, as I began to dress, I almost started when it occurred to me that it was my birthday.

William Macready

1835   Went to the gypsies early this morning & according to promise, gave Ed. Boswell's wife (who is expecting to be shortly confined) sundry old carpet ends & an ancient piece of drugget, as the covering of her tent was very scanty. They were highly delighted & insisted on my breakfasting with them, which of course I did. We had bread & cream & cold beef & capital tea. They are very hospitable, civil & industrious. Their conversation was really superior & the wit at times quite sparkling. We are all high friends. If Mrs Boswell's child be a boy it is to be christened Barclay in honour of your humble servant.

Barclay Fox

1946   Mama and I were alone in the evening. We looked through old letters which depressed us very much. They are emblems of mortality. She gave me a beautiful photograph of my grandmother.

Elsie Pethard called this morning and was overjoyed to see me. Talked nineteen to the dozen and kept repeating, 'Isn't he beautiful? Oh, I shouldn't say it, but isn't he beautiful?' For these words I kissed her affectionately when she left. She was my nursemaid when I was two, and sees me at that age today.

James Lees-Milne

4 March

1648   A very snowy morning, much time wherin I kept in was weather, not very fitt for mee to stirre out in; my water brake very ragged and a litle red sediment it argued as I conceive a remainder of ill humours in mee and that nature was concocting and expelling them: my water almost continually when cold had as it were a cover of fat over it, floting upon the same, my throate was banked and soare, they said the pallate of my mouth was downe, but I rather thinke it was streyned with hauking up the phlegme or with coughing, and sweld partly with rheume fallen into it, I tooke some hot broth with pepper and found it eased presently.

The Reverend Ralph Josselin

1815   Read, talk, and nurse. Shelley reads the *Life of Chaucer*. Hogg comes in the evening and sleeps.

Mary Shelley

1950   Never a dull moment, I think to myself when I look back over four years with Queenie [his dog]. What a rare thing to be able to say of any relationship.

That is why one is never free from anxiety and fear. Life is so insecure. Happiness is so insecure. At any moment, some disaster. Now, travelling to Notts., I look at my watch and say, 'She's having a fine walk on Wimbledon Common with Nancy.' Then I think, Perhaps at this very moment she has been run over and is screaming in her death agony.

Georges [Duthuit] said of dogs: 'How sad and frustrating for them: never quite able to say, to convey, what they wish and try to convey.'

Georges also said, about women: 'Each one believes herself to be the centre of the cosmos.'

J. R. Ackerley

---

5 March

1815   Shelley and Clara go to town. Hogg here all day. Read *Corinne* and nurse my baby. In the evening talk. Shelley finishes the *Life of Chaucer*. Hogg goes at 11.

Mary Shelley

1832   A melancholy event indeed – my poor friend Henry B. destroyed himself this morning in his room at Limmer's Hotel, Conduit-street. Continued losses at play and other pecuniary embarrassments drove him to despair, and he cut his own throat, after shaving and dressing himself completely, while the breakfast was preparing by his servant. It was an infatuation of long standing; his father had twice paid his debts to a large amount, and they were unfortunately not on speaking terms for some time past. His poor mother was burnt to death not two months ago, and he never saw her in her last moments. This sad event, and the recollection of his intimate friend —, who last year drowned himself in the Serpentine from the same dreadful cause, most probably accelerated this catastrophe. He left no letter to anyone – merely the following words, scribbled on the back of a kind note, which he had received the preceding evening from his friend the Duke of Dorset, 'I cannot pray, and am determined to rush unbidden into the presence of my God!' What a sickening thought.

Thomas Raikes

1912   I was offered by the Public Prosecutor a ticket admitting me to the trial of the Seddons, a couple accused of having poisoned an old woman who was their lodger, for her money. Although much of the evidence was of a dull nature, watching the prisoners was to me intensely interesting. They were the most respectable, commonplace-looking people imaginable. Seddon, an insurance agent, looked like a superior tradesman and

Mrs Seddon like a self-respecting, pretty servant. He appears far older than forty, and she younger than thirty-four.

What I found strange and unnatural in their behaviour was the way in which they constantly talked to one another, and his laughter at anything in the proceedings which could be considered as comic, such as the pompous way in which an old gentleman took the oath.

Marie Belloc Lowndes

6 March

1787 I spent almost all this morning with her Majesty, hearing her botanical lesson, and afterwards looking over some prints of Herculaneum, till the Princess Augusta brought a paper, and a message from Mr Turbulent, with his humble request to explain it himself to her Majesty. It was something he had been ordered to translate.

'Oh, yes!' cried the Queen readily, 'let him come; I am always glad to see him.'

He came immediately; and most glad was I when dismissed to make way for him: for he practises a thousand mischievous tricks, to confuse me, in the Royal presence; most particularly by certain signs which he knows I comprehend, made by his eyebrows; for he is continually assuring me he always discovers my thoughts and opinions by the motion of mine, which it is his most favourite gambol to pretend constantly to examine, as well as his first theme of gallantry to compliment, though in a style too high-flown and rhodomontading to be really embarrassing, or seriously offensive. Nevertheless, in the Royal presence, my terror lest he should be observed, and any questions should be asked of the meaning of his signs and tokens, makes it seriously disagreeable to me to continue there a moment when he is in the room.

Fanny Burney

1815 Find my baby dead. Send for Hogg. Talk. A miserable day. In the evening read *Fall of the Jesuits*. Hogg sleeps here.

Mary Shelley

1832 My birthday! [her twenty-sixth] – My thoughts will go to the past – the past – to the ever ever beloved! [her mother] – My happy days went away with her! – If I were to count up every happy hour since, how few they wd. be! – But there is no use in all this! The tears which I am shedding at this moment are as vain – as if they were smiles! – In another year, where shall I be – & what shall I have suffered? – A great deal I dare say – and my heart appears to be giving way even now.

Elizabeth Barrett

1836 Dined at Miss Rogers's, R., and I, and Sydney going there together. Company: the Hollands, the Langdales, Lady Davy, Surgeon Travers, and Rogers's nephew. Sydney highly amusing in the evening. His description of the *dining* process, by which people in London extract all they can from new literary lions, was irresistibly comic. 'Here's a new man of genius arrived; put on the stew-pan: fry away; we'll soon get it all out of him.' On this and one or two other topics, he set off in a style that kept us all in roars of laughter.

Thomas Moore

---

7 March

1662 I was basely poisoned in my soule by a base dreame the last night. A base impression made on my fancy y^t in some circumstances will be not easly shaken out.

The Reverend Henry Newcombe

1815 Shelley and Clara go after breakfast to town. Write to Fanny. Hogg stays all day with us; talk with him, and read the *Fall of the Jesuits* and *Rinaldo Rinaldini*. Not in good spirits. Hogg goes at 11. A fuss. To bed at 3.

Mary Shelley

1818 Get on but slowly with Bede and here I have to record the loss of an old and faithful friend in my little dog Pam who was unfortunately killed by my son's horse laying upon him in the stable where he was sent to dry himself after having been washed and was forgotten to be taken into the house again at night. He was 12 years old, very sagacious and affectionate, particularly handsome and never had any descendants at all equal to him in beauty. For many years he slept in our room. He was of a very amiable disposition and had as far as I am able to judge no evil propensity. He was grave but could be gay. Interpreter not only of looks and actions but often as I thought of words also. He remembered his friends at any distance of time and expressed himself with pleasure at seeing them after a long or short absence.

The Reverend Benjamin Newton

1934 My 35th birthday. Actually I have lied so much about my age that I forget how old I really am. I think I look 28, and know I feel 19.

'Chips' Channon

8 March

1581 It was the 8 day, being Wensday, hora noctis 10, 11, the strange noyse in my chamber of knocking; and the voyce, ten tymes repeted, somewhat like the shrich of an owle, but more longly drawn, and more softly, as it were in my chamber.

John Dee

1720 I got up, and after my breeches only were slipped on (but not fastened at the knees) I put on everything excepting my shoes, and completely dressed myself in two minutes by my wife's watch which I desired her to observe.

Dr Claver Morris

1796 Obliged to get up in the night and take some mint-water, which instantly relieved me. Must be very careful what I eat: blame pease-soup for this.

The Reverend W. J. Temple

1941 Just back from L.'s speech at Brighton. Like a foreign town: the first spring day. Women sitting on seats. A pretty hat in a teashop – how fashion revives the eye! And the shell-encrusted old women, rouged, decked, cadaverous at the teashop. The waitress in checked cotton.

No: I intend no introspection. I mark Henry James's sentence: Observe perpetually. Observe the oncome of age. Observe greed. Observe my own despondency. By that means it becomes serviceable. Or so I hope. I insist upon spending this time to the best advantage. I will go down with my colours flying. This I see verges on introspection; but doesn't quite fall in. Suppose, I bought a ticket at the Museum; biked in daily & read history. Suppose I selected one dominant figure in every age & wrote round & about. Occupation is essential. And now with some pleasure I find that its seven; & must cook dinner. Haddock & sausage meat. I think it is true that one gains a certain hold on sausage & haddock by writing them down.

Last night I analysed to L. my London Library complex. That sudden terror has vanished; now I'm plucked at by the H. Hamilton lunch that I refused. To right the balance, I wrote to Stephen & Tom: & will write to Ethel & invite myself to stay; & then to Miss Sharp who presented me with a bunch of violets. This to make up for the sight of Oxford Street & Piccadilly which haunt me. Oh dear yes, I shall conquer this mood. Its a question of being open sleepy, wide eyed at present – letting things come one after another. Now to cook the haddock.

Virginia Woolf

9 March

1660 All night troubled in my thoughts how to order my business upon this great change with me, that I could not sleep; and being overheated with drink, I made a promise the next morning to drink no strong drink this week, for I find that it makes me sweat in bed and puts me quite out of order.

Samuel Pepys

1815 Read and talk. Still think about my little baby. 'Tis hard, indeed, for a mother to lose a child. Hogg and Charles Clairmont come in the evening. C. C. goes at 11. Hogg stays all night. Read Fontenelle, *Plurality of Worlds.*

Mary Shelley

1949 I distrust myself so deeply, that is what I mean. How does one know what one is like? I hide from other people. I hide, too, from myself. The savage, the monkey within me, it cleverly conceals itself. That is civilization, of course. But not cleverly enough. Crises occur, and the façade breaks – as Jack [Sprott] saw with me over Irene: 'Why this hatred, Joe?' – the grinning ape looks through. 'Joe is so kind,' people say. Some people. 'People are frightened of you,' William [Plomer] has said. What am I really like? How do I behave, on balance? What do I do in secret, concealing it from myself, so that even I shall not look into the dreadful depths?

I woke in the middle of the night and thought, She [his sister, Nancy] cried herself often to sleep. She told me so. Oh dear, oh dear, that was dreadful. I should have never allowed that. I should have done something at once. I did feel for her too. When I visited her in that wretched sort of room in Portland Road, and saw her washing up in a tin basin on the wash-hand stand, I used to think to myself with a dreadful pity, compassion, Oh no, this mustn't go on. It's too dreadful. This is death. But I let it go on, out of fear. And of course she herself could do nothing. She had no initiative, no 'go'. I ought really to have given that its true value. It was simply her character not to be able to do things, not to be able to pay a day visit to London, or move, or go to lawyers by herself. It was part of the weakness of her character not to be able to do these things. And I – judging others by oneself, as we always do – thought it just tiresomeness, and that she should be driven, forced to do these things, obliged to do them by not being helped. But she killed herself instead.

The truth – that is what is so worrying and impenetrable in these matters, and fills my notebooks with such miserable arguments. Whatever Nancy may be, she is not a liar, a calculating schemer, a person one can expose. It is much more difficult than that. Bored and tired by her perverse –

apparently perverse – behaviour, her capacity for looking always for scapegoats for her own mistakes, I said to Morgan once lately, I remember, that I didn't know whether to tell her the truth or not – that *she* was the troublemaker, and that the disorders of our life were due to her uncontrolled bad temper and jealousy – and Morgan said, 'I should certainly tell her the truth, why not?' Jack [Sprott] on the contrary shook his head, and said it was no good. Jack was right. I did try to tell her the truth. How, I thought, was it possible for her ever to improve if she did not see her own faults, and admit them? So I tried to tell her the truth, and in the end she went out of her mind. Why? Because she saw the truth too – but her truth was different from mine.

J. R. Ackerley

10 March

1666   Thence home and to the office, where late writing letters; and leaving a great deal to do on Monday – I home to supper and to bed. The truth is, I do indulge myself a little the more pleasure, knowing that this is the proper age of my life to do it, and out of my observation that most men that do thrive in the world do forget to take pleasure during the time that they are getting their estate but reserve that till they have got one, and then it is too late for them to enjoy it with any pleasure.

Samuel Pepys

1853   As we turned the corner of a lane during our walk, a man and a bull came in sight; the former crying out, 'Ladies, save yourselves as you can!' the latter scudding onwards slowly but furiously. I jumped aside on a little hedge, but thought the depth below rather too great – about nine or ten feet; but the man cried 'Jump!' and I jumped. To the horror of all, the bull jumped after me. My fall stunned me, so that I knew nothing of my terrible neighbour, whose deep autograph may be now seen quite close to my little one. He thought me dead, and only gazed without any attempt at touching me, though pacing round, pawing and snorting, and thus we were for about twenty minutes. The man, a kind soul but no hero, stood on the hedge above, charging me from time to time not to move. Indeed, my first recollection is of his friendly voice. And so I lay still, wondering how much was reality and how much dream; and when I tried to think of my situation, I pronounced it too dreadful to be true, and certainly a dream. Then I contemplated a drop of blood and a lump of mud, which looked very real indeed, and I thought it very imprudent in any man to make me lie in a pool – it would surely give me rheumatism. I longed to peep at the bull, but was afraid to venture on such a movement. Then I thought, I shall probably be killed in a few minutes, how is it that I am not taking it more solemnly? I tried to do so, seeking rather for preparation for death than restoration to life. Then I checked myself with the thought, It's only a dream, so it's really quite profane to treat it in this way; and so I went on oscillating. There was, however, a rest in the dear will of God which I love to remember; also a sense of the simplicity of my condition – something to do to involve others in suffering, only to endure what was laid upon me. To me the time did not seem nearly so long as they say it was; at length the drover, having found some bullocks, drove them into the field, and my bull, after a good deal of hesitation, went off to his own species. Then they have a laugh at me that I stayed to pick up some oranges I had dropped before taking the man's hand and being pulled up the hedge; but in all this I acted as a somnambulist, with only fitful gleams of unconsciousness and memory.

Caroline Fox

11 March

1758   At home all day. Very piteous.

Thomas Turner

1838   The Queen sat for some time at table, talking away very merrily to her neighbours, and the men remained about a quarter of an hour after the ladies. When we went into the drawing-room and huddled about the door in the sort of half-shy, half-awkward way people do, the Queen advanced to meet us, and spoke to everybody in succession, and if everybody's 'palaver' was as deeply interesting as mine, it would have been worth while to have had Gurney to take it down in shorthand.

I shall now record my dialogue with accurate fidelity:

Q. Have you been riding today, Mr Greville?

G. No, Madam, I have not.

Q. It was a fine day.

G. Yes, Ma'am, a very fine day.

Q. It was rather cold though.

G. (*Like Polonius*) It *was* rather cold, Madam.

Q. Your sister, Lady Francis Egerton, rides, I think, does she not?

G. She does ride sometimes, Madam.

(*A pause, when I took the lead, though adhering to the same topic.*)

G. Has your Majesty been riding to-day?

Q. (*With animation*) Oh, yes, a very long ride.

G. Has your Majesty got a nice horse?

Q. Oh, a very nice horse.

Gracious smile and inclination of head on part of Queen, profound bow on mine, she turned again to Lord Grey. Directly after I was (to my satisfaction) deposited at the whist table to make up the Duchess of Kent's party, and all the rest of the company were arranged about a large round table (the Queen on the sofa by it), where they passed about an hour and a half in what was probably the smallest talk, interrupted and enlivened, however, by some songs which Lord Ossulston sang. We had plenty of instrumental music during and after dinner. To form an opinion or the slightest notion of her real character and capacity from such a formal affair as this, is manifestly impossible. Nobody expects from her any clever, amusing, or interesting talk; above all, no stranger can expect it. She is very civil to everybody, and there is more of frankness, cordiality, and good-humour in her manner than of dignity. She looks and speaks cheerfully: there was nothing to criticize, nothing particularly to admire. The whole thing seemed to be dull, perhaps unavoidably so, but still so dull that it is a marvel how anybody can like such a life. This was an unusually large party, and therefore more than usually dull and formal; but it is much the same sort of thing every day.

Charles Greville

12 March

1769   I read Prayers and preached this morning at Ansford Church. I read prayers and preached this afternoon at C. Cary Church.

Mem: As I was going to shave myself this morning as usual on Sundays, my razor broke in my hand as I was setting it on the strop without any violence. May it be always a warning to me not to shave on the Lord's Day or do any other work to profane it pro futuro.

I dined, supped and spent the evening at Parsonage.

The Reverend James Woodforde

1898   The room into which I was shown in Gower Street was, I think, the ugliest, the most *banal* I have seen. From the twisted columns of the furniture to the green rep of the upholstering, everything expressed Bloomsbury in its highest power. This was a boarding-house. My hopes sank, and they were not raised by the appearance of Mrs L., who combines the profession of a landlady with that of a 'mental healer'. She looks the typical landlady, shabbily dressed, middle-aged, and with that hardened, permanently soured expression of eyes and lips which all landladies seem to acquire. She fitted with and completed the room.

She asked me about my stammering and my health generally, talking in a quiet, firm, authoritative voice. I noticed the fatigue of her drooping eyelids and the terrific firmness of her thin lips. She told me how she had been cured of nervousness by Dr Paterson of America, and gave a number of instances of his success and her own in 'mentally treating' nervous and physical disorders. Some of them were so incredible that I asked myself what I, notorious as a sane level-headed man, was doing in that galley. However, as Mrs L. talked I was rather impressed by her sincerity, her strong quietude, and her sagacity. I asked what the patient had to do.

'Nothing,' she said. I explained my attitude towards 'mental healing' – that I neither believed nor disbelieved in it, that certainly I could not promise her the assistance of my 'faith'.

'Can you cure me of my stammering?'

'I am quite sure I can,' she answered with quiet assurance, 'but it will take some time. This is a case of a lifelong habit, not of a passing ailment.'

'Shall you want to see me often?'

'I shall not want to see you at all; but if you feel that you want to see me, of course you can do so. I shall look after your general health too. If you have a bad headache, or a liver attack, send me a word and I will help you.'

I nodded acquiescence but I was nearly laughing aloud, and telling her that I preferred to dispense with these mysterious services. As I was arranging terms with her, I marvelled that I should be assisting at such an interview. And yet – supposing there were after all something in it! I was not without hope. She had distinctly impressed me, especially by odd phrases here and there which seemed to indicate a certain depth of character in her. I went away smiling – half believing that the whole business was a clever fraud, and half expecting some happy result.

Tonight I sent her a cheque. I wondered, as I wrote it out, whether twelve months hence I should be wanting to burn these pages which recorded my credulity, or whether with all the enthusiasm of my nature I should be spreading abroad the report of Mrs L.'s powers.

Arnold Bennett

13 March

1815   Shelley and Clara go to town. Stay at home; net, and think of my little dead baby. This is foolish, I suppose; yet, whenever I am left alone to my own thoughts, and do not read to divert them, they always come back to the same point – that I was a mother, and am so no longer. Fanny comes, wet through; she dines, and stays the evening; talk about many things; she goes at half-past 9. Cut out my new gown.

Mary Shelley

1904 I finished *A Great Man* at 11.30 this morning, having written about ten thousand words in the last five days. I am more satisfied with it than I thought I should be. I began it with an intention merely humorous, but the thing has developed into a rather profound satire. I began the book about the 10th December; during two weeks of the time between then and now (Xmas) I put it aside, and during three other weeks I put it aside in order to write the play with Eden. So that I have been engaged on it nine weeks altogether. It is 60,000 words in length, and my eighth novel of one sort of another.

On Friday and Saturday I had an extremely severe cold in the head, but nothing could prevent me from finishing that novel. I was in the exact mood for writing, and had all the ideas arranged in my head.

Arnold Bennett

1923 Today I rode Higham Destiny in the Open Race at the Beaufort Point-to-Point. There were twenty-two starters. Going to the post my mare was very excited, bucking and yawing, going sideways through the spectators, and giving me an uncomfortable time. She is (as Norman Loder remarked sagely) 'very highly strung'! I can't say I felt very confident while she bounded across a stubble-field under a dark lowering sky that looked like a heavy rain-storm impending. But the excitement was exhilarating. At the post everyone seemed to be pushing and shoving and turning round while the Starter made ineffective attempts to get the unruly riders into some sort of line. Finally he allowed us to go, regardless of further formalities. I had ranged my mare alongside Geoffrey Pease, who uneasily asked 'whether she jumped straight'. 'I'll take damned good care she does,' I muttered indomitably, and a few moments later we were hurtling down to the first fence, which I jumped among the first half-dozen. As usual in Open Races there were some very wild riders, and I was thankful when I was over the first four fences and the field was getting strung out . . .

As I jumped the eleventh fence I heard Phyllis Loder's voice shout 'Go on, Sig!'

The voice seemed to come from a long way off, but pleased me. At the thirteenth fence – an awkward one on a bank, with an old cart-road and a ditch on the take-off side – a man just in front fell and his horse rolled head over heels, and I had to pull across to the left to avoid being brought down by landing on him. (Rather a clever bit of riding, I thought.) There was a nice long stretch of grass before the next fence, so I counted the horses in front of me. There were seven, so I wasn't doing badly, but the race was being run very fast and the course was sticky after last night's rain. Higham Destiny seemed to be 'dying away' a bit; I hit her twice and she responded with a spurt and jumped four more fences nicely. I was then four fences from the finish and the leaders were racing away from me, so I circumspectly pulled up and jogged blissfully back to the paddock, to be welcomed by Norman and Phyllis, who thought it 'a very good show'.

Siegfried Sassoon

14 March

1793   The most melancholy day ever happened to me. This morning about 20 minutes after eleven my beloved wife was taken from me and my dear children. We had lived six and twenty years together, being married the 6th of August 1767 at Berwick by the Rev. Mr T. Thorpe, Vicar of that town.

She had been ill about three weeks, but her apothecary, Mr Street, and her physician, Dr Gould never gave us any idea she was in any danger till about half an hour before her decease. It being totally unexpected I was struck with horror. It began with loss of appetite, universal coldness, complaint in her bowels and stomach, perpetual reachings so that nothing would stay on her stomach, pain in her side, breast and in all the muscles. Most of these were subdued, but then succeeded want of sleep and great difficulty of breathing. Dr Gould suspected a paralysis and seemed to think the vital powers were totally decayed and worn out, yet she was but 46, and never been what one could call ill before.

The Reverend W. J. Temple

1796   This, two years ago, the most melancholy day in my life: my beloved wife was taken from me. What have I suffered since and how have I missed her in every way! What future prospect of comfort? Anne too will probably soon leave me. Laura too young and giddy. No one with whom I can mingle minds. Reproach myself for not using more exertion. My time steals away unprofitably. Nothing done for the good of my Family. Blessed Saint look down, encourage and confirm me. They may know what passes here; why not? They may be permitted imperceptibly to influence our minds. Let my thoughts dwell on this dear object of my affection. But I dare not turn to the pages of this book that paint her last days, or to her Letters. Last year it was too much for me. I may, however, recollect a thousand tender passages of our lives. Incapable of doing any thing all this day. In the evening read again Mr Burke's Pamphlet.

The Reverend W. J. Temple

1876   A chemist here is selling bottles of scent, each of which is warranted to contain a sum of money from a farthing upwards, and one bottle in a thousand contains £5. Most of the coins are farthings, of course, but several have found sovereigns and half-sovereigns, and a poor woman yesterday actually bought the bottle which contained £5. She is half mad with joy!

The Reverend Benjamin Armstrong

1957   With Val to see play *Look Back in Anger* by John Osborne, whom I once interviewed on television without being able to get anything out of him. Play quite execrable – woman ironing, man yelling and snivelling, highbrow smut, 'daring' remarks (reading from Sunday paper; Bishop of . . . asks all to rally round and make hydrogen bomb). Endured play up to point where hero and heroine pretended to be squirrels.

Malcolm Muggeridge

15 March

1737   I set out for London, in the Marlborough coach, which had been robbed morning and evening, for four days before. This fifth morning we passed unmolested. Scarce was I got to town, when they fell to robbing again.

Charles Wesley

1766 A tender query: doth thy evening refreshment interrupt thy communion with thy Maker? Some doubt about it.

Dr John Rutty

1952 I am alone and revelling in my solitude. I spent my evening reading a life of Pepys; his diaries covered only nine years, from 1660 to 1669 – from when he was 27 to 36. Mine are far longer and more, at times, although such is not their intention, improper.

'Chips' Channon

1969 Jack, Hughie and Les Cannon came in at 10 a.m. Hughie apologized for keeping me waiting while they 'clarified' their 'misunderstanding'. He told me that the penal clauses presented the major obstacle; they wanted a 'total revaluation of the agreement' but recognized that this, together with the withdrawal of the penal clauses, must inevitably mean the suspension of some of the benefits – i.e. the £25 bonus and the guaranteed week. Discussions should take place with the company as soon as possible, either with me or without me. I assured them that Blakeman and Ramsey would be plenipotentiaries and that I would try to get them round. At lunchtime Charles Birdsall urged that none of us should go out because the building was besieged by the press, to say nothing of a few militants, culled from far and wide, who were demonstrating with banners outside the door. Our hearts sank at the thought of a day on nothing but sandwiches. Nothing daunted, Charles said he would ask Wheeler's to send us something in. That, I said firmly, would make the most unhelpful news story of the day: oysters and black velvets wheeled in while strikers starved. With that incredible dedication of his Charles refused to admit defeat and sent the two typists out on a foray to Lyons instead. We spent the interval giggling about it all (Roy Hattersley having sacrificed his weekend not to miss the 'fun'), and when Les Cannon came out of the waiting-room to ask when they were going to get something to eat, I went in to have a chat in the most relaxed way possible with the three of them, explaining that we didn't think sandwiches were good enough for them. It's an odd business, industrial relations! Eventually Charles and his girls returned triumphantly with smoked salmon and tongue salads, cheese, chocolate éclairs and bottles of Chablis and we had quite a picnic in my room.

Barbara Castle

16 March

1766 The women are taking your crowns from off your heads, O ye boobies and earthlings of men!

Dr John Rutty

1796 At breakfast, wrote to Miss Stowe, my dear wife's eldest sister. Interrupted by Mrs Treene and her daughter, who came to beg assistance. Drove with Anne to Enys to see the Miss Carlyons there. Mentioned Mrs Treene to Mrs Enys. Bible. Barrow. Walked after dinner. In the evening wrote to Mr Boswell enclosing a £30 bill on Frederic's account. Wrote to Sir C. Hawkins. A little in Xenophon &c. Still this is doing nothing.

How unfeelingly people talk of the distress of others. No consideration for former situations, notions, prejudices. Mrs Enys thought these people might work like common servants, tho' brought up in abundance and accustomed to attendance.

How much of our time is engrossed by sleep, meals, riding, walking, intruding and uninteresting talk! It is almost surprising how anything is done. Yet what immense and laborious Works some persons atchieve!

The Reverend W. J. Temple

1904 Felt very ill at work today – my chest hurt and my throat was sore.

Have entered for Chamber of Commerce Shorthand examination and National Union of Teachers Book-keeping. Bought No. 1 of C. B. Fry's Magazine. Jolly good!!

Looked up advertisements for clerks for Hong Kong and Brussels. Went with Dan to Drury Lane Pantomime – Dan Leno in *Humpty Dumpty*. Excellent!

Tonight I saw Loretta. She was with Joe! I think he *must* be my rival; although he told me he was in love with somebody else. He is a great swimmer and a tall, handsome fella.

Sydney Moseley

1943 I began to walk up the road past May's house and then I did hear footsteps. I stood at the side of the road, and as the figure came up he must have thought I was peepeeing, for he gave me a cheery call and said, 'How is it?' I laughed and started to walk at his side. He must have been Canadian. He was not very tall, with dark hair and a small moustache – glistening, like Ramon Novarro of my childhood.

We walked along and he said chaffingly, 'Did it get frost-bitten?' Then he told me of his leave and how he did 'it' twice a night. 'That's twenty times in ten days!' He laughed, showing all his teeth. He talked of girls and asked me where mine was and where I lived.

'Have you got a nice bed to go back to?' he asked. 'That's the main thing.'

He asked me more questions and I became uneasy. How I hate to answer questions! He went on saying that he was well set up for three weeks. He looked an extraordinarily vital, compact little man with his showy, handsome head, under the moon.

Everything was wrong. He wanted to find out about me and he wanted to talk about his women. Probing and bragging.

'Taking precautions is like paddling in your socks,' he said in a businesslike voice. He spoke of flesh touching flesh – it was all so gruesome and brotherly.

I left him, turning off the road and walking down a lane some way to shake him off. I had the fear that he was waiting to see if I would return again.

At last I came back and longed for him, for everything, to be different in the world; and for my poems to be good, not smeary as his love affairs were smeary.

Denton Welch

17 March

1814 I have been sparring with Jackson for exercise this morning; and mean to continue and renew my acquaintance with the muffles. My chest, and arms, and wind are in very good plight, and I am not in flesh. I used to be a hard hitter, and my arms are very long for my height (5 feet 8½ inches). At any rate, exercise is good, and this the severest of all; fencing and the broadsword never fatigued me half so much.

Redde the *Quarrels of Authors* (another sort of *sparring*) – a new work, by that most entertaining and researching writer, Israeli. They seem to be an irritable set, and I wish myself well out of it. 'I'll not march through Coventry with them, that's flat.' What the devil had I to do with scribbling? It is too late to inquire, and all regret is useless. But, an it were to do again – I should write again, I suppose. Such is human nature, at least my share of it; though I shall think better of myself, if I have sense to stop now. If I have a wife, and that wife has a son – by any body – I will bring up mine heir in the most anti-poetical way – make him a lawyer, or a pirate, or – any thing. But, if he writes too, I shall be sure he is none of mine, and cut him off with a Bank token.

Lord Byron

1940 She has gone. There is nothing to show that she has been here except the toothbrush glass of faded violets and some talcum powder on top of the dressing-table – that and my own feeling that other people do not exist, have no solidity or meaning, that they are figures cut out of illustrated papers, photographs of people. I am alone in the flat. I wonder whether I could sit through a dinner at the club. No – I do not think so. The sight of those pink-faced, silver-haired old boys and those well-kept young men drinking their claret and eating their jugged hare would be too much. The whole settled order of daylight comfort and daytime wisdom has become insufferable. I am beyond any consolation to be derived from the cosiest and most sympathetic friend. My heart hurts – I should like to have it removed and taken away on a silver salver.

Charles Ritchie

1943 Time's passing; time's passing. Horace Walpole said, even while one thinks of one's pain one can know that it is passing. And I know it now, that every moment passing is washing out its pain and happiness, and will leave me a blank state at last. What happiness this gives – to know that one can lay plans and be busy because the labour will not go on for ever. How is it that we are born with this fixed idea that we shall live for ever? It poisons and perverts us. It is the chief reason for our hopeless lethargy.

Now as I lie in bed at quarter to eleven and hear the drunk soldiers sing and shout as they crawl back to their billet I am filled with satisfaction, for it is all passing, which is the only reason for wanting to preserve it.

Denton Welch

18 March

1775 Being waked at three in the morning, when it is dark, occasions a kind of convulsion in the frame of man. It is an untimely and violent birth from insensibility or unconsciousness to life, and shocks our sensibility. There is a coldness in the body and a dreariness in the mind; and the cessation of human existence or activity, which then prevails, affects one with gloom. Formerly, when my nerves were bad, such a scene was terrible to me. Now that they are vigorous and well-braced, I shudder a little, but soon recover.

James Boswell

1828 I was sorely worried by the black dog this morning, that vile palpitation of the heart – that *tremor cordis* – that histerical passion which forces unbidden sighs and tears and falls upon a contented life like a drop of ink on white paper which is not the less a stain because it conveys no meaning. I wrought three leaves however and the story goes on.

Walter Scott

1866 I fret because I do not realize ambition, because I have no active work, and cannot win a position of importance like other men. Literary success would compensate me: yet, the first steps to this seem always thwarted. Intellectual, moral, and physical qualities in combination are required for this success. I have the intellectual; the physical is always giving way without my fault, and the moral flags by my cowardly inertia. I am an over-cultivated being, too alive to all sensibilities to walk on one path without distraction, and so keenly appreciative of greatness in art and literature that I am disdainful of small achievements. Yet, these gloomy reflections serve as spurs to goad me on. 'Venture, and thus climb swift to Wisdom's height.' A man has but one life to lose; he can but strive; and if he fails at last and dies with nothing done, an unremembered weed, a sea-wrack on the barren shore, why, so have lived and died, hoped and despaired, petulantly struggled and then calmly sunk, thousands before him.

J. A. Symonds

19 March

1815   Dream that my little baby came to life again; that it had only been cold, and that we rubbed it before the fire, and it lived. Awake and find no baby. I think about the little thing all day. Not in good spirits. Shelley is very unwell. Read Gibbon. Charles Clairmont comes. Hogg goes to town till dinner-time. Talk with Charles Clairmont about Skinner Street. They are very badly off there. I am afraid nothing can be done to save them. C. C. says that he shall go to America; this I think a rather wild project in the Clairmont style. Play a game of chess with Clara. In the evening Shelley and Hogg play at chess. Shelley and Clara walk part of the way with Charles Clairmont. Play chess with Hogg, and then read Gibbon.

Mary Shelley

1910   Over a fortnight has passed since I joined the *Daily Express*. Now I am a journalist – in *reality*; and we Fleet Street men (!) have little time for private dreaming in diaries! What we write we give to the world!

Sydney Moseley

1940   We talked of the varying intensities at which people required to live. I said, thinking it was axiomatic, that my great – almost my only – object in life was to be as intensely conscious as possible. To my surprise neither Ralph nor David agreed in the least. What I most dread is that life should slip by unnoticed, like a scene half glimpsed from a railway-carriage window. What I want most is to be always reacting to something in my surroundings, whether a complex of visual sensations, a physical activity like skating or making love, or a concentrated process of thought; but nothing must be passively accepted, everything modified by passing it through my consciousness as a worm does earth. Here too comes in my theory that pleasure can be extracted from experiences which are in themselves neutral or actually unpleasant, with the help of drama and curiosity, and by drama I mean the aesthetic aspect of the shape of events. The exceptions are physical pain and anxiety, the two most stultifying states; I can't hold intensity of experience to be desirable in them.

Frances Partridge

1941   I am sick of my present hectic life – the work, the miscellaneous loveless affairs and the mixed drinks. I wish I lived in a small provincial town and spent the evenings reading aloud the Victorian novelists to my wife and my adoring daughters.

Charles Ritchie

20 March

1664   *Lords day*. Kept my bed all the morning, having laid a poultice to my cods last night to take down the tumour there which I got yesterday; which it did do, being applied pretty warm and soon after the beginning of the swelling – and the pain was gone also. We lay talking all the while; among other things, of religion, wherein I am sorry so often to hear my wife talk of her being and resolving to die a Catholique; and endeed, a small matter I believe would absolutely turn her, which I am sorry for.

Samuel Pepys

1910 Bad dreams. Why – *why?* Feel wretched, and, not having the patience to wait until I go home and eat there, I am spending more money on supper. Depressed – until I get my steak and chips! Journalism is a hard master. Late hours don't matter, but stories are absolutely altered by impersonal and impassive sub-editors . . .

Find that my Letchworth inquest story has not been used. Very disappointed and down-hearted. Even now I have not quite learnt the lesson that a soft heart is no use in the battle of life . . . Take this *Express* Fund to assist the horse-bus drivers who are being driven off the street by the new motor-buses. I was asked to go to some of the busmen's houses and then report on how the Fund should be used. I wrote a factual – perhaps sentimental account giving varied human sidelights on these impoverished old chaps. I was really much touched on seeing the state they lived in. But R.D.B. (Ralph Blumenfeld, the editor) comes rushing into the Reporter's Room and exclaims: 'I did not ask you to write an old woman's embroidery account. Write a plain report!' I replied coldly: 'Very well! You shall have it.' It was hurtful. (My original story was a real slice of life as I saw it . . . wasted!) Now I simply wrote two brief sentences giving my blunt view on how the money should be spent; I suggested a Pension Fund for the old men . . . R.D.B. couldn't complain this time.

All the same, I seem to be making some progress on the *Express*.

Sydney Moseley

1949 No need to say what tonight has been like. Wonderful. I play two very small parts [in Richard III], still I don't mind. I am Dorset, the son of some Queen (Elizabeth, I think) and a messenger. Am just a little worried as I have never had to speak Shakespeare before . . .

Joe Orton

21 March

1787 The seven year old Howick ox was killed at Alnwick, amazingly fat, and weighed as follows: the carcase 152 st 8 lbs, the tallow 16 st = 168 st 8 lbs. Bolton and Embleton, butchers. The head and feet of this ox were not weighed. It was sold at tenpence per pound, in pieces, and stakes of it at one shilling; calculated to have sold, adding every article together, for the sum of £100 or thereabouts. Very remarkable to be fed in Northumberland.

Nicholas Brown

1860 Finished this morning *The Mill on the Floss*, writing from the moment when Maggie, carried out on the water, thinks of her mother and brother. We hope to start for Rome on Saturday, 24th.
Magnificat anima mea!
   The manuscript of *The Mill on the Floss* bears the following inscription: –
'To my beloved husband, George Henry Lewes, I give this MS of my third book, written in the sixth year of our life together, at Holly Lodge, South Field, Wandsworth, and finished 21st March 1860.'

George Eliot

1944 I am in a nostalgic mood, occasioned by too many late nights, too much gin and by the receipt of a late birthday present of food sent by my poor mother. She must have arranged for it nearly a year ago, since she died in June. I was touched and saddened and as I ate her chocolate, I thought of her frustrated life.

'Chips' Channon

1950 Tonight I am alone, *desœuvré*, and depressed; even lonely; I am dissatisfied with my mode of life and ask myself why I go on being an MP. In fact, why do I do so much that both bores me, and for which I am unsuited? I really only like frivolity, and society; or else solitude, writing and love.

'Chips' Channon

22 March

1870   I asked the Brentford boys about a ghost story they had told me before that. At Norris's market gardens by Sion Lane there is a place where according to tradition two men (and some boys, I think) were ploughing with four horses: in bringing the plough round at the headland they fell into a covered well which they did not see and were killed. And now if you lean your ear against a wall at the place you can hear the horses going and the men singing at their work. There are other ghosts belonging to Sion House, e.g. there is an image (of our Lady, if I remember) in a stained window which every year is broken by an unseen hand and invisibly mended again.

Gerard Manley Hopkins

1906   While I was speaking to Loretta a vulgar urchin shouted: 'What a Nose!' Untrained Barbarians!

Sydney Moseley

1957   Drove down to Robertsbridge in the early morning with Illingworth – glorious morning with mist gradually clearing as we drove along. Spirits rose as we got further from London, clearing at last the interminable suburban belt and into the country. Described to Illingworth how, the evening before, I'd kept my spectacles on by accident, and looked down at plate of beef, all bloody, like an animal's platter; how terrific reaction against such food had seized me. Spoke of growing desire to escape altogether from senses – not in itself admirable; indeed, possibly the opposite if dictated by will to self-denial; but admirable if governed by awareness of more subtle, spiritual sensibility released by eschewing the grosser, material form. Also said that my own present trend towards asceticism related to deep conviction I had that troubled times were coming – a sort of training derived from mood very like one I'd experienced in years before 1939. (Very like life that shortly after this seized by happily fugitive, gross, fleshly desire.)

    Reflected later that concept of dying in the flesh in order

to live in the spirit most profound of all. Ah, how I long and long for this.

Malcolm Muggeridge

1967 Seat belt testing at the British Standards Laboratory premises at Hemel Hempstead. And another good spate of publicity. The joy of being a Minister is that one can *do* things.

Barbara Castle

23 March

1602 I dyned with Dr Parry in the Priuy Chamber, and understood by him, the Bishop of Chichester, the Deane of Canterbury, the Deane of Windsore, &c. that hir Majestie hath bin by fitts troubled with melancholy some three or four monethes, but for this fortnight extreame oppressed with it, in soe much that shee refused to eate anie thing, to receive any phisike, or admit any rest in bedd, till within these two or three dayes. Shee hath bin in a manner speacheles for two dayes, verry pensive and silent; since Shrovetide sitting sometymes with hir eye fixed upon one obiect many howres togither, yet shee alwayes had hir perfect senses and memory, and yesterday signified by the lifting up of hir hand and eyes to heaven, a signe which Dr Parry entreated of hir, that shee beleeved that fayth which shee hath caused to be professed, and looked faythfully to be saved by Christes merits and mercy only, and noe other meanes. She tooke great delight in hearing prayers, would often at the name of Jesus lift up hir handes and eyes to Heaven. Shee would not heare the Archbishop speake of hope of hir longer lyfe, but when he prayed or spake of Heaven, and those ioyes, shee would hug his hand, &c. It seemes shee might have lived yf she would have used meanes; but shee would not be persuaded, and princes must not be forced. Hir physicians said shee had a body of a firme and perfect constitucion, likely to have liued many yeares. A royall Maiesty is noe priviledge against death.

John Manningham

1906 Excited talk in the office about my letter in the *Daily Express*. Under the heading 'At great expense' I attack the wearing of corsets:

> Would your lady correspondents have us believe they expect any right-minded man to accept a ludicrous attempt at revising nature at the expense of health?
>
> 'Astounded'

This was in answer to a letter saying that corsets *did* help to 'keep the female figure'. Instead, of course, it crushes her organs to the detriment of her health. I maintain a dignified calm!

Sydney Moseley

1946 I had a poem in my head last night, flashing as only those unformed midnight poems can. It was all made up of unexpected burning words. I knew even in my half-sleep that it was nonsense, meaningless, but that forcing and hammering would clear its shape and form. Now not a word of it remains, not even a hint of its direction. What a pity one cannot sleepwrite on the ceiling with one's finger or lifted toe.

Denton Welch

24 March

1602 This morning about three at clocke hir Majestie departed this lyfe, mildly like a lambe, easily like a ripe apple from the tree, *cum leue quadam febre, absque gemitu*. Dr Parry told me that he was present, and sent his prayers before hir soule; and I doubt not but shee is amongst the royall saints in Heaven in eternall joyes.

About ten at clocke the Counsel and diverse noblemen having bin a while in consultacion, proclaymed James the 6, King of Scots, the King of England, Fraunce, and Irland, beginning at Whitehall gates; where Sir Robert Cecile reade the proclamacion which he carries in his hand, and after reade againe in Cheapside. Many noblemen, lords spirituell and temporell, knights, five trumpets, many heraulds. The gates at

Ludgate and portcullis were shutt and downe, by the Lord Maiors commaund, who was there present, with the Aldermen, &c. and untill he had a token besyde promise, the Lord Treasurers George, that they would proclayme the King of Scots King of England, he would not open.

Upon the death of a King or Queene in England the Lord Maior of London is the greatest magistrate in England. All corporacions and their governors continue, most of the other officers authority is expired with the princes breath. There was a diligent watch and ward kept at every gate and street, day and night, by householders, to prevent garboiles: which God be thanked were more feared then perceived.

The proclamacion was heard with greate expectacion and silent joye, noe great shouting. I thinke the sorrowe for hir Majesties departure was soe deep in many hearts they could not soe suddenly showe anie great joy, though it could not be lesse then exceeding greate for the succession of soe worthy a king. And at night they shewed it by bonefires, and ringing. Noe tumult, noe contradicion, noe disorder in the city; every man went about his busines, as readylie, as peaceably, as securely, as though there had bin noe change, nor any newes ever heard of competitors. God be thanked, our king hath his right! *Magna veritas et prevalet.*

John Manningham

1856 We are now at the 24th of March 1856, and from this point of time, my journal, let us renew our daily intercourse without looking back. Looking back was not intended by nature, evidently, from the fact that our eyes are in our faces and not in our hind heads. Look straight before you, then, Jane Carlyle, and, if possible, not over the heads of things either, away into the distant vague. Look, above all, at the duty nearest hand, and what's more, do it. Ah, the spirit is willing, but the flesh is weak, and four weeks of illness have made mine weak as water.

Jane Welsh Carlyle

1962 White's. 7 p.m. I sit alone in the hall. A member known to me by sight but not by name, older than I, of the same build, but better dressed, said: 'Why are you alone?' 'Because no one wants to speak to me.' 'I can tell you exactly why; because you sit there on your arse looking like a stuck pig.'

Evelyn Waugh

25 March

1792   Day of [Mother's] funeral. I did not find myself much affected; the same thoughts as for some time past occupied my mind, but they had lost much of their effect. Should some thoughts which passed in my mind during the period spent in church, be the happy foundation of a system of belief, less liable to doubt and uncertainty than any that I have hitherto formed, I shall have reason to number this occasion among the happiest of my life, and to add this to what I already owe my mother for early habits of piety and devotion.

William Windham

1865   I am in deep depression, feeling powerless. I have written nothing but beginnings since I finished a little article for the *Pall Mall*, on the 'Logic of Servants'. Dear George is all activity, yet is in very frail health. How I worship his good humour, his good sense, his affectionate care for every one who has claims on him! That worship is my best life.

George Eliot

1949   Beautiful days, cloudless, windless, cool in the night, warm by day. Faintly misty. The sky pale blue. On Wimbledon Common every morning immense orchestration of birds. How they pipe and trill. A rabbit this morning fled out of a clump of bracken almost under my feet. Queenie [his dog] was hunting elsewhere and did not see it. I began to give a shout to attract her; but the day was so beautiful, why stain it with blood. We had the place quite to ourselves from eight until ten; just ourselves and the birds, and the rabbit. Queenie had a meal of dead bracken. I never saw her do that before, she tore off and munched quite a lot. Perhaps a rabbit had pissed on it.

There was a certain amount of new broken glass about,

which I tidied away. Spring and summer – they mean broken bottles, and perhaps cut feet. Still, one can't stop it, one can only pick up the glass when one comes upon it.

J. R. Ackerley

26 March

1872 Snow fallen upon the leaves had in the night coined or morselled itself into pyramids like hail. Blade leaves of some bulbous plant, perhaps a small iris, were like delicate little saws, so hagged with frost. It is clear that things are spiked with the frost mainly on one side but why this is and how far different things on the same side at the same time I have not yet found.

Gerard Manley Hopkins

1930 On to the *Daily Express* office about books. I see an intolerable man who treats both me and literature as if they were dirt. I am so depressed by the squalor of this interview that I return home in a nerve-storm. To make it worse, I am sent out to represent the *Standard* at the Knights of the Round Table dinner. There is no seat for me and I creep away in dismay and humiliation. I never foresaw that writing for the Press would be actually so degrading. What I dread is that I might get to like it: the moment I cease to be unhappy about it will be the moment when my soul has finally been killed.

Harold Nicolson

1940 Had to leave at six to go to Sadler's Wells with Rowena. During the interval we had cocoa and Welsh rarebit at the Angel Café, while Rowena told me about her 'uncle', and how nice sex is. She says it's the best indoor recreation she has yet discovered, particularly in the afternoon which is the only time he can get away from his wife. She says it's like an old French song which just goes on and on, and I really ought to try it. I asked her what she did to prevent herself from getting pregnant, and she said there are things called

Volpar Gels which are quite effective, but the best thing is to go to the Marie Stopes clinic and get a Dutch cap.

I told her all about Gerhardt and Jo, and she said it sounded very boring and rather decadent. Of course I'm not decadent at all really, I only wish I was.

Joan Wyndham

27 March

1668　This day at noon comes Mr Pelling to me and shows me the stone cut lately out of Sir Tho. Adam's (the old comely Alderman) body, which is very large endeed, bigger I think then my fist, and weighs above 25 ounces – and which is very miraculous, never in all his life had any fit of it, but lived to a great age without pain, and died at last of something else, without any sense of this in all his life.

Samuel Pepys

1768　ADDRESSED TO A CERTAIN MISS NOBODY
Poland Street, London, March 27.
To have some account of my thoughts, manners, acquaintance and actions, when the hour arrives in which time is more nimble than memory, is the reason which induces me to keep a Journal. A Journal in which I must confess my *every* thought, must open my whole heart! But a thing of this kind ought to be addressed to somebody – I must imagion myself to be talking – talking to the most intimate of friends – to one in whom I should take delight in confiding, and remorse in concealment – but who must this friend be? to make choice of one in whom I can but *half* rely, would be to frustrate entirely the intention of my plan. The only one I could wholly, totally confide in, lives in the same house with me, and not only never *has*, but never *will*, leave me one secret to tell her. To *whom*, then, *must* I dedicate my wonderful, surprising and interesting Adventures? – to *whom* dare I reveal my private opinion of my nearest relations? my secret thoughts of my dearest friends? my own hopes, fears, reflections, and dislikes? – Nobody!

To Nobody, then, will I write my Journal! since to Nobody can I be wholly unreserved — to Nobody can I reveal every thought, every wish of my heart, with the most unlimited confidence, the most unremitting sincerity to the end of my life! For what chance, what accident can end my connections with Nobody? No secret *can* I conceal from Nobody, and to Nobody can I be *ever* unreserved. Disagreement cannot stop our affection, Time itself has no power to end our friendship. The love, the esteem I entertain for Nobody, Nobody's self has not power to destroy. From Nobody I have nothing to fear, the secrets sacred to friendship Nobody will not reveal when the affair is doubtful, Nobody will not look towards the side least favourable.

I will suppose you, then, to be my best friend, (tho' God forbid you ever should!) my dearest companion — and a romantick girl, for mere oddity may perhaps be more sincere — more tender — than if you were a friend in propria persona — in as much as imagionation often exceeds reality. In your breast my errors may create pity without exciting contempt; may raise your compassion, without eradicating your love. From this moment, then, my dear girl — but why, permit me to ask, must a *female* be made Nobody? Ah! my dear, what were this world good for, *were* Nobody a female? And now I have done with preambulation.

Fanny Burney

1889 Wrote a long letter to Carte, stating my feelings on the subject of my position in the theatre as contrasted with Gilbert's, and also protesting against the manner the stage rehearsals were conducted by G. wasting everybody's time, and ruining my music. If Gilbert will make certain concessions to me in the construction and manner of producing the pieces, I will go on writing as merrily as ever.

Arthur Sullivan

28 March

1756 I went down to Jones, where we drank one bowl of punch and two muggs of bumboo; and I came home again in liquor. Oh!

with what horrors does it fill my heart, to think I should be guilty of doing so, and on a Sunday too! Let me once more endeavour never, no never to be guilty of the same again.

Thomas Turner

1765 In the afternoon rode over to Chiddingly, to pay my charmer, or intended wife, or sweetheart, or whatever other name may be more proper, a visit at her father's, where I drank tea, in company with their family and Miss Ann Thatcher. I supped there on some rasures of bacon. It being an excessive wet and windy night I had the opportunity, sure I should say the pleasure, or perhaps some might say the unspeakable happiness, to sit up with Molly Hicks, or my charmer, all night. I came home at forty minutes past five in the morning – I must not say fatigued; no, no, that could not be; it could be only a little sleepy for want of rest. Well, to be sure, she is a most clever girl; but however, to be serious in the affair, I certainly esteem the girl, and think she appears worthy of my esteem.

Thomas Turner

1814 This night got into my new apartments, rented of Lord Althorpe, on a lease of seven years. Spacious, and room for my books and sabres. *In* the *house*, too, another advantage. The last few days, or whole week, have been very abstemious, regular in exercise, and yet very *un*well.

Yesterday, dined *tête-à-tête* at the Cocoa with Scrope Davies – sat from six till midnight – drank between us one bottle of champagne and six of claret, neither of which wines ever affect me. Offered to take Scope home in my carriage; but he was tipsy and pious, and I was obliged to leave him on his knees praying to I know not what purpose or pagod. No headach, nor sickness, that night nor today. Got up, if anything, earlier than usual – sparred with Jackson *ad sudorem*, and have been much better in health than for many days. I have heard nothing more from Scrope. Yesterday paid him four thousand eight hundred pounds, a debt of some standing, and which I wished to have paid before. My mind is much relieved by the removal of that *debit*.

Lord Byron

29 March

1776 I was in a kind of brutal fever, went to the Park, and was relieved by dalliance.

I supped at Mrs Stuart's. Her husband did not come home. Oswald and Aberdeen were there. I madly drank a bottle of claret by myself, none of them drinking with me, and this, meeting what I had taken at dinner, made me brutally feverish. So I sallied to the Park again, and again dallied. But, what was worse, as I was coming home to General Paoli's, I was picked up by a strumpet at the head of St James's Street, who went with me to the entry to the passage from Hay Hill by Lord Shelburne's, and in my drunken venturousness, I lay with her. Oh, what a sad apprehension then seized me! I got home between three and four, or a little earlier.

James Boswell

1843 The Rabbi's wife told me that all her uncles and aunts are deaf; they may scream as loud as they like in their Uncle Jacob's ear to no purpose, but, by addressing his nose, he becomes quite accessible; an aunt's mode of approach is her teeth.

Caroline Fox

1943 My birthday, so I went to Tunbridge Wells and nearly bought a Georgian teapot, but then I didn't, because the engraved shield had no crest on it, and I hate signet rings or engraved shields with no crest on them. They looked naked. Before the silver shop I went to Mrs Heasman's and found two charming, stumpy cut glasses for 2s 6d each.

She stood in the doorway talking to me, telling me how when her husband came home on his last leave in the last war she didn't know him. 'I heard a knock at the door,' she said, 'and I thought, oh, that's only someone come to borrow something. Then there was another knock, louder. We used to use the back room then as a dining-room, so I came out of it and go to the door and open it and almost fall back with surprise. There he was with his equipment up to his eyes and a thin growth of beard all round his face. I hardly recognized him. Of course, after a bath and a shave and a good lay down he looked all right again.' Her eyes glittered and smiled behind her winking glasses. 'Then bless me if it wasn't the Armistice ten days after he'd arrived home. He had to go back again to France though, and he said the difference! Why, it was as quiet as quiet. No guns. Quite uncanny, he said.' She mused for a little and smiled again. I had no idea she loved her husband. I had only heard him, once before, shouting angrily up the stairs for his dinner. Isn't it strange to think of the continuity of lives? In the same shop and home for the space between the wars. It seemed to me quite like the landed gentry.

Denton Welch

30 March

1712   A certain barbarous Sect of People arose lately in London who distinguish themselves by the Name of Mohocks. There are great Numbers of them, and their Custom is to make themselves drunk and in the Night-time go about the Streets in great Droves and to abuse after a most inhumane Manner all Persons they meet, by beating down their Noses, prickling the fleshy Parts of their Bodys with their swords, not sparing even the Women, whom they usually set upon their Heads and committ such Indecencies towards them as are not to be mentioned; nor indeed shall I descend to any other particulars about these Brutish People, against whom there is a Proclamation issued by the Tender of a considerable Reward for Discovery of any of them. Divers have been taken up, and strict Watches are kept every Night. They are found to be young, lewd, debauched Sparks, all of the Whiggish Gang, and the Whiggs are now so much ashamed of this great Scandal (provided Whiggs can be shamed) that they publickly give out there have been no such People, nor no such Inhumanities committed, thereby indeavouring to perswade People out of their Senses. But this is only one Instance of their abominable Lying, &c.

Thomas Hearne

1755 This morn my wife and I had words about her going to Lewes tomorrow; Oh, what happiness must there be in the married state, when there is a sincere regard on both sides, and each partie truly satisfied with each other's merits! But it is impossible for tongue or pen to express the uneasiness that attends the contrary.

Thomas Turner

1948 Usual Heinemann meeting. Business of publishing, I have come to the conclusion, is really rather more depressing, if anything, than journalism. Nearly all the manuscripts I have so far been shown exceedingly tedious. In journalism there is at least the reality – news – on which the whole phoney business is based. In books there is not even this reality . . .

Started reading Goebbels' *Diary*. Interested to note that he, too, writer *manqué* who had begun by producing a bad novel and a play which no theatre would put on. Most men of action seem to be writers *manqué*, and correspondingly most writers, men of action *manqué*. Interesting theme.

Malcolm Muggeridge

31 March

1594 A great fit of the stone in my left kydney: all day I could do but three or four drops of water, but I drunk a draught of white wyne and salet oyle, and after that, crabs' eys in powder with the bone in the carp's head, and abowt four of the clok I did eat tosted cake buttered, and with suger and nutmeg on it, and drunk two great draughts of ale with it; and I voyded within an howr much water, and a stone as big as an Alexander seed. God be thanked!

John Dee

1668 I called Deb to take pen, ink, and paper and write down what things came into my head for my wife to do, in order to her going into the country; and the girl writing not so well as she would do, cried, and her mistress construed it to be sullenness and so was angry, and I seemed angry with her too; but going to bed, she undressed me, and there I did give her good advice and beso la, ella weeping still; and yo did take her, the first time in my life, sobra mi genu and did poner mi mano sub her jupes and toca su thigh, which did hazer me great pleasure; and so did no more, but besando-la went to my bed.

Samuel Pepys

1793 Employed a considerable time in endeavours to improve my hand, by trial of different methods of holding my pen; by one, in particular, apparently very little promising, but which I saw lately used by Nepean. I cannot yet much boast of my success, yet the attempt must not be relinquished. After what I have remarked myself, confirmed by the remark which I once heard made by Burke, I am convinced that a good hand is not wholly without connection with a good style.

William Windham

1835 A gypsy, Elias Barclay Boswell, was born today at 6 a.m., just steering clear of Fools' day for the honour of the name.

Barclay Fox

1718 A doctor layd a gentleman a wager that he could not eat two eggs after every dinner for a year and never drink till an hour after, he laid it (it was his estate to, etc.) and died before the year ended – He was opened, and a hard thing about his heart – which his relation kept – made a cane head of it, lying near some radishes it dissolved – he laid the same wager with the doctor for the same estate, and won it, the eating of radishes dissolved the eggs.

The Reverend John Thomlinson

1787 The weather still continues mild: never known so promising a spring, wind continuing south-east.

Nicholas Brown

1819 Made Bessy turn her cap awry in honour of the day.

Thomas Moore

1858 Received a letter from Blackwood containing warm praise of *Adam Bede*, but wanting to know the rest of the story in outline before deciding whether it should go in the Magazine. I wrote in reply refusing to tell him the story.

George Eliot

1941 Sid and Mummy stayed over at the Grail House last night, so was alone in London for the first time since the blitz started. Went up to Sid's bedroom and read all her juicy books about psychopaths and sexual abnormalities and the symbolism of dreams. There was one by Kraft Ebbing that got me so excited that I remembered something Leonard had told me and took a candle from the little altar. Now I suppose I'm completely beyond the pale as far as the Church is concerned.

Joan Wyndham

2 April

1552 I fell sick of the measles and the smallpox.

King Edward VI

1775 I passed the evening at Sir John Pringle's. Much was talked of Mr Johnson's *Journey*. I sat awhile with Sir John after his company were gone, and got home quietly a little after twelve, which was extraordinary for me. My landlord always gets up and lets me in. It vexes me somewhat to disturb him so much; and it has come into my mind that such violent exercise, agitation of spirits, and want of sleep might bring on a fever. But my avidity to put as much as possible into a day makes me fill it till it is like to burst.

James Boswell

1790 My Journal has been neglected, it must be confessed; but in return my neglects in other articles have been less than at any former period. It is in some respects consolatory and in others grievous, to consider how different my life has been this time from what it ever was before. I have now began to discover, for the first time, that as much may be done in London as at any other place. To what is this change owing? Is it a fact that has always been true and only now discovered; or is it, that some change, not depending on myself, has really made the difference? I suspect that there is a concurrence of causes, but that the principal is in my own determination. Let us say in what this change consists. Internally and substantially, I make a greater progress in all sorts of employment. I possess my faculties in greater perfection and enjoy throughout the day, in every situation, either of solitude or company, a higher degree of happiness.

William Windham

1914 I have begun to sleep badly again and I've decided to tear up everything that I've written and start again. I'm sure that is best. This misery persists, and I am so tired under it. If I could write with my old fluency for *one day*, the spell would be broken. It's the continual effort – the slow building-up of my idea and then, before my eyes and out of my power, its slow dissolving.

Katherine Mansfield

---

3 April

1724 Good-Friday. Went to Church. Mr Johnson Preach'd. I neither Eat nor Drank, nor so much as took any Snuff at all, 'till past 7, in the Evening.

Dr Claver Morris

1940 This morning I polished up an old box I found upstairs – it is of walnut with black and yellow inlay and a brass crest on the lid. It makes a beautiful box for relics – so in went all the letters, pressed flowers, Niersteiner corks, handkerchiefs, *Tilia platyphyllos*, etc. It will still hold a few more letters, though it is quite nicely filled. I wonder what will happen to it. If I were to die tomorrow I should either have it sent back to him or buried with me (probably the latter) – but as it seems not very likely that I shall, I daresay it may be in my possession for years and years, until one day it becomes junk again and the box returns to the place where I found it – perhaps with the relics still in it. Dust to dust, ashes to ashes . . . What a great pleasure and delight there is in being really sentimental. I thought about this as I picked flowers in the garden this morning – violets – a great patch of them smelling lovely, sweeter than the lids of Juno's eyes, primroses plain and coloured, scyllas and wild celandines, so very much spring flowers. People who are not sentimental, who never keep relics, brood on anniversaries, kiss photographs good-night and good morning, must miss a good deal. Of course it is all rather self-conscious and cultivated, but it comes so easily that at least a little of it must spring from the heart. I could write a lovely metaphysical poem about the relics of love in a box. Perhaps I will – for his seventieth birthday (in March 1989).

Barbara Pym

1949 [During rehearsals for *Richard III*]
Must check growing tendency to think
a) Nigel Pochin (he plays Rivers, Norfolk, and Largest Messenger) got his part through influence (his dad's assistant stage manager).
b) That because quite often I sit and read on my own (I hardly know anyone) people think how lonely I must be (which is ridiculous).

Joe Orton

4 April

1835 I was told last night that the scene of noise and uproar which the House of Commons now exhibits is perfectly disgusting. This used not to be the case in better, or at least more gentlemanlike, times; no noises were permissible but the cheer and the cough, the former admitting every variety of intonation expressive of admiration, approbation, assent, denial, surprise, indignation, menace, sarcasm. Now all the musical skill of this instrument is lost and drowned in shouts, hootings, groans, noises the most discordant that the human throat can emit, sticks and feet beating against the floor. Sir Hedworth Williamson, a violent Whig, told me that there were a set of fellows on his side of the House whose regular practice it was to make this uproar, and with the settled design to bellow Peel down. This is the *reformed* House of Commons.

Charles Greville

1854 Coming from Lord Monteagle's, I suffered myself to be swindled. A fellow with a bad grinning countenance, very dirty in appearance, accosted me by my name. I said I did not recollect him. 'You knew my father.' – 'It is – Julius, I suppose?' – He said 'Yes.' And then a scene like that in a comedy followed, I playing fool, and he knave; confirming all I said by assent, and saying himself nothing. 'Are you going home now?' – 'Why, no; I am going to the Athenæum.' – 'Had you been going, I should have asked you to accommodate me with a sovereign. It would save me a walk to the Custom House, where I want to fetch some articles from abroad.' Ass! this ought to have opened my eyes. I should be further off the Custom House here than there. I was infatuated. 'You are a clergyman?' – 'Yes.' – 'But why in such a dress?' – 'Oh, I would rather follow any other profession.' I could fill a page with recounting all the circumstances that ought to have told me the fellow was a knave. Opening my purse, he said, 'Could you let me have two?' I gave him one sovereign and a half, and the moment he left me, saying he would bring it in the morning, I saw my stupidity.

Henry Crabb Robinson

1945   When I got home I read in the evening paper that poor Ava [Lord Dufferin] had been killed. Ava was with Tom the friend I most admired at my private school, and at Eton, where the three of us edited magazines together. I saw little of him at Oxford, and rarely met him afterwards. He had the best brain of my generation, and was at school a brilliant scholar, winning prizes after doing the minimum amount of work, always at the last moment. As a boy he was an eccentric in that, during intense concentration, he would literally eat his handkerchief and suck ink from the end of a pen without realizing what he was doing. I think he was ruined for life by the late Lord Birkenhead, who at Oxford taught him and others of his group to drink. Consequently he became a sad physical wreck before he was thirty.

James Lees-Milne

5 April

1750   I read over great part of Gerard's *Meditationes Sacræ* – a book recommended to me in the strongest terms. But alas! how was I disappointed! They have some masterly strokes, but are in general trite and flat, the thoughts being as poor as the Latin. It is well every class of writers has a class of readers, or they would never have come to a second impression.

John Wesley

1797 Rev. Mr Barclay I called on, and had a long conversation with him. He considers my inconveniences of feeling as arising from suppressed gouty humours. He advises a disuse of wine – particularly Port Wine – and to substitute a little Brandy & Water. To eat roasted Apples for supper, – White Biscuits instead of Bread – to avoid eating web-footed Animals – Salmon, Mackrell. To eat in preference Venison, all game, Fowls; Beef & Mutton are less to be preferred than the former. *Large* Cod, – whitings, Soles, Haddocks – Turbot, all good. To avoid Pork entirely. He asked me if I had warm feet, I said, Yes, *that* He replied was a good sign. To regulate the Bile ought to be the great object of life – the oppressions caused by it when in a vitiated state destroys mankind. Avoid Milk, I remarked on it being the natural food of Children, and what, said He, is so bilious as a young Child. Sea bathing would be bad for me – Those constitutions only can stand sea bathing which perspire very freely. Do you start in your sleep sometimes – that is irritation from Bile. When you awake in the night or in the morning, are you *instantly broad awake?* No; then you have not *that* Symptom of irritation. Are you much troubled with Phlegm collecting in the Stomach? Not to be sensible of it. That is a bilious symptom. (I observe Sir George often labours with Phlegm). Avoid vegetables.

Take my Pills at night, going to rest – one, two or three as you find necessary – if in the morning they have no effect, take one, two or three more. An hour after breakfast, an Hour after Dinner, and an Hour after Supper take two tea spoon full of the *Specific*, in a third of pint of *soft* water. At any time of the day that you may find yourself uneasy take of the *Volatile Cordial* 4 or 6 tea spoons full in water as above.

Joseph Farington

1980 Children and grandchildren arrive. Cold wind, hot sun, blue sea. Read Ruskin, walk on the beach, play snakes and ladders. Feel well blessed. What did Thomas More say to his children? 'I have given you, forsooth, kisses in plenty and but few stripes ... If ever I have flogged you 'twas but with a peacock's tail.'

Hugh Casson

6 April

1766   Fine Day. After Matins, I told the Clark, William Wood, who has laid at my House these 6 years, (ever since Jo: Burgess left me, & whose Son Tom was too little to be safe in the House in Case of any Accident), & who consequently always supped here, that for the future he might lie at his own House, with his Wife at Mrs Page's, & not dine at my House on a Sunday, but when particularly invited: as I would not make it a Custom to be demanded of Right. This I did, as he had been drunk for a Week together, & was so drunk this morning that I was sent to, to desire that Will Turpin might officiate as Clark, he being Sexton. His wife sent the Message to me by my Man, his son. I was sorry to do this, as he is a quiet, good-tempered Man, & no Fault but Drunkenness: he had not laid at my House these 2 or 3 Nights, but at an Ale House at F. Stratford, the Sink of all that is bad. However, not to disgrace him at once, I told Tom to ask him to Dinner in the Kitchin to Day, & that he might lie here a few Nights 'till his Mother, Mrs Page, & he were a little reconciled.

William Cole

1961   I am very happy these spring days. Each morning I wake between 4 a.m. and 5 a.m.; then make tea, read for a while, work until 7.30, when I go for a walk. Through the window I watch the day begin, from first grey light to full sunrise, as, in the evening, I watch it end. It is a great joy to see each day's first and last light. After breakfast I read the papers, then work until lunch time. After lunch, I lie down with a book, and usually sleep for an hour or so; then walk or do gardening, mostly mowing the grass; followed by a late tea, work until about 7.30, another short stroll, supper, a game of cards with Kitty, and bed. This quiet and serenity set one apart from public affairs. The newspapers, which I still avidly devour, seem to be about another world than mine. I continue to want to know about it, but not to visit it.

A paperback series of religious books has, for its first volume, St Augustine's *Confessions*, and for its second *Sex, Love and Marriage*. In contemporary terms, anything about fornication is religious, as anything about raising the standard of life, and ameliorating its material circumstances, is Christian. In this sense fornication can be seen as sacred, an act of Holy Communion – which, as Euclid says, is absurd.

Malcolm Muggeridge

---

7 April

1847 A day sadly spoiled by my growing infirmity – absence of mind. After going to University College Committee, I went to J. Taylor's, to exchange hats, having taken his last night; but he had not mine there. I took an omnibus to Addison Road, drank tea with Paynter, and then went to Taylor's to restore his hat; and then found that I had a second time blundered by bringing Paynter's old hat; and I lost an hour in going to and from Addison Road, and from and to Sheffield House. Is this infirmity incurable? I fear it is; though I record it here to assist me in becoming more on my guard. It is a wise saying of Horace Walpole's: 'There is no use in warning a man of his folly, if you do not cure him of being foolish.'

Henry Crabb Robinson

1875 We took tea with Mr Hipperson of Hoe. The whole thing was done rather as a joke, and the old lady provided hot cockles, which our party had never tasted before, and which we are in no hurry to taste again.

The Reverend Benjamin Armstrong

1940 Today I have been reading *Of No Importance* – Rom Laudau's diary of February–October 1939. Many things in it I understand so well – the reluctance to sit down and begin writing so that one finds oneself doing all sorts of unnecessary tasks to postpone that moment of starting. And also the feeling that no day is really satisfactory if one hasn't done some sort of work – preferably a few pages of writing, but anyway something useful. Why is it that one is still surprised to discover that other people feel these things too? I am beginning to be less surprised now. I used to think that I was the only person who the night before setting out to go abroad – even for a holiday – had the feeling that I'd give anything not to be going. But Jock says he feels it too and Mr Barnicot – both hardened travellers.

My days pass so pleasantly and uneventfully but really with nothing *accomplished*. I have done so little writing this year. But writing is not now quite the pleasure it used to be. I am no longer so certain of a glorious future as I used to be – though I still feel that I may ultimately succeed. Perhaps I need some shattering experience to awaken and inspire me, or at least to give me some emotion to recollect in tranquillity. But how to get it? Sit here and wait for it or go out and seek it? Join the ATS and get it peeling potatoes and scrubbing floors? I don't know. I expect it will be sit and wait. Even the idea of falling violently in love again (which is my idea of an experience!) doesn't seem to be much help in the way of writing. I seem to have decided already the sort of novels I want to write. Perhaps the war will give me something. Perhaps the Home Front novel I am dabbling with now will get published. Perhaps . . .

But women are different from men in that they have so many small domestic things with which to occupy themselves. Dressmaking, washing and ironing, and everlasting tidying and sorting of reliques. I think I could spend my whole day doing such things, with just a little time for reading, and be quite happy. But it isn't *really* enough, soon I shall be discontented with myself, out will come the novel and after I've written a few pages I shall feel on top of the world again.

Barbara Pym

8 April

1725 Busied in Mulling Red-Wine, & the Funeral of my Dear Wife.

Dr Claver Morris

1815 There is nothing like the sight of a lovely Woman! Nothing so subdues one, so controuls one; I feel the influence of her eyes if they wander down my form just like electrical air from a point. I sat by one this morning at a lecture of Spurzheim's, and without one atom of appetite or passion felt an affectionate desire to put her sweet arm round my neck and nestle my own cheek on her lovely bosom – with pure heartfelt softness. She looked so gentle, so delicate, so soft, so yielding, that one's manly feelings of protection were roused, and one's gentle emotions of tenderness were excited.

The principle implanted by Nature that the feelings of consciousness as to manhood should be encreased by gratifying the other Sex, often pushes us to the gratification without reference to the object for which that sensation was given.

B. R. Haydon

1942   A proud and pleasant day. Lunched with Gladys, Joyce and Lorn in dressing-room. At three o'clock the King and Queen arrived with the two Princesses, Dickie and Edwina. We took them first to Stage 5, where the King took the salute. Then I did the Dunkirk speech. The ship rolled, the wind machine roared, in fact everything went beautifully. All the time they were perfectly charming, easy and interested and, of course, with the most exquisite manners to everyone. The Queen is clearly the most enchanting woman. The Princesses were thrilled and beautifully behaved. Altogether it was an exhibition of unqualified 'niceness' from all concerned and I hope it impressed the studio as much as it should have – not just because the King and Queen and Princesses of England put themselves out to make everyone they met happy and at ease. There are many who might say, 'So they should, for it's part of their job.' This is perfectly true. It was also part of Pavlova's job to dance perfectly and part of Bernhardt's job to act better than anyone else. I'll settle for anyone who does their job that well, anyhow.

Noël Coward

9 April

1922   I feel thoroughly immersed in the sporting life and feel strong cravings to acquire a smart point-to-point horse for next year.

The one undeniably good thing about athletic sport is that it forces one to keep healthy.

But extreme physical fitness does not go with intellectual alertness and creative intensity. I think that periods of physical fitness are a preparation for emotional expression. Army life was the same.

Siegfried Sassoon

1943   This evening I saw a white bicycle; and whenever I see a white bicycle it spells madness to me, for when I was small the doctor's wife in our village was mad, and she rode a white bicycle.

Dressed in her mauve riding-habit and her thick veil she could be seen all over the village, riding her white bicycle, pouring milk down the drains (to feed the German prisoners confined down there), carrying her badminton racket, going round to each house in an attempt to get people to join her badminton club.

Once, my aunt told me, she was discovered directing the traffic dressed in football boots and shorts.

The poor doctor also had his Sunday joint thoroughly washed under the tap, to get rid of the poison.

Often the doctor's wife slept in a barn in the hay, but at other times she would go home and sleep in her room as she used to do.

It was after the last war that she finally went mad. My aunt said that she had always been a little eccentric.

I remembered wondering, even as a child, how it was that she was left entirely to roam freely.

'But mightn't she do something dangerous? Mightn't she hurt herself?' I asked.

'The doctor says that it is much kinder to let her lead the kind of life she likes. She doesn't do anyone any harm,' my aunt answered.

I think she and the doctor were right, although it is obvious to me now that the reason for leaving the mad woman unmolested was an economic one.

She really seemed to lead a vital life, however fantastic and ridiculous she made herself. Shut up in a home, or with a keeper, she could not direct the traffic, could not be of heroic service to poor imprisoned aliens, could not organize thrilling badminton clubs, sleep in the hay, wear mauve riding-habits, decontaminate the Sunday joint, ride on her romantic white bicycle over the common in the evening, talking and singing to herself mysterious and important words.

Oh, how my heart bled for her! I thought of her alone in the hay – the whole wreck of her life – the fiendish laughter of the village children who were worse than devils.

It was shaming, utterly shaming to think that no one cared what she did; that no one would ever take anything she did seriously.

Denton Welch

10 April

1862   Took my elder daughter to a concert to hear Jenny Lind sing. She is a great favourite in Norwich. The other celebrities were Sims Reeve and Belletti. The 'Swedish Nightingale' was, however, the great attraction; certainly her powers of song are marvellous. The sustained note on the highest key, the shakes and above all the 'echo' in the Swedish song, are astonishing, and partake of the nature of ventriloquism.

The Reverend Benjamin Armstrong

1905   In a very bad plight. Boots all broken. No money. Things are going worse at home. . .

The only way I will ever release my heart of feelings will be to *write*, write! write!!

Sydney Moseley

1922   I motored to Colwall Park Steeplechases, through Cheltenham and Tewkesbury. At present I find race-meetings very interesting. The behaviour and appearance of the racing folk are absolutely Hogarthian. They go there to make money; or because they have a passion for 'a bit of a gamble'; or to kill time (which probably includes the first two as well).

And they can never lose interest in the day's sport, because no one loses interest in acquiring money. Many of them are losing, but they soon recover from their depression and try again. It is all very simple.

Siegfried Sassoon

1944 I am terribly distressed about my state and about my behaviour with the children. They don't know how to take me at all. And the years are passing so quickly. I had a bath before supper tonight for the first time for many years, I think. It made me think of the time when I had this regularly, and then dressed in dinner jacket suit, and sat down to my evening meal with Muriel like a gentleman. I don't suppose I shall ever do this again. I sometimes look at my old diary 'enclosures' volumes when I was 'the most powerful man in the country next to the PM' and such like. *Ichabod* indeed.

John Reith

11 April

1681 I took early in the morning, good dose of elixir, and hung three spiders about my neck, and they drove my ague away – *Deo gratias*.

Elias Ashmole

1856 Today also I lighted upon an interesting man. It was in our baker's shop. While the baker was making out my bill he addressed some counsel to a dark little man with a wooden leg and a basket of small wares. That made me look at the man to watch its effect upon him. 'I'll tell you what to do,' said this Jesuit of a baker; 'Go and join some Methodists' chapel for six months; make yourself agreeable to them, and you'll soon have friends that will help you in your object.' The man of the wooden leg said not a word, but looked hard in the baker's face with a half-perplexed, half-amused, and wholly disagreeing expression. 'Nothing like religion,' went on the tempter, 'for gaining a man friends. Don't you think so, ma'am?' (catching my eye on him). 'I think,' said I, 'that whatever this man's object may be, he is not likely to be benefited in the long run by constituting himself a hypocrite.'

The man's black eye flashed on me a look of thanks and approbation. 'Oh,' said the baker, 'I don't mean him to be a hypocrite, but truly religious, you know.' 'If this man will be advised by me,' I said, 'he will keep himself clear of the *true religion* that is purposely put on some morning to make himself friends.' 'Yes,' said the poor man pithily, 'not that at *no* price!' In my enthusiasm at his answer, and the manner of it, I gave him — sixpence! and inquired into his case.

Jane Welsh Carlyle

1972 I have a feeling the National Theatre is going to go wrong. It makes me think one can only make small decisions from day to day, from hour to hour. The big decisions are somehow made for one. And yet I resent that thought. I have always believed passionately that one makes one's own luck. I have tried to make mine all my life. The truth is that at this moment I don't know whether I want to go to the National Theatre or not. It is flattering to be asked. The status is enormous. The possibility of doing good work is boundless. The impression it makes on people is ridiculous. But I grasp eagerly at every possibility that it may go wrong. What will be the outcome?

Peter Hall

12 April

1789 A number of well-dress'd people descending the mountain paths and hastening to exhibit their holiday apparel at the Church in this village.

Lady Eleanor Butler

1802 Had the mantua-maker. The ground covered with snow. Walked to T. Wilkinson's and sent for letters. The woman brought me one from William and Mary. It was a sharp, windy night. Thomas Wilkinson came with me to Barton, and questioned me like a catechizer all the way. Every question was like the snapping of a little thread about my heart — I was so full of thought of my half-read letter and other things. I was glad when he left me. Then I had time to look at the moon while I was thinking over my own thoughts. The moon travelled through the clouds, tinging them yellow as she passed along, with two stars near her, one larger than the other. These stars grew or diminished as they passed from, or went into, the clouds. At this time William, as I found the next day, was riding by himself between Middleham and Barnard Castle, having parted from Mary. I read over my letter when I got to the house.

Dorothy Wordsworth

1870 Last night the Swan was very quiet, marvellously quiet and peaceful. No noise, rowing or fighting whatever and no men as there sometimes are lying by the roadside all night drunk, cursing, muttering, maundering and vomiting.

The Reverend Francis Kilvert

13 April

1718 Mr Werg reported to have offered to lay with two or three men's wifes in Alnwick – one was the day before sacrament – she asked him how he durst, when he knew he was the next day to administer sacrament and she to receive it – he replyed love was a noble passion, and God would indulge it. This sent up to London, and they say he is stopt of the living.

The Reverend John Thomlinson

1737 Having had bohea to breakfast, and drank green tea with Mr Seward whom I met in the Strand after I had been to enquire for the Fulham coach, which was full, and having talked with Mr Seward about his correction upon *Timon*, I walked to Putney, it was very windy and dusty, or else pleasant walking; I called at Fulham and had two Brentford rolls and a glass of wine 5d, and a little after two I went to Mr Gibbon's, where the dinner was just going up; Mr Law was in the dining parlour by himself, I went in and came out again, and he said, Are you but just come in? and I sat down by the fire and they came in to dinner, and being asked, I excused myself and said that I had dined, and Mr Gibbon saying

Where? I said, On the other side the bridge. He asked, among other questions, how shorthand went on, and I said that more persons were desirous to learn. After dinner I sat to the table and drank a few glasses of champagne; Mr Law eat of the soup, beef, &c., and drank two glasses of red wine, one, Church and King, the other, All friends; Mr Gibbon fell asleep.

John Byrom

1946 An amazing thing has happened; they have written from my father's office to say that Bill has asked for his Air Force gratuity, about ninety-nine pounds, to be handed over to me on my birthday! How heartless and dead of them not to have told me of this on my birthday, instead of several weeks afterwards. It would have overjoyed me, for I got no letters that day – although some arrived the next. I have never had a present like this before. It delights one all over.

Denton Welch

14 April

1775 This being Good Friday, I resolved as usual that it should be solemnly spent. I breakfasted with Mr Johnson, drank a good deal of tea, and eat cross-buns. Dr Levett made tea to us. I observed Mr Johnson took no milk to his tea. I suppose because it is a kind of animal food. Nor did he eat any bread at all. I was not quite so strict; and I will own that the minute circumstance of the buns being marked with the cross had *some* effect on my mind.

James Boswell

1789 Glorious day. A Plough at one end of the field, plough man whistling melodiously. A Harrow in another part. Sheep and lambs dispersed about, some grazing, some at play, others lying down. Smoke ascending from the cottages with which the sides of the mountains are dotted. Writing beside the window. I must write down the Scenery which adorns this field at this moment. Richard Griffith's Plough is under the window. Edward Evans with a Harrow. Evan Williams sowing oats. The Pinahin man's cart with Dung in a remote corner of the field for Potatoes. The Miller and his horse laden with sacks of corn coming from the Mill to the village. Sun shining, birds singing, lambs bleating. Ploughmen and sowers whistling and singing. Village bells ringing for Church.

Lady Eleanor Butler

1862   I went down to see Tennyson, who is very peculiar-looking, tall, dark, with a fine head, long black flowing hair, and a beard; oddly dressed, but there is no affectation about him. I told him how much I admired his glorious lines to my precious Albert, and how much comfort I found in his *In Memoriam*. He was full of unbounded appreciation of beloved Albert. When he spoke of my own loss, of that to the nation, his eyes quite filled with tears.

Queen Victoria

15 April

1765   After dinner I set out for Malling, to pay Molly Hicks, my intended wife, a visit, with whom I intended to go to church, but there was no afternoon service. I spent the afternoon with a great deal of pleasure, it being very fine, pleasant weather, and my companion very agreable. Now, perhaps, there may be many reports abroad in the world of my present intentions, some likely condemning my choice, others approving it; but as the world cannot judge the secret intentions of my mind, and I may therefore be censured, I will take the trouble to relate what really and truly are my intentions, and the only motive from which they spring (which may be some satisfaction to those who may happen to peruse my memoirs). First, I think marriage is a state agreable to nature, reason, and religion; I think it the duty of every Christian to serve God and perform his religious services in the most calm, serene, and composed manner, which, if it can be performed more so in the married state than a single one, it must then be an indispensable duty ... As to my choice, I have only this to say: the girle, I believe, as far as I can discover, is a very industrious, sober woman and seemingly endued with prudence, and good nature, with a serious and sedate turn of mind. She comes of reputable parents, and may perhaps, one time or other, have some fortune. As to her person, I know it's plain (so is my own), but she is cleanly in her person, and dress, which I will say is something more than at first sight it may appear to be, towards happiness. She is, I think, a well-made woman. As to her education, I own it is not liberal; but she has good sense, and a desire to improve her mind, and has always behaved to me with the strictest honour and good manners — her behaviour being far from the affected formality of the prude, on the one hand; and on the other, of that foolish fondness too often found in the more light part of the sex. For myself, I have nothing else in view but to live in a more sober and regular manner, to perform my duty to God and man in a more suitable and religious manner, and, with the grace of the Supreme Being, to live happy in a sincere union with the partner of my bosom.

Thomas Turner

1870   *Good Friday*
Took cross-buns to Hannah Whitney, Sarah Williams, Margaret Griffiths, Catherine Ferris, Mary Jones, five widows.

The Reverend Francis Kilvert

16 April

1766   Will Wood junr, who wants to be married to Henry Travel's Daughter, the prettiest Girl in the Parish, being uneasy with his Grandmother, (who can't afford to settle him), went away from her for 3 or 4 Days. The Times are so hard, small Farms so difficult to be met with, the Spirit of Inclosing, & accumulating Farms together, making it very difficult for young People to marry, as was used; as I know by Experience this Parish, where several Farmers' Sons are forced to live at Home with their Fathers, tho' much wanting to marry &

settle, for Want of proper Places to settle at. Which sufficiently shews the baneful Practice of Inclosures, & that the putting any the least Restraints upon Matrimony, (as the last Marriage Act did, contrived by Lord Chancellor Hardwicke on selfish Family Motives, as it was commonly said), is of great Disservice to the Nation.

The Reverend William Cole

1855 Out to pay Rent – about 3 pound left in pocket. Tax-man called I think for the 4th time for poor rate; sent him about his business – worked at the sketch of 'Last of England'. To day I am 34, a dull thing to consider. How little done, Oh Lord, & how much gone through? How many changes, how many failures? Is it fate, is it fault? Will it end or must it end me? A bad cold on my chest with pain therein these 3 days (6 hours).

Ford Madox Brown

1936 Kit is in hospital. I went to see her this afternoon. After I'd left the hospital, I walked along the Embankment worrying about her, imagining how I'd react if she died, then realizing that I was turning even the possibility of her death into a kind of sensuality.

Malcolm Muggeridge

1938 Dined at Windsor Castle. The invitation had said I was to bring knee breeches and trousers so I phoned Hill Child [Master of the Household] and he said it was a mistake. I had enquired if one were meant to turn up in pants with both alternatives ready; if not which would he tip. At 7.45 I suddenly thought that, with ordinary breeches, buckles wouldn't be worn on pumps. Phoned up – told yes. Much relief. A few minutes later phoned back – bows. Much consternation. I got the governess to use a black evening tie. It was excellent and there was much amusement at the Castle when I told them about it.

John Reith

17 April

1870 *Easter Day*

The happiest, brightest, most beautiful Easter I have ever
spent. I woke early and looked out. As I had hoped the day
was cloudless, a glorious morning. My first thought was
'Christ is Risen'. It is not well to lie in bed on Easter morning,
indeed it is thought very unlucky. I got up between five and
six and was out soon after six. There had been a frost and the
air was rimy with a heavy thick white dew on hedge, bank
and turf, but the morning was not cold. There was a heavy
white dew with a touch of hoar frost on the meadows, and as
I leaned over the wicket gate by the mill pond looking to see if
there were any primroses in the banks but not liking to
venture into the dripping grass suddenly I heard the cuckoo
for the first time this year. He was near Peter's Pool and he
called three times quickly one after another. It is very well to
hear the cuckoo for the first time on Easter Sunday morning. I
loitered up the lane again gathering primroses.

The village lay quiet and peaceful in the morning sunshine,
but by the time I came back from primrosing there was some
little stir and people were beginning to open their doors and
look out into the fresh fragrant splendid morning.

There was a very large congregation at morning church, the
largest I have seen for some time, attracted by Easter and the
splendour of the day, for they have here an immense reverence
for Easter Sunday. The anthem went very well and Mr
Baskerville complimented Mr Evans after church about it,
saying that it was sung in good tune and time and had been a
great treat. There were more communicants than usual: 29.
This is the fifth time I have received the Sacrament within four
days. After morning service I took Mr V. round the
churchyard and showed him the crosses on his mother's,
wife's, and brother's graves. He was quite taken by surprise
and very much gratified. I am glad to see that our primrose
crosses seem to be having some effect for I think I notice this
Easter some attempt to copy them and an advance towards
the form of the cross in some of the decorations of the graves.
I wish we could get the people to adopt some little design in
the disposition of the flowers upon the graves instead of

sticking sprigs into the turf aimlessly anywhere, anyhow and with no meaning at all. But one does not like to interfere too much with their artless, natural way of showing their respect and love for the dead. I am thankful to find this beautiful custom on the increase, and observed more and more every year. Some years ago it was on the decline and nearly discontinued. On Easter Day all the young people come out in something new and bright like butterflies. It is almost part of their religion to wear something new on this day. It was an old saying that if you don't wear something new on Easter Day, the crows will spoil everything you have on.

Between the services a great many people were in the churchyard looking at the graves. I went to Bettws Chapel in the afternoon. It was burning hot and as I climbed the hill the perspiration rolled off my forehead from under my hat and fell in drops on the dusty road. Lucretia Wall was in chapel looking pale and pretty after her illness. Coming down the hill it was delightful, cool and pleasant. The sweet suspicion of spring strengthens, deepens and grows more sweet every day. Mrs Pring gave us lamb and asparagus at dinner.

The Reverend Francis Kilvert

1975 At rehearsal this afternoon John [Gielgud] asked Harold [Pinter] what the Briggs/Spooner scene was for at the beginning of Act II. What did it give the audience? What did it convey? Harold paused. 'I'm afraid I cannot answer questions like that, John. My work is just what it is. I am sorry.'

Peter Hall

18 April

1785 Saw the first Swallow this Season this Morning.

The Reverend James Woodforde

1819 Took my little Bible to church with me, in order to search in it for a subject that would suit a fine triumphant air of Novello's

I have to put words to. Found an admirable one in Jeremiah, and wrote four lines during service – War against Babylon: much better employed than I should have been in listening to the drawling parson and snuffling clerk. Let nobody see me though, having the pew to myself and the two little girls.

Thomas Moore

1899   Today I sat on a Coroner's Jury at Fulham and heard four cases, including one suicide through religious mania. I was struck by several things:
   The decency of people in general.
   The common sense and highly trained skill of the coroner.
   The dramatic quality of sober fact. In two instances, the deceased persons had died from causes absolutely unconnected with the superficial symptoms. Thus a woman who had brought on a miscarriage and died, had died from heart disease.
   The sinister influence of the ugliness amid which the lower classes carry on their lives.
   The enormous (as it were) underground activity of the various charitable and philanthropic agencies which spread themselves like a network over London. It would seem that nothing could happen, among a certain class of society, without the cognizance of some philanthropic agency.
   The dullness and the conscientiousness of a jury.
   The absolute thoroughness with which suspicious deaths are inquired into.

Arnold Bennett

1906   Bought nearly new bike: £3. Pay by next Friday. Ride to Kingsway, when bars became loose, and so have to walk with bike home.

Sydney Moseley

1937   A quiet day with my accounts and finances . . . I find a new, unexpected joy at the age of nearly forty, in accumulating money and watching it grow.

'Chips' Channon

19 April

1661 To London, and saw the bathing and rest of the ceremonies of the Knights of the Bath, preparatory to the Coronation; it was in the Painted Chamber, Westminster. I might have received this honour, but declined it.

John Evelyn

1921 Walked three miles out of Gloucester and up a gorse-clad hill, and back over some lush green meadows. A lovely morning; apple-blossom; and a peacock in a farmyard, shaking out his tail-feathers, and turning to face me with his array of eyes and barbaric dignity.

Siegfried Sassoon

1945 We went into the church and wandered about, admiring the candelabra and wishing I had a small one like it for the dolls' house. Then into the churchyard. I was getting tired and it was hot.

Suddenly, under a large yew we came upon iron railings round the opening of a vault. The top grating had been removed, and the gate at the top of the stairs was open. Ferns grew in the wall and stretched out their fronds over the opening. Eric began to walk down the steps, and as I watched him, he looked like the perfect figure of an explorer going down into the secret tunnel.

At the bottom of the steps was another iron gate with thick wire netting all over it, but this had been pulled away at one corner, and through it Eric looked; then he called me to come down quickly. I ran down, pushed myself in front of him, and looked in. There, quite plain before me, was a bare white-washed little room, and on a framework three coffins, a graceful, other-century shape. In the darkness they seemed to be of perished leather, studded with nails, but this may have been an illusion. For a moment I was only conscious of extreme stillness (although children were shrieking and playing in the rectory garden above us) and of three human beings in the coffins. I saw them through the lids of the coffins, and it seemed as if they were sleeping there till some later date when they would rise up again. The horror of the nailed down lids over those faces was very real, and the feeling too that here for more than a century was something untouched, undisturbed, protected and now perhaps on the eve of being molested, spoilt, obliterated.

We both realized that it was something that we might never see again. Three old coffins, extraordinarily refined, civilized and ordered, lying in their vault, in the coolness, the darkness. The world up above rushing by year after year and none of its heat and pain and misery meaning anything in that subterranean room.

I climbed up the steps again and went to look at the altar tomb memorial that was also enclosed in the iron railing. There I saw the name Arundel and a date in the early eighteen-thirties. There were other names too I have forgotten already, and a later date. One at least was a woman; perhaps all were women. I will go back one day and look properly.

Denton Welch

1945   The black-out is to end officially on Monday and on Tuesday Big Ben will be lit up after a five years' eclipse. Slowly life reverts to normal.

'Chips' Channon

20 April

1828   I preached in the morning on the subject of Balaam and Balak: very few at Church on account of the rain; this prevented my walking between the services. There was a churching in the evening, and two burials. Some of the boys behaved very badly at the funerals by talking and laughing out loud, so I desired the clerk to take a stick and chastise them. This is a most untoward race, and it is impossible to deal with them.

The Reverend John Skinner

1915   I don't want to go back at all. Everything has changed so much since I was at college six weeks ago. On reading parts of my diary from the beginning of the year just now it struck me as curious how very little I said about Roland during last term, though he was in my mind so much. I think I loved him then, but it was nothing to what I do now. The development of my feelings towards him has been rapid & quite carried me away; it is almost terrible. When one loves deeply, it is almost impossible to remember what the time was like before one did. Yet I must go on trying to work – thinking that he may never read the letter I have so loved writing to him, or that the one I have received from him may be the last. I wrote him a long one today telling him much the same things as I have been writing just now. How I love writing to him!

Vera Brittain

1925 Happiness is to have a little string onto which things will attach themselves. For example, going to my dressmaker in Judd Street, or rather thinking of a dress I could get her to make, & imagining it made – that is the string, which as if it dipped loosely into a wave of treasure brings up pearls sticking to it.

Virginia Woolf

21 April

1911 London. Palace Theatre. Pavlova dancing the dying swan. Feather falls off her dress. Two silent Englishmen. One says, 'Moulting'. That is all they say.

Arnold Bennett

1915 Sometimes I can hardly believe I am I. I feel as if I were writing a novel about someone else, & not myself at all, so mighty are the things happening just now. If, that summer just after I came out & things seemed as though they would always be stagnant & dull, someone had said to me 'Before three years are over you will not only have fallen deeply in love with someone, but that very person will be fighting on the battlefields of France in the greatest war ever known to man. And your anguish of anxiety on his account will be greater than anything you have dreamed possible,' I should not have believed it could really ever happen. Tonight – not only when I heard from Roland but before – I have been full of a queer excitement – almost exultation. There has been no apparent reason for it, so I very much wonder why.

Apparently the hill we have taken near Ypres is a real advantage to us, but our losses are reported to be heavy. That means terrible long casualty lists within the next few days.

Vera Brittain

1968   Ted and I were sitting by the telly listening to the six o'clock news when there suddenly was Enoch Powell, white-faced and tight-lipped, delivering his Wolverhampton speech on immigration. As we listened to his relentless words – 'I see the Tiber running with blood' – intense depression gripped us. I knew he had taken the lid off Pandora's box and that race relations in Britain would never be the same again. This is certainly a historic turning point, but in which direction? I believe he has helped to make a race war, not only in Britain but perhaps in the world, inevitable.

Barbara Castle

22 April

1659   *After the berthe of my son John*
My God and my Lord, my defender, and protectur, reseue I most Humbely beseche thee my acknoledgments of thy mercy, and my thanksgeuings for my saue deleueranc from the payne and perill of Childe berthe, and for the grete blesing of an outher Sone, Lord multyply thes thy blesings uppon me, making me truly sensabull of thy mercis and my owne mesery, Lorde what am I that thou shouldest thus regarde me, I am nothing but a dede doge without thee, but thou supportest me on euery side, *therefor I will be glade and reioyce, in thy Saluation, I will prayse thee amungst much pepul.*

Amen

Viscountess Mordaunt

1835 Read at breakfast the beautiful ode of Horace 'Ad Lollium,' Ode IX, Book 4. How much do I desire to obtain that 'animus secundis temporibus dubiisque rectus'. The concluding stanzas I have prefixed to this diary: they really delight me. Walked for about an hour and a half and thought occasionally on *Hamlet*.

Read with the dictionary one or two stanzas of Tasso, and with an earnest desire of acting Hamlet well, lay down on the bed after dinner striving to keep it in my mind. Went refreshed and rather confident to the theatre, but very much disappointed in my own performance. I might find an excuse for my inability to excite the audience in the difficulty of ascertaining where the audience was, but I allow no plea of reservation in the question of playing as I ought or not. I did not satisfy myself. My only consolation was that, though provoked once or twice, I manifested not the slightest appearance of anger. How is it that, with the pains and precautions I take, I should thus disappoint myself? Am I too fastidious and too careful? Were I less so, what would become of me?

In the opening speeches to the king and queen I was better than usual – more direct, and with more meaning and more feeling. My soliloquy was, at least the latter part of it, flurried, not well discriminated, not well given in regard to action – it wants finish and study. The scene with Horatio, &c., still requires study and earnestness; the interview with and address to the Ghost, rearrangement, except the latter part, which I did well tonight. The last scene of the first act was amended tonight, but needs study, finish, clear discrimination.

Act second – scene with Polonius – more ease, abstraction, and point; with Rosencrantz and Guildenstern, more ease and dignity and purpose; with the players, more point and discrimination. The soliloquy also requires a little finish.

Act third – soliloquy requires, and always will require, study and practice. I was pretty well tonight; with Ophelia, a little softening and practice; with the players, throughout, rearrangement and study; the scene with Horatio, a little more melancholy and tenderness. The music beginning *piano* is very good, the play scene is good, and the remainder of the act. The closet scene requires a little revision and correcting.

Act fourth – try over that scene often.

Act fifth – requires much earnestness and much study; it was, as a whole, the best part of the play tonight.

William Macready

---

23 April

1696   I went to Eton, and din'd with Dr Godolphin, the Provost. The schoolmaster assur'd me there had not been for 20 years a more pregnant youth in that place than my Grandson. I went to see the *King's house* at Kensington. It is very noble, tho' not greate. The gallery furnish'd with the best pictures from all the houses, of Titian, Raphael, Corregio, Holbein, Julio Romano, Bassan, Vandyke, Tintoret and others; a greate collection of Porcelain; and a pretty private library. The gardens about it very delicious.

John Evelyn

1856   The Countess sat an hour with me in the morning. She is sure I 'don't *eat* enough'. I could not walk further than half-way to Sloane Square! Oh dear, oh dear! this living merely *to live* is weary work!

Jane Welsh Carlyle

1948   Yesterday I had a letter from Count Carlo John Russoni who said that he had stayed up till four a.m. reading *Maiden Voyage*. He seemed to think that it exactly mirrored his own experiences as an adolescent. He needed to feel somebody really near him and my book had made him feel it. 'Your book was like a rope thrown out to one in the deep waters. I hope you won't disappoint by showing me that the rope was an end in itself. If I follow the rope I must find you. I hope you will forgive my writing in such an exacting manner. The fact is that I need some help very badly, and it may be your help I need. I have been in your country for six months, and I am afraid I have failed entirely in whatever may have been my purpose in coming here.'

He gives me his Florence address: Via Leone X, Firenze,

Italy, then finished off, 'Try to contact me soon, will you, as in a few weeks it may be too late.'

I have asked him down to lunch. One can never stop being a little curious about people who write such letters, they are often so strangely unlike their letters; witness Peter Verreker. Another part of one is only pushed into having them because they seem to expect it. This part is always reluctant, 'put upon', ill at ease and irritated, because it is so aware of the disappointment in store for them. How outrageous it is of them to expect an oracle, a miracle or some other equally monstrous thing! And that is exactly what they do expect. Is it only the very simple who write such letters?

Denton Welch

---

24 April

1718 Secker preached a marriage sermon – some call 'em evils, plague of man, etc. But we should not play the butcher upon that naked sex who have no arms, but for embraces. Some think any wives good enough, who have but goods enough – But take heed, for sometimes the bag and baggage go together. Marriages are stiled matches – yet amongst those many that are married, how few are there matched. Husbands and wives are like locks and keys, that rather break than open, except the wards be answerable.

The Reverend John Thomlinson

1902 (My fortieth birthday) . . . – Now let me write a little sober survey of my life, as it turns upon the hinge. It is just half-past six, about which hour I was born.

'I am fairly happy – full of little plans and ambitions and interests. But I fear that most of these are very selfish. I don't think I want to serve; neither do I want to rule . . . My face is set away from Eton, and towards the Meadows of Ease, that delicate place. Should I be happier? A.C.A. says bluntly that I should not, but I think that only money keeps me back. I have nearly £700 a year of my own, and a pension would make it £800; so that it could not be imprudent to leave. Certainly my heart is more and more in writing, and less and less in teaching or administration. A very small thing would dislodge me hence. I put aside all ambition for the headmastership as merely futile . . .

'And so I enter on a new phase, and I try to survey the plains of middle age with fortitude and faith. I hope I may slay some Canaanites. But what good is it to look forward? I am in the hands of God.'

A. C. Benson

1943   Today is an anniversary – I mean six months since my poor darling declared his ill-fated love and started me on this great chunk of misery.

After breakfast Honor and I went shopping in Clifton and came back with our string bags bulging – treacle and Shredded Wheat and cakes and buns. We discussed the technique of misery on the way back, then had tea in the kitchen. In the afternoon I washed my hair and parted it in the middle again.

Barbara Pym

25 April

1803   I was very indifferent all day and safe delivered of a little girl soon after five o'clock.

Elizabeth Fremantle

1804   William Fremantle called to ask Betsey to chapron Miss Hervey to the play, she therefore accepted and at about 7 we went to Covent Garden. It was *The Merry Wives of Windsor* and *Valentine and Orson*. The first was very laughable and the latter surpassed everything in scenery; really in their last scene the stage appears a sole mass of gold; I was excessively entertained as well as Emma but Tom was sleepy and stupid. The box being small I was stuffed to death. Kemble was admirable in his part of Ford. Mrs Siddons was in the box opposite and looked quite ugly. It was a very shewy evening and the music pretty.

Harriet Wynne

1813   I felt this morning an almost irresistible inclination to go down to Greenwich and have a delicious tumble with the Girls over the hills. I fancied a fine, beamy, primy, fresh, green, spring day (as it was), a fine creature in a sweet, fluttering, clean drapery, spotted with little flowers, a slight, delicate, muslin, white scarf crossed over her beating bosom, with health rosing her shining cheeks, & love melting in her sparkling eyes, with a soft warm hand & bending form ready to leap into your arms, confiding & loving! After a short struggle, I seized my brush with a spasmatic effort, knowing the consequences of yielding to my disposition, & that tho' it might begin today, it would not end with it.

B. R. Haydon

1878   The E. wind worse than ever. Thinking to amuse some guests staying with us, I proposed a day at Cromer (of all places in the world when the E. wind was tremendous). Cromer is always disappointing on a first visit, and the gale disturbed some of the party and filled them with grievances. They could see nothing to admire or appreciate. Everything was bad and wrong. It is a caution not to be over-anxious to amuse one's guests.

The Reverend Benjamin Armstrong

26 April

1768   I came to Aberdeen.
     Here I found a society truly alive, knit together in peace and love. The congregations were large both morning and evening, and, as usual, deeply attentive. But a company of strolling players, who have at length found place here also, stole away the gay part of the hearers. Poor Scotland! Poor Aberdeen! This only was wanting to make them as completely irreligious as England.

John Wesley

1865   For the present, everything is forgotten in the assassination of President Lincoln, the intelligence of which came today.

Henry Crabb Robinson

1938 Ottoline's burial service. Oh dear, oh dear, the lack of intensity; the wailing and mumbling; the fumbling with bags; the shuffling; the vast brown mass of respectable old South Kensington ladies. And then the hymns; and the clergyman with a bar of medals across his surplice; and the orange and blue windows; and a toy Union Jack sticking from a cranny. What all this had to do with Ottoline, or our feelings? Save that the address was to the point: a critical study, written presumably by Philip and delivered, very resonantly, by Mr Speaight the actor: a sober, and secular speech, which made one at least think of a human being, though the reference to her beautiful voice caused one to think of that queer nasal moan: however that too was to the good in deflating immensities.

Virginia Woolf

1941 The station dance. Great excitement, everyone hoping to get off with a pilot. Wings, of course, are the thing; if you don't have wings you don't stand a chance, but the men turned out to be dreadful, all mechanics and technical chaps. The hut was small and crowded, boiling hot and smelling of Brylcreem and sweat.

We had a bet in our hut to see who could get the most – I got five, each one worse than the last, and a date for tea at the Regal.

Samantha is laid up with a sprained ankle. She fell over a slag-heap running away from a mechanic after the dance last night.

Joan Wyndham

27 April

1755 A little before I took horse, I looked into a room as I walked by, and saw a good old man, bleeding almost to death. I desired him immediately to snuff vinegar up his nose, and apply it to his neck, face, and temples. It was done; and the blood entirely stopped in less than two minutes.

The rain began about five, and did not intermit till we came to Haworth; notwithstanding which, a multitude of people were gathered together at ten. In the afternoon I was obliged to go out of the church, abundance of people not being able to get in. The rain ceased from the moment I came out, till I had finished my discourse. How many proofs must we have that there is no petition too little, any more than too great, for God to grant?

John Wesley

1935 All desire to practise the art of a writer has completely left me. I cannot imagine what it would be like: that is, more accurately, I cannot curve my mind to the line of a book: no, nor of an article. Its not the writing but the architecting that strains. If I write this paragraph, then there is the next & then the next. But after a months holiday I shall be as tough & springy as — say heather root; & the arches & the domes will spring into the air as firm as steel & light as cloud — but all these words miss the mark.

Virginia Woolf

1940 Mummy's birthday party. Alfred came with his new friend Basil. Sid doesn't seem to like him any better than Bertie, calling him decadent and perverted. Alfred did his take-off of Madame Butterfly's entrance in Act I, in red silk shawl with a parasol and a flower behind his ear. Mummy and I did the *Swan Lake* adagio.

Alfred has a new word he uses rather a lot, which is 'camp'. He uses it mainly when he is talking about the opera. He says it's got nothing to do with Boy Scouts but just means anything outrageous, or over the top — camp in fact! He thinks Basil's new tie is camp.

Joan Wyndham

28 April

1807 Wordsworth said, He thought Historical subjects shd. never be introduced into Landscape but where the Landscape was to be subservient to them. Where the Landscape was intended principally to impress the mind, figures, other than such as are general, such as may a thousand times appear, and seem accidental, and not particularly to draw the attention, are injurious to the effect which the Landscape shd. produce as a scene founded on an observation of nature.

Joseph Farington

1838 Such is my life – Aujourd'hui j'ai reçu cent guinées sterling, hier au soir actuellement sans quatre schellings! Telle est ma vie! – un jour au sommet, pendant le jour suivant au bout de besoin et misère!

Grace au Dieu pour sa bonté! ce matin, ½ past *one*. Was there ever any thing like it? This moment j'ai reçu de Liverpool l'autre £50! Cent cinquante cinq livres dans un jour – apres la plus grande necessité. Grace au Dieu encore.

B. R. Haydon

1922 The last ten hours have been interesting, and have given me a headache. I doubt whether I can 'make any use of the material'. Getting up late, I was wondering whether I'd go down to Kew for the afternoon, which seemed to be fine and warmer. But E. M. Forster turned up at 2 o'clock, just as I was going out. He had been lunching at the Tate Gallery (rather the sort of obscure place he *would* lunch at) so we went back there and he watched me eat stewed ox-tail in the basement restaurant. He was carrying a volume of Marcel Proust. After he had talked about Proust for a few minutes I felt that I knew more about him than Middleton Murry and all the other critics would tell me in twenty volumes. (Bennett said the other day that E.M.F. is 'the best reviewer in London'. And, by the way, F. said that he had definitely decided to do no more reviewing.)

We spent the whole afternoon together, and it was extremely pleasant. We laughed a lot; E.M.F. is certainly one of the nicest men I know. He told me that, at parties, he always feels 'self-conscious *and* contemptuous', which exactly describes my own feelings at old Lady Lewis's party a month ago. Walking through St James's Park, I said, 'Perhaps we suffer from living in an exhausted age'.

F. 'Isn't that only one of your *dodges*? – to say that.'

S. 'What *is* the matter with us?'
F. 'Resignation.'

I wrote earlier that F. makes me feel 'youthful, impetuous, and intellectually clumsy'. The description is quite accurate. This afternoon I found myself chattering away in an inconsequent headlong chuckle-headed style; F. seemed to enjoy it; so I went on.

Siegfried Sassoon

29 April

1789 Rain. The cuckold for the first time this year.

Lady Eleanor Butler

1815 This week has really been a week of great delight. Never have I had such irresistible, perpetual, & continued urgings of future greatness. I have been like a man with air balloons under his arm pits and ether in his soul. While I was painting, or walking, or thinking, these beaming flashes of energy followed & impressed me! O God, grant they may not be presumptuous feelings. Grant they may be the fiery anticipations of a great Soul born to realize them. They came over me, & shot across me, & shook me, & inspired me to such a degree of intensity, that I lifted up my heart, & thanked God.

B. R. Haydon

1871 I first heard the cuckoo but it has been heard before.

Just caught sight of a little whirlwind which ran very fast careering across our pond. It was made by conspiring cats-paws seeming to be caught in, in a whorl, to the centre . . . I saw that there was something eery, Circe-like and quick about it.

Gerard Manley Hopkins

1933 Oh, ever to be remembered day. Lorenzo spoke to me! I saw him in the Bod. and felt desperately thrilled about him so that I trembled and shivered and went sick. As I went out Lorenzo caught me up – and said 'Well, and has Sandra finished her epic poem?' – or words to that effect. He talks curiously but very waffily – is very affected. Something wrong with his mouth I think – he can't help snurging. I was almost completely tongue-tied. I said, 'Er – No'. He asked me if I was still keeping up the dual personality idea – he had caught me out. 'But you don't know who I am,' I said. 'Of course I do,' replied Lorenzo. 'Everybody does.' Oh Misery or the reverse! Then I said, 'By the way I hope you don't mind my calling you Lorenzo – it suits you you know.' 'Oh does it – how *awfully* flattering!' He snurged and went on up the Iffley Rd while I walked trembling and weak at the knees into Cowley Place.

Barbara Pym

30 April

1706 Memorandum that tho' Dr Tyndal of All-Souls be a noted Debauchee and a man of very pernicious Principles, yet he is so sly and cunning, and has that command over his Passions, that he always appears calm and sedate in company, and is very abstemious in his Drink, by which means he has no small advantage over those he discourses with, and is the more able to instill his ill Notions.

Thomas Kearne

1829 Dr Johnson enjoins Bozzy to leave out of his diary all notices of the weather as insignificant. It may be so to an inhabitant of Bolt Court in Fleet Street who need care little whether it rains or snows except the Shilling which it may cost him for a Jarvie. But when I wake and find a snow shower sweeping along destroying hundreds perhaps of young lambs and famishing their mothers I must consider it as worth noting. For my own poor share I am as indifferent as any Grubstreeter of them all

> *– and since tis a bad day*
> *Rise up rise up, my merry men,*
> *And use it as you may.*

I have accordingly been busy.

Walter Scott

1836 I now conclude the fifth volume of my journal, which I have kept for six years, including a short diary during the year 1830. I find it such an useful practice, and so entertaining, that I am fully resolved to continue it all my life. It was first suggested to me by the possession of a small pocket-book, given me by a pupil when I was ten years old. I have ordered a sixth volume to be made by Fraser at Potton, and I shall have it on Monday, when I shall forthwith begin it. I have been long convinced that, as Abbot says in his *Young Christian*, the use of the pen is amongst the most valuable means of improving the mind.

Emily Shore

1870 This evening being May Eve I ought to have put some birch and wittan (mountain ash) over the door to keep out the 'old witch'. But I was too lazy to go out and get it. Let us hope the old witch will not come in during the night. The young witches are welcome.

The Reverend Francis Kilvert

1839   Our petty sessions at Whittington. Pye and Taylor attended; nothing of consequence; two assault cases, and the commitment of a very young thief, quite a child, only nine years old, for stealing and carrying away from a plough a ploughshare. We agreed on account of the youth of the *felon* to admit him to bail. The ploughshare was nearly as long as the boy was high. He was detected when carrying it off, and seen to throw it into the canal.

William Dyott

1922   Oh, what will this beloved month bring?

Katherine Mansfield

1945   I worked and dined alone in Brooks's. At 10.30 a member rushed into the morning room announcing that Hitler's death had just come through on the tape. We all ran to read about it. Somehow, I fancy, none of us was very excited. We have waited, and suffered too long. Three years ago we would have been out of our minds with jubilation and excitement – and with prognostications of a happy issue out of all our afflictions.

James Lees-Milne

1978   Dinsdale Landen told today a wonderful story of his days as assistant stage manager at Worthing. He was a walk-on when Wolfit was there as guest star, playing Othello, but was not told what to do until the dress rehearsal, at which the great man said it would be a very good idea for Othello to have a page who followed him everywhere. He handed Dinsdale a loin cloth, told him to black-up, and said he'd got the part. Dinsdale did not know the play and just went wherever Wolfit went, the complete dutiful page, always in attendance. But at one point he found himself in a scene in which he felt rather ill at ease; he had an instinct about it. Suddenly he heard the great man's voice roaring, 'Not in Desdemona's bedroom, you cunt.'

Peter Hall

2 May

1550 Joan Bocher, otherwise called Joan of Kent, was burned for holding that Christ was not incarnate of the Virgin Mary, being condemned the year before but kept in hope of conversion; and the 30th of April the Bishop of London and the Bishop of Ely were to persuade her. But she withstood them and reviled the preacher that preached at her death.

King Edward VI

1735 We had a bottle of red wine, of which we returned a pint, and bread and butter and radishes, he would pay and did, 18d, the wine very harsh, like slow poison. There was a poor woman sat upon a stone in Chancery Lane with a child, I gave her 1½d, and being very thankful, 6d, at which she seemed mightily affected, and said that God had inspired a gentleman to give her 6d; I asked the watchman if he knew her, he went to her and brought her to the upper end of the lane, where he got her ¾ of beer, and I gave him about 4d in farthings to see her safe home in Drury Lane, and I followed them, and he brought her part of the way and then gave her a piece of candle, and she went on and through a dark lane with her candle out, at the other end of which I saw her again, having gone round about, and gave her 1s there, and the watchman 1d to see her home; she was much moved, and still talked of the gentleman that had given her sixpence. I have had many thoughts of this poor creature, who cried, 'What will my end be?' lives I think near St Thomas's street, has a husband but had not seen him today, had been with his sister for relief, but could not have it, was lost, she said, for want; I wish I had gone with her and the watchman to the place where she lived, but I came home and had a glass of water and went to bed.

John Byrom

1945 Gradually, picking up the threads of life.

I lunched with Tony and Violet Powell and T. S. Eliot. Eliot has improved enormously, largely, I understand, because his wife has been put in an asylum. We were gloomy together in a good-humoured way. I say to myself all day long: 'I must work, I must work' and don't work.

Saw Hughie Kingsmill after lunch and talked about Mussolini's end and Hitler's; laughed about all the strange events now happening. I felt a great desire to describe it all, to write contemporary history. Of all my friends I most enjoy Hughie's company.

Malcolm Muggeridge

---

3 May

1551   The challenge at running at ring performed, at the which first came the King, sixteen footmen, and ten horsemen, in black silk coats pulled out with white silk taffeta; then all lords having three men likewise appareled, and all gentlemen, their footmen in white fustian pulled out with black taffeta. The other side came all in yellow taffeta. At length the yellow band took it twice in 120 courses, and my band tainted often – which was counted as nothing – and took never – which seemed very strange – and so the prize was of my side lost. After that, tourney followed between six of my band and six of theirs.

King Edward VI

1787   Dined at home; and though I ate only some minced veal, some spinach, and eggs, in moderate quantity, felt myself greatly oppressed, so as to afford a strong instance in confirmation of the opinion, that a solitary dinner, for whatever reason, does not so soon pass away as one ate in company. The reason first occurring would be, that for a dinner ate in company some time was taken; but the fact does not seem to correspond; for I have made, if I am not mistaken, as many intervals in dining alone, and have yet found that digestion does not take place so quickly. Besides the effect that company may have on the mind, much, I apprehend, is to be ascribed to the action given to the lungs and stomach by talking.

William Windham

1946 Lord Ilchester joined us at dinner, telling us how corrupt the police are. He instanced the case several months ago when he was fined for driving through a military zone at Wilton. It goes against the grain for me to criticize the police, naively believing all policemen to be like our dear old Sergeant Haines at Wickhamford and Badsey who spanked the boys for stealing apples and succoured old women and lame cats; and, after the Vicar, was the pillar of village society.

James Lees-Milne

4 May

1663 The Dancing Maister came; whom standing by seeing him instructing my wife, when he had done with her he would needs have me try the steps of a *coranto*; and what with his desire and my wife's importunity, I did begin, and then was obliged to give him entry-money, 10*s* – and am become his Scholler. The truth is, I think it is a thing very useful for any gentleman and sometimes I may have occasion of using it; and though it cost me, which I am heartily sorry it should, besides that I must by my oath give half as much more to the poor, yet I am resolved to get it up some other way; and then it will not be above a month or two in a year. So though it be against my stomach, yet I will try it a little while; if I see it comes to any great inconvenience or charge, I will fling it off. After I had begun with the steps of half a *coranto*, which I think I shall learn well enough, he went away and we to dinner.

Samuel Pepys

1945 I am dreading the victory celebrations and have no sort of heart for them. I am feeling absolutely rotten and utterly soured of everything even religion if an essential is loving one's neighbour and feeling kindly to them – for I hate and loathe them. It seems to me that anyone who has decency, unselfishness, kindliness, public spirit and such like is a fool. He is put on. It is the opposite sort of qualities which bring success and contentment. Everything is upside down. The undesirable are subsidized from birth to grave at our expense:

they are given everything and nothing is expected of them. We who pay for it all are pushed about, insulted and soon will be driven out of existence.

Lord Reith

1948   I quite often look back at the pleasures and pains of youth – love, jealousy, recklessness, vanity – without forgetting their spell but no longer desiring them; while middle-aged ones like music, places, botany, conversation seem to be just as enjoyable as those wilder ones, in which there was usually some potential anguish lying in wait, like a bee in a flower. I hope there may be further surprises in store, and on the whole do not fear the advance into age.

Frances Partridge

1961   It is a common feature of all but the most recent fiction that a character is falsely suspected of a misdemeanour and is able to recognize his true friends from the false by their irrational belief in his innocence. How many of my friends should I believe innocent of what crimes? If I heard, e.g., that Andrew Devonshire was arrested for sodomy, Ann Fleming for poisoning her husband, Bob Laycock for burglary, should I not think: how surprising and amusing?

Evelyn Waugh

5 May

1663   Being envited to goe to Banforlonge to Ann Greinsworth, I was goeing, and was in Roger Naylor's, and word was sent me my Master was pasd to shopp, soe I went after and overtooke hime, but he was not offended. Afterwards I went to Banforlonge. Att my comeing home I cald att Roger Naylor's and partly ingagd to come beare them company that night; I comeing downe to shop and stayd awhile, and then went againe and privatly ingagd to Mary to sit up awhile to let us discourse, which she promisd; and the maine question was because we lived seaverally that we wuld not act soe publickely as others, that we might live privately and love firmely, that we might be faithfull to each other in our love till the end: all which was firmely agreed upon. This was the first night that ever I stayd up a wooing ere in my life.

Roger Lowe

1785 Went up in balloon. Much satisfied with myself; and, in consequence of that satisfaction, dissatisfied rather with my adventure. Could I have foreseen that danger or apprehension would have made so little impression upon me, I would have insured that of which, as it was, we only gave ourselves a chance, and have deferred going till we had a wind favourable for crossing the Channel. I begin to suspect, in all cases, the effect by which fear is surmounted is more easily made than I have been apt to suppose. Certainly the experience I have had on this occasion will warrant a degree of confidence more than I have ever hitherto indulged. I would not wish a degree of confidence more than I enjoyed at every moment of the time.

William Windham

1938 Pouring now; the drought broken; the worst spring on record; my pens diseased, even the new box; my eyes ache with *Roger* and I'm a little appalled at the prospect of the grind this book will be. I must somehow shorten and loosen; I *can't* (remember) stretch it to a long painstaking literal book: later I must generalize and let fly. But then, what about all the letters? How can one cut loose from facts, when there they are, contradicting my theories? A problem. But I'm convinced I can't, physically, strain after an RA portrait. What was I going to say with this defective nib?

Virginia Woolf

1977 On the train back to London I wondered what I got from this life, why I did it, and why I seem incapable of calming down. I ate a large breakfast to reassure myself.

Peter Hall

6 May

1763 I awaked as usual heavy, confused, and splenetic. Every morning this is the case with me. Dempster prescribed to me to cut two or three brisk capers round the room, which I did, and found attended with most agreeable effects. It expelled the phlegm from my heart, gave my blood a free circulation, and my spirits a brisk flow; so that I was all at once made happy. I must remember this and practise it. Though indeed when one is in low spirits he generally is so indolent and careless that rather than take a little trouble he will just sink under the load.

James Boswell

1780 Now I am here again how solitary I feel. Hardly know anybody. Home is the place for little people who are little known. No living in London without servants and a carriage.

The Reverend W. J. Temple

1870 As I entered the fold of Gilfach y rheol, Janet issued from the house door and rushed across the yard and turning the corner of the wain-house I found the two younger ladies assisting at the castration of the lambs, catching and holding the poor little beasts and standing by whilst the operation was performed, seeming to enjoy the spectacle. It was the first time I had seen clergyman's daughters helping to castrate lambs or witnessing that operation and it rather gave me a turn of disgust at first.

The Reverend Francis Kilvert

1945 I am the worst possible example for the children in almost every way. I am so embittered and soured by the treatment I have had. The best years of life have gone and I have missed such a terrible lot when there was plenty of money and the children were young. I had so very much to be thankful for; but I was always wanting much more to do than I had to do, and never content. Oh God, what a disposition I have.

Lord Reith

7 May

1802 William had slept uncommonly well, so, feeling himself strong, he fell to work at *The Leech Gatherer*; he wrote hard at it till dinner time, then he gave over, tired to death – he had finished the poem. I was making Derwent's frocks. After dinner we sate in the orchard. It was a thick, hazy, dull air. The thrush sang almost continually; the little birds were more than usually busy with their voices. The sparrows are now full fledged. The nest is so full that they lie upon one another, they sit quietly in their nest with closed mouths. I walked to Rydale after tea, which we drank by the kitchen fire. The evening very dull – a terrible kind of threatening brightness at sunset above Easedale. The sloe-thorn beautiful in the hedges, and in the wild spots higher up among the hawthorns. No letters. William met me. He had been digging in my absence, and cleaning the well. We walked up beyond Lewthwaites. A very dull sky; coolish; crescent moon now and then. I had a letter brought me from Mrs Clarkson while we were walking in the orchard. I observed the sorrel leaves opening at about 9 o'clock. William went to bed tired with thinking about a poem.

Dorothy Wordsworth

1879 I am certain that theatres and exhibitions are not what they used to be. People are well satisfied now with what would not have satisfied them thirty years back.

The Reverend Benjamin Armstrong

1956 Children have all returned to school. The weather is delicious, the house is silent, there is no reason for me not to work. I will try one day soon. I did a little work.

Evelyn Waugh

8 May

1883 At the [Scottish] National Gallery. In the portrait room, John Wilson full length in hunting costume! scarlet coat cut away from just under the chin yet buttoning quite across the upperpart of the chest intensely and permanently ridiculous because not coinciding with any natural divisions of the human form. Sir N. Paton's *Oberon & Titania*. Fairies beautiful and graceful. Perhaps the Pre-Raffaelites would call them 'conventional'. But beauty and grace are essentially 'conventional', because all men agree in finding them attractive & pleasing, as they find awkwardness, stiffness and affectation repulsive, and will do so to the end of the chapter, in spite of the transient whimsies whether of clever people or dullards.

Alfred Domett

1941   This is the eighth day of my renunciation of smoking. It gets more difficult rather than less difficult. But I do observe that it is a thought which suggests a pang rather than a pang which suggests a thought. Thus an aching tooth twitches into consciousness and says 'I have a toothache.' But this nicotine hunger is only stimulated by some outside occurrence such as the sight of someone else smoking or an advertisement of Craven A. Then the pang lights up. Apart from that it is a vague feeling of something missing as if one had had no breakfast.

Harold Nicolson

1945   *Victory Europe Day*, London.
A wonderful day from every point of view. Went wandering through the crowds in the hot sunshine. Everyone was good-humoured and cheerful. In the afternoon the Prime Minister made a magnificent speech, simple and without boastfulness, but full of deep pride.
    In the evening I went along to the theatre and had a drink with the company. We all had cold food and drinks at Winnie's: Joyce [Cary], Lilian, Alfred and Lynn, Lorn [Loraine], Gladys [Calthrop], Dick, etc. We listened to the King's broadcast, then to Eisenhower, Monty and Alexander. Then I walked down the Mall and stood outside Buckingham Palace, which was floodlit. The crowd was stupendous. The King and Queen came out on the balcony, looking enchanting. We all roared ourselves hoarse. After that I went to

Chips Channon's 'open house' party which wasn't up to much. Walked home with Ivor. I suppose this is the greatest day in our history.

Noël Coward

1957 Increasingly bored by *Punch* routine. Ought really to give up job, sometimes think of doing so; then hesitate because it's easy way of earning money, and, by virtue of being Editor, other things turn up.

Malcolm Muggeridge

9 May

1666 So away to my Lord Treasurer's; and thence to Pierce's, where I find Knipp and I took them to Hales's to see our pictures finished; which are very pretty, but I like not hers half so well as I thought at first, it being not so like, nor so well painted as I expected or as mine and my wife's are. Thence with them to Cornehill to call and choose a chimney-piece for Pierce's closet; and so home, where my wife in mighty pain, and mightily vexed at my being abroad with these women – and when they were gone, called them 'whores' and I know not what; which vexed me, having been so innocent with them. So I with them to Mrs Turner's and there sat with them a while; anon my wife sends for me; I come, and what was it but to scold at me, and she would go abroad to take the ayre presently, that she would. So I left my company and went with her to Bow, but was vexed and spoke not one word to her all the way, going nor coming – or being come home; but went up straight to bed. Half an hour after (she in the coach leaning on me, as being desirous to be friends), she comes up, mighty sick with a fit of the Cholique and in mighty pain, and calls for me out of the bed; I rose and held her; she prays me to forgive her, and in mighty pain we put her to bed – where the pain ceased by and by; and so had some sparagus to our beds-side for supper, and very kindly afterward to sleep, and good friends in the morning.

Samuel Pepys

1871 A simple behaviour of the cloudscape I have not realized before. Before a N.E. wind great bars or rafters of cloud all the morning and in a manner all the day marching across the sky in regular rank and with equal spaces between. They seem prism-shaped, flat-bottomed and banked up to a ridge: their make is like light tufty snow in coats.

Gerard Manley Hopkins

1925 [Easton Glebe]
How pleasant it is – to get into a small car and drive away from London on a fine Saturday afternoon. As one gets nearer open country, one slows down to watch half a minute of local cricket. By the time the bowler has started to deliver his next ball one is out of sight. Easton Park is an ideal destination. At the lodge-gate one turns into the untidy deer-dotted park, with its rooks and rabbits and derelict-looking old trees; half a mile across the green levels there is H.G.'s cosy house, demure and Jane Austenish. This weekend wasn't noteworthy.

Siegfried Sassoon

10 May

1652 Passing by Smithfield I saw a miserable creature burning who had murder'd her husband. I went to see some workmanship of that admirable artist Reeves, famous for perspective and the turning of curiosities in ivorie.

John Evelyn

1940 Today Germany invaded Holland and Belgium. It may be a good thing to put down how one felt before one forgets it. Of course the first feeling was the usual horror and disgust, and the impossibility of finding words to describe this latest *Schweinerei* by the Germans. Then came the realization that the war was coming a lot nearer to us – airbases in Holland and Belgium would make raids on England a certainty. People one met were either gloomy (Mr Beauclerk, the electrician and Mr Cobb, the wireless shop), slightly hysterical (Miss

Bloomer) or just plainly calm like Steele. I think I was rather frightened, but hope I didn't show it, and anyway one still has the 'it couldn't happen to us' feeling. Then there is the very real, but impotent, feeling of sympathy for these poor wretches who are the latest victims. In the news the Dutch and Belgian Ministers spoke and the Dutch Minister sent a greeting to his wife and children and grandchildren. Then it was the most difficult thing to control oneself, and I know that if I had been alone I couldn't have done. Later came the news of Mr Chamberlain's resignation and his speech, in that voice which brings back so many memories mostly of crisis. But even if he has failed, and we can't be sure yet that he has, there is no more courageous man in the government or indeed anywhere, I'm sure of that. But Winston Churchill will be better for this war – as Hilary said, he is such an old beast! The Germans loathe and fear him and I believe he can do it.

Barbara Pym

1942   Yesterday was a day of flowers. The tulips are out in St James's Park – they are at their time of perfection – not one has fallen out of the ranks. Three unattractive little girls were picking the faded bluebells that grew on the bank above me and stuffing them into a shabby leather handbag that must have belonged to one of their mothers. It irritates me that since the railings have gone people pick the flowers and trample the grass in the parks until it becomes hard dry earth. The lilac is out. It gives me a feeling of urgency – its time is so short – only about a fortnight.

Something of the panic of middle age is coming over me. It is the bald spot beginning on the back of my head. This morning I combed the longer hair from the sides back over the place where it is thin. I felt as if I were adjusting a wig which the wind might blow out of place. I seem surrounded by nice but ugly girls.

Charles Ritchie

1943   A filthy day, very wet and stormy. But I wore my fur-lined boots and took an extra jersey. Now I can see how people get eccentric.

Barbara Pym

1977   I heard this afternoon that there was a letter from the Prime Minister at Wallingford. I rang my father and asked him to open it, thinking it was something to do with the NATO foreign ministers who are visiting the National this week. It was the recommendation for a knighthood. I don't want it, I really don't: I'm too young to be labelled a member of the Establishment. Yet there's no doubt it will help combat all the mischief-makers and the horrors.

Peter Hall

11 May

1654   I now observed how the women began to paint themselves, formerly a most ignominious thing and us'd only by prostitutes.

John Evelyn

1830   The first place we visited today was a shop, in which we remained an hour and a half, during which time Papa studied with his book and pencil very quietly, notwithstanding the noise and bustle of the shop and the frequent appeals of the shopkeeper to his taste, such as 'This is a very neat colour, sir; only four shillings a yard; very cheap I assure you, sir.' To which sally Papa replied that in Scotland the adjective 'neat' was applied to form, not to colour. 'Yes, sir,' said the man, 'we do not always apply our words correctly; we call this a *quiet* colour,' pointing to a brown. If any of my readers object to the above colloquy on the ground of its being too highly coloured, let me assure them that I am a faithful reporter, more so than he of *The Times* newspaper, who was cruel enough to prevent a poor innocent man from enjoying his breakfast by the insertion of a letter in his name. We proceeded to Walworth and dined with my Uncle, and immediately after dinner went to the House of Commons, found Mr Hay waiting for us, who conducted us to the ventilator where ladies can hear the speakers and even see them sometimes through the holes in the roof. We found a good many ladies there, among others two very gay ones who laughed in convulsions at some of the members who came under their scrutiny. 'Oh! Good God! What a pair of eyes! I declare he is looking up! La! what frights in boots! I could speak better myself!' and various similar instructive and amusing exclamations formed the tenor of their conversation. But to return to the business of the house. Its members do not sit gravely and sedately on their benches as wise legislators ought to do. (I beg their pardon – if I had said so in their presence they would have bawled out 'Order! Order!' until I had said 'as I should have supposed wise legislators would have done from their well-known prudence and discretion in all other matters.') They walk about and talk to each other unless an interesting person is speaking, and call out 'Hear! hear! Order!' – I suppose at random, for they certainly do not *seem* to pay much attention. Then they like so much to exercise their privilege of wearing their hats, and appear constantly in boots, so that their general appearance is by no means dignified.

Anne Chalmers

12 May

1649   I did not medle with my navel for above a weeke, but the lint stucke in it, I perceive it is not best to lett the lint stick in it, but wash it out, of this day I found it was somewhat sore, whereupon I washed it as formerly, it savoured very much was full of white stuffe; it looked a litle red and open. I thinke yett that it was not rawe it continued well above 8 weekes through gods mercy unto mee and I hope in god he will command his blessing on me therein.

The Reverend Ralph Josselin

1826   Worked lazily – saw nothing distinctly. The model was exhausted and I was dull; and so, after five hours' twaddling I gave up.

B. R. Haydon

1834   Here begins another *volume* of my '*strange eventful history*'. Whether I may live to complete the numerous pages, God only knows. I feel truly gratefull to the Almighty Providence for having vouchsafed to protect me to my present age with the enjoyment of health and the blessing of my three beloved children. Their society I have been lately enjoying for a longer time than I can ever hope to see them together again. Dick is fast recovering from his accident, and must soon return to his regiment. Bill making preparations for his ordination on the 26th, and after to settle at his curacy at Glen. I must then be left with my darling dear daughter, the solace and comfort of my life.

William Dyott

1887 It is a long time since I made an entry – partly from failing health and partly from the absence of anything to record.

The Reverend Benjamin Armstrong
[Final entry]

13 May

1828 There were to be five men executed, and I was desirous to witness for once the ceremony within the prison. At half-past seven I met the Under Sheriff, Foss, at the gate. At eight we were joined by Sheriff Wilde, when some six or eight of us walked in procession through long narrow passages to a long, naked, and wretched apartment, to which were successively brought the five unhappy creatures who were to suffer. The first, a youth, came in pale and trembling. He fainted as his arms were pinioned. He whispered some inaudible words to a clergyman who came and sat by him on a bench, while the others were prepared for the sacrifice. His name was Brown. The second, a fine young man, exclaimed, on entering the room, that he was a murdered man, being picked out while two others were suffered to escape. Both these were, I believe, burglars. Two other men were ill-looking fellows. They were silent and seemingly prepared. One man distinguished himself from the rest – an elderly man, very fat, and with the look of a substantial tradesman. He said, in a tone of indignation, to the fellow who pinioned him, 'I am not the first whom you have murdered. I am hanged because I had a bad character.' (I could not but think that this is, in fact, properly understood, the only legitimate excuse for hanging any one; – because his *character* (not reputation) is such that his life cannot but be a curse to himself and others.) A clergyman tried to persuade him to be quiet, and he said he was resigned. He was hanged as a receiver of stolen horses, and had been a notorious dealer for many years. The procession was then continued through other passages, to a small room adjoining the drop, to which the culprits were successively taken and tied up. I could not see perfectly what took place, but I observed that most of the men ran up the steps and addressed the mob. The second burglar cried out, 'Here's another murdered man, my lads!' and there was a cry of 'Murder' from the crowd. The horse-stealer also addressed the crowd. I was within sight of the drop, and observed it fall, but the sheriffs instantly left the scaffold, and we returned to the Lord Mayor's parlour, where the Under Sheriff, the Ordinary, two clergymen, and two attendants in military dress, and I, breakfasted.

The breakfast was short and sad, and the conversation about the scene we had just witnessed. All agreed it was one of the most disgusting of the executions they had seen, from the want of feeling manifested by most of the sufferers; but sympathy was checked by the appearance of four out of five of the men. However, I shall not soon see such a sight again.

Henry Crabb Robinson

1940   Return of Jo from Cornwall. I went round to the café at eleven, wearing my new hat that I got from Woolies – cyclamen with a veil – that really knocked Jo's eye out. He was looking pretty good too because he was brown, in a blue linen shirt open to the waist, wicked and amorous and laughing like hell all the time. He filled me with vitality and I found myself thinking he was really quite attractive.

We had a wonderful morning, all young and excited again like it was at the beginning, kissing and fighting and hurling insults, laughing till we had to stuff our fingers in our mouths. Jo bit me till my neck was marked, and said, 'Oh how good and soft you are to feel! How do I feel? Do you like it?' But I wouldn't let him undo my blouse.

'Christ, this is bad for me,' Jo said. 'I really shouldn't do it, it gets me all worked up and nowhere to go, because if there's one thing I don't do it's sleep with virgins.'

'Too much trouble, I suppose.'

'My God, yes, and no fun for the virgin either. I'll give you one word of advice – when it does happen go all out and give it everything you've got, don't hold back or have any inhibitions, because if you do it's the one thing that can turn a young girl into a lesbian. Didn't your mother ever talk about these things?'

'No, she never told me much – I don't think she knew much herself, in spite of being married. Oh, she sort of told me how it's done, driving around Hyde Park in her little Austin 7, with the engine revved up very loud to hide her embarrassment – actually, her own mother didn't tell her very much either, just to use lots of scent and not let her husband see her cleaning her teeth.'

Joan Wyndham

---

14 May

1800 Wm. and John set off into Yorkshire after dinner at ½ past 2 o'clock, cold pork in their pockets. I left them at the turning of the Lowwood bay under the trees. My heart was so full that I could hardly speak to W. when I gave him a farewell kiss. I sate a long time upon a stone at the margin of the lake, and after a flood of tears my heart was easier. The lake looked to me, I knew not why, dull and melancholy, and the weltering on the shores seemed a heavy sound. I walked as long as I could amongst the stones of the shore. The wood rich in flowers; a beautiful yellow, palish yellow, flower, that looked thick, round, and double, and smelt very sweet – I suppose it was a ranunculus. Crowfoot, the grassy-leaved, rabbit-toothed white flower, strawberries, geranium, scentless violets, anemones two kinds, orchises, primroses. The heckberry very beautiful, the crab coming out as a low shrub. Met a blind man, driving a very large beautiful Bull, and a cow – he walked with two sticks. Came home by Clappersgate. The valley very green; many sweet views up to Rydale head, when I could juggle away the fine houses; but they disturbed me, even more than when I have been happier; one beautiful view of the Bridge, without Sir Michael's. Sate down very often, though it was cold. I resolved to write a journal of the time till W. and J. return, and I set about keeping my resolve, because I will not quarrel with myself, and because I shall give Wm. pleasure by it when he comes home again. At Rydale, a woman of the village, stout and well dressed, begged a half-penny; she had never she said done it before, but these hard times! Arrived at home with a bad headach, set some slips of privett, the evening cold, had a fire, my face now flame-coloured. It is nine o'clock. I shall soon go to bed. A young woman begged at the door – she had come from Manchester on Sunday morn. with two shillings and a slip of paper which she supposed a Bank note – it was a cheat. She had buried her husband and three children within a year and a half – all in one grave – burying very dear – paupers all put in one place – 20 shillings paid for as much ground as will bury a man – a stone to be put over it or the right will be lost – 11/6 each time the ground is opened. Oh! that I had a letter from William!

Dorothy Wordsworth

---

15 May

1839   Epsom races, and actually snow at the 'Derby.'

Colonel Peter Hawker

1896   At noon precisely I finished my first novel, which was begun about the middle of April last year; but five-sixths of the work at least has been performed since the 1st October. Yesterday I sat down at 3 p.m. to write, and, with slight interruptions for meals etc., kept at it till 1 a.m. this morning. The concluding chapter was written between 9 and 12 today.

My fears about *In the Shadow* are (1) that it is not well knit, (2) that it is hysterical, or at any rate strained in tone. Still, I should not be surprised if it impressed many respectable people. The worst parts of it seem to me to be in front of my *Yellow Book* story, which came in for a full share of laudation.

Arnold Bennett

1946 *Early. Just awake.*

Wonderful morning of coldness and sun – frost, only little birds chirping, and my Regency chair standing, silent against the white door, its black glistening, its brass gleaming with the remains of the old lacquer. I am making a squab seat for it out of eight layers of my old rug – rug that I bought with my mother just before going to my prep school.

She said, 'That one is nice.' It was expensive, with camel hair on one side. I wondered that she could spend so much on a rug; but she said: 'It will keep you warm.'

And it kept me warm for years and years until the fire of 1941 spoilt it and pitted it all over.

Denton Welch

1981 Indecent Displays Bill. The Pornography Report had recommended a three-pronged attack on pornography: the milder forms should not be displayed in public, the harder forms should not be sold at all; the exploitation of performers should be rendered a criminal offence (some steps have been taken in the last direction). The present Bill deals only with display. I described it as a small step forward. Mary Whitehouse, with whom I had coffee just before the debate, doubts whether it is even that . . .

I did not speak for long. After some hesitation I told an oft-repeated story: 'A taxi driver dropped me at my flat and said to me, "Excuse my asking your name. I know you are Lord Porn, but what's your other name?" ' The *Guardian* quotes it this morning, as does *The Times*, which adds 'laughter'. I suppose that a successful joke cannot be repeated too often. But I avoid the eye of noble lords who must have heard this one more than once already.

Lord Longford

---

16 May

1826 She died at nine in the morning after being very ill for two days – easy at last. I arrived here late last night. Anne is worn out, and has had hystericks which returned on my arrival. Her broken accents were like those of a child, the language as well as the tones broken but in the most gentle voice of submission. 'Poor Mama – Never return again – gone for ever – a better place – ' Then when she came to herself she spoke with sense freedom and strength of mind till her weakness returnd. It would have been inexpressibly moving to me as a stranger – what was it then to the father and the husband? For myself, I scarce know how, I feel sometimes as firm as the Bass rock sometimes as weak as the wave that breaks on it. I am as alert at thinking and deciding as I ever was in my life – yet when I contrast what this place now is with what it has been not long since I think my heart will break. Lonely – aged – deprived of my family all but poor Anne – impoverishd, an embarrassd man, I am deprived of the sharer of my thoughts and counsels who could always talk down my sense of the calamitous apprehensions which break the heart that must bear them alone. Even her foibles were of service to me by giving me things to think of beyond my weary self-reflections.

I have seen her – The figure I beheld is and is not my Charlotte – my thirty years' companion – There is the same symmetry of form though those limbs are rigid which were once so gracefully elastic – but that yellow masque with pinchd features which seems to mock life rather than emulate it, can it be the face that was once so full of lively expression? I will not look on it again. Anne thinks her little changed because the latest idea she had formed of her mother is as she appeard under circumstances of sickness and pain. Mine go back to a period of comparative health. If I write long in this way I shall write down my resolution which I should rather write up if I could. I wonder how I shall do with the large portion of thoughts which were hers for thirty years. I suspect they will be hers yet for a long time at least. But I will not blaze cambrick and crape in the publick eye like a disconsolate widower, that most affected of all characters.

Walter Scott

1856 Remarkable for being the day of my *second* Oratorio! Oh, goodness me! how my sensibility to music must have diminished, or how my sense of 'the fitness of things' must have increased, since my *first* Oratorio in Edinburgh old Parliament House! *Jephtha's Daughter*, in the Parliament House, carried me away, away into the spheres! At the first crash of the Chorus, I recollect a sensation as of cold water poured down my back, which grew into a positive physical cramp! The *Messiah* at Exeter House, tho' perfectly got up – 'given' they call it – left me calm and critical on my rather hard bench; and instead of imaginary cold water, I felt stifled by the real heat of the place! Geraldine said her sister, the 'religious Miss Jewsbury,' in contradistinction to Geraldine – wouldn't let her go to the *Messiah* when a girl, because 'people,' she thought, 'who really believed in their Saviour, would not go to hear *singing* about him'. I am quite of the religious Miss Jewsbury's mind. Singing about him, with *shakes* and white gloves and all that sort of thing, quite shocked my religious feelings – tho' I have no religion.

Jane Welsh Carlyle

17 May

1818   This melancholy second Sunday since my irreparable loss [her husband's death] I ventured to church. I hoped it might calm my mind and subject it to its new state – its lost – lost happiness. But I suffered inexpressibly; I sunk on my knees, and could scarcely contain my sorrows – scarcely rise any more! but I prayed – fervently – and I am glad I made the trial, however severe. Oh, mon ami! mon tendre ami! if you looked down! if that be permitted, how benignly will you wish my participation in your blessed relief!

Fanny D'Arblay (Burney)

1871   I have several times seen the peacock with train spread lately. It has a very regular warp, like a shell, in which the bird embays himself, the bulge being inwards below but the hollow inwards above, cooping him in and only opening towards the brim, where the feathers are beginning to rive apart. The eyes, which lie alternately when the train is shut, like scales or gadroons, fall into irregular rows when it is opened, and then it thins and darkens against the light, it loses the moistness and satin it has when in the pack but takes another grave and expressive splendour, and the outermost eyes, detached and singled, give with their corner fringes the suggestion of that inscape of the flowing cusped trefoil which is often effective in art. He shivers it when he first rears it and then again at intervals and when this happens the rest blurs and the eyes start forward. I have thought it looks like a tray or green basket or fresh-cut willow hurdle set all over with Paradise fruits cut through – first through a beard of golden fibre and then through wet flesh greener than greengages or purpler than grapes – or say that the knife had caught a tatter or flag of the skin and laid it flat across the flesh – and then within all a sluggish corner drop of black or purple oil.

Gerard Manley Hopkins

1874   Bright. Took Br Tournade to Combe Wood to see and gather bluebells, which we did, but fell in blue-handed with a gamekeeper, which is a humbling thing to do. Then we heard a nightingale utter a few strains – strings of very liquid gurgles.

On the way home, from about 4.30 to 5 p.m. but no doubt longer, were two taper tufts of vapour or cloud in shape like the tufts in ermine, say, touched with red on the inside, bluish at the outer and tapering end, stood on each side of the sun at the distance, I think, the halo stands at and as if flying outward from the halo. The left-hand one was long-tailed and curved slightly upwards. They were not quite diametrically opposite but a little above the horizontal diameter and seemed to radiate towards the sun. I have seen the phenomenon before.

Gerard Manley Hopkins

18 May

1709   I visited Mr Young's Child, at Somerton, where there was still a very great Flood occasion'd by a storm of Rain with Thunder & Lightning very dreadfull, that fell Monday last there, & all along by Masson, Shirborn & the Places adjacent with that fierceness for about 6 hours time that the like had never been seen by any Man; It so overfilling the Rivers that Kingsmoor was even this day (when I rode in sight of it) all over cover'd very deep with Water; & many Houses were beat down, 8 at Masson. Such a weight of Water broke out of the River & ran into Shirborn Church that it beat down many seats, & broke up the Pavement of the Church all over & was reckon'd to have done in that Town 5000£ dammage. There were Hailstones that fell in Immensurable Quantities, said to be 6 Inches in the Circumference. Mr Shirley measured one of 3 Inches & half. The Thunder was incessant. I lodg'd at Charleton at my Brother Farwel's. There fell on Monday no Rain at Wells, and there was very little Thunder heard.

Dr Claver Morris

1839 On the 4th of April I broke a blood-vessel, and am now dying of consumption, in great suffering, and may not live many weeks. God be merciful to me a sinner.

God be praised for giving me such excellent parents. They are more than any wishes could desire, or than any words can sufficiently praise. Their presence is like sunshine to my illness.

Emily Shore

1943 Today I am by the river below East Peckham. I'm writing letters, roasting in the sun, sweating, burning, turning red. The feathers of the grass tickle me and I am almost stupefied. Oh, how lovely it is. Bang in front is a concrete pill-box covered with nets, slowly being swallowed up by weeds. *They'll* win, every time.

Denton Welch

19 May

1907 What incredible folly one gives way to! I have spent a *miserable* twenty-four hours since yesterday at 11.0 when I consented to preach. Why miserable? I don't know. I had a neat typewritten simple sermon ready. I had only to stand up for ten minutes and read it out to a congregation of some twenty people, all of whom I know, and whose opinion I do not really regard. But the thing has hung over me like a black cloud. A fear of breaking down, of turning faint, of hurrying out, etc., etc. I have enacted a dozen possible scenes over and over. My sleep last night was broken with fearful dreams — a huge function at Eton, which I was to address ... A vast, incongruous party was assembled. Last of all papa came in and was very gracious. I waited and went away with him, and he was in his easiest, simplest, most loving mood; he suggested a walk, that we might have a long talk; 'It is such an age since I have seen you, dearest boy,' he said — and smiled.

Then the recollection of the function which was then proceeding, and probably waiting for me, came on me, and I ran from him in stricken haste, while he waited smiling by the gate.

So it went on all night — waking in misery; but I got a good deal of sleep. Of course it shows that my nerves are a good deal in rags. Then I read a little, breakfasted, read more — and went in feeling fairly cheerful. But in the middle of the service my terrors came on me, and I felt I could not stand it — my legs quivered, my voice became husky. Then came the hymn. Then my own voice making the invocation. And then I read the whole sermon, clearly and strongly, with due emphasis, without a touch of nervousness, gazing benignantly round — and it was that performance I have dreaded for twenty-four hours! Yet no amount of deriding myself as a fool, or even the prudential thought that fretting over it was the very thing to bring the catastrophe about, will help me ...

Simpson came in to lunch — pleasant and intelligent — and we talked on many matters. I don't quite understand the lie of his mind; but he is fond of good literature and austere books. Then I went out, really feeling rather tired. It was cold and fresh, but with gleams of sun. I went along the Backs, and how I hated the good-humoured, ugly, shoving, noisy democracy! I turned into King's garden and walked there a long time round and round. The place is very beautiful, and always suggests to me paradise. The way in which the lawns run in smooth inlets, in and out of the shrubberies, the edges of the beds all fringed with a foam of flowers, is very sweet.

The real misfortune is that the garden has fallen into the hands of a botanist, whose idea is to cut down trees and do everything for the sake of having specimens of flowers, with names on tin labels. It is like turning a country-house into a school . . .

But I felt somehow that I was nearing the end, or near the end, of my tapestry of life. I have used up my strength, such as it was, and my reserves. I am tired, and my only way of fighting tiredness is to tire myself afresh. It takes people in different ways, and that is my way.

A. C. Benson

1945 Made a little progress musically today, but my mind and hands feel heavy. It will pass soon, I hope. I know nothing so dreary as the feeling that you can't make the sounds or write the words that your whole creative being is yearning for.

Noël Coward

20 May

1940 He seemed very pleased to see me and we bought apple tarts to take back for tea at number 34. After we had munched our way through them, he sat facing me and set out, I think, to shock me. That cultured, rather charming voice, and those clear grey eyes made what he was saying even more intriguing. He started off by saying, 'Do you find yourself shocked by the things that are happening to you now? You know you really shouldn't, there's something fine and human and large about the person who's never shocked, a lovely robustness of outlook. I'm going to ask you something now that would have shocked me at your age – you'll think me terrible – maybe I'd better not!'

'Oh no, go on, please ask me,' I said, expecting something terrific.

'Well,' Leonard went on in bell-like tones, 'I was going to ask you if you'd mind if I peed in your sink.'

I laughed so much that I choked and became red in the face. When my voice came back I wiped my eyes and said weakly,

'No, no, please do, only make sure that you move the tea things first!' and went off into further spasms.

'You see,' he went on, ignoring my hilarity, 'I always pee in the sink at home, it's so much easier than going down to the lavatory which is two floors down, and Agnes doesn't mind. I really thought you'd be shocked,' he went on, seeming rather annoyed. 'I didn't know you'd find it funny.' Really men are amazing.

After he had finished peeing he sat down again and started teaching me words like bugger, fuck, cunt, cock etc., which he thinks should not be thought of as vulgar but should become part of the English language.

After he had gone on about this for quite a long time with the air of an Oxford don, he moved his chair nearer to me and said, 'I'm being terribly curious, and I suppose your friends would think me either silly or a cad to speak to a young girl like this, but have you ever thought that you would like to indulge in certain erotic practices other than mere face-to-face copulation?'

I told him that quite honestly I didn't know there were any, which is probably why I had never thought about it. Leonard looked rather taken aback, but went on to describe, with scholarly enthusiasm, how a woman could lie on top of a man or sit astride him, or how she could kneel upright with a man coming in behind, or how they could do it standing up, or the woman could lean back over a table.

'But of course,' he went on, 'it's more difficult for a woman to come in those attitudes than when you're face to face – do you follow? I'll demonstrate if you like?'

'Oh no – thank you very much, I'd really rather you didn't – what does come mean?'

Leonard stared at me in amazement. 'An orgasm, of course. My goodness, I keep forgetting how young you are.'

'So what else can a woman do?' I went on, beginning to get interested.

'Well, she can hold the man's penis in her mouth – the only objection to that is that it's rather difficult to know what to do with the semen when it comes. I know some women like swallowing it – it acts like a tonic and makes them feel marvellous.'

I said I couldn't really see myself enjoying that very much, so he steered the conversation back on to masturbation, which we had just been starting on the day Holland and Belgium were invaded. When I said I had never done it, he seemed very startled and said, 'Good heavens, not even at your convent? I thought all convent girls did it? Well you really ought to, you've missed a lot! Goodness,' he went on, looking for some more cake, 'I'm being extraordinarily perverse this afternoon.'

Leonard believes that any normally attractive man can get any woman in the end if he is patient and soft with her. I looked at Leonard's skinny legs and decided it wasn't true.

After he had gone I sat thinking for a long time and my face was terribly flushed because I have never really discussed these things before. Funnily enough, he reminded me of Mother Mary Damian giving a sex talk at school.

Joan Wyndham

21 May

1925 For some reason I am fresh and alert, although today has been exacting, and I slept atrociously last night. I had two vivid 'surface dreams' in which I was in a state of poetic afflatus and quite confident that I was really doing 'the big stuff' at last. The second afflatus concerned a poem about driving a motor-car in a snowstorm, and the only extant line is 'And there the ship lay with her funnel'. Freud would assert that this signified something sexual. But he would be wrong, I think. The line arose from my needing a rhyme to 'tunnel'. But perhaps 'tunnel' is sexual too!

From 1 to 6 I was with Mother. I called at her club, with the car, and drove her to the Heads', where we lunched well and she got on beautifully with that couple of middle-aged angels. They, too, were charmed by Mother, and I had a pleasantly creative feeling, as I always do when I am 'bringing together' people who are dear to me, and who were intended by nature to become known to one another. More and more I want to weave this texture (or context) of my friends into a tapestry of human understanding. It is like someone building a house and furnishing it slowly and wisely. My friends are my house. I have no other refuge on earth.

Siegfried Sassoon

1947   Motored Eardley to Somerset. We reached Stourhead at 3 o'c. By that time the sun had penetrated the mist, and was gauzy and humid. The air about lake and grounds of a conservatory consistency. Never do I remember such Claude-like, idyllic beauty here. See Stourhead and die. Rhododendrons and azaleas full out. No ponticums, but pink and deep red rhododendrons – not so good – and loveliest of all, the virginal snow white ones, almost too white to be true. Azaleas mostly orange and brimstone. These clothe the banks of the lake. The beech are at their best. We walked leisurely round the lake and amused ourselves in the grot trying to remember Pope's four lines correctly by heart, and forgetting, and running back to memorize.

James Lees-Milne

1970   The phone never stopped ringing all day. No. 10 again: this time to tell me to get a reply out to the Tories on the unemployment figures. And there is so much to do in the garden! I have been shovelling barrowloads of earth from our old mound to reveal the outline of the original farm road. I find the challenge of the garden as obsessive as that of politics: I work off my aggression by beating it into shape.

Barbara Castle

---

22 May

1682   This night, scratching the right side of my buttock, above the fundament, thence proceeded a violent sharp humour.

Elias Ashmole

1826   The head this morning looked well. So true is that which Wilkie has often said to me, 'Never rub out in the evening of the day you have worked hard, if your labour should appear a failure.' Your nature, strained from over-excitement, is apt to be either disconcerted at your imagination being so much more noble than your attempts, or your digestion being deranged by long thinking affects the brain and fills it with gloomy apprehensions. I was exhausted last night; this morning got up refreshed and everything looked smiling.

B. R. Haydon

1830   We walked to the Zoological Garden in Regent's Park. It is a most delightful spectacle, the animals have so much more liberty than in common menageries. The enclosures are large, and all except the wild animals are kept in the open air during the daytime. The tiger seemed to feel annoyed at being looked on in what it esteemed a state of degradation, and walked up and down its narrow prison as if it would fain increase its boundaries, and the lion lay asleep – perhaps dreaming of its own native forests, or of a delicious banquet which it tasted only *once*, but remembers with continued zest, consisting of a young negro which had been brought to it by its mother. Many more animals and birds were there than I can enumerate, but I shall mention the monkeys, whose tricks were very diverting. I brought them some nuts and biscuits, and whenever they saw them there was a commotion in their cages, and paws were stretched out in all directions for them. While I was bending to give a weak one a nut, which a superior was taking from it, my bonnet was seized from a cage above and the front nearly torn from it. The keeper let them out from their confinement into large arbours in the open air, where were hung swings and ropes, and certainly the gymnastics of the Greenwich boys were far exceeded by these agile creatures. They flung themselves from rope to rope and to the side of the cage with immense celerity. Next in agility to the monkeys were the bears, though in a more clumsy style. They begged for buns, and clambered up a long pole to amuse the bystanders, who rewarded them with cakes. Mamma was quite pleased with the beaver for showing itself both on land and water, she said it was very obliging and exceedingly gentlemanly of it.

Anne Chalmers

23 May

1792   Received a letter from my old Pigmy Friend J. Walker. How remarkable was the adventure on his Wedding Night. Somewhat before Bed Time a Carriage drew up to his Door. Some Gentlemen in great haste requested to speak with him for a moment. He came to the door – they seized him – dragged him into the Chaise which drove furiously away and without uttering a word conveyed him to a Common some 7 miles from the town. There left him to his meditations. By daybreak he found his way home. A strange occurrence and in so large a City as Norwich. Many conjectured that the Story was a fiction and that he had committed a Rape upon himself. Strange if so. Upon the Death of his 1st Wife an Ugly Old Woman with £10,000 in her Pocket proposed herself to Jack as a Bedfellow for life. 'Madam,' says he, 'I thank you for the offer but I had rather have Your Daughter.' 'My Daughter,' says she, 'an Elegant Young Woman with £5,000 at her disposal would never think of such a whipper-snapper Chap as You.' 'Whipper-snapper tho' I be,' replies Jack, 'and knowing as You are, You are mistaken. Read this.' Here he gave her a Billet from her Daughter to read. The Old Woman having perused the Paper burst into tears but wisely recollecting herself said, 'Seeing things are as they are I can have no objection to my daughter marrying a Man whom I could have wished to have married myself.' So an amicable agreement took place. The ring was bought. The Bride Maid was sent for, the Day was fixed, when, such is the Perverseness of Fate, the Young Lady was seized with a Fever and died. My Little Friend consoled himself with courting the Bride Maid and she is his Present Wife.

The Reverend William Bagshaw Stevens

1947   *The Loved One* goes very slow, snakes and ladders progress. Some time ago an American from Cambridge wrote to ask me for an interview. I said if he would come here I would see him. Today he came. A very very humourless Boston Irishman. All the topics he raised bored me so much I would only say, 'No, No.'

'Do you consider that in a democratic age the radio and cinema will develop into great arts?'

'No. No.'

'Do you think the Renaissance villain represents the individual at war with society?'

'No. No.'

'Do publishers have an influence on modern writing comparable to the patron of the eighteenth century?'

'No. No.'

Then I ordered him eggs for tea as he had a long journey back and he spilt one on his trousers. I gave him sherry and a copy of *Campion* and sent him back on his long journey to Cambridge.

Evelyn Waugh

24 May

1833 To-day is my birthday. I am to-day fourteen years old! How *very old*!!

Princess Victoria

1837 Today it is my 18th birthday! How old! and yet how far am I from being what I should be. I shall from this day take the *firm* resolution to study with renewed assiduity, to keep my attention always well fixed on whatever I am about, and to strive to become every day less trifling and more fit for what, if Heaven wills it, I'm some day to be!

Princess Victoria

1839 This day I *go out of my teens* and become 20! It sounds so strange to me! I have much to be thankful for; and I feel I owe more to *two* people than I can every repay! my dear Lehzen, and my dear excellent Lord Melbourne! I pray Heaven to preserve them in health and strength for *many, many* years to come, and that Lord Melbourne may remain at the Head of Affairs; not only for my own happiness and prosperity, but for that of the whole Country and of all Europe; and lastly that I may become every day less unworthy of my high station!

Queen Victoria

1900 Again my old birthday returns, my eighty-first! God has been very merciful and supported me, but my trials and anxieties have been manifold, and I feel tired and upset by all I have gone through this winter and spring . . .

  The number of telegrams to be opened and read was quite enormous, and obliged six men to be sent for to help the two telegraphists in the house. The answering of them was an interminable task, but it was most gratifying to receive so many marks of loyalty and affection.

Queen Victoria

25 May

1652 After drowth of neare 4 monethes there fel so violent a tempest of haile, raine, wind, thunder, and lightning, as no man had seene the like in this age; the haile being in some places four or five inches about, brake all glasse about London, especially at Deptford, and more at Greenwich.

John Evelyn

1716 On Sunday May 13th 1716 (being this Year) one George Ward (commonly called for his loose way of Living Jolly Ward), AM and Fellow of University College, and a Tutor of the House, and in Priests Orders, was found with a common strumpet in his Chamber of the College, in the time of Evening Service in the Afternoon. Which strumpet lives in Oxford, and is very notorious. She was with this Ward two or three Hours, and was conveyed to him by an elderly woman that he had imployed. The same Strumpet hath been often with one Fiddes, AM and Fellow of All Souls, as also with our debauched and irreligious (for so he is) Professor of Astronomy, Dr John Keil. Ward went out of Town the next day, the matter being divulged and brought before the Master of Univ. Coll., Dr Charlett, at that time Pro-vice-chancellor. And Fiddes is likewise out of Town. But Ward being a Favourite of the Master's, nothing is done against him, tho' he ought to be expelled both the College and University. Nor is the Strumpet punished, but permitted to go away; only the old woman that conveyed her hath been corrected a little in Bridewell. I put these things down, not that I think the University ought to be reflected on upon this Account, but only some particular Men who encourage Idleness and Debauchery and the greatest wickedness, this Ward being a vile Fellow, and the very same man that hath most scandalously debauched the present Young Lord Brooke, with whom he often is both in Town and Country, and they enjoy their Whores (as I am well informed) in common.

Thomas Hearne

1932 Now I have 'finished' *David Copperfield*, and I say to myself can't I escape to some pleasanter atmosphere? Can't I expand and embalm and become a sentient living creature? Lord how I suffer! What a terrific capacity I possess for feeling with intensity – now, since we came back, I'm screwed up into a ball; can't get into step; can't make things dance; feel awfully detached; see youth; feel old; no, that's not quite it: wonder how a year or so perhaps is to be endured. Think, yet people do live; can't imagine what goes on behind faces. All is surface hard; myself only an organ that takes blows, one after another; the horror of the hard raddled faces in the flower show yesterday: the inane pointlessness of all this existence: hatred of my own brainlessness and indecision; the old treadmill feeling, of going on and on and on, for no reason: Lytton's death; Carrington's; a longing to speak to him; all that cut away, gone: ... women: my book on professions: shall I write another novel; contempt for my lack of intellectual power; reading Wells without understanding; ... society; buying clothes; Rodmell spoilt; all England spoilt: terror at night of things generally wrong in the universe; buying clothes; how I hate Bond Street and spending money on clothes: worst of all is this dejected barrenness. And my eyes hurt: and my hand trembles.

Virginia Woolf

26 May

1783 The great extent of London makes visits or business very inconvenient to me. Never wish to be here without a carriage.

Neither strength nor spirits to run about here. Should stay at home and be content. How provoking it is to take a long walk and then not find the person you want. No attachments here. Every one is indifferent to another. Neither Literature nor anything appears of consequence.

The Reverend W. J. Temple

1829 The 26th my dear son Dick attained his twenty-first year, an event I had looked forward to with much anxiety, not alone on his account so much as avoiding the necessity for *borrowed* trustees, etc., for all my beloved children. He, I am very confident, will prove himself a steady guardian in every particular. May Almighty Providence long protect him, and send him a long life of happiness and health to enjoy dear Freeford after my days have passed away. There was a jolly day, and *beards wagged all* in the hall to celebrate the happy event. The labourers and their wives had a dinner and flowing cups of strong ale brewed for the occasion, of which they took full measure, and reached their homes by various ways, some in wheelbarrows, etc. The servants invited their friends to a ball and supper, the sports of which continued until four o'clock the next morning. There were fifty persons entertained in the course of the day, all, I trust and believe, most happy with the enjoyments of the feast. It is many years since such an event took place at Freeford. My father having been the last of the family who came of age as the heir, which must have been on the 12th April 1744, eighty-five years ago.

William Dyott

1932 And now today suddenly the weight on my head is lifted and I can think, reason, keep to one thing and concentrate. Perhaps this is the beginning of another spurt. Perhaps I owe it to my conversation with L. last night. I tried to analyse my depression: how my brain is jaded with the conflict within of two types of thought, the critical, the creative; how I am harassed by the strife and jar and uncertainty without. This morning the inside of my head feels cool and smooth instead of strained and turbulent.

Virginia Woolf

27 May

1650 This day a quarter past two in the afternoone my Mary fell asleepe in the Lord, her soule past into that rest where the body of Jesus, and the soules of the saints are, shee was: 8 yeares and 45 dayes old when shee dyed, my soule had aboundant cause to blesse gode for her, who was our first fruites, and those god would have offered to him, and this I freely resigned up to him, it was a pretious child, a bundle of myrrhe, a bundle of sweetnes, shee was a child of ten thousand, full of wisedome, woman-like gravity, knowledge, sweet expressions of god, apt in her learning, tender hearted and loving, an obedient child to us. it was free from the rudenesse of litle children, it was to us as a boxe of sweet ointment, which now its broken smells more deliciously then it did before, Lord I rejoyce I had such a present for thee, it was patient in the sicknesse, thankefull to admiracion; it lived desired and dyed lamented, thy memory is and will bee sweete unto mee.

The Reverend Ralph Josselin

1743 David Taylor informed me, that the people of Thorpe, through which we should pass, were exceeding mad against us. So we found them, as we approached the place, and were turning down the lane to Barley-hall. The ambush rose, and assaulted us with stones, eggs, and dirt. My horse flew from side to side, till he forced his way through them. David Taylor they wounded in his forehead, which bled much: his hat he lost in the fray. I returned, and asked what was the reason a Clergyman could not pass without such treatment. At first the rioters scattered; but their Captain, rallying, answered with horrible imprecations, and stones that would have killed both man and beast, had they not been turned aside by an hand unseen. My horse took fright, and hurried away with me down a steep hill, till we came to a lane, which I turned up, and took a circuit to find our brother Johnson's. The enemy spied me from afar, and followed, shouting. Blessed be God, I got no hurt, but only the eggs and dirt. My clothes indeed abhorred me, and my arm pained me a little by a blow I received at Sheffield. David Taylor had got just before me to Barley-hall, with the sisters, whom God had hid in the hollow of his hand.

I met many sincere souls assembled to hear the word of God. Never have I known a greater power of love. All were drowned in tears; yet very happy. The scripture I met was, 'Blessed be the Lord God of Israel; for he hath visited and redeemed his people.' We rejoiced in the God of our salvation, who hath compassed us about with songs of deliverance.

Charles Wesley

1839 I feel weaker every morning, and I suppose am beginning to sink; still I can at times take up my pen. I have had my long back hair cut off. Dear papa wears a chain made from it. Mamma will have one too.

Emily Shore

28 May

1757 O thou inflammable jack-straw!

Dr John Rutty

1833 I acted Hamlet although with much to censure, yet with a spirit and feeling of words and situations that I think I have never done before. The first act was the best, still, at the exit of the Ghost in both scenes and afterwards, polish and self-possession is requisite. In the second act, almost general revision. Third act, the soliloquy wants a more entire abandonment to thought, more abstraction. Ophelia's scene wants finish, as does the advice to the players. The play scene was very good, and most of the closet scene, but in parts my voice is apt to rise, and I become rather too vehement; latter part wants smoothness. End of the play was good. Energy! Energy! Energy!

William Macready

1977 Looking around me as I sit locked in my cell with the natural light pouring in through the window, I think of how last week

I thought of this week and how it would be the same. It is. Now look and think and see the barbarity of it. The lock shut tight alone in the early evening – it's not as though I would be a lonely person by choice. I am a private person who likes to retain his own identity but this is an imposed solitude. I think of the image of the past and how it is no longer me, yet it hangs around me, clinging. I look at the barbed wire that hangs outside my window and want to throw myself at it, not to climb over but as a gesture of defiance. It wouldn't be meant as a gesture of self-destruction though that would be the obvious consequence. It would be more a cry to humanity, to the people of the world as to what they are doing. It's all about these very strong passionate and very tender feelings deep within that have been buried for so long, that have been expressed in snide ways. I always knew they existed but didn't know what they were or what they meant. Having gained this knowledge and having learned a lot about my life and society, I feel my earlier life has been stolen from me.

Jimmy Boyle

29 May

1837   The King is believed to be suffering from asthma and water on the chest, and if the latter is not removed, a fortnight more may see a new reign. The heiress of the throne, the Princess Victoria of Kent, attained her eighteenth birthday on Wednesday last, and is capable of ascending the throne without a regency, as Queen in her own right.

The Reverend Francis Witts

1954   To Oxford to see Burgo, and after lunch to watch the Eights-week races among crowds of variously elegant and dandified young men, many wearing beautiful snow-white flannels, straw hats and huge button-holes. There was a great feeling of youth, high-spirits and promiscuous élan; also a lot of pretty girls with peach-like complexions and ugly clothes. Drizzle fell sparsely, the river glittered like tin under a grey sky flaming with sunlight at the horizon; the races created intermittent moments of excitement and roars of 'House! House!' like a cheerful dog barking. Ralph wore his Leander tie, and in the boat-house we saw an oar with his name painted on it. An afternoon of youthful glamour and gaiety.

Frances Partridge

1977 Last night I went to bed at 8.35 p.m. as I couldn't face looking at the cell walls, doors and windows. I felt exhausted and was soon sound asleep. This morning I wakened and went outside to do my running exercises. While doing so I thought, in the freshness of the morning, of my thoughts of the night before. I thought of the soil and my returning to it. It's inevitable at some point, and the daily struggle in here has reached a level where I am facing each day in a condition of rawness, where exposure to the actual surroundings is excruciatingly painful. Strangely enough the one moment of respite I got this morning was when I lifted a 400 lb weight. I don't know why but somehow the heavy weight matched what I felt. I showered, shaved and dressed. While doing so I looked at myself in the mirror. I looked very healthy and thought of how the external belies the internal . . .

This afternoon my aunt Peggy and cousin came to visit me bringing my two children, James and Patricia, with them. I put on a 'mask' and sat with them, but it was flat, and yet I felt so terribly close to them. I managed to get my children away on their own and have a chat with them. Here I am in this situation just as in previous nights. Is it this, or am I using the confinement as an excuse to avoid the deeper issues lying inside me? Why do I feel as though all that is inside me is blocked in my throat? I feel the best thing I can do is to remain away from everyone for a day or two till I work this thing through. Thank God for the music that is playing – a Brandenburg Concerto.

There was a time when the things that now hurt me never would have as I would have been too insensitive to them. Therefore, is sensitivity a bad thing in a situation, or, more to the point, in a world such as this? No, the answer must be no.

Jimmy Boyle

30 May

1722 Mr Nooth telling my Son his Fault three or 4 times in Holding his Pen, & he committing the same again I struck him a Slap on the Hinder part of his Head with the Palm of my Hand; But that did not make him mend it.

Dr Claver Morris

1800 Day of Divorce Bill. Up late. Unusually languid and incapable of exertion. So perplexed between the two things I had to do, viz. the business of the Divorce Bill and motion about Soldiers' Children, that in the state of bodily languor in which I was I could do nothing.

William Windham

1933 Yes, but of all things coming home from holiday is undoubtedly the most damned. Never was there such aimlessness, such depression. Cant read, write or think. Theres no climax here. Comfort yes: but the coffee's not so good as I expected. And my brain is extinct – literally hasnt the power to lift a pen. What one must do is to set it – my machine I mean – on the rails & give it a push. Lord – how I pushed yesterday to make it start running along Goldsmith again. Theres that half finished article. Lord Salisbury said something about dished up speeches being like the cold remains of last nights supper. I see white grease on the pages of my article. Today its a little warmer – tepid meat: a slab of cold mutton. Its coldish, dullish here. Yes, but I hear the clock tick, & suspect, though I must not look, that the wheels are just beginning to turn on the rails. We go to Monks House for Whitsun, which is Monday – the suburban, the diminished Monks House. No, I cant look at *The Pargiters*. Its an empty snail shell. And I'm empty with a cold slab of a brain. Never mind. I shall dive head foremost into *The Pargiters*. And now I shall make my mind run along Italian – whats his name – Goldoni. A few verbs I think.

It occurs to me that this state, my depressed state, is the state in which most people usually are.

Virginia Woolf

1966 The thought of old age is, not unnaturally, in my mind a great deal nowadays. The weeks and months and years pass with disconcerting swiftness. In only thirteen years' time I shall be eighty! I cannot say that this realization doesn't depress me a little because it does, but not to an excessive degree for the simple reason that there is *nothing* I can do about it. I don't mind whether the final curtain falls in Jamaica, Japan or Fiji, but I am determined that the last act shall be set mainly in 'This realm, this dear, dear land', in which the people are sillier than ever and the succeeding governments also are idiotic, but my roots are sunk deep in it.

Noël Coward

31 May

1662 And had Sarah to comb my head clean, which I find so foul with poudering and other troubles, that I am resolved to try how I can keep my head dry without pouder. And I did also in a sudden fit cut off all my beard, which I have been a great while bringing up, only that I may with my pumice-stone do my whole face, as I now do my chin, and so save time – which I find a very easy way and gentile. So she also washed my feet in a bath of hearbes; and so to bed.

This month ends with very fair weather for a great while together. My health pretty well, but only wind doth now and then torment me about the fundament extremely.

Samuel Pepys

1669 Up very betimes, and so continued all the morning, with W. Hewer, upon examining and stating my accounts, in order to the fitting myself to go abroad beyond sea, which the ill condition of my eyes, and my neglect for a year or two, hath kept me behindhand in, and so as to render it very difficult now, and troublesome to my mind to do it; but I this day made a satisfactory entrance therein. Dined at home, and in the afternoon by water to Whitehall, calling by the way at Michell's, where I have not been many a day till just the other day; and now I met her mother there and knew her husband to be out of town. And here yo did besar ella, but have not opportunity para hazer mas with her as I would have offered if yo had had it. And thence had another meeting with the Duke of York at Whitehall with the Duke of York on yesterday's work, and made a good advance; and so being called by my wife, we to the park, Mary Batelier, a Duch gentleman, a friend of hers, being with us. Thence to the World's end, a drinking-house by the park, and there merry; and so home later.

And thus ends all that I doubt I shall ever be able to do with my own eyes in the keeping of my journall, I being not able to do it any longer, having done now so long as to undo my eyes almost every time that I take a pen in my hand; and therefore, whatever comes of it, I must forbear; and therefore resolve from this time forward to have it kept by my people in longhand, and must therefore be contented to set down no more then is fit for them and all the world to know; or if there be anything (which cannot be much, now my amours to Deb are past, and my eyes hindering me in almost all other pleasures), I must endeavour to keep a margin in my book open, to add here and there a note in shorthand with my own hand. And so I betake that course which is almost as much as to see myself go into my grave – for which, and all the discomforts that will accompany my being blind, the good God prepare me.

Samuel Pepys
[Final Entry]

1 June

1792 This day had been long engaged for breakfasting with Mrs Dickenson and dining with Mrs Ord.

The breakfast guests were Mr Langton, Mr Foote, Mr Dickenson, jun., a cousin, and a very agreeable and pleasing man; Lady Herries, Miss Dickenson, another cousin, and Mr Boswell.

This last was the object of the morning. I felt a strong sensation of that displeasure which his loquacious communications of every weakness and infirmity of the first and greatest good man of these times have awakened in me, at his first sight; and, though his address to me was courteous in the extreme, and he made a point of sitting next me, I felt an indignant disposition to a nearly forbidding reserve and silence. How many starts of passion and prejudice has he blackened into record, that else might have sunk, for ever forgotten, under the preponderance of weightier virtues and excellences!

Angry, however, as I have long been with him, he soon insensibly conquered, though he did not soften me: there is so little of ill design or ill nature in him, he is so open and forgiving for all that is said in return, that he soon forced me to consider him in a less serious light, and change my resentment against his treachery into something like commiseration of his levity; and before we parted we became good friends. There is no resisting great good-humour, be what will in the opposite scale.

Fanny Burney

1941 I like to remember the mornings after I have spent a night out when I have got up very early to be away before the daily charwoman arrives and standing in the damp grey morning air waiting to get one of the first buses with the people starting out for their day's work coughing and gossiping and grousing and waiting stolidly – patiently – for the bus – working men with coat collars turned up and stout women going scrubbing who spent last night at the local. I am unshaven and drifting and happy and with all the pores open to physical sensation and the tight core of will melted. Then to get into my smart pseudo-New York flatlet that always smells of whatever they clean the carpets with, and I have a hot bath and sausages for breakfast to celebrate the fact that I feel fine.

Love affairs. In my youth (that is until this year, for my youth was one of the protracted kind) I used to be bewildered by my own lack of feeling in affairs of the heart. I felt that my love affairs were not up to scratch. I did not yearn or suffer enough – not nearly enough. I still feel that – I believe it to be a much more common state than people suppose. For to hear me talking of my love you would think me to be a creature of burning passion and palpitating feelings, particularly if I am telling a woman of my ecstasies and sufferings in love's lists. This is just advertising one's own temperament by exaggerating what one is capable of feeling in love. Most other people knowingly or not must employ the same trick. It is true that promiscuous love-making knocks a lot of the nonsense out of one, and at the same time it 'hardens a' within and petrifies the feelings!'

Charles Ritchie

2 June

1658   *In the yere of our Lorde 1658, on the first of June, my Deare Husband was tryed for his Life by a Corte, calede the Highe Corte of Justis, and on the second day of June, was cleerd by one uoys only, 19 condemning of him and 20 sauing of him, and thos twenty had not preualed, but by God's emedeate Hand, by striking one of the Corte with an illnes, which forsed him to goe out, in whous absens, the uots wer geuen, and recorded, so that his returne no way preiudis'd Mr Mordaunt tho' in his thoughts he resolued it, (Prid was the person) many outher meracolus blesings wer shod in his preseruation for which Blesed Be God.*

   He was the first exampule that pleded not gilty, that was cleerd befor thes Cortes.

Viscountess Mordaunt

1797   Visited the Royal Exhibition. Particularly struck with a sea view by Turner – fishing vessels coming in, with a heavy swell, in apprehension of a tempest gathering in the distance, and casting, as it advances, a night of shade; while a parting glow is spread with fine effect upon the shore. The whole composition, bold in design, and masterly in execution. I am entirely unacquainted with the artist; but if he proceeds as he has begun, he cannot fail to become the first in his department.

Thomas Green

1806 I said a great deal to Campbell, as much as I could and dared, but was often interrupted, by others coming up to us, my want of courage, and his own evident wish to avoid an explanation – How painful it is for a Woman to talk on such a Subject! – I am sure that I likewise put him in pain, Walter unluckily dragg'd him away to Mrs Greville's Masquerade just as I should have got him to speak – However I went so far as to beg he would soon make up his mind and tell me his determination when he had – But did he understand me? – God alone knows! – it makes me quite miserable – but it was necessary that I should speak – We came home at about four o'clock – I was tired, dull and unhappy –

Eugenia Wynne

3 June

1767 Excessive Flood at Eaton & great Rain all Day. It has now rained 18 Days successively.

The Reverend William Cole

1806 We were assail'd with tiresome visitors all the morg – Campbell to my surprize and sorrow never came near me – Before we went out to an early dinner at Mrs Bankes, I wrote to explain my meaning of last night, and to ask for a decision, which he can no longer deny me – my heart breaks, when I think that now the dye is cast and that we shall perhaps part for ever – Mrs Bankes approves of what I have done – We staid with her till she went out when she set us home – I returned miserable, sick at heart, and overcome to find that

Campbell had sent no answer – when shall I know my fate –
Mrs Bankes takes great interest in the whole affair, and spoke
to me with all the kindness of a mother on the subject – But if
I love him, can anything make me amends for his loss! –

Eugenia Wynne

1875　Admiral Hall always has an old waddling terrier with him, a
great pet of his daughter's. He says their kitchen is terribly
infested with black beetles, and the dog always sleeps there at
night and has become so fond of them that if any one, even
himself, goes in after the servants are gone to bed, and
attempts to kill any of them, the dog will try to bite him, and
do all he can to prevent their being molested by barking and
showing his anger. 'Flying at' the intruders is out of the
question. No doubt the dog lying awake, or in a dog-sleep, so
much alone, has come to like the companionship even of the
beetles, perhaps feels their rushing about even an amusement.

Alfred Domett

1888　Strange how sternly I am possessed of the idea that I shall not
live much longer. Not a personal thought but is coloured with
this conviction. I never look forward more than a year at the
utmost; it is the habit of my mind, in utter sincerity, to expect
no longer tenure of life than that. I don't know how this has
come about; perhaps my absolute loneliness has something to
do with it. Then I am haunted with the idea that I am
consumptive. I never cough without putting a finger to my
tongue, to see if there be a sign of blood. Morbidness – is it? I
only know that these forecasts are the most essential feature
of my mental and moral life at present. Death, if it came now,
would rob me of not one hope, for hopes I simply have not.

George Gissing

4 June

1676　Being hard bound in my body I was five hours before I could
go to stool, and suffered much torment.

Elias Ashmole

1763   It was the King's birthnight, and I resolved to be a blackguard and see all that was to be seen. I dressed myself in my second-mourning suit, in which I had been powdered many months, dirty buckskin breeches and black stockings, a shirt of Lord Eglinton's which I had worn two days, and little round hat with tarnished silver lace belonging to a disbanded officer of the Royal Volunteers. I had in my hand an old oaken stick battered against the pavement. And was not I a complete blackguard? I went to the Park, picked up a low brimstone, called myself a barber and agreed with her for sixpence, went to the bottom of the Park arm in arm, and dipped my machine in the Canal and performed most manfully. I then went as far as St Paul's Church-yard, roaring along, and then came to Ashley's Punch-house and drank three threepenny bowls. In the Strand I picked up a little profligate wretch and gave her sixpence. She allowed me entrance. But the miscreant refused me performance. I was much stronger than her, and *volens nolens* pushed her up against the wall. She however gave a sudden spring from me; and screaming out, a parcel of more whores and soldiers came to her relief. 'Brother soldiers,' said I, 'should not a half-pay officer roger for sixpence? And here has she used me so and so.' I got them on my side, and I abused her in blackguard style, and then left them. At Whitehall I picked up another girl to whom I called myself a highwayman and told her I had no money and begged she would trust me. But she would not. My vanity was somewhat gratified tonight that, notwithstanding of my dress, I was always taken for a gentleman in disguise. I came home about two o'clock, much fatigued.

James Boswell

1806   I had a Letter, from Campbell this morning which cost me many tears, and I repented most heartily that I had not followed my own inclinations and feelings on the subject, but yeilded to the solicitations of others – I have plainly offended him – he however answered all my questions and it is as plain that he does not mean to marry me unless he obtains some situation.

Eugenia Wynne

1831 I wonder if I shall burn this sheet of paper like most others I have begun in the same way. To write a diary, I have thought of how very often at far & near distance of time: but how could I write a diary without throwing upon paper my thoughts, all my thoughts – the thoughts of my heart as well as of my head? – & then how could I bear to look on *them* after they were written? Adam made fig leaves necessary for the mind, as well as for the body. And such *a* mind as I have! – So very exacting & exclusive & eager & head long – & *strong* – & so very often *wrong*! Well! but I will write: I must write – & the oftener wrong I know myself to be, the less wrong I shall be in one thing – the less *vain* I shall be! –

Elizabeth Barrett

5 June

1800 I sate out of doors great part of the day and worked in the garden – had a letter from Mr Jackson, and wrote an answer to Coleridge. The little birds busy making love, and pecking the blossoms and bits of moss off the trees; they flutter about and about, and thrid the trees as I lie under them. Molly went out to tea, I would not go far from home, expecting my Brothers. I rambled on the hill above the house, gathered wild thyme, and took up roots of wild columbine. Just as I was returning with my load, Mr and Miss Simpson called. We went again upon the hill, got more plants, set them, and then went to the Blind Man's for London Pride for Miss Simpson. I went up with them as far as the Blacksmith's, a fine lovely moonlight night.

Dorothy Wordsworth

1828 Old Harris was buried after dinner: several attended his inanimate corpse who never pay any attention to the soul which animates their own.

The Reverend John Skinner

1873 With M. D. to Christie and Manson's sale room. Pictures by Phillips, Egg &c. A beautiful one of Etty's – the *Rape of Proserphine* with 'gloomy Dis' '*gathering* her' in a chariot with rearing piebald horses. Nothing like this of his in our National Gallery. Our wondrous custodians prefer giving 2 or 3 thousand pounds for some hideous flat distortions of the human frame, womanly or infantine, miscalled Venuses and Cupids, by 'Botticelli' or other preRaffaellite, things at best only *historically* interesting to pedants in Art as recording the early stages it went through in its imperfect development. Of course, this is dreadfully heterodox and unfashionable doctrine to preach, but in spite of occasional liveliness and truth of *conception* or expression, these pictures evince, one cannot help thinking the public will one day or other come to such an estimate of them.

Alfred Domett

1932   A fine morning – I went with Rupert up to Boars Hill – we went into a wood and sheltered from the showers under trees. He was very Theocritean and loving. I got a wee bit sick of it – but tried to please him as I was determined to treat him as kindly as possible as he'd Schools on the 9th.

Barbara Pym

6 June

1825   As I strolled for an hour in the Park today and distantly contemplated the string of fashion – how like ants! I thought. There goes a little yellow-looking box, and two little things with four legs & one little insect driving them, & one behind the box, and something, a living insect, behind inside, and these little boxes & insects constituted superiority! and other little insects that seemed crawling by the side seemed to do so in great ease, for these boxes and four legged insects gave evidence of fashion & rank. These were the queen insects, and yet no insect there but had a consciousness of existence, as if it was a God! fancied itself born to be immortal! to live in endless bliss, endless torment.

No man can have a just estimation of the insignificance of his species, unless he has been up in an air balloon.

B. R. Haydon

1842 To the Carlyles', where we were received with great cordiality in the library, which looks well suited to the work performed there. Wax medallions of Edward Sterling and his son hang over the chimney-piece. Thomas Carlyle came in in his blouse, and we presently got, I know not how, to Swedenborgianism. Swedenborg was a thoroughly practical, mechanical man, and was in England learning shipbuilding. He went into a little inn in Bishopsgate Street, and was eating his dinner very fast, when he thought he saw in the corner of the room a vision of Jesus Christ, who said to him, 'Eat slower.' This was the beginning of all his visions and mysterious communications, of which he had enough in his day.

Caroline Fox

1906 Back again to business. Great Scott! – startling changes. Ambitions checked. Dan has been given Overall's job, not me. He is well in front. Mr Almond says I have thrown my chances away. I can't see it . . . I take Dan's place.

Holiday leaves me the same, except for sun-tan. At my age one cannot be in fixed health.

Sydney Moseley

1939 On the hottest day of the year I saw two nuns buying a typewriter in Selfridges. Oh, what were they going to do with it?

Barbara Pym

7 June

1800 A very warm cloudy morning, threatening to rain. I walked up to Mr Simpson's to gather gooseberries – it was a very fine afternoon. Little Tommy came down with me, ate gooseberry pudding and drank tea with me. We went up the hill, to gather sods and plants, and went down to the lake side, and took up orchises, etc. I watered the garden and weeded. I did not leave home, in the expectation of Wm. and John, and sitting at work till after 11 o'clock I heard a foot go to the front of the house, turn round, and open the gate. It was William! After our first joy was over, we got some tea. We did not go to bed till 4 o'clock in the morning, so he had an opportunity of seeing our improvements. The birds were singing, and all looked fresh, though not gay. There was a greyness on earth and sky. We did not rise till near 10 in the morning. We were busy all day in writing letters to Coleridge, Montagu, Douglas, Richard. Mr and Miss Simpson called in the evening, the little boy carried our letters to Ambleside. We walked with Mr and Miss S. home, on their return. The evening was cold and I was afraid of the toothach for William. We met John on our return home.

Dorothy Wordsworth

1843   A lecture on aeronautic navigation was delivered soon after we came in. The principle of the new invented mode of flying does not appear to be unphilosophical but the practical difficulty is the weight of the engine. The inventor asserts, however, that he has overcome that difficulty, having constructed a steam engine of 20 horse-power weighing only 200 lbs. There is no doubt that sails rapidly revolving will raise a weight if not too cumbersome, but how to keep up that rotation and preserve lightness? However time will prove this as it proves everything else.

Barclay Fox

1943   I have been eating my lunch in the fields nearby (Ryvita, cheese, apricot jam, chocolate, bar of squashed dried fruits, coffee), sitting on my coral aircushion, given me by May, reading for the fourth or fifth time an outline of the Brontë sisters' lives.

Charlotte's success, as always, delights and excites me. I cannot help thinking of my own book. I keep wondering if mine can really be called a success. Edith Sitwell says it is the best reception of a first book she can remember. I have letters and wires and lovely reviews, but how and when does one know? When the fat cheque rolls in? Is that what one is waiting for?

Denton Welch

8 June

1741 I found myself much out of order. However, I made shift to preach in the evening: but on Saturday my bodily strength quite failed, so that for several hours I could scarce lift up my head. Sunday, 10. I was obliged to lie down most part of the day, being easy only in that posture. Yet in the evening my weakness was suspended, while I was calling sinners to repentance. But at our love-feast which followed, beside the pain in my back and head, and the fever which still continued upon me, just as I began to pray, I was seized with such a cough, that I could hardly speak. At the same time came strongly into my mind, 'These signs shall follow them that believe.' I called on Jesus aloud, to 'increase my faith', and to 'confirm the word of his grace'. While I was speaking my pain vanished away; the fever left me; my bodily strength returned; and for many weeks I felt neither weakness nor pain. 'Unto thee, O Lord, do I give thanks.'

John Wesley

1794 A Fire happened at Oatlands yesterday which damaged some of the out buildings. The King had been there, and brought back a little dog belonging to the Duchess of York, who seemed more anxious abt. her animals than abt. the House. She has 18 dogs. The King observed that affection must rest on something. Where there were no children Animals were the objects of it.

Joseph Farington

1948 With a high temperature these last few weeks I can read for long stretches, a thing I have not been able to do for months and months, but I do not seem able to write at all. Through the day I stop and wonder enviously how it is done. I wonder however I have done it in the past. I wonder how I could ever have believed even a little in what I wrote. Such emptiness and rubbish is in my mind that I would have no one ever see it.

Denton Welch

9 June

1797 I was much amused this evening with a ventriloquist; the most perfect in his art I have ever met with. He maintained a spirited dialogue with himself, and sung an air, with good effect, in this assumed voice. The deception is highly curious. That it is in the power of the professors of this art, according to the vulgar notion, to cast their voice wherever they please, is certainly untrue: the delusion they produce, may, I think, thus be accounted for. Though I cannot admit with Reid (Enquiry into the Human Mind, chap. 4, sect. 1) that sound does not indicate the quarter from whence it proceeds, since, as I have often observed, a dog, with nothing to direct him, will instantly turn towards the point from whence his master calls; yet unquestionably this indication is very vague and slight, and leaves the mind in considerable suspense. When the ventriloquist first inwardly articulates, we are prompted to refer the sound to *him*; but observing that not a muscle in his countenance stirs, and hearing a voice entirely different from that in which he had just addressed us, we naturally cast about to some other quarter for the speaker: the ventriloquist always takes care to lead the imagination, with much address, to that quarter from which he wishes us to suppose that the ideal speaker is talking: and we eagerly refer thither, those accents for which we could otherwise assign no place whatever.

Thomas Green

1914 The days are more interesting when I talk to B.S., whom I have not seen since Saturday. To fall in love with him would be a perfect impossibility, but it is very easy to be in love with love. To hear a man's voice say 'you' in a tone which he uses to no one else on earth, is in itself a gigantic temptation to make him go on saying it like that, & to go on listening. It is wrong of me to think of such things, still worse to take pleasure in them, but then I am not good, & in spite of high purposes, only a very human girl. Still, that's no excuse!

Vera Brittain

1938 How many nights have I sat alone in my room listening to the laughter in the streets, looking furtively at my watch to see if I could get up and go to bed. All those nights in my stuffy little room in Paris, in my room at Oxford with the clock of Tom Tower striking nostalgia on the night air, at school with the movements and muffled voices of the boys in the corridors, and at home at the table which faced the window looking out on the lawn with the single oak tree. And always this piece of staring, white paper in front of me with the few and feeble words strung across it. These wasted nights are most remarkable. Nothing could be more stubborn than my devotion, nothing more stupid than my persistence. After all, I have written nothing – I will write nothing. Twenty years have not been enough to convince me of my lack of talent.

Charles Ritchie

---

10 June

1758 I went to Lewes on foot to know the result of Counsellor Humphrey's oppinion of Mr Virgoe's will; and now what I am going to relate makes me shudder with horrour at the thoughts of it. It is, I got very much in liquor; but let me not give it so easy a name, but say I was very drunk, and in consequence no better than a beast. I got on horseback at the Cats, and proceeded on my way home, and met Mr Langham and several more, but who they were I cannot remember. There was formerly a dispute between Mr Langham and I, about a bill, and I imagine I must tell him of that. Whether they, seeing me more in liquor than themselves, put upon me, I do not remember; but Mr Langham pulled me by the nose and struck at me with his horsewhip, and used me very ill. Mr Adams told them he thought there was enough for a joke, upon which they used him very ill, and whilst they were a-fighting, I, free from any hurt, and like a true friend and bold hearty fellow, rode away upon poor Peter's horse, leaving him to shift for himself, and glad enough I got away with a whole skin. What can I say in my own behalf, for getting drunk? Sure I am a direct fool.

Thomas Turner

1833 [Liverpool.] At twelve I got upon an omnibus, and was driven up a steep hill to the place where the steam-carriages start. We travelled in the second class of carriages. There were five carriages linked together, in each of which were placed open seats for the traveller, four and four facing each other; but not all were full; and, besides, there was a close carriage, and also a machine for luggage. The fare was four shillings for the thirty-one miles. Everything went on so rapidly, that I had scarcely the power of observation. The road begins at an excavation through rock, and is to a certain extent insulated from the adjacent country. It is occasionally placed on bridges, and frequently intersected by ordinary roads. Not quite a perfect level is preserved. On setting off there is a slight jolt, arising from the chain catching each carriage, but, once in motion, we proceeded as smoothly as possible. For a minute or two the pace is gentle, and is constantly varying. The machine produces little smoke or steam. First in order is the tall chimney; then the boiler, a barrel-like vessel; then an oblong reservoir of water; then a vehicle for coals; and then comes of a length infinitely extendible, the train of carriages. If all the seats had been filled, our train would have carried about 150 passengers; but a gentleman assured me at Chester that he went with a thousand persons to Newton fair. There must have been two engines then. I have heard since that two thousand persons and more went to and from the fair that day. But two thousand only, at three shillings each way, would have produced £600! But, after all, the expense is so great, that it is considered uncertain whether the establishment will ultimately remunerate the proprietors. Yet I have heard that it already yields the shareholders a dividend of nine per cent. And Bills have passed for making railroads between London and Birmingham, and Birmingham and Liverpool. What a change will it produce in the intercourse! One conveyance will take between 100 and 200 passengers, and the journey will be made in a forenoon! Of the rapidity of the journey I had better experience on my return; but I may say now, that, stoppages included, it may certainly be made at the rate of twenty miles an hour!

I should have observed before that the most remarkable movements of the journey are those in which trains pass one another. The rapidity is such that there is no recognizing the features of a traveller. On several occasions, the noise of the passing engine was like the whizzing of a rocket. Guards are stationed in the road, holding flags, to give notice to the drivers when to stop.

Henry Crabb Robinson

1919   I have discovered that I cannot burn the candle at one end and write a book with the other.

Katherine Mansfield

---

11 June

1607   This day fell in Colyton, not far from the town, rain, being as it seemed a thunder shower, and some thunder heard withall, among which were certain drops fell like blood, which stained those things as it fell on. I saw a partlet slain therewith, and it seemed as it had been blood; my mother's maid, viz. Scar's wife, and one Joan Milles, showed the same coming home from milking.

Walter Yonge

1699   Now died the famous Dutchess of Mazarine, she had ben the richest lady in Europe. She was niece of Cardinal Mazarine, and was married to the richest subject in Europe, as is said. She was born at Rome, educated in France, and was an extraordinary beauty and wit, but dissolute and impatient of matrimonial restraint, so as to be abandon'd by her husband, and banish'd, when she came into England for shelter, liv'd on a pension given her here, and is reported to have hasten'd her death by intemperate drinking strong spirits.

John Evelyn

1837   'A dripping June brings all in tune.'

The Reverend Francis Witts

1922   After dinner (mollified by a demi-bottle of Sauterne) I read Freud's new book for two hours. Freud can't see straight about sex, but he has discovered a lot about the mechanism of the human mind.

This afternoon I enjoyed myself in Brompton Road. First I went to the International Theatre Exhibition at the Victoria & Albert Museum. But I was more inclined to look at the human exhibits than the art-products of Appia and Craig.

Then I popped into Brompton Oratory; the choral Mass seemed *the last word in dope.* (I noticed the drugged look in the faces of the audience as they came out.) The choir sang a bit of Elgar's *Apostles* very finely. It was a pleasant and interesting intermezzo, that Catholic celebration. I sat next to a red-haired youth whose beauty added to the interest of the proceedings.

Siegfried Sassoon

12 June

1560 The xij day of June dyd ryd in a care a-bowtt London ij men and iij women; one man was for he was the bowd, and to brynge women unto strangers, and on woman was the wyff of the Bell in Gracyous-strett, and a-nodur the wyff of the Bull-hed be-syd London stone, and boyth wher bawdes and hores, and the thodur man and the woman wher brodur and syster, and wher taken nakyd together.

Henry Machyn

1832 I do not think that in all my experience I ever remember such a season in London as this has been; so little gaiety, so few dinners, balls, and *fêtes*. The political dissensions have undermined society, and produced coolnesses between so many of the highest families; and between even near relations, who have taken opposite views of the question. Independent of this feeling, the Tory party – whose apprehensions for the future are most desponding, who think that a complete revolution is near at hand, and that property must every day become less secure – are glad to retrench their usual expenses, and are beginning by economy to lay by a *poire pour la soif*. Those who have money at command are buying funds in

America or in Denmark, which they think least exposed to political changes. Those who have only income are reduced to retrench; but all seem impressed with the idea that they cannot long depend on their present prosperity; and these very means of precaution may tend to accelerate the crisis, if such there is. The London tradesmen are first affected; the *petit commerce* declines, which creates discontent; the orders to the country are diminished, which disappoints the manufacturer; he in return must discard workmen, which augments the number of those already out of employ; and thus the apprehensions on one side create distress on the other, till at length that which was only imaginary creates for itself an alarming reality.

Thomas Raikes

1840   After leaving my name among the innumerable calls of congratulation at Buckingham Palace, I went to inspect the supposed two bullet marks on the wall near where the would-be assassin, Edward Oxford, fired two pistols at her Majesty and Prince Albert on the evening of the 10th. From what I could learn the villain was only about three paces off when he fired; and the bullet marks, if such they were, measured thirteen paces apart, and were evidently well directed, except rather behind. Her Majesty was driven at a quick trot; and by the blessing of Divine Providence, the scoundrel omitted to make the proper allowance for a cross shot.

Colonel Peter Hawker

13 June

1811   After tea a call on C. Lamb. His brother with him. A chat on puns. Evanson, in his *Dissonance of the Gospels*, thinks Luke most worthy of credence. P— said that Evanson was a *luke* - warm Christian. I related this to C. Lamb. But in a pun he likes a dash of the ridiculous. He was reading with a friend a book of Eastern travels, and the friend observed of the Mantschu Tartars, that they must be cannibals. This Lamb thought better. The large room in the accountant's office at the East India House is divided into boxes or compartments, in each of which sit six clerks, Charles Lamb himself in one. They are called Compounds. The meaning of the word was asked one day, and Lamb said it was 'a collection of simples'.

Henry Crabb Robinson

1831 The gnats kept Arabel & me & half the house besides up half the night: witness my swelled finger – witness this *eccentric* writing. I will *gnat* sleep in that room again, until the weather changes. I will go into the Bamboo room. No letters on Monday, & if it had been Tuesday, I should have expected none.

Elizabeth Barrett

1849 Steamed to Chelsea, and paid Mrs Carlyle a humane little visit. I don't think she roasted a single soul, or even body. She talked in rather a melancholy way of herself and of life in general, professing that it was only the Faith that all things are well put together – which all sensible people *must* believe – that prevents our sending to the nearest chemist's shop for sixpennyworth of arsenic; but now one just endures it while it lasts, and that is all we can do. We said a few modest words in honour of existence, which she answered by, 'But I can't enjoy Joy, as Henry Taylor says. He, however, cured this incapacity of his by taking to himself a bright little wife, who first came to him in the way of consolation, but has now become real simple Joy.' Carlyle is sitting now to a miniature-painter, and Samuel Laurence has been drawing her; she bargained with him at starting not to treat the subject as an Italian artist had done, and make her a something between St Cecilia and an improper female. She caught a glimpse of her own profile the other day, and it gave her a great start, it looked such a gloomy headachy creature.

Caroline Fox

1932 I had a note from Rupert and Miles asking me to go to the flicks. I dashed to Carfax at 7.30 and we went to *Goodnight Vienna* at the Queener. It was lovely, and somehow appropriate. We sat at the back in the corner and I had two arms around me for the first time in my history. The flick was over at 10, so we stopped at the coffee stall by Cowley Place on our way back. We drank to each other in chocolate Horlicks.

Barbara Pym

---

14 June

1789   We then all walked out, and had a very delightful stroll: but, in returning, one of the dogs (we have twelve, I believe, belonging to the house) was detected pursuing the sheep on the common. Miss Thrale sent one of the men after him, and he was seized to be punished. The poor creature's cries were so dreadful, that I took to my feet and ran away.

When, after all was over, they returned to the house, the saucy Captain Fuller, as soon as he saw me, exclaimed, 'Oh, some hartshorn! some hartshorn for Miss Burney!'

I instantly found he thought me guilty of affectation; and the drollery of his manner made it impossible to be affronted with his accusation; therefore I took the trouble to try to clear myself, but know not how I succeeded. I assured him that if my staying could have answered any purpose, I would have compelled myself to hear the screams, and witness the correction, of the offending animal; but that as that was not the case, I saw no necessity for giving myself pain officiously.

'But I'll tell you,' cried he, 'my reason for not liking that ladies should run away from all disagreeable sights: I think that if they are totally unused to them, whenever any accident happens, they are not only helpless, but worse, for they scream and faint, and get out of the way; when, if they were not so frightened, they might be of some service. I was with a lady the other day, when a poor fellow was brought into her house half-killed: but, instead of doing him any good, she only shrieked, and called out – "Oh! mercy on me!" and ran away.'

There was an honesty so characteristic in this attack, that I took very serious pains to vindicate myself, and told him that, if I had any knowledge of myself, I could safely affirm that, in any case similar to what he mentioned, instead of running away, I should myself, if no abler person were at hand, have undertaken not merely to see, but to bind the man's wounds: nor, indeed, can I doubt but I should.

Fanny Burney

1815   My feelings, my heart, yearn & are sick for a sweet woman on whose bosom I could lay my head & in whose heart I could confide. I would marry her from any class of life if she had elegant & tender feelings, but alas, I have seen so much of the weakness of women, or perhaps their vices, that I often sigh with agony that we can call these delicate creatures ours, but not *their appetites.* My love, my enthusiasm, my reverence for a woman of susceptibility & virtue is unbounded; to women I owe the change of my taste since Macbeth; their loveliness & softness & beauty have worked a reformation in my Soul, have expanded my sensations, & softened the fierceness of my Nature. Could I but meet with one! But even if I could, I must yet sacrifice my feelings till their gratification will not interrupt the great object of my being. How many feelings am I obliged to curb with iron grasp till that be accomplished.

At a house where I visited, a most elegant, lovely servant opened the door; an exchange of feeling took place in our eyes. When she came in nothing could be more graceful. The Mistress & family talked of her kindness of heart, elegance of manner, and said she had a mind above her situation. This affected me. I longed for her to be pure & virtuous, but alas, the next time I went a hang of the head & smile of intelligent meaning gave indications of an easy conquest. I was melancholy, as I have often been, at such disappointments, to me at least when I had highest views, than corrupting their hearts [the rest of the page is torn away].

B. R. Haydon

15 June

1673   About one a clocke in the morning my eldest sonne Thomas and my most deare child ascended early hence to keepe his everlasting Sabbath with his heavenly father, and Saviour with the church above, his end was comfortable, and his death calme, not much of pain til the Satturday afore. in my course this morning I read Josh; 1: which had words of comfort, god making his word my counsellour and comfort. He was my hope. but some yeares I have feared his life, god hath taken all my first brood but Jane. Lett all live in thy sight sanctified. A wett morning, the heavens for some time have mourned over us.

The Reverend Ralph Josselin

1837   I proceeded to Stow to take evidence with the view to the committal of a prisoner charged with stealing two sovereigns and a half out of a poor blind man's box. The case had already been before me and Mr Pole at my house on the 12th, when we had remanded the man for re-examination. After hearing the evidence of one witness, we were obliged by the pressure of other business to suspend the examination and sent him to the lock-up house about 12 o'clock. When about 5 in the afternoon the officer was sent to bring the prisoner before us, he was found dead, having strangled himself by forcibly tightening his neck cloth, a wretched example of living without God in the world, a wild, reckless, hardened life of idleness and vice.

The Reverend Francis Witts

1841   Dr Calvert joined us at dinner, and we all lounged under our drooping spruce, with Balaam the ape, which I had borrowed for the afternoon, in the foreground, and the kid near by, quite happy in our companionship . . . Aunt Charles's wit seemed to do him good, but he speaks of himself as physically very miserable. She has given him a Neapolitan pig which is an amusement to him; he has it washed and shampooed every morning.

Caroline Fox

16 June

1787   From whatever cause, it happened – whether from continuing too long in bed, or from the same as occasioned what is stated above – I felt all this day low in spirits and feeble in mind. I was so drowsy as to be obliged to betake myself to the couch, where I continued fast asleep till I was waked by Mrs Lukin coming under the window in the phaeton.

William Windham

1789   The sweetest softest silent night. Clouds to the West of a gleaming red. We leaned over the gate, admiring the solemnity of the scene and the profound Silence which reigned around as if we were the only inhabitants of this sweet Valley. Suddenly we heard a sweet pipe. Enquired who was the Performer. 'Thomas Jones the Glazier is playing on the Wall of the Churchyard which is over the Dee.' We listened till the Village struck ten.

Lady Eleanor Butler

1798   From illness of horse, have left off riding and walked about without boots; for some reason uncommonly well.

William Windham

1914   Oh I am so *sick* of this everlasting Latin & Mathematics – if only I could do some interesting work. I really am weary & bored with everything – strange as it is for me – but nothing seems to go very right; I have no legitimate cause for complaint, but yet life is short of something & I am miserable.

Vera Brittain

---

17 June

1781   There passed, some time ago, an agreement between Mr Crutchley and Mr Seward, that the latter is to make a visit to the former, at his country-house in Berkshire; and today the time was settled: but a more ridiculous scene never was exhibited. The host elect and the guest elect tried which should show least expectation of pleasure from the meeting, and neither of them thought it at all worth while to disguise his terror of being weary of the other. Mr Seward seemed quite melancholy and depressed in the prospect of making, and Mr Crutchley absolutely miserable in that of receiving, the visit. Yet nothing so ludicrous as the distress of both, since nothing less necessary than that either should have such a punishment inflicted. I cannot remember half the absurd things that passed; but a few, by way of specimen, I will give.

'How long to you intend to stay with me, Seward?' cried Mr Crutchley; 'how long do you think you can bear it?'

'Oh, I don't know; I shan't fix,' answered the other: 'just as I find it.'

'Well, but – when shall you come? Friday or Saturday? I think you'd better not come till Saturday.'

'Why yes, I believe on Friday.'

'On Friday! Oh, you'll have too much of it! what shall I do with you?'

'Why on Sunday we'll dine at the Lyells, Mrs Lyell is a charming woman; one of the most elegant creatures I ever saw.'

'Wonderfully so,' cried Mr Crutchley: 'I like her extremely – an insipid idiot! She never opens her mouth but in a whisper; I never heard her speak a word in my life. But what must I do with you on Monday? will you come away?'

'Oh no: I'll stay and see it out.'

'Why, how long shall you stay? Why I must come away myself on Tuesday.'

'Oh, I shan't settle yet,' cried Mr Seward, very drily. 'I shall put up six shirts, and then do as I find it.'

'Six shirts!' exclaimed Mr Crutchley; and then, with equal dryness added – 'Oh, I suppose you wear two a-day.'

And so on.

Fanny Burney

1888 I have lived in London ten years, and now, on a day like this when I am very lonely and depressed, there is not one single house in which I should be welcome if I presented myself, not one family – nay, not one person – who would certainly receive me with good will. I wonder whether any other man would make such a statement as this with such absolute truth. Thought I might have written today, but found it impossible. No gleam of sunshine, and still very cold.

George Gissing

1943 I have sunk very low. I emptied tea leaves out of the window.

Barbara Pym

18 June

1824 What a divine night it is! I have just returned from Kentish Town; a calm twilight pervades the clear sky; the lamp-like moon is hung out in heaven, and the bright west retains the dye of sunset. If such weather would continue, I should write again; the lamp of thought is again illumined in my heart, and the fire descends from heaven that kindles it. Such, my loved Shelley, now ten years ago, at this season, did we first meet, and these were the very scenes – that churchyard, with its sacred tomb, was the spot where first love shone in your dear eyes. The stars of heaven are now your country, and your spirit drinks beauty and wisdom in those spheres, and I, beloved, shall one day join you. Nature speaks to me of you. In towns and society I do not feel your presence; but there you are with me, my own, my unalienable!

I feel my powers again, and this is, of itself, happiness; the eclipse of winter is passing from my mind. I shall again feel the enthusiastic glow of composition, again, as I pour forth my soul upon paper, feel the winged ideas arise, and enjoy the delight of expressing them. Study and occupation will be a pleasure, and not a task, and this I shall owe to sight and companionship of trees and meadows, flowers and sunshine.

England, I charge thee, dress thyself in smiles for my sake! I will celebrate thee, O England! and cast a glory on thy name, if thou wilt for me remove thy veil of clouds, and let me contemplate the country of my Shelley and feel in communion with him!

I have been gay in company before, but the inspiriting sentiment of the heart's peace I have not felt before to-night; and yet, my own, never was I so entirely yours. In sorrow and grief I wish sometimes (how vainly!) for earthly consolation. At a period of pleasing excitement I cling to your memory alone, and you alone receive the overflowing of my heart.

Beloved Shelley, goodnight. One pang will seize me when I think, but I will only think, that thou art where I shall be, and conclude with my usual prayer – from the depth of my soul I make it – May I die young!

Mary Shelley

19 June

1550　I went to Deptford, being bidden to supper by the Lord Clinton, where before supper I saw certain men stand upon the end of a boat without hold of anything and ran one at another until one was cast into the water. At supper Mons. Vidame and Hunaudaye supped with me. After supper was there a fort made upon a great lighter on the Thames, which had three walls and a watchtower in the midst, of which Mr Winter was captain, with forty or fifty other soldiers in yellow and black. To the fort also appertained a galley of yellow color with men and munition in it for defense of the castle. Wherefore there came four pinnaces with their men in white handsomely dressed, which, intending to give assault to the castle, first drove away the yellow pinnace, and afterward with clods, squibs, canes of fire, darts made for the nonce, and bombards they assaulted the castle; and at length they came with their pieces and burst the outer walls of the castle, beating them of the castle into the second ward, who afterward issued out and drove away the pinnaces, sinking one of them, out of which all the men in it, being more than twenty, leaped out and swam in the Thames. Then came the Admiral of the Navy with three other pinnaces and won the castle by assault and burst the top of it down and took the captain and under-captain. Then the Admiral went forth to take the yellow ship and at length clasped with her, took her, and assaulted also her top, and won it by composition and so returned home.

King Edward VI

1668　To a new play with several of my relations, *The Evening Lover*, a foolish plot, and very profane; it afflicted me to see how the stage was degenerated and polluted by the licentious times.

John Evelyn

1947 Last week I had six copies of *Maiden Voyage* in German. So sad it was on its grey lavatory paper on which steel filings seemed to glint. The binding, too, one felt might split in half if one attempted to open the book to read. But I can't read any German.

Then I had a letter from my translator; it was a touching letter. He is sixty years old and was interned on the Isle of Man in the last war. He has written a book about the British and their Empire, and also novels. He says my book arouses great interest in Germany. They have published five thousand. He regrets that they are not allowed to publish another five thousand.

Denton Welch

20 June

1837 I was awoke at 6 o'clock by Mamma, who told me that the Archbishop of Canterbury and Lord Conyngham were here, and wished to see me. I got out of bed and went into my sitting-room (only in my dressing-gown), and *alone*, and saw them. Lord Conyngham (the Lord Chamberlain) then acquainted me that my poor Uncle, the King, was no more, and had expired at 12 minutes p. 2 this morning, and consequently that I am *Queen*. Lord Conyngham knelt down and kissed my hand, at the same time delivering to me the official announcement of the poor King's demise. The Archbishop then told me that the Queen was desirous that he should come and tell me the details of the last moments of my poor, good Uncle; he said that he had directed his mind to religion, and had died in a perfectly happy, quiet state of mind, and was quite prepared for his death. He added that the King's sufferings at the last were not very great but that there was a good deal of uneasiness. Lord Conyngham, whom I charged to express my feelings of condolence and sorrow to the poor Queen, returned directly to Windsor. I then went to my room and dressed.

Since it has pleased Providence to place me in this station, I shall do my utmost to fulfil my duty towards my country; I am very young and perhaps in many, though not in all things, inexperienced, but I am sure, that very few have more real good will and more real desire to do what is fit and right than I have.

Queen Victoria

1886   Have entered the fiftieth year of my reign and my Jubilee year. I was upset at the thought of those no longer with me, who would have been so pleased and happy, in particular my beloved husband, to whom I owe everything, who are gone to a happier world.

There were beautiful and most kind articles in *The Times*, *Standard* and *St James's*. I don't want or like flattery, but I am very thankful and encouraged by these marks of affection and appreciation of my efforts.

Queen Victoria

21 June

1662   Having from my wife and the maids complaints made of the boy, I called him up and with my whip did whip him till I was not able to stir, and yet I could not make him confess any of the lies that they tax him with. At last, not willing to let him go away a conqueror, I took him in task again and pulled off his frock to his shirt, and whipped him till he did confess that he did drink the Whay, which he hath denied. And pulled a pinke, and above all, did lay the candlesticke upon the ground in his chamber, which he hath denied this Quarter of this year. I confess it is one of the greatest wonders that ever I met with, that such a little boy as he could possibly be able to suffer half so much as he did to maintain a lie. But I think I must be forced to put him away. So to bed, with my arme very weary.

Samuel Pepys

1806   We drank tea with Mrs Bankes – met George Jenkinson there – We afterwards went to Mrs Jenkinson's where I had appointed Campbell to meet us, and there I experienced what I can hardly bear to think of now and what I hope he may never make me feel again – He had an air of triumph, and a sort of flow of *false spirits* like a person who is doing wrong, who knows it, and yet *cannot help* doing it – He was going to meet Mrs S. at a Concert, and left me at cards notwithstanding the pressing entreaties of everyone present – I alone did not dare say one word because I knew, *why* he was so anxious to go – but I felt so mortified, so hurt and so wretched, that the tears actually ran down my cheeks – but he did not see it, and went to gratify his vanity at the expense of my heart – Vanity is his prevailing fault and he cannot resist this abominable woman – I could not sleep and cryed all night – to be thus slighted by a Man whom I love with so much sincerity and tenderness and to be slighted for an unworthy object, who at best can only feel a whim for him, is too much for me to bear – it kills me –

Eugenia Wynne

1953   Ben today made a strange remark while we were discussing what an effect a private school had on little boys, and how they separated their home from their school life. 'It is an effect,' says Ben, 'which lasts all one's life. To this day I have a horror of rendering myself conspicuous or of seeming different from other people.' Considering that his hair is like that of a gollywog and his clothes noticeable the other end of Trafalgar Square, this is an odd assertion. Yet it was made in absolute sincerity, and with that naiveté which is part of his compelling charm.

Harold Nicolson

22 June

1807   He [Dr Smith] spoke of Alderman Herring of Norwich, who has by perseverance obtained a Bill for paving & lighting that City, but is in respect of education a remarkably ignorant Man. Being deputed to wait upon the King with an Address, His Majesty observed to Him that Norwich is an ancient City to which the Alderman replied 'Please your Majesty It Has been a very ancient city.' He recd. a letter signed Anonymous,

and on being told by a person that He heard He had recd. an
Anonymous letter, He replied, 'Yes, very anonymous.'

Joseph Farington

1846   God forgive – me – Amen.
                              Finis
                               of
                          B. R. Haydon
            'Stretch me no longer on this tough World' – Lear.
                              End –

B. R. Haydon
[Final Entry]

1937   Isnt it shameful to write here first thing, not to tackle
Congreve? But my brain after talking to Miss Sarton, to
Murray, to Ann [Stephen] gave out after dinner, so that I
cdn't read *Love for Love*. And I won't do 3 Gs. till Monday –
till I've had a quiet breather. Then the Prof. Chapter: then the
final . . .

So now to draw the blood of that brain to another part –
according to H. Nicolson's prescription, which is the right
one. I wd. like to write a dream story about the top of a
mountain. Now why? About lying in the snow; about rings of
colour; silence . . . & the solitude. I cant though. But shant I,
one of these days, indulge myself in some short releases into
that world? Short now for ever. No more long grinds: only
sudden intensities. If I cd. think out another adventure. Oddly
enough I see it now ahead of me – in Charing X road
yesterday – as to do with books: some new combination.
Brighton? A round room on the pier – & people shopping,
missing each other – a story Angelica told in the summer. But
how does this make up with criticism? I'm trying to get the 4
dimensions of the mind . . . life in connection with emotions
from literature – A days walk – a mind's adventure:
something like that. And its useless to repeat my old
experiments: they must be new to be experiments.

Virginia Woolf

23 June

1796 Therm. 65. W. Bible, Barrow, Denina. To please them let Master Fuller and Octavius drive me alternately in the Gig. Laura returned in the evening from Falmouth. Rude and disagreeable. Miss Stephens and her sister B. drank tea with Anne. Octavius's propensity to perverseness must be checked. Children when young are always bickering. To be a parent without an assistant is a hard task. Always doing something to discompose and interrupt tranquillity.

The Reverend W. J. Temple

1906 Left off straw hat. Too heavy.

Although Vice-Captain, I am left out of cricket team. They lost disgracefully. By the by, I saw a fellow get killed while batting. Bit of a damper. Shadows before my eyes. I wonder what is the reason for it.

Sydney Moseley

1932 Rupert and I went to buy some things for lunch – as we intended to take it with us on the river. We then took Miles up to Boars Hill as he had to see Prof. Griffith. Rupert and I went to a pub to get some gin and then waited for Miles in the car. There it was that Rupert said to me Marvell's 'To his Coy Mistress' and 'Definition of Love'. And I had never heard them before. The more one talks with him the more one realizes that he really *is* brilliant – in all sorts of ways. Then on to the river, from the Cherwell Arms, where we drove in the car. Getting into the punt I half fell in – and Miles got his trousers entirely wet trying to rescue me. We had an amusing time getting dry. I lay on my tummy in the middle of the punt – Rupert punted and Miles sat at the other end with his trousers on the end of a paddle. I rushed back to St Hilda's and changed, then we met at 131 Iffley Road and decided to dine out of Oxford. We went to the Spreadeagle at Thame – Lovely! Before dinner we wandered about in the charming garden – the flowers seem to grow at random but it is very well planned. Then we ate a marvellous dinner – at which everything ordinary (i.e. fish) tasted extraordinarily good. We finished with yellow Chartreuse – Rupert laughed at me because it made me cough.

Barbara Pym

1937   Its ill writing after reading *Love for Love* – a masterpiece. I never knew how good it is. And what exhilaration there is in reading these masterpieces. This superb hard English! Yes, always keep the Classics at hand to prevent flop.

Virginia Woolf

---

24 June

1805   We first asked if the Miss Lowndes were at home, and as they had just set out for Oxford we continued our route and as we got up the lane we met John looking quite hidious, with his hair in powder, a pink neckcloth blue Waistcoat nankin inexpressibles and blue coat, he really was a sight, and soon went on, and when we got to the turning the Miss Pouletts were just coming – We stopped and I got in their carriage and they took my place and I had a very pleasant journey home talking the whole while, they remained some time with us and after making us promise to dine with them on Thursday – They departed – I gave Lucy a little cat and she is to give me a Canary.

Harriet Wynne

1872   A double rainbow, and I noticed that the sky was darker between the two bows, so that the effect was that of a broad bridge with two coloured brims. It is no doubt the excess of the red colour that made the inside brownish and so of the purple outside.

Gerard Manley Hopkins

1981   I told Prue [Lady Windlesham] that in my opinion normal men didn't dress with a view to appearing attractive. She disagreed totally. She assured me that men dressed either to create an impression of power (e.g. Kissinger, 'Power is the supreme aphrodisiac') or for servitude. I insisted that men of seventy-five and upwards dressed for impotence. I must have been reading too much *King Lear*.

Lord Longford

25 June

1830 Breakfasted at eleven o'clock, and then set off in a carriage with Mr Hoffender, Papa, and Mary Rose, although it was pouring of rain, to have a drive in a steam engine. Mr Charles and Pat rode in the phaeton. Upon arriving at the destined spot we climbed a steep bank to await its arrival, but after standing in the rain for some time we were told it had passed an hour before, so we returned the way we came; but before we had gone far we passed the railroad and saw the steam engine *in propria persona*. There had been some mistake about it which I did not take the trouble to comprehend, but we got into the waggon and rode five miles in it in ten minutes, sometimes faster and sometimes slower, and once at the rate of thirty-four miles an hour. The motion is imperceptible, and the feeling of moving so quickly most exhilarating; we wrote each a sentence while we were at full speed, and would have done so with perfect ease had not the rain, which was very heavy, blotted the writing. Afterwards we went to the entrance of the tunnel and met there Mr De Cappleton and Mr Scoresby. We here entered a waggon, and being pushed off, the motion accelerated, and we passed through the tunnel one mile and a quarter in four minutes.

Anne Chalmers

1905 Arthur hurt me when he said I had round shoulders. Little does he know how sensitive I am on physical perfection.

Had to sleep on floor at home. Could not sleep. We had sold Alf's bed, thinking he would not come back.

Sydney Moseley

1923 Tonight Turner gave me a ticket for *Tristan*. I missed Act I (missing an Act always increases one's enjoyment of Wagner) and left at Isolde's entrance in the last Act. I found myself feeling violently antagonistic to the Wagnerian tradition of *Love*! Surely it is an utterly obsolete notion of romantic passion. The spectacle of that corpulent couple galumphing about in their ocean of melodious eroticism appeared grotesque. And the audience! What do those old women with skimpy white hair feel as they sit for hours drowning in the Wagnerian ocean? What a colossal joke Wagner played on cultured humanity! When the lights were turned up after Act II, the faces, young and old, wore a drugged look. They had been witnessing one of 'the world's supreme love-dramas'. How many of them ever ask themselves whether *love* is like that now or was like that in Tristan's time?

Siegfried Sassoon

26 June

1830 On the 26th of June his Majesty King George the Fourth departed this mortal life after long suffering under various complaints, asthma, etc., occasioned probably by the liberty he had taken with a powerful constitution, for certainly few of his subjects had exercised the intestines with the stimulants his Majesty had. I always found his Majesty most gracious and condescending. A more accomplished Prince could not be as to address and manner, but as King of a great empire future historians will not have material to supply many princely traits of a great man.

William Dyott

1836 I accompanied Lady Dickson to the Zoological Gardens to see the new curiosities lately added to the collection, the giraffes most surprising animals, but so shapen they can be of no use to employ, and whether eatable I did not inquire.

William Dyott

1924 I did, I think, nothing.

Evelyn Waugh

1944 I went towards the river and I saw truck after truck with a huge red cross on it winding slowly along the road – quite fifty of them. And I thought of the soldiers inside – their wounds and torn bodies.

   I picnicked by the river in the boiling sun, in only my

shorts; then I bicycled right along the banks until I felt the sun burning into the dip between my shoulder blades.

At Yalding I sat down in the long grass, close to the medieval bridge, where the water falls away in a thunderous roar; and an Italian prisoner in pinkish chocolate battledress came up to me and asked if one could bathe at that spot. We got talking and he told me that his brother was a postman in Sicily and he himself was captured at Tobruk in 1941. His own people lived near Naples. We smoked cigarettes. He was nice. His face was brown and coarse and good-looking and his body thick-set.

Another prisoner approached, a more Egyptian-looking type, and the first one said, 'He is my cousin; caught the same day.'

We all sat together in the grass until about four-thirty, when they went to get back into their lorry to go home.

Denton Welch

---

27 June

1798   At Melborne – in the evening to Boaz. Two of his Tricks particularly surprized me.

1. He asked three ladies sitting at distances from each other simply to think of a card. He put no cards into their hands and he asked them no question. He then requested a Gentleman to open a sealed pack of Cards which lay upon the table and shuffle them. He then took them into his own hands and drew out three cards which he showed to the bystanders as the Cards the three Ladies had drawn. He then presented the Pack to each Lady separately and when the first said her card she thought of was not in the Pack – 'No, Ma'am, I have it in my hand' – the Card was the 10 of Diamonds – and so on to the second and so to the third.

2. The other trick was that he brought to Table two Letters sealed up. He desired me to mark them, then He let them lay a considerable time upon the table whilst he performed other deceptions. He then put into my hand one of the Letters and went to a Lady, Mrs Brown of Ingleby, my Parishioner, and desired her to think of a Card and then to draw that card out

of the Pack. 'Then tell the company, if you please, what is the number you thought of' – 'The ten of diamonds' – 'But did not you think of some other card before and changed your Mind?' 'Yes, I thought of the King of Hearts.' 'Now Sir,' to me, who was at a distance from him, 'be so good to break open the Letter and read the contents.' In the Paper was written in a large hand, 'The Lady shall think of the King of Hearts but dropping the Cards will change her mind and think of the Ten Diamonds.' Again after interspersing some other tricks he put the other Letter in like manner into my hand and asked Mrs Beale of Willington who sat at a distance from me to think at what hour she would please to rise in the morning – and then to take out the pack the Number of the Hour thought on.

The contents of the Letter as before corresponded with her mind and ran thus. 'The Lady will think of getting up at eight but will change her Mind to six though neither is her usual hour of getting up.' These tricks he exhibited both nights of his performance and to Persons who had never seen him that there could be no collusion.

The Reverend William Bagshaw Stevens

1830   I had to marry a couple at half-past eight; the bride was as round as a barrel, and according to custom, I suppose there will be a christening in the course of the honeymoon. On my return from the wedding, Mrs Jarrett's footman brought me her paper, mentioning the death of the King; it seems he departed on Saturday morning; if the storm was so violent at the time of his death as it was here in the evening, the oppression of the atmosphere might have accelerated his transition.

The Reverend John Skinner

1928   Evelyn and I were married at St Paul's, Portman Square, at 12 o'clock. A woman was typewriting on the altar. Harold best man. Robert Byron gave away the bride, Alec and Pansy the witnesses. Evelyn wore a new black and yellow jumper suit with scarf. Went to the 500 Club and drank champagne cocktails under the suspicious eyes of Winifred Mackintosh and Prince George of Russia. From there to luncheon at

Boulestin. Very good luncheon. Then to Paddington and by train to Oxford and taxi to Beckley.

Evelyn Waugh

---

28 June

1838   *Thursday, 28th June!* – I was awoke at four o'clock by the guns in the Park, and could not get much sleep afterwards on account of the noise of the people, bands, &c., &c. Got up at 7 feeling strong and well; the Park presented a curious spectacle; crowds of people up to Constitution Hill, soldiers, bands, &c. I dressed, having taken a little breakfast before I dressed, and a little after. At ½ p. 9 I went into the next room dressed exactly in my House of Lords costume; and met Uncle Ernest, Charles and Feodore (who had come a few minutes before into my dressing-room), Lady Lansdowne, Lady Normanby, the Duchess of Sutherland, and Lady Barham, all in their robes. At 10 I got into the State Coach with the Duchess of Sutherland and Lord Albemarle, and we began our Progress. It was a fine day, and the crowds of people exceeded what I have ever seen; many as there were the day I went to the City, it was nothing – nothing to the multitudes, the millions of my loyal subjects who were assembled in *every spot* to witness the Procession. Their good-humour and excessive loyalty was beyond everything, and I really cannot say *how* proud I feel to be the Queen of *such* a Nation . . .

At about ½ p. 4 I re-entered my carriage, the Crown on my head and Sceptre and Orb in my hand, and we proceeded the same way as we came – the crowds if possible having increased. The enthusiasm, affection and loyalty was really touching, and I shall ever remember this day as the *proudest* of my life. I came home at a little after 6 – really *not* feeling tired.

Queen Victoria

1838   We all posted off about 6 to see the raree-show. Dropped the girls at the Athenaeum & proceeded to my seat in the 'Abbey Box'. A squadron of life guards soon arrived & formed in front of the crowd so as to keep a clear space in front of the Abbey. From the time of my arrival at 7 to that of the procession at 11 there was one perpetual stream of the English nobility, principally peers & peeresses who all drove up to the door in their ermined scarlet robes with their coronets on their laps. At length the gun fired which told of the procession having started from St James's & in about half an hour it appeared, a most unutterably imposing array. From where I sat I could see them all dismount but had the best view as they passed in order in front. The Duchess of Kent is a very striking woman. Her coach was stopped just in the right place for about a minute during which we cheered her lustily & she bowed on all sides. Some of the peeresses were magnificent creatures. The maids of honour preceded her Majesty in twelve of the royal coaches. They were all in white like so many sylphs & from the back of their heads flowed a zephyr-like gauze veil which reached to the ankle. But all the enthusiasm shown before was as nothing to that on the appearance of the grand actress herself. Her Majesty was dressed in white satin with her hair simply arrayed & looked every inch a queen, only one could have wished there were a few more inches of her.

Barclay Fox

29 June

1806   I spent an agonizing morning in the midst of suspense and anxiety – Bankes call'd after his conference with Campbell, whom he persuaded to write to his Father to settle on him £700 per annum and to enable him to settle upon me and my children the Estate which it appears his Father is at liberty to sell during his Life time – Unless the Father agrees to this Bankes advises me not to think of the match – Campbell afterwards call'd and seems full of hopes that his Father will agree – I could feel happy even in this suspense, did not that unhappy story haunt me – but so convinced am I that no blame can be attached to Campbell in it, that I long to talk to himself on the subject; only it is too delicate to mention – We dined at the Wm. Fremantles with the Cathcarts – spent the

evening with Mrs Jenkinson where we met all the Campbells
– Robert was all affection to me and talks of nothing but our
future prospects of happiness which he seems certain we shall
enjoy – I was very near telling him every thing –

Eugenia Wynne

1922   I have no particular inclination to commit my thoughts to
paper. Yesterday evening I was happy enough, as I well might
be after seeing so much of old Hardy, who is more loveable
than ever. (Mrs H. also impresses me as being one of the good
and grave inhabitants of this unsatisfactory earth.) I say
'unsatisfactory' because nothing could have been more so
than my state of mind today; and the earth doesn't exist
except in this unreliable identity of mine.

It was all right until I arrived here at one o'clock. Reading
about Wagner's *Tannhäuser* difficulties in Paris in the train
seemed pleasant enough. And there was the prospect of seeing
Blunden receive the £100 Prize at three o'clock this afternoon.
But everything seemed to go wrong. First I found the usual
tiresome little batch of letters. The irritating ones always lie in
wait for me when I get back from the country. And Turner
was in bed after a severe attack of gastritis (talking about cool
beverages). Then, after lunching alone at the club, I was
obliged to converse with a man who always exasperates me
with pompous and reactionary pronouncements about art,
literature, and politics.

Siegfried Sassoon

30 June

1874   The Revd S. Blackburn speaking of the new mode of
pronouncing Latin and the admission of female students at
the University of Cambridge, told a story of a Professor with a
Ladies' class: the young lady translating says, in the old style
'*vicissim* – in turn'; 'No' the Professor corrects her, say '*we-
kiss-im* – in turn'. The Bishop of Gloucester's allusion to the
matter in a public speech at some Education meeting was still
better, when he remarked that for himself he was content with

reading Caesar's famous despatch in the old fashion, '*Veni, vidi, vici,*' though he supposed he ought to say 'Wany, weedy, weaky'.

Alfred Domett

1905 The chemist said that the pimples on my face have come because I am growing into manhood. Whilst others tell me to go with a woman! Many people hold such views and I feel ashamed.

I seem to inspire Loretta as she inspires me. She has left off wearing corsets because I convinced her it is bad for a girl's health.

Sydney Moseley

1914 There has been another assassination, this time of the heir of the Austrian Emperor. I do not quite know how it affects the political situation.

Wilfred Scawen Blunt

1955 The television people came at 10 and stayed until 6.30. An excruciating day. They did not want a dialogue but a monologue. The whole thing is to be cut to five minutes in New York and shown at breakfast time. They filmed everything including the poultry. The impresario kept producing notes from his pocket: 'Mr Waugh, it is said here that you are irascible and reactionary. Will you please say something offensive?' So I said: 'The man who has brought this apparatus to my house asks me to be offensive. I am sorry to disappoint him.' 'Oh, Mr Waugh, please, that will never do. I have a reputation. You must alter that.' I said later, not into the machine: 'You expect rather a lot for $100.' 'Oh, I don't think there is any question of payment.'

Evelyn Waugh

1 July

1838 I have been addicted of late to growing faint after breakfast. I do not much mind it myself, only that it alarms papa and mamma. Poor papa is so anxious about me, that one would think every cough I utter is my death-knell.

I suppose I am never to be strong again. It is nearly three months since I have walked into the Forest, and now I am always left behind when others go out. This evening I could almost have cried when I saw mamma, Aunt Charlotte, Cousin Susan, and the four children set forth joyously to ramble in some of the loveliest glades, and poor I was obliged to content myself with the dull drawing-room. It was a sweet, still summer's evening, such as is proper for the enjoyment of the Forest, and I would have given worlds to have gone too. However, I had a partner in misery, poor papa, who is at present equally unable to walk. So we remained quietly conversing at home, and certainly I enjoyed it very much. I grew envious again of the strong party, when they returned at nearly nine o'clock, extolling the beauties they had seen, and bringing in a handful of butterfly orchises, whose delicious fragrance scented all the room, and recalled me to those long-past days when I used to gather them at Woodbury.

Emily Shore

1946 Well, the atom bomb experiment was made last night, with apparently disappointing results. I would like it put on record that I think now, and always have thought, that far too much cock has been talked about atomic energy. I have no more faith in men of science being infallible than I have in men of God being infallible, principally on account of them being men. I have heard it stated that atomic energy might disturb the course of the earth through the universe; that it might cause devastating tidal waves; that it might transform climates from hot to cold or vice versa; make a hole in the bed of the ocean so that the seas would drain away and extinguish the fires of the earth; suddenly deflect our planet into the orbit of the sun, in which case we should all shrivel up, etc., etc., etc. I am convinced that all it will really do is destroy human beings in large numbers. I have a feeling that the universe and the laws of nature are beyond its scope.

Noël Coward

1954   Mother died yesterday at a quarter to two. I went round at eleven o'clock and she recognized me for a fleeting moment and said 'dear old darling'. Then she went into a coma. I sat by the bed and held her hand until she gave a pathetic little final gasp and died. I have no complaints and no regrets. It was as I always hoped it would be. She was ninety-one years old and I was with her close, close, close until her last breath. Over and above this sensible, wise philosophy I know it to be the saddest moment of my life. Owing to my inability to accept any of the comforting religious fantasies about the hereafter, I have no spurious hopes that we shall meet again on some distant Elysian shore. I know that it is over. Fifty-four years of love and tenderness and crossness and devotion and unswerving loyalty. Without her I could only have achieved a quarter of what I have achieved, not only in terms of success and career, but in terms of personal happiness. We have quarrelled, often violently, over the years, but she has never stood between me and my life, never tried to hold me too tightly, always let me go free. For a woman with her strength of character this was truly remarkable. She was gay, even to the last I believe, gallant certainly. There was no fear in her except for me. She was a great woman to whom I owe the whole of my life. I shall never be without her in my deep mind, but I shall never see her again. Goodbye, my darling.

Noël Coward

2 July

1922   Turning back to my 1921 diary I find the following: 'March 27 Went to Anerley and spent five and a half hours with de la Mare and his delightful family.' Why have I allowed fifteen months to pass by without repeating that visit? In an old note-book I find a few pencil scribblings dated March 27. Apparently de la Mare spoke of 'the strained language of poetry' as 'literary shorthand – above reality'. Also I scribbled: 'Colin's queer eyes. An elf or plump-faced fairy. Colin kissing his father's forehead when he came in.'

'Colin's queer eyes' have probably something to do with the fifteen months' hiatus. He is an uncomfortably attractive creature – one of the most attractive I've met. I felt it the first time I went there (on 23 November 1918) when he was a month less than thirteen years old. I felt it more than ever today, when I spent six hours in that queer little suburban house. Instinct warns me once again to avoid seeing him often. Yet I always enjoy being among that family. I enjoy it with an unusual intensity.

Mrs de la Mare is a tired-looking silent grey woman. She scarcely utters a word. She looks as if she's spent a sleepless week in a haunted house, without being acutely frightened – merely very tired. But I expect it is only that she has had a harassing existence of small domestic worries – money shortage and so on.

De la Mare is the most wonderful and interesting and sympathetic and mystery-haunted manuscript he has ever written. He is a human being to whom I respond with the utmost enthusiasm. I am bubbling over with excitement when I am with him. I want to say so much that I am confused and discontinuous in my conversation, leaping to and fro like a grasshopper in my anxiety to exchange ideas with him. His mind is an enchanted landscape lit by unearthly gleams and fiery auguries. Thinking of him I am urged toward 'fine writing'. The 'strained language of poetry' allures my pen. And Colin is the sorcerer's child.

Siegfried Sassoon

1973 Had to do an interview for American TV on the lawns of Shepperton to promote *The Homecoming* film. 'Who would you like to be if you weren't Peter Hall?' said the interviewer. I have never considered this before. I had to be honest and say that I had no desire to be anybody else at all. I'd like to be a better me, a cleverer me, a more organized me. And wouldn't mind being a me of twenty-eight knowing what I knew at forty. But the thought of being somebody else is inconceivable. Not because I'm particularly pleased with myself – I just can't imagine *being* somebody else. Perhaps you only want to be somebody else when you are very much in love. You want to become the other person.

Peter Hall

3 July

1765 I have been so embarrassed with a multiplicity of business, that I was not able to continue my journal, being, on the 19th day of June, married, at our church, to Mary Hicks, servant to Luke Spence, Esq., of South Malling, by the Rev. Mr Porter; and for about fourteen days was very ill with a tertian ague, or, rather, an intermitting fever; then the ceremony of receiving visitors, and again the returning of them, has indeed, together with the business of my trade, taking up so much of my time, that I was obliged to omit that which would have given me the greatest pleasure imaginable to have continued; but, however, thank God, I begin once more to be a little settled, and am happy in my choice. I have, it's true, not married a learned lady, nor is she a gay one; but I trust she is good-natured, and one that will use her utmost endeavour to make me happy. As to her fortune, I shall one day have something considerable, and there seems to be rather a flowing stream. Well, here let us drop the subject, and begin a new one.

Thomas Turner

1838 I was at the ball at Court last night to which hundreds would have given hundreds to go, and from which I would have gladly stayed away: all was very brilliant and very tiresome.

Charles Greville

1861 I passed a very bad night, in the course of which I had this dream. I thought that papa and I were travelling, and were sleeping in adjoining rooms. We were in some hot country, and I had just come to the end of a night spent in great pain. Toward the morning I slept fairly, and when I woke the sun was shining hot upon my darkened room. For some reason or other papa had left his room, and I was alone. As I rose a horrid sense of impending evil oppressed me. I could hardly stand, and in great weakness I tottered to a chair that stood before a tall looking-glass. There I saw myself a hideous sight. My skin was leprous white, like parchment, and all shrivelled. From every pore burst a river of perspiration, and ran to my feet. My feet were cramped and blanched, and cockled up with pain. But the face was the most awful sight. It was all white – the lips white and parted – the eyes pale, and presenting a perfectly flat surface. They were dilated, and shone with a cold blue eerie light. I heard a noise in papa's room, and knocked. He said, 'Come in' in his usual tone, and I crept up to him. He was shaving and did not see me, till I roused him by touching him and saying slowly, 'Papa.' Then he turned round and looked intently at me and inquiringly. I shrieked, 'Papa, don't you know me?' but even while I cried the vision of my own distorted features came across me, and filled me with my utter loneliness. At last he cried, 'My son,' and, burying his face in his hands, he added, 'All in one night.' In an ecstasy of deliverance I clasped his neck, and felt that now I need not go back into that twilight room with its bed and the mystery behind its curtains. But he went on in a hesitating voice, 'My poor boy! what fiend – or demon?' I stopped the question with a yell. Something seemed to tear me, and I awoke struggling. Such was my dream – more horrible than it seems, for the terror of dreams bears no relation to the hideousness of their incidents, but to some hidden emotion.

J. A. Symonds

---

4 July

1813 I hastened to Freeford without loss of time by the mail, and arrived on the morning of the 4th to witness the most sad scene I ever beheld – that of an ever-beloved and most affectionate brother lying on his bed, deprived of his speech, and with little or no hopes of his ever rising to continue his comfort and happiness to his connections. Poor good soul, on my approaching his bedside, the mild, benign and kind look that ever animated his countenance appeared on his brow. He took my hand and pressed one to his cheek. What sorrow, what suffering I endured. He was perfectly sensible, but showed no inclination to communicate anything. I did not conceive it a proper time to ask him if he had any wish to express, as I imagined it must hurt him to feel he had not the power of utterance, and the question might also imply despair of his recovery.

William Dyott

1873 To Shakespeare's birthplace, Henley Street. The old house restored, where absolutely necessary, strictly in accordance with the oldest engravings or other representations of it extant. A modern lean-to in front removed, and the immediately adjoining houses, to prevent danger of fire. This I think has been done with the best taste and judgment; in spite of Ruskin's opinion somewhere that no part of the material or actual substance of such venerated old relics ought to be renewed or replaced. Surely it is better to renew such portion or portions of these buildings from time to time as would fall away and soon disappear altogether, taking scrupulous care that they only reproduce with the utmost possible exactness what had been there before, than to lose them utterly for ever.

Alfred Domett

1905 Buying books and more books, although I can hardly afford them – yet. I MEAN TO GET ON.

Sydney Moseley

1935 I am tired of being 'tiddly' by night and 'gaga' by day: the season has lasted long enough.

'Chips' Channon

5 July

1813 On the 5th the symptoms were more fatal, his breathing difficult, and towards the evening he had little appearance left of sensibility. I sat with him all night; he was perfectly quiet, but evidently growing weaker and his respiration more difficult. He continued weaker and weaker and his breathing more faint until twelve o'clock, when it ceased, and he expired like a dying ember without a groan or struggle. The only comfort left to his disconsolate connections was the hope he had suffered no bodily pain. Dr Darwin, my brother Phillip and myself were the only persons in the room at the time of his death, and when his soul took its departure, the dissolution was scarce perceptible. The Lord receive his spirit.

William Dyott

1856   Spent the forenoon reading in Battersea Fields. In the evening alone, as usual; a very sick and sad day with me, like many that have gone before, and many that will come after, if I live to the age that the Prophetess foretold for me, seventy-two.

Jane Welsh Carlyle

1904   Bought some chocolate and gave it to Loretta. She accepted it! Her whole aspect is changed for good towards me!! . . . Dived off second board.

Sydney Moseley

1976   [Barlinnie Prison]
There is no doubt about it, these bastards are trying to destroy me mentally. Blows come in psychological form, ripping through my defences, tearing me apart internally. In the face of this new, but very effective game of destruction I cry like a child. Shattered! No injuries are apparent. What is going on, why?

Retaliation is called for. This violent typewriter shouts bloody anger. Punching holes in the fucking enemy with each tap of the key. Fingers filled with fire and vengeance as they press each lettered key – hatehatehatehatehate. Fuckers causing mental anguish, I HATE YOU.

They would like to see it. Oh God, they would like to see it. If I were to strike out and hit one of them. 'See!' they would shout. 'Look, the bastard is an animal.' All would turn to me and point. 'Animal, animal,' they would cry.

What the fucking hell am I doing sitting here suppressing all this natural anger and keeping it under the surface? Does this make me any more civilized? I'm supposed to sit here like some vegetable with a mandarin smile accepting it all.

Jimmy Boyle

---

6 July

1746 After talking, largely with both the men and women leaders, we agreed it would prevent great expense, as well of health as of time and of money, if the poorer people of our society could be persuaded to leave off drinking of tea. We resolved ourselves to begin and set the example. I expected some difficulty in breaking off a custom of six-and-twenty years' standing. And, accordingly, the three first days, my head ached, more or less, all day long, and I was half-asleep from morning till night. The third day, on Wednesday, in the afternoon, my memory failed, almost entirely. In the evening I sought my remedy in prayer. On Thursday morning my headache was gone. My memory was as strong as ever. And I have found no inconvenience, but a sensible benefit in several respects, from that very day to this.

John Wesley

1751 We were hardly met, when the sons of Belial poured in upon us, some with their faces blacked, some without shirts, all in rags. They began to 'stand up for the Church', by cursing and swearing, by singing and talking lewdly, and throwing dust and dirt all over us; with which they had filled their pockets, such as had any to fill. I was soon covered from head to foot, and almost blinded. Finding it impossible to be heard, I only told them I should apply to the Magistrates for redress, and walked up stairs. They pressed after me, but Mr Walker and the brethren blocked up the stairs, and kept them down. I waited a quarter of an hour; then walked through the midst of them to my lodgings, and thence to the Mayor's.

I spent an hour with him, pleading the poor people's cause. He said, he had never before heard of their being so treated; that is, pelted, beat, and wounded, their house battered, and windows, partitions, locks broke; that none had applied to him for justice, or he should have granted it; that he was well assured of the great mischief the Methodists had done throughout the nation, and the great riches Mr Whitefield and their other teachers had acquired; that their societies were quite unnecessary, since the Church was sufficient; that he was for having neither Methodist nor Dissenter.

I easily answered all his objections. He treated me with civility and freedom, and promised, at parting, to do our people justice. Whether he does or not, I have satisfied my own conscience.

Charles Wesley

1936   What a bore weekends are, forty-eight hours social crucifixion. Ours this summer have been curious. 13 June, the Dufferins, in a hideous villa, with cocktails, gramophones, Pekes and bridge. 20 June, Sutton Courtenay, roses, the river, and the youth of England splashing in the Thames, and Norah, the sublime Norah. Russian ballet food in the courtyard, Chopin, colour, gardening, a riot, but a healthy riot of the senses, and a deep thirst for life. 27 June, Villa Trianon, Versailles, super sophistication. Toile-de-Jouy, French princesses, Sèvres, gardens lit by Wendel, flowers, one feels, by Cartier. 4 July, Tredegar; glorious house, but the feel and even smell of decay, of aristocracy in extremis, the sinister and the trivial, crucifixes and crocodiles.

'Chips' Channon

7 July

1833   Took some luncheon at Mitchell. After resting an hour there we walked on to Lower St Colomb where we dined on a rasher of bacon & some bread. An original old man was there with whom we were much amused. He told John Richards he was a drunken farmer. John Richards asked him if his health didn't suffer by it? No, he was as healthy as any man in the parish. If his affairs weren't the worse for it? No, he always struck a better bargain drunk than sober. If his conscience did not prick him for it? Not in the least. If the Parson didn't scold him for it? Parson – law, bless your heart the parson ha' got drunk with me scores of times. Thus beaten on every point John Richards was obliged to sound a retreat.

Barclay Fox

1922 Wine certainly sets the mind alight and sets the wits dancing round the central bonfire of genial emotion. But it is an affair of rosy and capricious illuminations, a sunset of inspiration, a showery sunset with a rainbow that soon departs.

Walking home this evening along the embankment toward Westminster after half a bottle of Rhine-wine at an old-fashioned eating-house in the Strand, I felt that I *could* write. I was one with all the Whibleys and crapulous flushed adorers of Elizabethan prose. I bethought me, in that riverside dusk where the rain had ceased and the lamps were not yet lit – what did I actually bethink me?

Ah well, I was very wise; and I'd been reading Lamb and Hazlitt (on Hogarth) and my style was rich and racy. And I'd been to the Soane Museum before tea, and had made a prolonged and appreciative inspection of *The Rake's Progress* and *The Election*. I want to write poems as Hogarth painted humanity. Oh yes, I knew a hell of a lot about life after that half-bottle of Braunberger. And I recollect one of my conclusions.

It is better to be inspired by Hock (or anything elegantly alcoholic – none of your gross beverages, of course) rather than to dine austerely off cold meat and cold water and then go and get half drunk on Swinburne or the César Franck Symphony or any violently emotional art-product. The man who is half-intoxicated by his five shillings' worth of wine has some chance of thinking his own thoughts. Whereas the aesthetic voluptuary mixes his material with whatever it is he's been inspired by. Can you detect the faintest flavour of Lamb in what I've just written? Anyhow I've got considerable satisfaction out of today.

Siegfried Sassoon

1930 I lunched at the Ritz with Noël Coward. He has a simple, friendly nature. No brains. A theatrical manner. We talked about Catholicism. He said, 'Go round the world.' He said, what a shame he knew a Dominican prior who wanted all the time to be a play actor with the result that he was found, quite dotty, in his hostess's underclothes.

Evelyn Waugh

8 July

1733 Half an hour after 5 Clock yesterday in the afternoon was another Performance, at 5s a ticket, in the Theater by Mr Handel for his own benefit, continuing till about 8 clock. N.B. his book (not worth 1d) he sells for 1s.

Thomas Hearne

1916 [Training in Scotland]
The CSM getting more unpopular. Organized 'Boo's' surge up from the ranks against him; they get louder and louder.

Two men per hut were told off to fetch coal for officers' mess in the afternoon, and missed parade. They will not let us off parade to do orderly work in the huts, but don't mind our coming off to carry coal for them. There were plenty of the staff who could have done it.

Arthur Graeme West

1923 This entry in my diary is an example of inadequate and unskilful diarizing. But, when all is said and done, leading a good life is more important than keeping a good diary.

Siegfried Sassoon

1950 Ate lunch on hill overlooking Coulsdon. Hadn't been there for thirty years. Now little trace of countryside, houses everywhere. Still, however, vague traces remaining of walks I went on with my father. How confident he was that his intelligence and will were sufficient to measure up against the universe! How utterly subsequent events have proved their inadequacy.

Went on to have tea with my mother and Ingrid, and as

usual disturbed by them. Ingrid going to Berlin, but unsure whether she ought to go. Mother wanting to get her out of the house, and I wanting to get her out likewise for my mother's sake – this little personal contretemps projection of massive world conflict. My mother, at 84, told me she wanted to go on living as long as possible. Reflected that in the very old, egotism, the will to live, becomes quite vicious; suppose that in order to live to 80 such a development of one's ego is necessary.

Malcolm Muggeridge

9 July

1551 At this time came the sweat into London, which was more vehement than the old sweat. For if one took cold, he died within three hours, and if he escaped, it held him but nine hours, or ten at the most. Also, if he slept the first six hours, as he should be very desirous to do, then he raved and should die raving.

King Edward VI

1594 In the morning began my hed to ake and be hevy more then of late, and had some wambling in my stomach. I had broken my fast with sugar sopps, &c.

John Dee

1810 A man that begins to Study at Six in the morning will have gained 8 years when he has studied 50 years, over him who begins only at 8 – vice versa, he that lies abed till eight will have lost 8 years – 2 hours a day for meals – when you have lived 50 years you will have spent 8 years in eating.

One hour a day   365 hours in a year
                     50 years
                _____

                18,250 hours – at one hour a day
                 2
                _____

                36,500 hours at two a day in 50 years

$$3{,}041.8$$
$$12\,\sqrt{36{,}500}$$
$$36$$
—
$$50$$
$$48$$
—
$$20$$
$$12$$
—
$$8$$

$$8 \text{ days}$$
$$365 \text{ days in a year}\,\sqrt{3041 \text{ days}}$$
$$2980$$
—
$$61$$

In 25 years you will have lost 4 years

$12\frac{1}{2}$ .... 2 years
$6\frac{1}{4}$ .... 1 year
3 and Six weeks .... $\frac{1}{2}$ year
1 Six months & 3 weeks .... $\frac{1}{4}$ year
9 Months 1 week 3 days $\frac{1}{2}$ .... 6 weeks
$4\frac{1}{2}$–5 days & $\frac{1}{4}$ .... 3 weeks
$2\frac{1}{4}$–2 days $\frac{1}{2}\frac{1}{8}$ .... 10 days $\frac{1}{2}$
13 days $\frac{1}{2}$ 1 day $\frac{1}{4}\frac{1}{16}$ .... 5 days $\frac{1}{4}$
$\frac{1}{2}\frac{1}{2}$ day $\frac{1}{4}\frac{1}{2}$ .... 2 days $\frac{1}{2}$
$\frac{1}{4}$ .... 1 day

B. R. Haydon

1905   Started new method of diet. Inspired by Eustice Miles's *Muscle, Brains and Diet.* Felt very weak. Did not go to cricket.

Sydney Moseley

---

10 July

1807   Mr Le Vivier, a French priest who resides at Newport, and had been mentioned to me by Mr Cathcart, walked over to read Prayers, the distance must be at least thirteen miles, and I am quite surprised how this poor man can take such a long walk, before his breakfast, he was here by ten and went back before twelve, promising to come every Sunday.

Elizabeth Fremantle

1826   This morning I was visited by a Mr Lewis, a smart cockney, whose object is to amend the handwriting. He uses as a mechanical aid a sort of puzzle of wire and ivory which is put upon the fingers to keep them in the desired position like the puzzle on a dog's nose to make him bear himself right in the field. It is ingenious and may be useful. If the man come here as he proposes in winter I will take lessons. Bear witness, good reader, that if W. S. writes a cramp hand as you can bear witness is the case he is desirous to mend it.

Walter Scott

1950   War has broken out in Korea and for several days loomed larger. Yesterday the first British casualties were announced. It is inevitable (but depressing) to what a degree it has revived feelings from 1939, and nightmare images also, such as being in a small boat slowly but inexorably moving towards Niagara Falls. Yet a sort of excitement seemed to possess our weekend visitors, Judy and Dick and Quentin, at the thought of the bravery of soldiers in wartime. Talk is quite openly anti-foreign: all Germans are monsters impossible to shake by the hand, the Italians beneath contempt, and the French and Russians as bad as the Germans. Nor is this by any means meant as a joke. Benjamin Britten is a 'bloody man' (and *therefore* a bad composer) because he went to America instead of fighting the Germans.

Frances Partridge

11 July

1798   Viewed Miss Linwood's Exhibition of Needle Work; which might be mistaken for painting, but for the excessive deadness of the surface, and the stiffness and harshness of some of the contours. The Woodman, from Barker, struck me as the best piece. The Madonna, from Raffael, is, I dare say, exact; but, with all his excellencies, Raffael must, in this case, have retained something of the hardness of manner of the first artists. After all, this is a species of ingenious imitation which one does not wish to see prevail. The principal delight it affords, arises from the difficulty surmounted: the needle, though it may laboriously copy the effects, can never emulate the free, spirited, and masterly execution, of the pencil; and its productions are most grievously exposed to the molestations of moth and dust.

Thomas Green

1831 How tired I was, & unwell this evening. As, on our return, I was sitting by myself in our bedroom, I heard what I used to hear in the summer of 1828, & only *then* – the *deathwatch*. I grew sick & pale, & dizzy – & slept miserably all night – solely I believe from the strong unaccountable impression produced on me, by this circumstance. I have mentioned it to nobody, & dont much like mentioning it here. There never was a more foolishly weakly superstitious being than I am.

Elizabeth Barrett

1975 To Alan Ayckbourn's theatre at Scarborough to see *Bedroom Farce*, well directed by Ayckbourn himself. Supper with him afterwards. He told me that the play had been announced and publicized as the centre of the new Scarborough season even before it was written. It was due to rehearse on a Monday; he started writing it on the previous Wednesday, wrote all day Wednesday and most of the night, all day Thursday and most of the night, all day Friday and most of the night; on Saturday he typed it out, and on Sunday armed with some duplicated copies he drove up to Scarborough. He gave it to the cast on Monday morning, and after the reading collapsed in bed for two days. He said this was the kind of pressure he needed, and usually induced, to write a play.

Peter Hall

---

12 July

1823 The talk of the day is Lord Fitzwilliam's extraordinary marriage to old Lady Ponsonby; they are both about 75. At first it is impossible not to laugh, but on second thoughts it seems very rational. Two people long acquainted and strongly attached, one wanting society and the other fortune, have wisely determined to pass the remainder of their days together and brave the ridicule an envious and ill-natured world may try to throw upon their union.

Henry Edward Fox

1832   The cholera is here, and diffuses a certain degree of alarm. Some servants of people well known have died, and that frightens all other servants out of their wits, and they frighten their masters; the death of any one person they are acquainted with terrifies people much more than twenty of whom they knew nothing. As long as they read daily returns of a parcel of deaths here and there of A, B, and C, they do not mind, but when they hear that Lady Such-a-one's nurse or Sir Some-body's footman is dead, they fancy they see the disease actually at their own door.

Charles Greville

1843   Hay making day! Too much recreation . . . gave porter to six poor men and broth to three, they need strengthening at such a season. I have had too much exertion.

The Reverend W. W. Andrew

1873   Lunched at Browning's. He, Miss B. and a Miss Smith there.
        Looking at the copy of his wife's portrait by Richmond (the original of which is in the National Portrait Gallery at South Kensington) he said, 'That was taken when she was at her best,' and that 'the eyes were very like'. He added that Hiram Powers the American Sculptor who professed 'belief in Phrenology' declared that the 'organs of Imagination' were larger in her head than in his (B.'s) own, and that he (B.) had the biggest 'organ of Veneration' he had ever seen.
        Powers probably meant by organs of Imagination, the 'organ of Ideality' so called. But if he meant to infer that Mrs B.'s power or powers of *imaging* things, were greater than her husband's, all one can say is, that phrenology, interpreted by Mr Powers, gave no indication of the actual facts of the case.

Alfred Domett

13 July

1796 Am discomposed with Octavius, who grows very rude and troublesome. Holidays too long. What uneasiness do children give one from the very first. Miss Stephens came before we had finished dinner. In the evening, Bowyer again but read with no pleasure. Harassed, out of spirits. Make no progress, do nothing. How difficult it is to be regular in any thing one wishes!

The Reverend W. J. Temple

1832 At dinner at Lord Hertford's the conversation chiefly turned on the cholera, and though the table was loaded with every luxury, the entrées, the champagne, the ices, and fruits were neglected for plain meats, port, and sherry, the fear of this dreadful malady making all so cautious.

Thomas Raikes

1839 Grand teetotal festival. The ranks of the saints paraded the streets in procession with ribbons & evergreens, music playing, & banners waving. Amongst the devices was a dismal drunken scene, the wife dropping the child headlong from her lap, & the husband, too far gone to lift the last glass of spirits to his mouth, is kindly aided by the Arch Enemy, who is guiding his wrist.

Barclay Fox

1905 Re-start meat again. My health diet gives them trouble at home. Bought grape nuts, Hovis bread – Coal Tar soap. Still studying health culture and diet. Yet I still look pale, and at work still row with my boss.

Sydney Moseley

14 July

1787 We made use of the license, by driving to Mr Bryant at Cypenham. We found him in his garden, encompassed with his numerous family of dogs. His fondness for these good animals is quite diverting; he makes them his chief companions, and speaks to them as if they were upon terms of equality with him. He says they regularly breakfast with him, and he then gives them his principal lesson how to behave themselves.

After all, where is the philosopher wise enough to be all-sufficient to himself? A man had better arrange himself with a family of human beings, after the common mode, at once.

It was extremely amusing to see his anxiety that his children should not disgrace themselves. My dear Susan is not more solicitous for her Fanny and Nordia. 'Come, now, be good! Be good, my little fellows! – don't be troublesome! Don't jump up on Mrs Delany! Miss Burney, I'm afraid they are in your way. Come, my little fellows, keep back! – pray do. There! – there's good dogs! – keep back!'

And then, when they persevered in surrounding Mrs Delany – too kind and too easy to mind them – he addressed them quite with pathos: 'My sweet dogs! – Oh, my sweet dogs! – don't! – don't! – my sweet dogs!'

Well! – we are all born to have some recreation, and I should certainly do the same, had I nothing else alive about me.

Fanny Burney

1948 I was married – and how debonair and confident I was – 15 years ago today. I rose early, dressed slowly, went to Delhez, the fashionable Figaro, to be shaved and coiffed, and there my best man, Freddie Birkenhead, met me: I then entertained 15 ushers to luncheon at Buck's Club – I remember every detail. Today was different.

'Chips' Channon

1955 I am amazed that life seems to get more and more interesting as one gets older – and also perhaps saner, serener, more tough. It is no doubt the Indian Summer before the hand of decrepitude strikes and health crumbles.

Frances Partridge

15 July

1758 A most prodigious mellancholy time, and very little to do. I think that luxury increases so fast in this part of the nation, that people have little or no money to spare to buy what is really necessary.

The too-frequent use of spirituous liquors, and the exorbitant practice of tea-drinking has corrupted the morals of people of almost every rank.

Thomas Turner

1782 As I was coming down stairs, the carpet slipped from under my feet, which, I know not how, turned me round, and pitched me back, with my head foremost, for six or seven stairs. It was impossible to recover myself till I came to the bottom. My head rebounded once or twice from the edge of the stone stairs. But it felt to me exactly as if I had fallen on a cushion or a pillow. Dr Douglas ran out, sufficiently affrighted. But he needed not. For I rose as well as ever; having received no damage, but the loss of a little skin from one or two of my fingers. Doth not God give his angels charge over us, to keep us in all our ways?

John Wesley

1786 After breakfast I walked out a fishing. Had not put my Line in Water more than five Minutes before I caught a fine Trout of one Pound and a Quarter with a Grasshopper. It measured in length 14 Inches and in the highest Season. Mrs Pounsett Senr dined and spent the Aft: with us. After Tea this Aft: walked out again with my Rod and Line up the Bruton River and there caught another fine Trout which weighed 1 Pound and $\frac{1}{4}$ and measured $14\frac{1}{2}$ inches. Mr Sam: Pounsett supped and spent the Evening with us.

The Reverend James Woodforde

1937 Exhausted socially and mentally I slept for two hours this afternoon in the Library of the House of Commons! A deep House of Commons sleep. There is no sleep to compare with it – rich, deep, and guilty.

'Chips' Channon

16 July

1653 We went to another uncle and relative of my wife's, Sir John Glanvill, a famous lawyer, formerly Speaker of the House of Commons; his seate is at Broad-Hinton, where he now liv'd, but in the Gatehouse, his very faire dwelling house having ben burnt by his owne hands to prevent the rebells making a garrison of it. Here my cousin Will. Glanvill, his eldest sonn, shew'd me such a lock for a doore, that for its filing and rare contrivances was a master-piece, yet made by a country black-smith. But we have seene watches made by another with as much curiositie as the best of that profession can brag of; and not many yeares after, there was nothing more frequent than all sorts of Iron-work more exquisitely wrought and polish'd than in any part of Europ, so as a dore-lock of a tolerable price was esteem'd a curiositie even among forraine princes.

Went back to Cadenham, and on the 19th to Sir Ed. Baynton's at Spie Park, a place capable of being made a noble seate; but the humourous old Knight has built a long single house of 2 low stories on the precipice of an incomparable prospect, and landing on a bowling greene in the park. The house is like a long barne, and has not a window on the prospect side. After dinner they went to bowles, and in the meanetime our coach-men were made so exceedingly drunk, that in returning home we escap'd great dangers. This it seems was by order of the Knight, that all gentlemen's servants be so treated; but the custome is a barbarous one, and much unbecoming a Knight, still lesse a Christian.

John Evelyn

1793 Rose at 7. This is the 12th day of uninterrupted fine weather, and generally very hot. At 4 this afternoon the Thermometer stood on my staircase, to the North, at 89; the window open.

Joseph Farington

1818 Ripon Market, the thermometer in the sun at 9 a.m. 118. Heard that the heat this day in the sun at Ripon Market was so great that three butchers broiled their steaks for dinner on their cleavers in the sun without fire.

The Reverend Benjamin Newton

1845   As busy as busy could be from morning till night.

Colonel Peter Hawker

---

17 July

1738   At Newgate I preached on death (which they must suffer the day after tomorrow). Mr Sparks assisted in giving the sacrament. Another Clergyman was there. Newington asked me to go in the coach with him. At one I was with the Black in his cell; James Hutton assisting. Two more of the malefactors came. I had great help and power in prayer. One rose, and said, he felt his heart all on fire, so as he never found himself before; he was all in a sweat; believed Christ died for him. I found myself overwhelmed with the love of Christ to sinners. The Black was quite happy. The other criminal was in an excellent temper; believing, or on the point of it. I talked with another, concerning faith in Christ: he was greatly moved. The Lord, I trust, will help *his* unbelief also.

I joined at Bray's with Hutton, Holland, Burton, in fervent prayer and thanksgiving. At six I carried Bray and Fish to Newgate again, and talked chiefly with Hudson and Newington. N. declared he had felt, some time ago in prayer, inexpressible joy and love; but was much troubled at its being so soon withdrawn. The Lord gave power to pray. They were deeply affected. We have great hopes of both.

Charles Wesley

1785   And now I have filled this book and perhaps shall not fill another. I have learned by keeping this journal that I have been discontented more than was profitable, and that it is not proper for a tradesman to keep a journal without he has enough time and a plentiful fortune.

I begun Sunday, the 8th of August, 1784, and conclude Sunday, the 17th of July, 1785, at 7 o'clock in the evening.

Strother
[Final entry]

1833   Went to Drury Lane to see Paganini. His power over his instrument is surprising; the tones he draws from it might be thought those of the sweetest flageolet and hautboy, and sometimes of the human voice; the expression he gives to a common air is quite charming. His playing 'Patrick's Day' was the sweetest piece of instrumental music I ever heard; but he is a quack.

William Macready

18 July

1738   The Ordinary read prayers and preached. I administered the sacrament to the Black, and eight more; having first instructed them in the nature of it. I spake comfortably to them afterwards.

In the cells, one told me, that whenever he offered to pray, or had a serious thought, something came and hindered him; was with him almost continually; and once appeared. After we had prayed for him *in faith*, he rose amazingly comforted, full of joy and love; so that we could not doubt his having received the atonement.

At night I was locked in with Bray in one of the cells. We wrestled in mighty prayer. All the criminals were present; and all delightfully cheerful. The soldier, in particular, found his comfort and joy increase every moment. Another, from the time he communicated, has been in perfect peace. Joy was visible in all their faces. We sang,

> *Behold the Saviour of mankind,*
> *Nail'd to the shameful tree!*
> *How vast the love that him inclined*
> *To bleed and die for thee, &c.*

It was one of the most triumphant hours I have ever known.

Charles Wesley

1837 I started at five o'clock on Sunday evening [from London by coach] got to Birmingham at half-past five on Monday morning, and got upon the railroad at half-past seven. Nothing can be more comfortable than the vehicle in which I was put, a sort of chariot with two places, and there is nothing disagreeable about it but the occasional whiffs of stinking air which it is impossible to exclude altogether. The first sensation is a slight degree of nervousness and a feeling of being run away with, but a sense of security soon supervenes, and the velocity is delightful. Town after town, one park and *château* after another are left behind with the rapid variety of a moving panorama, and the continual bustle and animation of the changes and stoppages make the journey very entertaining. The train was very long, and heads were continually popping out of the several carriages, attracted by well-known voices, and then came the greetings and exclamations of surprise, the 'Where are you going?' and 'How on earth came you here?' Considering the novelty of its establishment, there is very little embarrassment, and it certainly renders all other travelling irksome and tedious by comparison.

Charles Greville

1949 Dear Queenie [his dog] is in heaven. Her journey down excited her so much, and finding herself in this bunnyland, that, on our first night here, she shit in the house. Not in my room, of course, but in the best bedroom that communicates with it. The door was open unfortunately. I should never have known about it if Miss Benn, Siegfried [Sassoon]'s housekeeper, not understanding whether I wanted breakfast in my room or downstairs, brought it up to this adjacent room and, setting the tray down on a table, stepped in Queenie's very loose shit which Queenie, I must praise her, such an intelligent dog, had deposited on a dark mat by this table instead of on the beautiful, thick, white pile carpet which covers the floors of most of the rooms in the house. However, her forethought was of no avail, for Miss Benn, having unwittingly stood in it, then walked over the white carpet of my room and wondered how she came to leave brown stains everywhere. Coming upstairs after breakfast I found the poor woman trying to clean up the mess with ammoniated water – and Queenie, outraged to find a stranger in her bedroom, menaced her and even nipped her ankle as a warning. But Miss B. has been a kennel maid luckily and understands dogs, and forgave Queenie both her shit and her nip, explaining, and quite rightly, both away as excitement and jealousy respectively. I debated whether or no to tell S. of this mishap. Was inclined to do so, then decided against, it seemed like sneaking on my dear doggie.

J. R. Ackerley

19 July

1738 I rose very heavy, and backward to visit them for the last time. At six I prayed and sang with them all together. The Ordinary would read prayers, and preached most miserably. Mr Sparks and Mr Broughton were present. I felt my heart full of tender love to the latter. He administered. All the ten received. Then he prayed; and I after him.

At half-hour past nine their irons were knocked off, and their hands tied. I went in a coach with Sparks, Washington, and a friend of Newington's (N. himself not being permitted). By half-hour past ten we came to Tyburn, waited till eleven: then were brought the children appointed to die. I got upon the cart with Sparks and Broughton: the Ordinary endeavoured to follow, when the poor prisoners begged he might not come; and the mob kept him down.

I prayed first, then Sparks and Broughton. We had prayed before that our Lord would show there was a power superior to the fear of death. Newington had quite forgot his pain. They were all cheerful; full of comfort, peace, and triumph; assuredly persuaded Christ had died for them, and waited to receive them into paradise. Greenaway was impatient to be with Christ.

The Black had spied me coming out of the coach, and saluted me with his looks. As often as his eyes met mine, he smiled with the most composed, delightful countenance I ever saw. Read caught hold of my hand in a transport of joy. Newington seemed perfectly pleased. Hudson declared he was never better, or more at ease, in mind and body. None showed any natural terror of death: no fear, or crying, or tears. All expressed their desire of our following them to paradise. I never saw such calm triumph, such incredible indifference to dying. We sang several hymns; particularly,

> *Behold the Saviour of mankind,*
> *Nail'd to the shameful tree;*

and the hymn entitled, 'Faith in Christ' which concludes,

> *'A guilty, weak, and helpless worm,*
> *Into thy hands I fall:*
> *Be thou my life, my righteousness,*
> *My Jesus, and my all.'*

We prayed Him, in earnest faith, to receive their spirits. I could do nothing but rejoice: kissed Newington and Hudson; took leave of each in particular. Mr Broughton bade them not be surprised when the cart should draw away. They cheerfully replied, they should not; expressed some concern how we should get back to our coach. We left them going to meet their Lord, ready for the Bridegroom. When the cart drew off, not one stirred, or struggled for life, but meekly gave up their spirits. Exactly at twelve they were turned off. I spoke a few suitable words to the crowd; and returned, full of peace and confidence in our friends' happiness. That hour under the gallows was the most blessed hour of my life.

Charles Wesley

---

20 July

1782   Mr Thomas spent the Morning with us Yesterday, he came to ask me to preach for him on Sunday but I could not, as I brought no Sermon with me – The last Time I was in the Country I had some Sermons with me and was never asked to preach therefore I thought it of no Use to bring any now.

The Reverend James Woodforde

1818   We arrive at Wensley where we found all the family well, about ½ past 2 and sat down at four to an excellent dinner and to an excellent story of my old friend about an acquaintance and I believe relative of his, the rector of Finchampstead in Essex, a man of fortune, who kept his coach and four and made his two sons postillion calling one son of a whore, whom he had by his wife who was his housekeeper before marriage, and the other son of a bitch whom he had by her afterwards.

The Reverend Benjamin Newton

1838   On the 20th I accompanied Hodgson to the levée to be presented to our young Queen. The crowd was *so obstreperous* and the hurry of the presentation so rapid, I really found it impossible to look her Majesty in the face. The instant of my approach the hand was already stretched out; I made my salute and floated on with the rapid stream. However, I performed my duty and was satisfied.

The next day there was a drawing-room, but I did not attend. London was a bumper in consequence of the preparation for the coronation of the 28th. Foreigners in abundance.

William Dyott

21 July

1664   Thence to Westminster and to Mrs Lane's lodging to give her joy. And there suffered me to deal with her as I used to do; and by and by her husband comes, a sorry simple fellow, and his letter to her, which she proudly showed me, a simple, silly nonsensical thing. A man of no discourse, and I fear married her to make a prize of; which he is mistaken in. And a sad wife I believe she will prove to him, for she urged me to appoint a time, as soon as he is gone out of town, to give her a meeting next week.

Samuel Pepys

1763   I remember nothing that happened worth relating this day. How many such days does mortal man pass!

James Boswell

1934 Duncan ill with very bad piles — operated on last night, or, since that sounds alarming, lanced. Spoke to Janie of the snobbishness of our sympathies. Cant really sympathize with that particular disease, though the pain is terrible. Must laugh.

Virginia Woolf

1949 In Warminster I could get no lunch. Neither the Bath Arms nor the Black Horse would admit Queenie [his dog] to the dining-room. No dogs allowed. I asked the proprietor of the former what he expected people who came walking into Warminster with a dog to do with it if they required lunch. He was irritable and offensive.

'I've made a rule. No dogs in the dining-room.'

'May I ask why not?' I asked.

'Because they're a nuisance. Do you know I once had a dog there that howled all through lunch!'

I said, 'But you might also have had a human being that howled all through lunch. There are some troublesome members of all species. Why penalize the majority?'

No good. No lunch. I ate some cheese sandwiches at the Anchor. And found that Queenie had stepped in some tar somewhere and that two of her paws were clogged and clotted with it, grit and stones embedded in it between her pads. Tiresome and dirty stuff. How to get it off? I asked an ironmonger, and he said turps and sold me a bottle of 'substitute' turps, some kind of alcohol. Doubtful about it, but Miss Benn did not think it would hurt Queenie, so I applied it to all her pads. It was certainly successful in removing the tar, but the poor girl resisted after a time — I quite poured it over her feet — and then, when I released her, flew about on the grass like a wild thing. I thought she was just playing, but she wasn't, it must have burnt the poor old thing. For two hours afterwards she was greatly distressed, hid in my bedroom, or ran about all over the house and garden like a cat on hot bricks, lying down and getting up, unable to find comfort anywhere, and panting and sweating profusely. I put olive oil on her feet then, but it didn't seem to help much, then warm water. In course of time the sting wore off. A day of adventure outside of the peace of Heytesbury,

yes, but unpleasant adventure in this unpleasant world. I
shan't walk out again.

J. R. Ackerley

22 July

1806   This was a memorable day – the most interesting, in my
whole Life – It made me feel very strange – I was afraid to
reflect or to think least I should lose the courage which every
Woman stands in need of on such an occasion – I was obliged
to dress in a hurry to attend my little Catholic Priest who
received my Confession, when that was over I found Robert
and Walter already arrived – My dear Bridegroom was even
perhaps more agitated than his Bride – We were instantly
married by the Catholic Priest and no Woman ever pronounced her vows with a happier heart – Robert pronounced his
with a firmness and at the same time a feeling which greatly
affected me – We had but just time to breakfast, and then I
had to dress for the second marriage – my *bridal array*
consisted of a white satin under dress and a patent net over it,
with a long veil – . . . my heart beat when we entered the
church, nor could I go thro' the second ceremony without
feeling even more affected – Miss Poole had been married a
few hours before me, and I signed my name under hers with a
steadier hand – I can never forget Jack's kindness to me
before we left the vestry – We immediately went to Argyle
House where we had a cold collation – Nothing can exceed
the kindness I met with from every member of Robert's family
– presents were pouring upon me, and Mr de Beaujolois gave
me a very handsome amethyst and diamond cross – at about
four *the happy pair* set out for L^y Elizabeth Cole's house
at Twickenham – My Sisters seemed to feel a great deal when
I left them – But they knew I was happy –

Eugenia Campbell (Wynne)

1832   Mrs Robert Smith was seized with the cholera this morning,
and died at eleven o'clock this evening. She was at the opera
last night in health and spirits, tonight she is no longer of this

world. How short a warning! Even the set at Crockford's was for a *moment* electrified at this sudden catastrophe! She was young, beautiful, daughter of the late Lord Forester, and sister of the present; niece to the Duke of Rutland; sister to Lady Chesterfield and to Mrs Anson. She was married to Mr Smith, eldest son of Lord Carington, who is disconsolate for her loss. Where will this scourge end? Each succeeding day increases the list of victims!

Thomas Raikes

1871   Mrs Nott told me that Louie of the Cloggau was staying in Presteign with her aunt Miss Sylvester, the woman frog. This extraordinary being is partly a woman and partly a frog. Her head and face, her eyes and mouth are those of a frog, and she has a frog's legs and feet. She cannot walk but she hops. She wears very long dresses to cover and conceal her feet which are shod with something like a cow's hoof. She never goes out except to the Primitive Methodist Chapel. Mrs Nott said she had seen this person's frog feet and had seen her in Presteign hopping to and from the Chapel exactly like a frog. She had never seen her hands. She is a very good person. The story about this unfortunate being is as follows. Shortly before she was born a woman came begging to her mother's door with two or three little children. Her mother was angry and ordered the woman away. 'Get away with your young frogs,' she said. And the child she was expecting was born partly in the form of a frog, as a punishment and a curse upon her.

The Reverend Francis Kilvert

23 July

1820   Every day I live I am more and more persuaded not to meddle in politicks; they separate the best friends, they destroy all social intercourse. And why? Is it for power? Is it for popularity? How unenviable they are separately! How seldom you see them combined; and most politicians have neither.

Henry Edward Fox

1874 To Beaumont: it was the rector's day. It was a lovely day: shires-long of pearled cloud under cloud, with a grey stroke underneath marking each row; beautiful blushing yellow in the straw of the uncut ryefields, the wheat looking white and all the ears making a delicate and very true crisping along the top and with just enough air stirring for them to come and go gently; then there were fields reaping. All this I would have looked at again in returning but during dinner I talked too freely and unkindly and had to do penance going home. One field I saw from the balcony of the house behind an elm tree, which it threw up, like a square of pale goldleaf, as it might be, catching the light.

Gerard Manley Hopkins

1949 I felt that he [Siegfried Sassoon] was thinking that I was drinking too much of his wine. He began very graciously, taking me down to the well-stocked wine cellar and asking me to choose what I'd like. But then, as time went on, I sensed he felt I was drinking too much – a glass of wine at a meal, not half a bottle, which I am used to. He was slower in bringing bottles up. And they turned into half-bottles instead of full ones.

I said at last, 'S. dear, I can't go on guzzling your drink like this. You've been immensely generous over it. I'm going to buy some *vin ordinaire* for myself instead.' He made no demur. So I've been buying cheap wine myself lately – 7s 6d a bottle – and he takes a glass or half-glass. He doesn't drink much himself owing to his ulcer. He never offers me sherry now. The rich are very strange.

Last night, speaking of Roderick Meicklejohn he said he liked him, but he was such a bore, he really felt he couldn't ask him down here. 'Also he'd drink up my cellar in no time.' Then he added, thinking perhaps of me, 'Not that I'd mind that, of course.' But he would. The rich are very odd. But we all are no doubt.

J. R. Ackerley

24 July

1749   I was riding over Hounslow-heath with my wife behind me, when an highwayman crossed the road, passed us, and robbed all the coaches and passengers behind us.

Charles Wesley

1806   I had a little fever in the night which alarmed Robert who flew for the Doctor and wanted to send for Sir Walter Farquhar – how much his agitation, and the affection he showed me endeared him to me – every instant makes me more sensible of my happiness in being united to a Being, I so dearly love, and who has such a heart and so much feeling with which he amply repays my affection – after all the uneasiness, the fears, my Love for him has cost me it is impossible for me to describe with what gratitude I look towards my God for having now placed me in a situation which sanctions all my tenderness and even makes it a duty – I spent half the day in bed and by following the prescriptions of Doctor Beauchamp I soon was much better, tho' I felt very weak – Robert would not leave me for an instant the whole day – He is the kindest and best Nurse –

Eugenia Campbell (Wynne)

1940   'By the way,' asked Rupert, as we sat in the cafeteria and ate a Lyon's fresh cream sandwich for tea, 'why are you a virgin?'

'I don't really know,' I said. 'It's never occurred to me to be anything else.'

He picked up my hand and studied my palm. 'I think it's because you sit aloof in an ivory tower, like me. We watch the saturnalia milling and beetling around below and wish we could join in – sometimes we venture down, but only for a moment. It does make life very boring, this aloof attitude. I expect if you had been more of the milling and beetling kind Gerhardt would have seduced you, in spite of everything. You're like me, you look as if you're always expecting something to happen, but it doesn't unless you make it. I'm the same, I bore myself to tears, but I'm far too lazy to try and make contact with life.'

When I got up to go home at six he said, 'How would you like it if I robbed you of your virginity?'

I thought for a minute.

'I don't *think* I should mind very much, but then I hardly know you well enough to say.'

Joan Wyndham

---

25 July

1926 At first I thought it was Hardy, and it was the parlourmaid, a small thin girl, wearing a proper cap. She came in with silver cake stands and so on. Mrs Hardy talked to us about her dog. How long ought we to stay? Can Mr Hardy walk much etc. I asked, making conversation, as I knew one would have to. She has the large sad lacklustre eyes of a childless woman; great docility and readiness, as if she had learnt her part; not great alacrity, but resignation, in welcoming more visitors; wears a sprigged voile dress, black shoes and a necklace. We can't go far now, she said, though we do walk every day, because our dog isn't able to walk far. He bites, she told us. She became more natural and animated about the dog, who is evidently the real centre of her thoughts – then the maid came in. Then again the door opened, more sprucely, and in trotted a little puffy-cheeked cheerful old man, with an atmosphere cheerful and businesslike in addressing us, rather like an old doctor's or solicitor's, saying 'Well now – ' or words like that as he shook hands. He was dressed in rough grey with a striped tie. His nose has a joint in it and the end curves down. A round whitish face, the eyes now faded and rather watery, but the whole aspect cheerful and vigorous. He sat on a three-cornered chair (I am too jaded with all this coming and going to do more than gather facts) at a round table, where there were the cake stands and so on; a chocolate roll; what is called a good tea; but he only drank one cup, sitting on his three-cornered chair.

Virginia Woolf

1944 Took the train to Henley and Eardley motored me to the Bothy. After dinner we sat on a table by the river, watching stream after stream of heavy bombers, with lights at the tips of their wings fly south-westwards. The roar was like that of Niagara waterfall. We could barely hear each other speak. Hundreds passed.

James Lees-Milne

1954   Incessant drenching rain, beating and soaking. The madonna lilies lie prostrate; it is disgustingly cold. Lord what a summer!

Frances Partridge

26 July

1836   Whilst at the Counting House Dr Fox appeared in pretty considerable affliction because his grandchild Edward had just been bitten by Blanco whom he feared was mad. I conveyed my medical cousin to our house to inspect the beast. He was chained & looked forlorn, refused water but lapped some milk, after which he tore the mat, rubbed his nose in the earth & performed other odd antics which much alarmed the physician. We collected evidence against the culprit who had snapped at a great number yesterday & today & Dr F. thought it advisable to proceed at once as if it were a case of hydrophobia. So having mustered Brougham & Appleton & Rachel Tregelles we visited the child. Dr F. left the house, Appleton & I held down the patient while Dr Brougham excised each tooth mark so as to make a clean wound of it, & then cauterized each with nitric acid. It was soon over. Whilst it lasted there was a sufficiency of kicking & squealing but a lollypop at the end seemed to set all right. I took Brougham to look at Blanco. He thought the symptoms suspicious of incipient madness. In the afternoon there was an alarm that Blanco had broken loose & was scampering off nobody knew where. A general hunt was established & he was taken in the garden in about 10 minutes, but in that time we found that he had bitten Harriet Tink in the hand very badly. Brougham attended her & treated her the same as the other. It made us all extremely anxious.

Barclay Fox

1935 I feel caddish, even treacherous sometimes keeping this diary from the eyes of my wife – yet it is our only secret. She knows I keep it, but if she were to read it, and I knew she were, it would lose much spontaneity, and cease to be a record of my private thoughts. Once or twice in the past I have dictated a few harmless paragraphs to a Secretary – and they have never been the same, becoming impersonal and discreet immediately. And what is more dull than a discreet diary? One might just as well have a discreet soul.

'Chips' Channon

1969 [Silver wedding]
Woke early to a glorious morning. The caterer and her minions were soon setting the bar up on a corner of the lawn, putting the little round tables and gilt chairs under the trees, and decorating the lunch table under the awning even better than I could have done it myself. And although the sun clouded over, it remained beautifully dry and warm so that people lolled on the grass just as we had dreamed. A real *fête-champêtre*, as Ruth Adam called it. Only two things embarrassed me: the lavishness of the presents we had never expected and the collapse of Harold's deck chair under him. I learned later that a *Sunday Express* photographer, trying to take pictures through the hedge, had been beaten off by the combined efforts of our neighbour Dick Moore, and Ted's friend, Tony Boram, while Sonya burst into tears with fury, nearly beating him with her fists. Harold joined in the fun in a relaxed way, making suitable cracks as he planted the commemoration tree, while our Tory friends were enchanted with Mary Wilson. An idyllic party in which I was actually able to join because I wasn't in the kitchen rustling up food. At 6 p.m., as the last guests were saying they ought to go, the first raindrops fell. God's watch must have been slow!

Barbara Castle

27 July

1738 In the coach to London I preached faith in Christ. A lady was extremely offended; avowed her own merits in plain terms;

asked if I was not a Methodist; threatened to beat me. I declared, I deserved nothing but hell; so did she; and must confess it, before she could have a title to heaven. This was most intolerable to her. The others were less offended; began to listen; asked where I preached: a maid-servant devoured every word.

Charles Wesley

1943 I have just been walking along the tow-path, wearing nothing but sandals and raw silk socks and khaki shorts I had eleven years ago, when I was seventeen. I walked along with the hot sun burning my back, eating plums, cutting the bruised parts off with my green-handled knife. It seemed so sad to be wearing the same shorts and silk socks I had when I was seventeen. I felt that I had changed much more than they had.

Denton Welch

1969 I've just got back from my royal weekend with the Queen Mother. She was charming, gay and entirely enchanting, as she always is. The Queen came over to lunch on Sunday looking like a young girl. It was all very merry and agreeable but there is always, for me, a tiny pall of 'best behaviour' overlaying the proceedings. I am not complaining about this, I think it is right and proper, but I am constantly aware of it. It isn't that I have a basic urge to tell disgusting jokes and say 'fuck' every five minutes, but I'm conscious of a faint resentment that I couldn't if I wanted to. I told the Queen how moved I had been by Prince Charles's Investiture, and she gaily shattered my sentimental illusions by saying that they were both struggling not to giggle because at the dress rehearsal the crown was too big and extinguished him like a candle-snuffer!

Noël Coward

28 July

1944 I went to bed soon after 11 in our cellar. At 12.15 a bomb fell with great noise. The basement was filled with fumes, so I guessed the bomb had been pretty close. Got out of bed, put on gumboots and Burberry, and walked into the road. Even in the clear light of the moon I could see a cloud of explosive steaming from the river in front of me. This fly bomb had cut out its engine, and recovered twice before finally falling. As I watched I heard people in the street shout, 'Look out, another's coming!' and they rushed down to their shelter. I was left transfixed, and knew there was no time to descend into my basement, down the rickety area steps. So I looked at the light of the bomb coming straight at me. Then the engine stopped, and I knew we were in for it. I lay flat on my face on the pavement, as close as could be to the embankment wall. I heard the bomb swish through the air. It too fell in the river, only closer than the last, and sent a spray of water over me. At dawn I met a policeman picking up a fragment of the bomb from the road. It was over a foot long. It must have hurtled over my head.

James Lees-Milne

1953 I love WCs as much as Queenie [his dog] does. She reacts instantly to their odours and with her ears and tail high investigates their urinal runnels with such an intensity of emotion that I feel that at any moment she might roll in them. She is always on the verge, swaying towards them with delight and her shoulder down, but since the configurations of the floor are not really satisfactory for turning upon one's back, she usually contents herself with rubbing herself ecstatically against the porcelain partitions. She is in her element here, and I understand and love to see her amusing herself.

I enjoy them for other and more intellectual reasons. I like to see humanity demeaning and humbling itself. I like to think that in the shut-up shit-house boxes respectable persons are behaving in a way of which they are slightly ashamed. At Waterloo Station for instance I am often fascinated by the sight of the lines and lines of cubicles all full with the shadows of the shitters' coats hanging up against the glass panels from pegs, while some embarrassed young man, who is bursting for a shit, hurries self-consciously up and down the line, with his cricket bag in his hands, trying in vain to get in. Who are occupying all those shit-houses? I think to myself gleefully, and populate them, in my imagination, with all the people I most despise, the eminently respectable and blimpish, the black-coated high-ups, let us say, of the BBC.

Possibly Sir John Reith is shitting there, I think to myself, and Sir Basil Nicolls, and Sir Ian Jacob. I like to think of them all with their black-striped trousers down, sitting with their pale legs apart, having a GOOD SHIT, and I like this because I know that they would not like me to think it. It is the people who put up the greatest show of not having any cocks or arseholes, who regard such interesting objects as rude and shameful, that I like to think of as having to admit to them, the people who preach and moralize and censor, they are the people with whom I fill my WCs, the people who religiously wash their hands, even if they have only taken out their penises, as though they had done some disgustingly defiling act.

J. R. Ackerley

29 July

1833   A most sad misfortune has happened. The day being very hot, we as usual spent it under the weeping ash, and, as is customary with us, took the lark with us in his cage. We allowed him to come out on our knees to eat little crumbs of bread, and, as he always popped back again, we apprehended no danger. At length he came out with no object but to ascertain the extent of the weeping ash, and then walked beyond it to the gravel walk. This looked rather alarming. Papa went in for flies, and I for a piece of bread to entice him back again. When I returned I held out a crumb to him, expecting him to eat it. Instead of that, he spread his wings and took a prodigious flight over the trees and across the yard. A hue and cry was instantly raised. But everybody expected him back again, and for at least an hour the children good-naturedly employed themselves, under a broiling sun, in toiling over the garden with his cage and looking for him. We spied him several times, flying or singing, extremely happy; the first flight he has taken since he was born. I hope he will not get into dangers abroad. He is very much missed by everybody, but I fear he will not return. I hung his cage out of my window to attract him back, and sat up till ten o'clock to watch for him; but, alas! he never came, and I must make up my mind to bear the loss. It is the more disappointing, because his tameness was daily increasing, so that he would even sit on my lap, and always came when called by almost any one. My only consolation is that he will be happier at liberty than in a cage.

Emily Shore

1837   Walked to Oxford Street, took cab home. The cabman insisted on two shillings, which I resisted; and, on his persisting, I made him drive me to the police office, where a deposit was made for the measurement of the ground. I walked home.

William Macready

1841   Buckland learnedly suggested something about snails which he discovered at the bottom of some extensive limestone borings near Boulogne. This led to a learned disquisition on snails, as to how they bored & where they bored, & why they bored & whether they really bored, or no. Thought I, if they don't, I know who does.

Barclay Fox

30 July

1798   We all went to see the house Fremantle wishes to buy, it is two miles from Winslow, about two miles from the turnpike road in the village Swanburn, very agreeably situated on a hill, it is a very nice place which would suit us on all accounts. It is to be sold for 1,000 guineas but we are endeavouring to get it for less − it is very cheap even at that price.

Elizabeth Fremantle

1905   Bus to Hyde Park. Heard band. In jolly fine luck today. Indeed I am! Find after paying debts I have only a few coppers left, and then my fare to Hyde Park is beyond my estimate − I had mistaken the longer route. Then, whilst sitting under a tree, a beautiful girl watching me from behind, some mischievous birds on top messed. Down it came on my suit. I got up sharply. I have never looked a greater fool! Ah! Cruel Fate! No money left.

Sydney Moseley

1907 *I wonder if I am a failure?* . . . Time goes on . . . There is no rise. Perhaps I will take a chance and go over to America.

Sydney Moseley

1943 We walked out of the restaurant into the heat, and down the embankment. We crossed London Bridge to the south side of the river, and ambled along Cardinal's Wharf. Jamesey was extolling in the most candid and engaging manner his age – he is twenty-six – his good looks and his successes, saying he did not believe he could ever die. He said, 'Our relationship is such a one that can never have existed in the past. I don't think anything marks the progress of civilization so vividly as improved personal relations.' I said, yes, I felt certain that before our time personal relations could never have been so intimate, though of course we could never tell what, for instance, Byron and Hobhouse talked about at nights in a tent during their travels in the Morea. I said that more people ought to keep diaries, but the trouble was that the most unscrupulous diarists were too scrupulous when it came to putting personal truths on paper. James said that Cecil [Beaton's] diary would be the chronicle of our age, that we would only live through it. I said Eddy Sackville West kept one. James said, 'We could not be hoisted to posterity on two spikier spikes.' We looked at bombed churches and sat in churchyards, and drank shandies in City pubs.

James Lees-Milne

31 July

1818 Rose at half-past 7. Thermometer 60, hard rain. It appears that the liberties in eating and drinking my wife had taken did pretty well as long as she was moving but the salmon, gooseberry, currant and apple pyes now she is stationary seem to tell. I gathered a few specimens of granite but the shore is very unproductive of pebbles or shells and has nothing of boldness about it. My wife was not able to dine at the ordinary and continued ill all day and all night and I was affected much in the same way and cannot account for it except by eating trout which gave me a violent lax which I have experienced from eating salmon. I ate indeed a good many shrimps but they are considered as wholesome and my wife ate none. We had for dinner trout, roast beef, ducks, rabbits, veal puddings and pyes, and a ball at the Ship in the evening to which were invited the party from the other inn amounting to three gentlemen and a lady. We supped at eleven and got home before twelve.

The Reverend Benjamin Newton

1933   After lunch I took some Yeastvite tablets and continued to take them after tea and supper. A slightly unromantic way of curing lovesickness I admit, but certainly I feel a lot better now. (Hilary is playing 'Stormy Weather' incessantly – my theme song I think!) After lunch I read Richard Aldington's new book, *All Men are Enemies* – it was rather interesting but intensely depressing. After tea I turned to Burton's *Anatomy of Melancholy* and began to read about Love Melancholy – but I haven't yet got to the part where he deals with the cure. Perhaps I'm suffering from the spleen too – in that case I may be completely cured by taking a course of our English poets – which all points to drowning my sorrows in work. I think I shall try to develop a 'Whatever is, is right' attitude of mind – and quite honestly I suppose all this *is* rather good for me – and an affair with Lorenzo probably wouldn't be!

Barbara Pym

1969   Lunch at the Royal Commonwealth Society with Bob. In the restaurant all those clergymen helping themselves from the cold table, it seems endlessly. But you mustn't notice things like *that* if you're going to be a novelist in 1968–9 and the 70s. The posters on Oxford Circus station advertising Confidential Pregnancy Tests would be more suitable.

Barbara Pym

1662 God forgive me, I was sorry to hear that Sir W. Pens maid Betty was gone away yesterday, for I was in hopes to have had a bout with her before she had gone, she being very pretty. I have also a mind to my own wench, but I dare not, for fear she should prove honest and refuse and then tell my wife.

Samuel Pepys

1719 I rode home to see my Hay-making; And Will Clarke and another Man who were making a Rick in Westley's Wood were both very fast asleep upon the top of a Load of Hay standing by the Rick in my Wagon.

Later I was at our Musick-Meeting; and Mr Ducket of Caune in Wiltshire play'd on a Flute one song with us: But Mr Hill's Harpsichord being near a note below Consort Pitch, and no sure Hand performing the Trebles (being only young Ladds of Wells and Shepton,) our Musick was very mean.

Dr Claver Morris

1767 A heart-searching time.

Sixty-eight and 7/12 years are past: Lord, cleanse from every alloy of impurity of flesh and spirit. Preserve and deliver not only from acts of drunkenness, gluttony, and ambition, but from the very spirit of those vices, even the living to eat and to drink, and to know; and so from eating, drinking, and studying for any other end, but the glory of God, and the real benefit of my neighbour, as well as of myself.

Memento, memento mori: but O my stupidity, whilst the organs begin to fail, even the ears, the eyes, and the grinders of the mill, and the flesh that covers thee! Awake, awake, O my soul! Death and judgement are at the door. Lord, search and cleanse!

Dr John Rutty

1791 We went on no farther than to Bagshot: thirty miles was the extremity of our powers; but I bore them very tolerably, though variably.

We put up at the best inn, very early, and then inquired what we could see in the town and neighbourhood.

'Nothing!' was the concise answer of a staring housemaid. We determined, therefore, to prowl to the churchyard, and read the tombstone inscriptions: but when we asked the way, the same woman, staring still more wonderingly, exclaimed, 'Church! There's no church nigh here!'

Fanny Burney

1909   Up to Arthur's. *Loretta no attraction now.* I am a man *now!*

Sydney Moseley

2 August

1786   You may have heard it wrong; I will concisely tell it right. His carriage had just stopped at the garden-door at St James's, and he had just alighted from it, when a decently dressed woman, who had been waiting for him some time, approached him with a petition. It was rolled up, and had the usual superscription – For the King's Most Excellent Majesty. She presented it with her right hand; and, at the same moment that the King bent forward to take it, she drew from it, with her left hand, a knife, with which she aimed straight at his heart!

The fortunate awkwardness of taking the instrument with the left hand made her design perceived before it could be executed; the King started back, scarce believing the testimony of his own eyes; and the woman made a second thrust, which just touched his waistcoat before he had time to prevent her; and at that moment one of the attendants, seeing her horrible intent, wrenched the knife from her hand.

'Has she cut my waistcoat?' cried he, in telling it – 'Look! for I have had no time to examine.'

Thank heaven, however, the poor wretch had not gone quite so far. 'Though nothing,' added the King, in giving his relation, 'could have been sooner done, for there was nothing for her to go through but a thin linen and fat.'

While the guards and his own people now surrounded the

King, the assassin was seized by the populace, who were tearing her away, no doubt to fall the instant sacrifice of her murtherous purpose, when the King, the only calm and moderate person then present, called aloud to the mob, 'The poor creature is mad! – Do not hurt her! She has not hurt me!'

He then came forward, and showed himself to all the people, declaring he was perfectly safe and unhurt; and then gave positive orders that the woman should be taken care of, and went into the palace, and had his levée.

There is something in the whole of his behaviour upon this occasion that strikes me as proof indisputable of a true and noble courage: for in a moment so extraordinary – an attack in this country, unheard of before – to settle so instantly that it was the effect of insanity, to feel no apprehension of private plot or latent conspiracy – to stay out, fearlessly, among his people, and so benevolently to see himself to the safety of one who had raised her arm against his life – these little traits, all impulsive, and therefore to be trusted, have given me an impression of respect and reverence that I can never forget, and never think of but with fresh admiration.

Fanny Burney

1916   Lying in a hospital train on his way to London he looks out at the hot August landscape of Hampshire, the flat green and dun-coloured fields – the advertisements of Lung Tonic and Liver Pills, the cows-neat villas and sluggish waterways – all these came on him in an irresistible delight, at the pale gold of the wheat-field and the faded green of the hazy muffled woods on the low hills. People wave to the Red Cross train – grateful stay-at-homes – even a middle-aged man, cycling along a dusty road in straw hat and blue serge clothes, takes one hand off the handlebars to wave feeble and jocular gratitude. And the soul of the officer glows with fiery passion as he thinks, 'All this I've been fighting for and now I'm safe home again I begin to think it was worth while.' And he wondered how he could avoid being sent out again.

Siegfried Sassoon

3 August

1778   But Dr Johnson's approbation! – it almost crazed me with agreeable surprise – it gave me such a flight of spirits, that I danced a jig to Mr Crisp, without any preparation, music, or explanation – to his no small amazement and diversion. I left him, however, to make his own comments upon my friskiness, without affording him the smallest assistance.

     Susan also writes me word, that when my father went last to Streatham Dr Johnson was not there, but Mrs Thrale told him, that when he gave her the first volume of *Evelina*, which she had lent him, he said, 'Why, madam, why, what a charming book you lent me!' and eagerly inquired for the rest. He was particularly pleased with the Snow-hill scenes, and said that Mr Smith's vulgar gentility was admirably portrayed; and when Sir Clement joins them, he said there was a shade of character prodigiously well marked. Well may it be said, that the greatest minds are ever the most candid to the inferior set! I think I should love Dr Johnson for such lenity to a poor mere worm in literature, even if I were not myself the identical grub he has obliged.

Fanny Burney

1830   I went yesterday to the sale of the late King's wardrobe, which was numerous enough to fill Monmouth Street and sufficiently various and splendid for the wardrobe of Drury Lane. He hardly ever gave away anything except his linen, which was distributed every year. These clothes are the perquisite of his pages, and will fetch a pretty sum. There are all the coats he has ever had for fifty years, 300 whips, canes without number, every sort of uniform, the costumes of all the orders in Europe, splendid furs, pelisses, hunting-coats and breeches, and among other things a dozen pair of corduroy breeches he had made to hunt in when Don Miguel was here. His profusion in these articles was unbounded, because he never paid for them, and his memory was so accurate that one of his pages told me he recollected every article of dress, no matter how old, and that they were always liable to be called on to produce some particular coat or other article of apparel of years gone by. It is difficult to say whether in great or little things that man was most odious and contemptible.

Charles Greville

1890   Day of blank misery.

George Gissing

4 August

1833   Drove to Regent's Park; Rogers told of Coleridge riding about in a strange shabby dress, with I forget whom at Keswick, and on some company approaching them, Coleridge offered to fall behind and pass for his companion's servant. 'No,' said the other, 'I am proud of you as a friend; but, I must say, I should be ashamed of you as a servant.'

Thomas Moore

1914   Late as it is & almost too excited to write as I am, I must make some effort to chronicle the stupendous events of this remarkable day. The situation is absolutely unparalleled in the history of the world. Never before has the war strength of each individual nation been of such great extent, even though all the nations of Europe, the dominant continent, have been armed before. It is estimated that when the war begins *14 millions* of men will be engaged in the conflict. Attack is possible by earth, water & air, & the destruction attainable by the modern war machines used by the armies is unthinkable & past imagination.

This morning at breakfast we learnt that war is formally declared between France & Germany, that the German ambassador has left Paris & the French ambassador Berlin. Germany has declared to Belgium that if her troops are allowed to pass unmolested through Belgian territory she will protect her interests in the Treaty at the end of the war. Belgium has indignantly refused any such violation of international honour, and the King of the Belgians has appealed to King George for aid. For an hour this morning I read a fine speech of Sir Edward Grey's, in which he manages successfully to steer the middle course between the extremists who on the one hand want neutrality & on the other immediate war. His two chief statements were that the British fleet would in the event of the French coast being attacked by Germany give France all the protection in her power, and also that she would see that Belgian neutrality was preserved. Sir E. Grey's statement that 'we are prepared' evoked tremendous cheering in the House. In consequence of their disagreement with this policy, Mr John Burns, Sir John Morley & Mr Masterman have all resigned their places in the Cabinet. It is rumoured that the Secretaryship for War has been offered to Lord Kitchener.

Vera Brittain

1973   To bed early. Began reading Mrs Gaskell's *North and South*. I have never read it before. I began with a great feeling of relief; I was reading something which had nothing to do with work. Within four chapters, I caught myself thinking of it as a film . . .

Peter Hall

5 August

1663   And in the afternoon to Westminster hall and there found Mrs Lane; and by and by, by agreement, we met at the parliament-stairs (in my way down to the boat, who should meet us but my Lady Jemimah, who saw me lead her but said nothing to me of her, though I stayed to speak to her to see whether she would take notice of it or no) and off to Stangate; and so to the Kingshead at Lambeth marsh and had variety of meats and drink; come to xs. But I did so towse her and handled her; but could get nothing more from her, though I was very near it. But as wanton and bucksome as she is, she dares not adventure upon that business – in which I very much commend and like her. Stayed pretty late, and so over with her by water; and being in a great sweat with my towsing of her, I durst not go home by water, but took coach. And at home, my brother and I fell upon Des Cartes, and I perceive he hath studied him well and I cannot find but he hath minded his book and doth love it. This evening came a letter about business from Mr Coventry, and with it a Silver pen he promised me, to carry inke in; which is very necessary. So to prayers and to bed.

Samuel Pepys

1826 In the course of the day I met my acquaintance Mr Charles Cripps, who resides here as manager of the Branch establishment of the Bank of England, which has recently commenced its operations at Gloucester. This is the only branch which the great bank has yet thrown out, and will serve as a model for others. Cripps is well calculated to superintend its operations, having long been the active partner with his father and uncle at Cirencester and Stow as country bankers, from which partnership, of course, he has withdrawn on undertaking the management of the Gloucester Branch Bank. At present it will disappoint the neighbourhood, as the latitude afforded by country bankers will not be given; no customer will be allowed to overdraw his account, no advances will be made on doubtful pledges etc.

The Reverend Francis Witts

1945 The world has been electrified, thrilled and horrified by the atomic bomb; one has been dropped in Japan today. It devastated a whole town and killed a quarter of a million people. It could mean the end of civilization.

'Chips' Channon

1979 I feel awful on waking but a bit better now sitting in the sun writing this, also trying to finish off my novel. Shall I write more in this notebook?

Perhaps what one fears about dying won't be the actual moment – one hopes – but what you have to go through beforehand – in my case this uncomfortable swollen body and feeling sick and no interest in food or drink.

Barbara Pym

6 August

1684   I rubbed the skin near my rump, whereupon it began to be very sore.

Elias Ashmole

1886   Girl, aged 17, remanded for a petty theft from her place, and that I may find a Home for her if she promises well. Her mother says she is beyond her control, runs away from her places and gets into bad company, and that she has never been right since she was 10, when a 'man' got six months for violating her. Two other girls, aged 13 and 9, were similarly treated by him, being waylaid on their way home from school. He was an accountant.

   Another girl of the same age and charged with a similar offence I send to another Home. Her mother is dead, her father in the workhouse, and she has been brought up in a workhouse school, which quite accounts for her dulness and obliquity of moral vision. The huge barrack schools are utter ruin for pauper girls in comparison with any other system. Why is the British rate-payer so slow to note that children in Sutton District School cost £30 a head, while in Cottage Homes, such as those at Marston Green, the cost is but £20 10s, and children boarded out (e.g., by the King's Norton Union) cost but £10 9s 10d a head per annum? I suppose they like to go on paying highest for the worst system and results, rather than lowest for the best.

   A third girl this morning will go hopefully into a Home. She is only 18, but has led an immoral life for six months, yet is modest and quiet in manner; an orphan likewise.

   An ex-prisoner is sent to me by a lady that I may help him. I find in conversation that a man for whom he worked twenty months is kindly disposed towards him and is now manager to a large firm. Yet it had never occurred to him to call on him! Verily, some men's idea of seeking employment is to lie on their back with their mouth open, expecting it to be filled.

**The Reverend J. W. Horsley
(Chaplain, Clerkenwell Prison)**

1962   Marilyn Monroe committed suicide yesterday. The usual overdose. Poor silly creature. I am convinced that what brought her to that final foolish gesture was a steady diet of intellectual pretentiousness pumped into her over the years by Arthur Miller, and 'The Method'. She was, to begin with, a fairly normal little sexpot with exploitable curves and a certain natural talent. I am sure that all the idiocies of her last few years, always being late on the set, etc., plus over-publicity and too many theoretical discussions about acting, were the result of all this constant analysis of every line in every part she had to play, and a desperate longing to be 'intellectual' without the brain to achieve it. It is a sad comment on contemporary values that a beautiful, famous and wealthy young woman of thirty-six should capriciously kill herself for want of a little self-discipline and horse-sense. Judy [Garland] and Vivien in their different ways are in the same plight. Too much too soon and too little often.

Noël Coward

7 August

1865   Today has been splendid. I worked at Lyly all the morning, and in the afternoon went with C. and Woolner to walk in Leigh Woods. They are just as beautiful as when I used to roam there years ago. The lights fall still as golden on those grey rocks streaked with red, on the ivy and the trees, the ferns and heather, and the bright enchanter's nightshade. Not a point is different except myself. This beauty sinks into my soul now as then; but it does not stir me so painfully and profoundly. I do not feel the hunger which I had; nor am I conscious of the same power, the same unlimited hopes, the same expectations solemn from their vagueness.

     C. has in a great measure effected this change. What is good in it I owe to her influence, and to the happiness which her love has brought me. She has raised my moral nature and calmed my intellectual irritability. But there is also a change for the worse. This is simply attributable to my long-continued physical weakness. No one who has not suffered in the same way can adequately feel how great is the sapping, corroding power of my debility. Eyes for more than two years useless. Brain for more than two years nearly paralysed – never acutely tortured, but failing under the least strain and vibrating to the least excitement. To feel as little as possible, to think and work as slightly as I could, to avoid strong enjoyments when they rarely offered themselves, has been my aim. I have done nothing in this period by a steady effort. Everything has come by fits and starts of energy, febrile at the moment, and prostrating me for days when they are over. Sometimes for weeks together I have not seen a ray of sunlight. At Florence, at Rome, in London, at Clifton, I have risen with the horror of these nights, have walked through the day beneath the burden of dull aching nerves, and have gone to bed in hopelessness, dry with despair and longing for death. Suddenly, in the midst of this despair, a ray of my old capacity for happiness has burst upon me. For a few hours my heart has beat, my senses have received impressions, my brain has coined from them vigorous ideas. But vengeance follows after this rejoicing. Crack go nerves and brain, and thought and sense and fancy die. The leaden atmosphere of despair closes around me, and I see no hope. Many are the men, no doubt, who have suffered as I have suffered. Last summer I spent six days in London, in Half-Moon Street. I had just been subjected to treatment which gave great pain, and made me very weak. If it succeeded it was to do wonders. In the midst of my weakness I hoped. I sat upon one chair with my legs upon another. I could not read. I was too desolate and broken to see friends. I scarcely slept, and heard all night London roar, with the canopy of flame in the hot sky, above those reeking thoroughfares. At three or four, day broke. In the evening I sat idle, and it was dark. All the while I hoped. This cure shall do wonders.

But the old evil broke out again. One night I woke. A clock struck two – it was the Victoria clock at Westminster. I bit the bedclothes, and bared myself upon the bed in anguish; and at last I sobbed. It was all over with me. I took up next morning the old cross.

How long is it since I last kept a connected diary? Three years. When that blow came upon me in the spring of 1863, I said, I will write no more in this book. And I did write no more. My happiness went first. Then my brain refused to work. Then my eyes were blinded. I went to Switzerland. How much of beauty I learned there. And at Mürren I saw C. Then followed my summer in London, and those days of mental, moral, physical annihilation. At the end of them I arose and found C. at Pontresina. On the 10th of last November we were married; and now we live together in our house, both happy, and she will ere long give me a child.

J. A. Symonds

8 August

1664 Being Ashton wakes, att this time I had a most ardent effection to Emm Potter, and she was in compeny att Tankerfeild's with Henry Kenion, and it greeved me very much. Henry Low came to me and would have me to go to Tankerfeild's to spend 2d., so we went to the next chamber to that they ware in. Att last they came by us and I movd Emm to stay to drinke with me, which she did, but would not stay with me, neither there nor no where els; would not come to me, tho she said she would; and I was in a very sad eflicted estate, and all by reason of her.

Roger Lowe

1684 I purged.

Elias Ashmole

1828 As my assistance was needed to play a rubber in the evening, I did so, and as a rare occurrence I note it: I was a winner of three shillings.

The Reverend John Skinner

1945 The papers are full of the atomic bomb which is going to revolutionize everything and blow us all to buggery. Not a bad idea.

Noël Coward

1956 Upon the concrete verandah the bars of my cage are cast, cast by the sun as it sinks below the balustrades. How pretty the pattern they make, the bars of my cage. They lie beside me, bars of shadow, bars of brightness, on the concrete ground, they lie upon my body as I sit in my deck chair and upon the body of my dog beside me. We are within our cage together, the cage we have chosen, as happy as it is possible to be with death drawing closer.

J. R. Ackerley

9 August

1684 I took leeches.

Elias Ashmole

1784 Supped at Mr Pearson's, in company with Messrs Levitt and Thompson. After supper the song and the glass went merrily round. The little liquour that I drank got into my head, and quite metamorphosed me to be dull and strangely stupid. When a man is in liquor, though but a small degree, it either makes a brute, a fool, or a madman of him – in short, he is fit for nothing. Drinking is thought by some to drive away care. It may, when a man's senses are drowned and stupefied, and he a little better than a living mass of clay. But when sobriety returns, the cares and sorrows return, with an additional force, because of the folly the man has committed, unless he is lost to reflection indeed.

Strother

1818 The Green Devils have haunted me all the way and all the while I have been out. If any one wishes to know what sort of things they are, I can only say they are not quite so bad as Blue Devils, being no other than green peas a month too old to be eaten by me who am very fond of them when young. I have heard Mr Wharton, the member for Beverley, says all women ought to be hung out of the way at forty; peas are like them and should never be brought to anything but pigs after the pods are full.

The Reverend Benjamin Newton

1941 Rather depressing financial discussion with Lorn. Obviously, however hard I work, I shall never be able to save any money.

Noël Coward

---

10 August

1684 I purged again.

Elias Ashmole

1764 Take care, take care, of the fumes of cyder and whiskey: tremble at the mixture. Such is the spirit of the true Quaker, and such was Joseph, who said, 'How shall I do this evil?' &c.

Dr John Rutty

1794 Dined at the Revd Mr Peach's at East Shene, who gave us excellent Port wine 19 years old. He said Dr Cadogan had told him that after any accidental excess, He was accustomed to take as much Rhubarb as would lay on a shilling — an equal quantity of ginger, & of magnesia, in peppermint water, which counteracted the effects of the excess.
Mr Peach always receives benefit from the Bath waters.

Joseph Farington

1823 I preached in the morning at Camerton a sermon, pointing out the advantages of education if properly directed, and the ills arising from the neglect of it. Mrs Jarrett, I thought, did not seem much to approve of some parts of the discourse, as I now and then noticed an emphatic 'hem'. However, I am too old a soldier to be alarmed at squibs!

The Reverend John Skinner

1838 I have heard of a lady, by birth, being reduced to cry 'muffins to sell' for a subsistence. She used to go out a-nights with her face hid up in her cloak, and then she would in the faintest voice utter her cry. Somebody passing by heard her cry – 'Muffins to sell, muffins to sell! Oh, I hope nobody hears me.'

Henry Crabb Robinson

11 August

1695 The weather now so cold that greater frosts were not always seene in the midst of Winter; this succeeded much wet, and set harvest extremely back.

John Evelyn

1764 Very unpleasant and irksome to myself to-day; the punch taken in too great a quantity last night, occasions my head to ach violently. A very fine pleasant day.

Thomas Turner

1921 A fortnight already gone. It goes too quick – too quick. If only one could sip slowly & relish every grain of every hour! For, to speak the truth, I've thought of making my will for the first time during these past weeks. Sometimes it seems to me that I shall never write out all the books I have in my head, because of the strain. The devilish thing about writing is that it calls upon every nerve to hold itself taut. That is exactly what I cannot do – Now if it were painting or scribbling music or making patchwork quilts or mud pies, it wouldn't matter.

Virginia Woolf

1925 Another solitary day. I received a letter from Heinemann's, objecting to my wanting 400 lines from *Selected Poems* for the 'Sixpenny Poets' edition. They say it will spoil the sales. I replied (during a violent thunderstorm) that I have no intention of altering my selection for the Sixpenny edition. This made me feel as if I'd done something strong. The alternative would be to print nothing but my new poems in the Sixpenny. This would infuriate Heinemann's. At present I am in the mood to be objectionable to everyone, myself included. How different I felt a fortnight ago. The sun came out after lunch, and I sat in Hyde Park till 5.30. Everything looked lovely; a Borzoi dog capered around on the grass with a brown French poodle, while the band played Mendelssohn's Wedding March brassily. But I felt ill and morose, and the sunlight only made my head ache. After dinner was a different story. Thank God for the Proms! Haydn, Mozart, and Mendelssohn (a piano concerto this time, and a very melodious one) made me feel quite happy and calm. I sat in the gallery and saw no one I knew.

Siegfried Sassoon

12 August

1684   I applied a plaster to it.

Elias Ashmole

1886   I wonder if this flower-girl, aged 18, used to sing the popular song, 'We are a happy family'. She is in for assaulting her mother with a poker, and has twice previously been in for drunkenness: the mother is living apart from her husband, and has spent ten months out of twelve in Millbank doing short terms for drunkenness: a younger brother and sister have been sent to Industrial Schools. Yet the wonder is that any members of some families do right, and not that many do wrong. On what a pinnacle of virtue, inaccessible to a countess, is the daughter of a convict father and gindrinking mother who keeps straight!

Twice this week have I written to the Reformatory and Refuge Union to set their special officer on children that I find to be living in houses of ill-fame, of which the denizens or keepers come here. In one case, at any rate, there seemed a dereliction of duty on the part of the police, who, when they apprehended the mother, should have rescued the children.

Fate is the convenient scapegoat of those whose 'can't' is a shuffling substitute for 'won't' or 'don't like'. This man is in for theft from a public-curse; he is badly consumptive through drinking long and heavily; his father died of alcoholic phthisis; he has often tried to abstain, but never for more than six weeks; he has been warned by a physician at a hospital of how he is committing suicide; but he 'supposes it is Fate'.

The Reverend J. W. Horsley
(Chaplain, Clerkenwell Prison)

1928   We had tea from bright blue cups under the pink light of the giant hollyhock. We were all a little drugged with the country; a little bucolic I thought. It was lovely enough – made me envious of its country peace; the trees all standing securely – why did my eye catch the trees? The look of things has a great power over me. Even now, I have to watch the rooks beating up against the wind, which is high, and still I say to myself instinctively 'What's the phrase for that?' and try to make more and more vivid the roughness of the air current and the tremor of the rook's wing slicing as if the air were full of ridges and ripples and roughnesses. They rise and sink, up and down, as if the exercise rubbed and braced them like swimmers in rough water. But what a little I can get down into my pen of what is so vivid to my eyes, and not only to my eyes; also to some nervous fibre, or fanlike membrane in my species.

Virginia Woolf

13 August

1717   Going this day through Christ Church, I took the opportunity to view distinctly the statue just put up in one of the niches within the college, by the dean's lodgings, of Bishop Fell. The statuary was at work. All people, that knew the bishop, agree 'tis not like him, he being a thin, grave man, whereas the statue represents him plump and gay. I told the statuary that it was unlike, and that he was made too plump. Oh, says he, we must make a handsome man. Thus the fellow. Just as if we were to burlesque the bishop, who is put in episcopal robes and yet by the statue is not represented above 20.

Thomas Hearne

1831 How depressed I felt yesterday evening. How I hung upon the past, as if my life as well as happiness were in it! How I thought of those words 'You will never find another person who will love you as I love you' – And how I felt that to hear again the sound of those beloved, those ever ever beloved lips, I wd. barter all other sounds & sights – that I wd. in joy & gratitude lay down before her my tastes & feelings each & all, in sacrifice for the love, the exceeding love which I never, in truth, can find again. Have I not tried this, & know this & felt this: & do I not feel *now*, bitterly, dessolately, that human love like her's [her mother's] I never can find again!

Elizabeth Barrett

1905 (Sunday) Shaved myself for first time. Arthur and I go to St Paul's.

Sydney Moseley

1940 Yesterday was my first night out in Soho, my first real dinner date, my first visit to the Café Royal and the second time I ever got drunk – quite a night to remember!

Joan Wyndham

14 August

1828 Still the same dreadful weather. I read before breakfast in the newspapers an ample and particular account of the execution of the horrible murderer, Corder. It occupied nearly two sides of the paper, that is, including his trial and remarks upon it. There needs not any other proof of the deplorable state of depraved feelings to which this country has gradually arrived through the instruction of novelists and fatalists, than this document.

I have before remarked (in my Journal) the eager curiosity with which people of all kinds and classes flocked to the barn in which the corpse of the unhappy woman had been interred, and that these pilgrims to the shrine and novelty took away portions of the barn floor as reliques! but the acme of depraved feelings was exemplified on the day of the execution, when the detestable wretch was launched into eternity. No less than 10,000 persons assembled on the plain surrounding the gallows: there well-dressed and delicate females exposed themselves to the rude jostling of the mob, and all the horrid language which generally is uttered by base and unfeeling men on the occasion, in order to witness the death of a fellow creature. These females pressed even to the foot of the gallows to witness his mental pangs and his bodily torments, which in all probability were very violent, for the executioner held by and pulled down the legs of the wretched sufferer for two minutes in order that his convulsive pangs might be shortened. Yet, notwithstanding this, even when *ten* minutes had elapsed the limbs were still convulsed.

The worst part of the recital is yet to come. So eager were the populace to retain some memorial of the transaction, and of the executed murderer, whose end ought to have excited the utmost horror and detestation, that they vied with each other in purchasing the cord with which he was hanged at a guinea an inch, and even the Sheriff took home in his carriage the pistols and sword [with which the murder was supposed to have been perpetrated], and declared he would not part with them for 100 guineas: there had been a quarrel as to the right of possession between the keeper of the prison and one of the constables – doubtless occasioned by the expectation of gain. Surely all these are indications of a dereliction of all sober sense and feeling, and an overruling folly which depraves the understanding, taking the sole possession of the vulgar mind.

I have read nothing nor heard of nothing of late which has so completely disgusted me as this horrid narrative.

The Reverend John Skinner

---

15 August

1684 Mr Agar applied a balsam.

Elias Ashmole

1886 Only twenty-three men and seven females admitted yesterday. Is London getting virtuous? No, but these are Thursday's offenders, and, 'it doesn't run to it' in the matter of drink by that time in the week.

The Reverend J. W. Horsley
(Chaplain, Clerkenwell Prison)

1916 Most people cannot see beyond the war at all; they cannot even realize that it is not the most important thing in the world, Truth and Beauty and Love being more so. How then shall they ever understand the truth that the world is an iota of the solar system, the solar system an iota of the universe, and the whole under the mindless rule of Primal force?

You can see how great a change it was to me, coming away from Box Hill and the free happy life of J. and M. and the baby and A. and lovely H. on Sundays, to the narrow society of ordinary people and to a world bounded by the columns of the *Morning Post*. I thought that when I went down to Box Hill, and I was quite bound to feel so, that I should not be really happy with them: I thought their happy carelessness would annoy me, that I would long for the company of those who had suffered, that the men with iron in their souls would be my only companions from the war days onwards.

I was mistaken. The view was dictated by a self-fostered gloominess perhaps, a selfishness at finding my own fearful experiences unaccounted of. I was happy to put them by, and fell in love with all the sublime life of Reason, Art, and Joy more than ever.

I come back here tonight to find a summons to go to W. in D. and join up with the X. Regiment.

As usual, the blow has quietened me. It has fallen, and now nothing can happen for a day or two.

I can barely convince myself that I am going back to the Army – that there is a war on at all.

Strong upon me tonight, with M.'s laugh and J.'s voice far away, is the now familiar feeling of unreality, of dream-existence.

What midgets we all are, what brief phantoms in a dream – a dream within a dream, this truly is my life, and how gladly would I end it now.

Arthur Graeme West

16 August

1664 I was this afternoone with William Chadocke and Thomas Heyes casting up their accounts, and after I had done with them I came to shop and shutt it up and went to William Hasleden's. They ware att prayer. After prayer Mr Woods' discourse was concerneinge wars and troubles that he and old William had beene in togather, so att far in night I came my way and came to the window that Emm Potter lay in chamber, and I would gladly have come in, but she durst not let me in; but she rise up to the windowe and we kisd, and so I went to bed.

Roger Lowe

1824 My boys engaged to attend young Newnham and Langford fishing in the brook; their two companions, with young Peter Hoare, came to breakfast: the whole party went afterwards to fish in the Cam. On my return I found the lads had had good success with their fishing, but young Newnham only caught one, as he thought it cruel to use a worm, and only fished with paste. I really believe he is an excellent young man, although he may in some instances carry his ideas too far.

The Reverend John Skinner

1838 The book came out today. And now I have the mortification before me, probably, of abuse, or more annoying indifference. Hitherto I have not had much of either to complain of.

Henry Crabb Robinson

1906 The question of the day is Morality. How can one be moral when so many books and papers really tempt one?

Sydney Moseley

1935 I cannot make a single note here, because I am so terrifically pressed re-writing – yes, typing out again at the rate, if possible, of 100 pages a week, this impossible eternal book. I work without looking up till one: what it now is, & therefore I must go in, leaving a whole heap of things unsaid: so many people, so many scenes, & beauty, & a fox & sudden ideas.

Virginia Woolf

17 August

1667 There was now a very gallant horse to be baited to death with doggs; but he fought them all, so as the fiercest of them could not fasten on him, till they run him through with their swords. This wicked and barbarous sport deserv'd to have ben punish'd in the cruel contrivers to get mony, under pretence that the horse had kill'd a man, which was false. I would not be persuaded to be a spectator.

John Evelyn

1669 To London, spending almost the intire day in surveying what progresse was made in rebuilding the ruinous Citty, which now began a little to revive after its sad calamitie.

John Evelyn

1684 The sore began to break.

Elias Ashmole

1932 Now I think I have corrected the *C.R.* [*Common Reader*] till I can correct no longer. And I have a few minutes' holiday before I need take the proofs in to L. Shall I then describe how I fainted again? That is the galloping hooves got wild in my head last Thursday night as I sat on the terrace with L. How cool it is after the heat! I said. We were watching the downs draw back into fine darkness after they had burnt like solid emerald all day. Now that was being softly finely veiled. And the white owl was crossing to fetch mice from the marsh. Then my heart leapt: and stopped: and leapt again: and I tasted that queer bitterness at the back of my throat; and the pulse leapt into my head and beat and beat, more savagely, more quickly. I am going to faint, I said, and slipped off my chair and lay on the grass. Oh no, I was not unconscious. I was alive: but possessed with this struggling team in my head: galloping, pounding. I thought something will burst in my brain if this goes on. Slowly it muffled itself. I pulled myself up and staggered, with what infinite difficulty and alarm, now truly fainting and seeing the garden painfully lengthened and distorted, back, back, back – how long it seemed – could I drag myself? – to the house: and gained my room and fell on my bed. Then pain, as of childbirth; and then that too slowly faded; and I lay presiding, like a flickering light, like a most solicitous mother, over the shattered splintered fragments of my body. A very acute and unpleasant experience.

Virginia Woolf

18 August

1721 There is also just come out a little thing, in 8vo, about Inoculating the small Pox, it being the Opinion of some that such as have it by Inoculation are nothing near so dangerously sick as otherwise. Experiments are to be made upon some Malefactors in Newgate.

Thomas Hearne

1921 Nothing to record; only an intolerable fit of the fidgets to write away. Here I am chained to my rock; forced to do nothing; doomed to let every worry, spite, irritation and obsession scratch and claw and come again. This is a day that I may not walk and must not work. Whatever book I read bubbles up in my mind as part of an article I want to write. No one in the whole of Sussex is so miserable as I am; or so conscious of an infinite capacity of enjoyment hoarded in me, could I use it. The sun streams (no, never streams; floods rather) down upon all the yellow fields and the long low barns; and what wouldn't I give to be coming through Firle woods, dirty and hot, with my nose turned home, every muscle tired and the brain laid up in sweet lavender, so sane and cool, and ripe for the morrow's task. How I should notice everything – the phrase for it coming the moment after and fitting like a glove; and then on the dusty road, as I ground my pedals, so my story would begin telling itself; and then the sun would be down; and home, and some bout of poetry after dinner, half read, half lived, as if the flesh were dissolved and through it the flowers burst red and white. There! I've written out half my irritation. I hear poor L. driving the lawn mower up and down, for a wife like I am should have a latch to her cage. She bites! And he spent all yesterday running round London for me. Still if one is Prometheus, if the rock is hard and the gadflies pungent, gratitude, affection, none of the nobler feelings have sway. And so this August is wasted.

Only the thought of people suffering more than I do at all consoles; and that is an aberration of egotism, I suppose. I will now make out a time table if I can to get through these odious days.

Poor Mdlle Lenglen, finding herself beaten by Mrs Mallory, flung down her racquet and burst into tears. Her vanity I suppose is colossal. I daresay she thought that to be Mdlle Lenglen was the greatest thing in the world; invincible, like Napoleon. Armstrong, playing in the test match, took up his position against the gates and would not move, let the bowlers appoint themselves, the whole game became farcical because there was not time to play it out. But Ajax in the Greek play was of the same temper – which we all agree to call heroic in him. But everything is forgiven to the Greeks. And I've not read a line of Greek since last year, this time, too. But I shall come back, if it's only in snobbery; I shall be reading Greek when I'm old; old as the woman at the cottage door, whose hair might be a wig in a play, it's so white, so thick. Seldom penetrated by love for mankind as I am, I sometimes feel sorry for the poor who don't read Shakespeare, and indeed have felt some generous democratic humbug at the Old Vic, when they played Othello and all the poor men and women and children had him there for themselves. Such splendour and such poverty. I am writing down the fidgets, so no matter if I write nonsense.

Virginia Woolf

19 August

1684   I fell into a looseness, which continued for two days.

Elias Ashmole

1773   We talked of composition, which was a favourite topic of Dr
Watson's, who first distinguished himself by lectures on
rhetoric. JOHNSON: 'I advised Chambers, and would advise
every young man beginning to compose, to do it as fast as he
can, to get a habit of having his mind to start promptly. It is so
much more difficult to improve in speed than in accuracy.'
WATSON: 'I own I am for much attention to accuracy in
composing, lest one should get bad habits of doing it in a
slovenly manner.' JOHNSON: 'Why, sir, you are confounding
doing inaccurately with the *necessity* of doing inaccurately. A
man knows when his composition is inaccurate, and when he
thinks fit he'll correct it. But if a man is accustomed to
compose slowly and with difficulty upon all occasions, there
is danger that he may not compose at all, as we do not like to
do that which is not done easily; and at any rate, more time is
consumed in a small matter than ought to be.' WATSON: 'Dr
Hugh Blair has taken a week to compose a sermon.'
JOHNSON: 'Then, sir, that is for want of the habit of
composing quickly, which I am insisting one should acquire.'
WATSON: 'Blair was not composing all the week, but only
such hours as he found himself disposed for composition.'
JOHNSON: 'Nay, sir, unless you tell me the time he took, you
tell me nothing. If I say I took a week to walk a mile, and have
had the gout five days and been ill otherwise another day, I
have taken but one day. I myself have composed about forty
sermons. I have begun a sermon after dinner and sent it off by
the post that night. I wrote forty-eight of the printed octavo
pages of the *Life of Savage* at a sitting, but then I sat up all
night. I have also written six sheets in a day of translation
from the French.' BOSWELL: 'We have all observed how one
man dresses himself slowly and another fast.' JOHNSON:
'Yes, sir, it is wonderful how much time some people will
consume in dressing: taking up a thing and looking at it, and
laying it down, and taking it up again. Everyone should get

297

the habit of doing it quickly. I would say to a young divine, "Here is your text; let me see how soon you can make a sermon." Then I'd say, "Let me see how much better you can make it." Thus I should see both his powers and his judgment.'

James Boswell

---

20 August

1813   (At Norwich). I defended a man for the murder of his wife and her sister by poison. It was a case of circumstantial evidence. There was a moral certainty that the man had put corrosive sublimate into a tea-kettle, though no evidence so satisfactory as his Tyburn countenance. I believe the acquittal in this case was owing to this circumstance. The wife, expecting to die, said, 'No one but my husband *could* have done it.' As this produced an effect, I cross-examined minutely as to the proximity of other cottages – there being children about – the door being on the latch, &c.; and then concluded with an earnest question – 'On your solemn oath, were there not twelve persons at least who *could* have done it?' – 'Yes, there were.' And then an assenting nod from a juryman. I went home, not triumphant. But the accident of being the successful defender of a man accused of murder brought me forward, and though my fees at two assize towns did not amount to £50, yet my spirits were raised.

Henry Crabb Robinson

1948   I was thinking of my mother. I suppose that her human relationships were unsatisfactory. She had always had a feeling for dogs and relied upon them for love up to almost the end. My father was dead, she and my sister never got on together, I abandoned her; she ended her sensible life with a housekeeper and a succession of Sealyham dogs. Upon them in the end she lavished all her love and care. I see that I have reached the same conclusion. Indeed, I find myself using the same peculiar phrases – they spring to my lips – that she herself would use, in her anxiety and reproofs, to my dog. I see that, in this much, I have returned to her. Owing to some psychological failure in us, we were both unable to manage a human relationship and turned instead to dogs. Dogs captivate the inadequate and unloved, and my mother's last Sealyham, Barbarita, like my Queenie with me, became the nearest thing to her heart. My conscience directs me to this sad thought. I failed my mother. She would have liked me to live with her, though she was too self-effacing and good to press such claims; she was a darling but a tiresome, talkative one. I would have been unkind, I would have gone mad, in her society; how can the young and the old be expected to live together?

Her life was drawing to its end, mine beginning; I resisted her slight pressures and set up house on my own, leaving her to a housekeeper and her dog. But I saw her regularly nevertheless once or twice a week until she died. Yes, we were fond of each other, but in the way that exists between people who have no intelligent understanding of each other's hearts. Her love for me, I know, contained a lot of awe: her tall, handsome, dear – ah all-too-dear – son. She herself was not clever. She was childish, gay, sentimental, romantic, and my love for her was as for a prattling, kittenish, sweet and tiring child. 'Do you luff me?' she would say. 'Love' would have been too serious and embarrassing a word, but it was what she meant. I did not take her seriously enough. Now I wish I had.

It was when she began to fade away and lose her faculties, when I saw that I should lose her, that I gave her, the sweet creature, in full measure, the love that she had always wanted and was now too dim to understand. Ah, how I would lavish upon her my demonstrative, kissing love and remorse, which I had not lavished upon her before although I had always loved her! But she no longer had the awareness to enjoy it. Barbarita had taken my place, as Queenie has now taken in my life the feelings of all the humans I have failed to attach and keep. My mother and myself. Like Queenie on mine, Barbarita slept on her bed and, in course of the night, growled as she moved. My mother did not mind, nor did she mind being nipped by the disturbed dog. My mother and myself; if Queenie gets as crotchety as that, *I* shall not mind either. I have gone the same way myself. She talked a lot to her dog, I talk endlessly to mine; sometimes I notice people looking strangely at me in the street and realize that I have been chattering to Queenie without thinking what I was doing. My mother and myself.

J. R. Ackerley

21 August

1862 [Balmoral]

At eleven o'clock started off in the little ponychair (drawn by the Corriemulzie pony, and led by Brown), Bertie, who had come over from Birkhall, on foot, the two girls on ponies, and the two little boys, who joined us later, for Craig Lowrigan; and I actually drove in the little carriage to the very top, turning off from the path and following the track where the carts had gone. Grant and Duncan pushed the carriage behind. Sweet Baby [Beatrice] we found at the top. The view was so fine, the day so bright, and the heather so beautifully pink – but no pleasure, no joy! all dead!

And here at the top is the foundation of the cairn – forty feet wide – to be erected to my precious Albert, which will be seen all down the valley. I and my poor six orphans all placed stones on it, and our initials, as well as those of the three absent ones, are to be carved on stones all round it. I felt very shaky and nervous.

It is to be thirty-five feet high, and the following inscription to be placed on it:

TO THE BELOVED MEMORY
OF
ALBERT, THE GREAT AND GOOD
PRINCE CONSORT
RAISED BY HIS BROKEN-HEARTED WIDOW,
VICTORIA R.
AUGUST 21, 1862

'He being made perfect in a short time fulfilled a long time;
For his soul pleased the Lord,
Therefore hastened He to take him
Away from among the wicked.'

Wisdom of Solomon, iv. 13, 14.

Walked down to where the rough road is, and this first short attempt at walking in the heather shook me and tired me much.

Queen Victoria

1947 Today is my Uncle Robert's birthday; and he died thirty years ago, cannon-fodder he was, and his name is known to a very few. Yet I shall remember him.

James Lees-Milne

---

22 August

1705 Yesterday Mr Gilby, Bach. of Law, Fellow of All-Souls Coll. and one of the Proctors in the vice-chancellor's court died of a consumption, which he said a little before he died he thought verily to have proceeded from a piece of cherry stone which some time since went down his wind-Pipe and caused a corruption in his Lungs. Which tho' it might be one cause, yet 'tis said the chief was hard Drinking. He is reported to have been a person of parts, and some Learning.

Thomas Hearne

1803 PORTSMOUTH. We dined at the Commissioners to meet Admiral Montagu's family, and Capt. Hanmar (son of Sr. Thos. Hanmar in the Flintshire Militia). A Haunch of Venison so stinking we could scarcely sit at table. A Welsh harper played during dinner, with much execution but the Harp had a peculiar sound and not a melodious one. Our musician was a tall stiff Sergeant, whose figure appeared ill contrasted to the Instrument. Miss Saxton's *melancolica*, il padre sempre gridanda – Looks at My Lady like a Duck upon a pole? When the poor old Lady is in the agony of getting over a stile or waddling in a boat. The Commissioner's House is a delightful one, but he seems to keep a shabby establishment.

Elizabeth Fremantle

1936 I've just been for a walk. It's a perfect morning. Dawn was an autumnal glow and the grass heavy with dew. As I walked along I tried to concentrate my thoughts on the necessity to escape from self and from the flesh if I was to know God. There was so much testimony that this was the way, and the only way. Self and the flesh, I thought, have only justified themselves in an occasional frolic, and then only partially, whereas their denial has led to all that is great in men's history. Even good became bad without this denial, as in egotistical humanitarians like C. P. Scott. Protracted sensuality always becomes despicable. At adolescence it seems a way to the absolute but this illusion can only be sustained by keeping adolescent. (Cf. Bertrand Russell.)

Malcolm Muggeridge

---

23 August

1742 About three in the afternoon I went to my mother, and found her change was near. I sat down on the bed-side. She was in her last conflict; unable to speak, but I believe quite sensible. Her look was calm and serene, and her eyes fixed upward, while we commended her soul to God. From three to four the silver cord was loosing, and the wheel breaking at the cistern; and then without any struggle, or sigh, or groan, the soul was set at liberty. We stood round the bed, and fulfilled her last request, uttered a little before she lost her speech: 'Children, as soon as I am released, sing a psalm of praise to God.'

John Wesley

1778 Awoke not long after I went to bed, exceeding ill indeed – I thought worse than ever and such uneasiness as can't be expressed. I really suspected after first waking I was going to die, scarce any pulse and otherwise in a shocking condition. I think I can't support it much longer – my left eye too daily empirant. Dined on cold boiled beef and currant tart.

John Baker

1778 At tea we all met again, and Dr Johnson was gaily sociable. He gave a very droll account of the children of Mr Langton,

'Who,' he said, 'might be very good children if they were let alone; but the father is never easy when he is not making them do something which they cannot do; they must repeat a fable, or a speech, or the Hebrew alphabet; and they might as well count twenty, for what they know of the matter: however, the father says half, for he prompts every other word. But he could not have chosen a man who would have been less entertained by such means.'

'I believe not!' cried Mrs Thrale: 'nothing is more ridiculous than parents cramming their children's nonsense down other people's throats. I keep mine as much out of the way as I can.'

'Yours, madam,' answered he, 'are in nobody's way; no children can be better managed or less troublesome; but your fault is, a too great perverseness in not allowing anybody to give them anything. Why should they not have a cherry or a gooseberry as well as bigger children?'

'Because they are sure to return such gifts by wiping their hands upon the giver's gown or coat, and nothing makes children more offensive. People only make the offer to please the parents and they wish the poor children at Jericho when they accept it.'

'But, madam, it is a great deal more offensive to refuse them. Let those who make the offer look to their own gowns and coats, for when you interfere, they only wish *you* at Jericho.'

'It is difficult,' said Mrs Thrale, 'to please everybody.'

Fanny Burney

---

24 August

1684   Mr Agar lanced the sore.

Elias Ashmole

1818   Arrived at my cottage. Always glad to return to it, and the dear girl who makes it so happy for me. Found heaps of letters, some of them from poets and authors, who are the pest of my life: — one sending me a 'Serio-Comic Drama of

Invasion, in Three Acts, including the Vision and the Battle,' and referring me for his poetic credentials to three admirals and 'the late comptroller of the navy'. Another begging to know whether I was acquainted with 'any man or woman to whom money was for a time useless,' who would venture £100 upon a literary speculation he had in hand.

Thomas Moore

1820 Went to Ampthill with Mr Shuttleworth. Read Ld John's book, which I admired very much, though I thought the description of ancient manners affected and many parts strained and forced expression, but on the whole lively, full of knowledge, observation and wit, but too cold and parental on *marriage* for a young man. Ampthill in beauty; but I hate the country and feel positive aversion for green fields and bleating flocks.

Henry Edward Fox

1939 A blazing hot day, just right for the treasure hunt. I was winning – I knew the last clue must mean the sundial in the rose garden. Suddenly I saw Granny almost running across the lawn, a letter in her hand, and while I was distracted Daddy pounced on the prize. He's such a cheat. The letter was from Mummy, saying I must go back to London right away – it looks as if war is inevitable.

I read it out and no one seemed to know what to say. Daddy opened his prize, a box of chocolates, and handed it round. I chewed a caramel slowly, feeling the sun on my face and smelling the roses. I thought, 'What a bore!'

Joan Wyndham

25 August

1818 Heard of a famous dandy at Harrowgate of the name of Stewart, a relative of Lord Castlereagh, who being asked by the Master of Ceremonies to dance enquired of him if the lady he meant to introduce him to was handsome, and being told she was he enquired if she was rich, and being told she had a good fortune asked if she danced well and being answered in the affirmative said, 'Trot her out.' When he came to her he took out his quizzing glass and having eyed the lady some time through it says to the MC 'Trot her back again.'

The Reverend Benjamin Newton

1821   When the news of Napoleon's death came, before the King had been informed of it by his Ministers, Sir E. Nagle, anxious to communicate the welcome tidings, said to him, 'Sir, your bitterest enemy is dead.' 'Is she, by God!' said the tender husband.

Henry Edward Fox

1897   Having recorded what has happened to-day (a crucial instance of E.'s behaviour) I hope to write no more such dreary stuff in my diary. Little Alfred was playing, just before tea-time, on the stairs leading out of our sitting-room, and he had got hold of my shaving-brush. The end of it came off and rolled down the stairs into the room, where, just then, I was sitting. I paid no attention, but after a lapse of a minute or two, E. came down from above (having heard the object roll) and began to search for the lost end of the brush. Oddly, it could not be found; the thing had mysteriously hidden itself in some corner. As her manner is, E. rapidly passed from annoyance at a futile search to irritation against the person nearest – myself; she asked me if I had taken up the missing object. I replied that I had not, but that I had heard it roll into the room. Her wrath growing, she next roundly accused me of secreting the thing. 'There's no knowing how nastiness will show itself,' she declared. The search was still vain, and presently we all sat down to tea – though not till E. had endeavoured to search my pockets. As the meal progressed, her anger reached the virulent stage (I had naturally begged her not to worry about such a trifle,) and at length she said to Walter: 'Why, your father jumped up as the thing rolled into the room, and I *saw* him take it up.' This was too much. I answered 'That is a deliberate lie' and asked Walter whether he thought me capable of lying so on such a subject. The boy, much upset, of course said, 'No.' At the sight of his tears, E. shouted: 'There, that's the second or third time you've made him cry with your ill temper.' I was very angry, and told her I would not be accused of lying before my own son. Thereupon she screamed, with a violent gesture: '*Hold your beastly noise, or you'll have this plate at your head!*' Hating the odious necessity of what I did, I turned to the boy, and said quietly, 'Walter, repeat to me the words your mother has just used.' He did so, poor little chap, with tears, and I wrote the sentence at once in my pocket-book. My reason, of course, was that E. invariably denies all her words and actions a day after they have been spoken or performed, and I was determined to allow her no possibility of that in the present monstrous instance. Still raging, she then addressed herself to Walter, and commiserated him on having such a father, a father unlike all others — who never bought him a toy (verbatim thus), and who was never in a decent humour — with much else of the usual kind.

There it is. Decisive, I should think, for ever.

George Gissing

26 August

1684   Being hard bound, I was two hours before I could go to stool, and then with exceeding trouble.

Elias Ashmole

1854   I hope I shall keep this one more regularly up than hitherto. Having now recommenced, must in earnest one would think after such a pause. Should every one keep a record of his daily acts & sentiments, the history of the world would be made out in a way that no historian could distort however illiberal or enthusiastic in his nature. However stupid a man might be could he be persuaded to set down what he thought or did, something would accrue from it. To judge by myself however many would have day after day to record blank. I have had a trouble to remember if it is one or two days that I have omitted to fill in for want of a book & now I know it to be two. I can remember yesterday but not the one before. I know them both to have been idle ones. A loathing of my vocation has seized me. I must rest. Work, work, work for ever muddles a mans brain and mine at times is none of the clearest. What have I done today – worked in the garden & weeded the back yard. Yesterday I turned a servant out of doors and we walked far enquiring for another. The day before I forget, I only know I did not work.

Ford Madox Brown

1940   A lovely morning. They raided London yesterday and we raided Berlin. I work at my broadcast talk. At noon I hear aeroplanes and shortly afterwards the wail of the siren. People are really becoming quite used to these interruptions. I find one practises a sort of suspension of the imagination. I do not think that the drone in the sky means death to many people at any moment. It seems so incredible as I sit here at my window [at Sissinghurst] looking out on the fuchsias and the zinnias with yellow butterflies playing round each other, that in a few seconds above the trees I may see other butterflies circling in the air intent on murdering each other. One lives in the present. The past is too sad a recollection and the future too blank a despair.

Dine at the Beefsteak. An air-raid warning sounds. I wait till 10.45 and then walk back to KBW. It is a strange experience. London is as dark as the stage at Vicenza after all the lights have been put out. Vague gleamings of architecture. It is warm and stars straddle the sky like grains of rice. Then there are bunches in the corners of searchlights, each terminating in a swab of cotton wool which is its own mist area. Suburban guns thump and boom. In the centre there are no guns, only the drone of aeroplanes which may be enemy or not. A few lonely footsteps hurry along the Strand. A little nervous man catches up with me and starts a conversation. I embarrass him by asking him to have a cigarette and pausing lengthily while I light it. His hand trembles. Mine does not. I walk on to the Temple and meet no one.

When I get into my rooms, I turn the lights off and sit at the window. There is still the drone of planes and from time to time a dull thump in the distance. I turn on my lights and write this, but I hear more planes coming and must darken everything and listen. I have no sense of fear whatsoever. Is this fatalism or what? It is very beautiful. I wait and listen.

There are more drones and then the search lights switch out and the all-clear goes. I shut my shutters, turn on my lights and finish this. The clocks of London strike midnight. I go to bed.

Harold Nicolson

27 August

1784   A gloomy, dull day. It is astonishing what an impression gloomy weather has on my mind.

Strother

1864   The day was devoted to looking over old letters – a necessary task, and the sense of its being a duty almost its only inducement. Some of the old letters were sour-sweet; but it was more painful than pleasant ruminating on them.

Henry Crabb Robinson

1886   A visiting wife describes her husband as a good one, and gives me as a definition, 'He doesn't get drunk *every* Saturday.'
        A lad, aged 17 says, 'My lawyer tells me to say that I reserve my defence, which, I suppose, is the thing to say when there is no defence.' Sharp lad that!

The Reverend J. W. Horsley
(Chaplain, Clerkenwell Prison)

1907   The book *God and My Neighbour* by Robert Blatchford, tells me there is no God. Very straightforward and seemingly logical. Yet to whom, then – to *whom* do they credit the many mysteries of life?

Sydney Moseley

1939   My inclinations are all to join the army as a private. Laura is better placed than many wives, and if I could let the house for the duration very well placed financially. I have to consider thirty years of novel-writing ahead of me. Nothing would be more likely than work in a government office to finish me as a writer; nothing more likely to stimulate me than a complete change of habit. There is a symbolic difference between fighting as a soldier and serving as a civilian, even if the civilian is more valuable.

Evelyn Waugh

28 August

1646 When the king was at supper, eating a pullet, and a piece of cheese, the room without was full, but the men's stomachs were empty for want of meat; the good-wife, troubled with the continual calling upon her for victuals, and haveing, it seems, but that one cheese, comes into the room where the king was, and very soberly asks if the king had done with the cheese, for that the gentlemen without desired it.

Henry Slingsby

1795 When the Ladies were seating themselves at Table, Miss Eardley obviously made way for me to sit by Her, but I durst not understand Her. Coutts desired me to take a chair at the top of the Table next to Mrs Oliver. This Situation made Fanny my left-hand neighbour and placed me opposite Miss Eardley. The Ladies drank Tea in an enclosed Garden at the back of the Woodhouse. When we left the Table to go to them, I found Fanny and Miss Eardley walking by themselves. I joined them, after some little Chat, 'Cannot we extend our Walk,' said Miss Eardley, 'a little further?' So we sauntered into the Wood and left the Company. The Scene was delicious. Fanny had hold of Miss Eardley's arm and My Arm was carelessly thrown round Fanny's Waist. Miss Eardley read to us from the Minstrel, read sweetly and commented well. She is a great reader of the Poets and has always some Book in her Pocket. I believe neither Fanny nor I much attended. Fanny's Heart beat. She was pleased with my attention. I felt happy. The reading was interrupted by Conversation. 'It is scarce possible to love another better than oneself,' said Fanny. I forget what introduced the remark. 'You don't speak as You think,' said Miss Eardley. 'Why this is the third time at least that Fanny has told me so today, therefore I should suppose she does speak as She thinks.' 'But from what she has been saying to me,' said Miss Eardley, 'I do not believe She speaks as She thinks.' Fanny smiled and said nothing. The remark probably arose from my having said Yesterday to Her among other things that I had a greater regard for Her than probably She had for herself – and the Sentiment I had repeated. Our Time of Departure arrived. We entered our respective Carriages. Miss Eardley, as Fanny said afterward, soon shut her Eyes and they had little conversation. She contemplated her favorite Planet the Moon.

This was one of those few privileged Days which I must exempt from the Number of the Painful or Unpleasurable.

The Reverend William Bagshaw Stevens

1947   Terribly upset by the announcement that the basic petrol ration is to be cut off and all foreign travel to cease.

James Lees-Milne

29 August

1800   We walked to Rydale to inquire for letters. We walked over the hill by the firgrove. I sate upon a rock, and observed a flight of swallows gathering together high above my head. They flew towards Rydale. We walked through the wood over the stepping-stones. The lake of Rydale very beautiful, partly still. John and I left Wm. to compose an inscription – that about the path. We had a very fine walk by the gloomy lake. There was a curious yellow reflection in the water, as of corn fields. There was no light in the clouds from which it appeared to come.

Dorothy Wordsworth

1873   Coming home by the underground Railway, our train got into a collision with the one ahead of us, in the tunnel between Gloucester Road and High St Kensington stations. There was a violent clap, the gas was suddenly extinguished; I was jerked on to the seat in front of me, losing my hat only. We heard no noise, except that of a lad in the same carriage bellowing in the utter darkness to be let out. He was quieted by some of the other passengers, and at last a man with a lantern came along the tunnel by our side and said the doors would be opened presently. They were so, and we walked along the tunnel a couple of hundred yards to High Street station where we found one or two persons being carried pigaback by others – one of them carried with a slight stream of blood trickling down his cheek, but apparently not very much damaged. Never heard the cause of the accident.

Alfred Domett

1923   I've been battling for ever so long with *The Hours*, which is proving one of my most tantalizing & refractory of books. Parts are so bad, parts so good; I'm much interested; can't stop making it up yet – yet. What is the matter with it? But I want to freshen myself, not deaden myself, so will say no more. Only I must note this odd symptom; a conviction that I shall go on, see it through, because it interests me to write it.

Virginia Woolf

30 August

1803   A shocking day; it rained and looked so dull that I was absorbed in thoughts and Melancholy took entire possession of my whole person. Others were likewise cross. Mr Clifton treated us to some punch. We had a nun night.

Harriet Wynne

1807   I felt extremely uncomfortable all day but walked out and dined at table. Mr Tookey was sent for in the evening and towards twelve o'clock I was happily delivered of another boy.

Elizabeth Fremantle

1810   I did not feel very well all day, but took a drive in the afternoon with all the Children – towards ten o'clock I sent for Dr Tookey, and was happily and safely brought to Bed a few minutes after twelve, of another Boy – the largest Child born of the whole lot, according to Tookey's report.

Elizabeth Fremantle

1836 Went to Tintern. Such visits do the mind positive good. Scenery like that which leads to this rare specimen of monastical architecture delights and entrances me; the inability to express our delight, the ever-changing effects of position or of light, make a confused and overflowing sort of pleasure in the mind, that is exhilarating – I was going to say, inebriating; it is very lovely, so sweet and rich, approaching to grandeur, but not reaching the sublime. The entrance to the abbey produces a complete change of emotion. I felt subdued, saddened, and softened by the surpassing beauty of the building, the bewildering and dazzling effect of the sort of tremulous light which glances in and up through the bay windows of the building upon the columns and arches. The sight of this edifice was as a talisman to evoke thoughts; speculative reflections on the tenants and founders of the pile; its actual connection with religion; fancies of the future; the use and end of life – what is it all worth?

William Macready

31 August

1665 Thus this month ends, with great sadness upon the public through the greatness of the plague, everywhere through the Kingdom almost. Every day sadder and sadder news of its encrease. In the City died this week 7,496; and of them 6,102 of the plague. But it is feared that the true number of the dead this week is near 10,000 – partly from the poor that cannot be taken notice of through the greatness of the number, and partly from the Quakers and others that will not have any bell ring for them.

Samuel Pepys

1684 I was again lanced, to prevent a fistula.

Elias Ashmole

1782 Dined at Flushing W^th Capt. Wauchope. Nothing passed to amuse. Shall associate only with those whose company may amuse or do me credit. A walk after dinner is infinitely preferable to wine and uninteresting conversation.

The Reverend W. J. Temple

1842 Thus ends August.

$$31 \text{ days}$$
$$\underline{4}$$
$$27$$
$$\underline{5} \text{ days Idle}$$

22 days at work. May the next month be a better balance.

For all thy mercies, O God, accept my gratitude, & for the troubles, may they keep my moral perfection. Amen.

B. R. Haydon

1904 That terrible sex urge! After warning boys of its dangers, I have to watch myself.

Sydney Moseley

1928 This is the last day of August and like almost all of them of extraordinary beauty. Each day is fine enough and hot enough for sitting out; but also full of wandering clouds; and that fading and rising of the light which so enraptures me in the downs; which I am always comparing to the light beneath an alabaster bowl. The corn is now stood about in rows of three four or five solid shaped yellow cakes – rich, it seems, with eggs and spice; good to eat. Sometimes I see the cattle galloping 'like mad' as Dostoievsky would say, in the brooks. The clouds – if I could describe them I would; one yesterday had flowing hair on it, like the very fine white hair of an old man. At this moment they are white in a leaden sky; but the sun behind the house, is making the grass green. I walked to the racecourse today and saw a weasel.

Virginia Woolf

1816 An entertaining German dined here who teaches the girls music and plays delightfully and sings well with no voice having been shot through the lung. A Mr Causer having been bit in a drunken frolic by a man of the name of Shipley in the leg last week is obliged to suffer amputation. During an armistice in which the Prussian and French officers were drinking together a son of Blücher gave for a toast the King of Prussia, which a French officer would not drink and soon after when it came to his turn gave Buonaparte which young Blücher would not drink, on which the officer went up to him and without saying anything struck him a smash in the face. Blücher said nothing but went out of the room and returned immediately with a pair of pistols, with one of which without uttering a word he shot the officer dead and then held up the other and said he had that ready for any man who would take up the quarrel. This came to his father's knowledge, who put him under arrest for six weeks. Rode to Bewdley, no corn cut. Write to J. Fendall and received letters from Ward and his son. NB Dinner eaten entirely up.

The Reverend Benjamin Newton

1831 I dreamt last night that I was married, just married; & in an agony to procure a dissolution of the engagement. Scarcely ever considered my single state with more satisfaction than when I awoke! – I never *will* marry: but if I ever were to do such a foolish thing, I hope I may not feel as I did last night! –

> '*Of such* stuff
> *My dreams are made! –* '

Oh! I *hope* there may be no letters today!! –
No letters: & no paper also. What can be the cause of *that?* . . .

Elizabeth Barrett

1842 My daughter was married this morning to Mr Charles Rhodes. If a man has any feeling in him, nothing, short of death, can more acutely try it than the parting thus from a child so dear to him as my darling Mary has ever been to me. May God be a Father to her wherever she goes, and inspire her husband with that ardent affection which she so justly deserves.

Colonel Peter Hawker

---

2 September

1667   From him I went to see a great match at tennis between Prince Rupert and one Capt. Cooke against Bab. May and the elder Chichly, where the King was and Court, and it seems are the best players at tennis in the nation. But this puts me in mind of what I observed in the morning; that the King, playing at tennis, had a Steeleyard carried to him, and I was told it was to weigh him after he had done playing; and at noon Mr Ashburnham told me that it is only the King's curiosity, which he usually hath, of weighing himself before and after his play, to see how much he loses in weight by playing; and this day he lost $4\frac{1}{2}$ lb. Thence home and took my wife out to Mile end green and there drank; and so home, having a very fine evening.

Samuel Pepys

1939   Awful news: they are planning to close the theatres! I rushed straight off to the New to see John and Edith Evans for the last time doing *The Importance*. Sat in the gallery. People in the street seemed really quite cheerful, and all the people in the gallery queue were talking to each other, which is unusual for the English!

When I got home Mummy and Sid were absolutely furious with me for going to the theatre. They seemed to think it was a dreadfully frivolous thing to do at such a time.

Joan Wyndham

1940   In the evening V. and I discuss the high-spots in our life. The moment when I entered a tobacconist's shop in Smyrna, the moment when we took Ebury Street, our early days at Long Barn, the night that Niggs was born so easily, the night at Kermanshah and so on. Viti says that our mistake was that we remained Edwardian for too long and that if in 1916 we had got in touch with Bloomsbury we should have profited more than we did by carrying on with Mrs George Keppel, Mrs Ronald Greville and the Edwardian Relics. We are amused to confess that we had never even heard of Bloomsbury in 1916. But we agree that in fact we have had the best of both the plutocratic and the bohemian world and that we have had a lovely life.

Harold Nicolson

1980 All day drawing. On the way to a quick office lunch pass a nun changing a wheel in Cromwell Road. Ashamed to say I don't stop to help.

Hugh Casson

3 September

1666 I had public prayers at home. The fire continuing, after dinner I took coach with my wife and and sonn and went to the Bank side in Southwark, where we beheld the dismal spectacle, the whole Citty in dreadfull flames neare the water side; all the houses from the Bridge, all Thames Street, and upwards towards Cheapeside, downe to the Three Cranes, were now consum'd: and so returned exceedinge astonished what would become of the rest.

The fire having continu'd all this night (if I may call that night which was light as day for ten miles round about, after a dreadfull manner) when conspiring with a fierce Eastern wind in a very drie season; I went on foote to the same place, and saw the whole South part of the Citty burning from Cheapeside to the Thames, and all along Cornehill (for it likewise kindl'd back against the wind as well as forward), Tower Streete, Fen-church Streete, Gracious Streete, and so along to Bainard's Castle, and was now taking hold of St Paule's Church, to which the scaffolds contributed exceedingly. The conflagration was so universal, and the people so astonish'd, that from the beginning, I know not by what despondency or fate, they hardly stirr'd to quench it, so that there was nothing heard or seene but crying out and lamentation, running about like distracted creatures, without at all attempting to save even their goods; such a strange consternation there was upon them, so as it burned both in breadth and length, the Churches, Public Halls, Exchange, Hospitals, Monuments, and ornaments, leaping after a prodigious manner from house to house and streete to streete, at greate distances one from the other; for the heate with a long set of faire and warme weather had even ignited the aire and prepar'd the materials to conceive the fire, which devour'd after an incredible manner houses, furniture, and every thing. Here we saw the Thames cover'd with goods floating, all the barges and boates laden with what some had time and courage to save, as, on the other, the carts, &c. carrying out to the fields, which for many miles were strew'd with moveables of all sorts, and tents erecting to shelter both people and what goods they could get away. Oh the miserable and calamitous spectacle! such as happly the world had not seene the like since the foundation of it, nor be outdon till the universal conflagration of it. All the skie was of a fiery aspect, like the top of a burning oven, and the light seene above 40 miles round about for many nights. God grant mine eyes may never behold the like, who now saw above 10,000 houses all in on flame; the noise and cracking and thunder of the impetuous flames, the shrieking of women and children, the hurry of people, the fall of Towers, Houses and Churches, was like an hideous storme, and the aire all about so hot and inflam'd that at the last one was not able to approch it, so that they were forc'd to stand still and let the flames burn on, which they did for neere two miles in length and one in bredth. The clowds also of smoke were dismall and reach'd upon computation neer 56 miles in length. Thus I left it this afternoone burning, a resemblance of Sodom, or the last day. It forcibly call'd to my mind that passage — *non enim hic habemus stabilem civitatem*: the ruines resembling the picture of Troy. London was, but is no more! Thus I returned home.

John Evelyn

1789 Discharged Betsy Haynes the kitchen maid for Idleness, dirt, and *Such a Tongue!*

Lady Eleanor Butler

4 September

1783 There were 20 of us at the Table and a very elegant Dinner the Bishop gave us. We had 2 Courses of 20 Dishes each Course, and a Desert after of 20 Dishes. Madeira, red and white Wines. The first Course amongst many other things were 2 Dishes of prodigious fine stewed Carp and Tench, and a fine Haunch of Venison. Amongst the second Course a fine Turkey, Poult, Partridges, Pidgeons and Sweatmeats. Desert – amongst other things, Mulberries, Melon, Currants, Peaches, Nectarines and Grapes. A most beautiful Artificial Garden in the Center of the Table remained at Dinner and afterwards, it was one of the prettiest things I ever saw, about a Yard long, and about 18 Inches wide, in the middle of which was a high round Temple supported on round Pillars, the Pillars were wreathed round with artificial Flowers – on one side was a Shepherdess on the other a Shepherd, several handsome urns decorated with artificial Flowers also &c. &c. The Bishop behaved with great affability towards me as I remembered him at Christ Church in Oxford. He was also very affable and polite to all the Clergy present.

The Reverend James Woodforde

1818 Went shooting with Mr Newsam who dined here, had no sport, at least killed only one hare at 14 shots, eight per Newsam and six per me.

The Reverend Benjamin Newton

1925 We went to tea at Racedown. W. and D. Wordsworth left here 128 years ago; the present occupants are the Pinneys (whose ancestor lent it to the Wordsworths). General Pinney's wife is Henry Head's sister. I served in Pinney's (33rd) Division in France, but was never spoken to by him then, as I wasn't under him long. To-day we got on very well. Fox-hunting, cricket, and infantry warfare were our points of contact and I exploited all three fully. (H.H. looked quite astonished, and must have thought me a bit of a chameleon.) The General cordially invited me to look them up any time I am passing that way and probably thinks me 'quite a decent young feller'. Lady P. showed me the inventory book of household effects, date 1795, with Wordsworth's manuscript notes in it. T. Hardy came to Racedown on August 19 and was much interested by it. The General remarked, 'My wife is getting quite poet-proud!' (a variation of '*house-proud*').

Siegfried Sassoon

---

5 September

1559   The sam day at non was shytt a thornderyng as was never hard a-for the tyme, for with a clap at Alalowes in Bred strett yt kyld a water spaniel at the chyrche syde, and fellyd a man on of the bedman of the Salters, ys nam ys Hare, and sexten of the sam chyrche, and more-over yt crakyd the stepull a-boyfe the batelment all of stone, that sum of it fluw owtt in pesses, that mony pepull resortyd theder to se that marvels thrugh-owt London. I pray God help! Thys was done between xij and on the v day of September.

Henry Machyn

1644   Stung I was with a bee on my nose, I presently pluckt out the sting, and layd on honey, so that my face swelled not, thus divine providence reaches to the lowest things. lett not sin oh Lord that dreadfull sting bee able to poyson mee.

The Reverend Ralph Josselin

1725   My briskly going Nagg which I bought of Mr Starr died, of a Gall of the Saddle; which suppurating, & being open'd, & the Matter beginning to be discharg'd, & stopped by an Ointment of Verdigrease by the Farrier Joyce (without my Consent or knowledge) a Gangrene suddenly ensued, & in less than 24 hours kill'd him.

Dr Claver Morris

1798   Eugenia, Fremantle, Capt. Hutchinson and myself called on Mrs de Salis at about twelve o'clock to go with us to Great Brickwell. It was a great disappointment to everybody that the day was showery as it would have been a most charming sight, but the rain prevented our seeing the yeomanry making the sword exercises etc. – . We dined under tents and had a charming ball and most elegant suppers – . Nearly all the county was there. We danced 24 couples till past four o'clock in the morning – I was well entertained but much fatigued.

Elizabeth Fremantle

---

6 September

1808   I should suppose that my nose fell of itself a-bleeding and continued so long, thought it necessary to send to Earle. Went to bed a little before two. Nose plugged up with lint and directions how to proceed, in case bleeding should recommence. Necessary, he thought, that some one should sit up: Mary Bean the person and very attentive. Released her from her attendance about five.

William Windham

1831   I have been unwell all the morning. *Nota bene*, never eat *new* honey. Lay in bed nearly all day, in consequence of that *nota bene* not having been noted yesterday.

Elizabeth Barrett

1843   Awoke again physically depressed. I got up saying, 'Is this B. R. Haydon? I'll see if I will be conquered by Cartoon or Woman.' I resolved to do some violent bodily exercise, so I moved out all my plasters, cleaned the windows myself (& don't wonder Servants have good appetites), I dusted, & got smothered, lifted till my back creaked, & rowed the Servant for not cleaning my *plate* (2 forks, 1 Table spoon & ½, 6 Tea Spoons, pepper box, & a Salt spoon). In fact by perspiration & violent Effort I cleaned out the Cobwebs, & felt my dignity revive. Now I'm safe.

B. R. Haydon

1916   I have succeeded in getting leave ... We reached London about seven. The sun was setting as I crossed Waterloo

Bridge, a red bubble behind the Houses of Parliament, but in Waterloo station the sunlight had still been intense, though of that thick, almost palpable radiance that low sunbeams have from autumn suns seen through glass. After the journey almost the vividest happiness is over: the ever-nearing imminence of London, the outlying commons dotted with children's figures playing, one I remember standing up amid a bush of dark green gorse, wearing a little red Corot-like cap.

You approach the wilderness of roofs, see the tall buildings so familiar to you far away over them, the train winds and twists bumpily over points and switches, you lean out of the window and look up the long vertebrate rod of carriages, watch them turn and tail round the curves, you pass Battersea and Vauxhall, more and more widths of line, shunting engines, pointsmen, forests of signals, the signal boxes perched right up above the line; the arch of the great station opens before you dark and gloomy beneath the dirty glass, the ends of the platforms stretch forth to meet you, you wonder which it will be, this side, this side, in you glide past the long line of porters and waiting friends: you alight, everyone is welcomed, you make your way out. London! London! I think the first piece of conscious unhappiness comes when you realize how alone you are.

Arthur Graeme West

7 September

1665 Came home, there perishing neere 10,000 poore creatures weekly; however I went all along the City and suburbs from Kent Streete to St James's, a dismal passage, and dangerous to see so many coffines expos'd in the streetes, now thin of people; the shops shut up, and all in mourneful silence, as not knowing whose turn might be next. I went to the Duke of Albemarle for a pest-ship, to wait on our infected men, who were not a few.

John Evelyn

1763 Had three bottles of Wine out of my room in ye BCR this afternoon and Waring had another, out of his room. Waring was very drunk and Bedford was but little better. NB I was very sober, as I had made a resolution never to get drunk again, when at Geree's rooms in April last, when I fell down dead, and cut my Occiput very bad indeed.

The Reverend James Woodforde

1805   Mr Delanos came for dinner, but Betsey was not able to sit it out, and afterwards her Misery began. We sent for Tookey who spent three hours with Mr Delanos, and about nine I called him upstairs he was not there long, for Betsey was soon delivered of a nice little girl. I was quite happy when it was over. She really had an uncommon good time. I slept with Emma in the little room and had a very good night. I *do* not think much of a Lying in.

Harriet Wynne

1921   Almost exactly ten years ago I came through Hereford, motoring from Rugby to Harlech. I haven't been here since then. How crude and innocent I was in those days! Ten years have brought me more success and more unhappiness than I could possibly have foreseen. But tonight I am conscious of my sterility of the last two years. I re-read my Exmoor story on Monday night, and it seemed wretched stuff. I wish I had the skill of Katherine Mansfield, whose stories I am reading with a mixture of enjoyment and aversion. They are vivid, adroit, and yet somehow unreal and insincere.

The last five months have been pleasant enough; divine weather; easy living; contrasts of places; meeting interesting people. And yet I seem to be wasting my time. I shall be thirty-five tomorrow.

My mind is sluggish; it ought to be intensely active. What is wrong with me? Is it this cursed complication of sex that afflicts me?

Siegfried Sassoon

1961   We, the English, too small for our boots.

Malcolm Muggeridge

8 September

1808   I had found myself yesterday more sensible to cold than usual, insomuch that I changed from nankeen pantaloons, and in the evening ordered for the first time, a fire. It seems to have been owing to the blood that I had lost, which Mr Earle, to my surprise, estimated at two pounds, i.e. thirty-two ounces.

William Windham

1845   It has occurred to me, and is an idea that I am disposed to adopt as a theory, that it is sufficiently improbable to be spoken of in common parlance as an impossibility that any educated woman – or rather, I should say, any fashionably educated woman, any one brought up with an express view to figure in society – can ever become a great or great tragic actress. All they are taught for their own particular rôle goes to extinguish the materials out of which an actress is formed – acquaintance with *the passions* – the feelings common to all, and indulged and expressed with comparative freedom in a poorer condition of life, but subjugated, restrained, and concealed by high-bred persons.

William Macready

1871   Perhaps this may be a memorable day in my life.
At 2 o'clock I walked to Llan Thomas. A gentleman was carrying chairs out of the house on to the lawn, a stranger to me, deeply sunburnt, but I soon recognized him as Lechmere Thomas, the Ceylon coffee-planter, from his likeness to Henry and Charlie. It was some time before the party began to arrive. The 3 Crichtons, 2 Miss Baskervilles and Miss Howard, Col. Balmayne and his niece Miss Baldwin, Mr and Mrs Webb and 2 Miss Estcourts of Gloucestershire, Tom Williams and Pope.
Some played croquet. Some went to archery. There were two croquet games going. I played with Daisy and a Miss Estcourt against Miss Baldwin, Tom Williams and Mrs and Major Thomas alternately. Daisy was very kind and charming, just home from school for good, she said. I sat next her at supper at the bottom of the side table in the window and

we were very merry. Her father wanted me to sit elsewhere, but she overruled him, saved my place, and kept me by her. I was telling her about Alice Davies of Cwm Sir Hugh. She became interested and when she heard what a treat fruit was to the sick child she sent the footman for a dish of grapes. 'Here,' she said, taking two bunches and putting them on my plate, 'take her these.' 'I do like you for that,' I said earnestly, 'I do indeed.' She laughed. I think she was pleased.

Today I fell in love with Fanny Thomas.

I danced the first quadrille with her and made innumerable mistakes, once or twice running quite wild through the figure like a runaway horse, but she was so good-humoured and long-suffering. It was a very happy evening. How little I knew what was in store for me when I came to Llan Thomas this afternoon.

The Reverend Francis Kilvert

1955   In the office 3.55 p.m. Even at this moment some dreadful thing may be happening – a husband deciding to leave his wife, a love affair being broken, somebody dying, languishing with hopeless love or quarrelling about the Church of South India in the Edgware Road as I nearly did with Bob on Sunday. And I sit typing, revising and 'translating' Harold Gunn's ms [changing the American spelling] waiting for tea.

Barbara Pym

9 September

1666   This weeke dolefull, a fire began in London in pudding lane at a French bakers about one of the clocke Sept: 2. being lords day, and on the 3. and 4 burnt down almost the whole city but a litle quarter from the tower to Moregate, and as low as Leadenhall Street, it burnt up all to Temple barre, few perishing in the flames, it ceasd the 5 at night, on which day being the fast wee prayed heartily, with teares and faith, that henceforward god would blesse us, wee are not too low for god to raise us up, and provide for us; a cheerfull audience, a good day, but dry season.

The Reverend Ralph Josselin

1857 Why time appears to fly more rapidly in old age than youth is ingeniously accounted for by Soame Jenyns. Each year is compared with the whole life. The twentieth at one time is the seventeenth at another, and that, of course, appears less; but in fact there is, perhaps, this real difference, that in a given time one does less in old age. All this day, for instance, was spent in reading less than a hundred pages of Froude.

Henry Crabb Robinson

1895 Fine, hot. Little boy's first day at school. Went off like a Trojan, and was perfectly good. Rather awed by the fact that a little girl had her hands caned.

George Gissing

1968 At last some sun has come back to drenched England. The day has been so warm and balmy that I couldn't bear to go home without my usual constitutional round St James's Park. As I strolled across the grass a man's voice from beneath a tree said, 'Good evening.' I was just ready to walk on haughtily with my head in the air when he added earnestly, 'The best of luck to you.' I can't walk across the park these days without getting accosted but always, I am glad to say, politically.

Barbara Castle

10 September

1684 By this time the sore, near my fundament, was healed.

Elias Ashmole

1940 Jo, Peggy and I drew Sallé. Jo asked me if I was still a virgin and I couldn't resist saying no, and old Jo said, 'Aah now you're a woman. Did you enjoy it?' and the model said in a bored sort of voice, 'No, of course she didn't.' I was dead tired and felt sick, and couldn't draw, and Jo wasn't too well either from getting drunk in air-raids. There was only a flicker of gas, so Sallé had to take up crouching poses, and in the middle of a pose the sirens went, and we had a machine-gun duel overhead, very exciting, so we all sat on the stairs with Madame Arcana and her dove, in case shrapnel came through the skylight.

Joan Wyndham

1942 Burgo and I went to a circus at Hungerford, too rare a treat to miss. A green awning cast a livid light as of extreme illness, not to say approaching death, on the faces of the audience and the mainly octogenarian performers, lending them a macabre beauty. We sat on rocking benches above the heaped excreta of horses, which gave off a hot smell. At one end, on seats draped with red plush, sat the children of the upper classes, with their mummies and nannies. The children were clean and brushed, white as worms, and their clothes spotless and well ironed; their little legs hung down limply in clean white socks. When they stood up they looked as though they were almost too weak to stand at all. The mummies and nannies pursed their mouths at the clown's obscene antics. The side benches were filled by the children of the proletariat, strong, active, brown and uproarious. It was the class war in concrete form and I saw it with proletarian eyes. The war has greatly emphasized this war between the classes, while paradoxically enough reducing the difference between them. Whereas the lower orders used to accept, God knows why, the idea that ladies should spend their time ordering meals and jealously preserving their beauty, now (when they flap about inefficiently with dusters) the cry is: Why the hell shouldn't they do more? Of course this only applies to the quiet domestic scene; danger and fear break the barriers instantly.

Frances Partridge

11 September

1784 It is the custom now to paint shop window stanchions yellow, and indeed it looks very pretty.

Strother

1874   A railway accident of most fearful character took place at Thorpe by Norwich last night, which has thrown the whole neighbourhood into consternation. The London express and the Yarmouth train dashed into each other at full speed, and twenty-four people were killed and about sixty fearfully injured. The Norwich official forgot the Yarmouth train was due when he allowed the express to start. It is a single line!

The Reverend Benjamin Armstrong

1916   I must try and make out what the officers among whom I move think of this war, its causes, its probable effects, its merits and demerits, and its remedies when it is over.

One sees, of course, that all the society in which one may find oneself is very fluid, and one doesn't like to hazard opinions, and they are not easily elicited.

I have mentioned the feelings against conscientious objectors, even in the minds of sentimental and religious people. Even R. speaks sneeringly of Bertrand Russell; no one is willing to revise his ideas or make clear to himself his motives in joining the war; even if anybody feels regret for having enlisted, he does not like to admit it to himself. Why should he? Every man, woman and child is taught to regard him as a hero; if he has become convinced of wrong action it lands him in an awkward position which he had much better not face. So everything tends to discourage him from active thinking on this important and, in the most literal sense, vital question.

They are, as one knows, many of them worthy and unselfish men, not void of intelligence in trivial matters, and ready to carry through this unpleasant business to the end, with spirits as high as they can keep them, and as much attention to their men as the routine and disciplinary conscience of their colonel will permit.

They are not often aggressive or offensively military. This is the dismal part of it: that these men, almost the best value in the ordinary upper class that we have, should allow themselves to suppose that all this is somehow necessary and inevitable; that they should give so much labour and time to the killing of others, though to the plain appeals of poverty and inefficiency in government, as well national as international, they are so absolutely heedless. How is it that as much blood and money cannot be poured out when it is a question of saving and helping mankind rather than of slaying them?

I suppose it is the suddenness and the threat of unusually terrible destruction, when war comes, that makes men respond so willingly to this singularly uninspiring appeal when they will not listen to the Socialist.

Arthur Graeme West

---

12 September

1773   We spoke of death. Mr Johnson gave us a short discourse worth any sermon, saying that the reflections of some men as to dying easily were idle talk, were partial views. I mentioned Hawthornden's *Cypress Grove*, where it is said that the world is just a show; and how unreasonable is it for a man to wish to continue in the show-room after he has seen it. Let him go cheerfully out and give place to other spectators. 'Yes,' said Mr Johnson. 'If he's sure he's to be well after he goes out of it. But if he is to grow blind after he goes out of the show-room, and never to see anything again; or if he does not know whither he is to go next, a man will not go cheerfully out of a show-room. No wise man will be contented to die if he thinks he is to go into a state of punishment. Nay, no wise man will be contented to die if he thinks he is to fall into annihilation. For however bad any man's existence may be, every man would rather have it than not exist at all. No, there is no rational principle by which a man can be contented, but a trust in the mercy of God, through the merits of Jesus Christ.' All this delivered with manly eloquence in a boat on the sea, upon a fine autumn Sunday morning, while every one listened with a comfortable air of satisfaction and complacency, had a most pleasing effect upon my mind.

James Boswell

1784   Mr Pitt has thought proper to tax hats with a duty of 5s upon every hat-maker by way of licence, owing, as it is supposed, by the people of Lancashire not being staunch friends to him, that county being famous for hatters. Manchester is the cheapest market for them, as well as for cotton goods, which he has taxed also.

Strother

1796   On this day, the twenty-seventh anniversary (as Gibbon, in stately language, would describe it) of my birth, I begin a register of my observations and reflections: − a task which I deeply lament has been so long deferred, but which I am resolved to prosecute with vigour, now it is begun; anticipating much delight from the review it will enable me to take of my occupations and pursuits, and of the feelings and opinions with which they were accompanied.

Thomas Green

1951   Worked as usual. Painted as usual. Ate as usual. Drank vegetable juice as usual. Went to bed early as usual.

Noël Coward

13 September

1871   An ever memorable day in my life. I went to the Vicarage at 10 o'clock and had a long talk with him on the lawn about my attachment to Daisy. Ways, means and prospects. I started off for Llan Thomas on foot rather nervous. As I crossed the bridge over the Digedi I wondered with what feelings I should cross the bridge an hour later. The whole family at home came into the drawing-room to see me and I was wondering how I could get Mr Thomas away for a private talk, when he said suddenly, 'Come out into the garden.' Daisy came into the room. I thought she coloured and looked conscious. Then we went out into the garden, her father and L. I said, 'You will be very much surprised but I hope not displeased at what I am going to say to you.' 'What is it?' he said eagerly, 'have you got the living of Glasbury?' 'No, something much nearer to you than that.' 'What is it?' I was silent a minute. I was frightfully nervous. 'I-am-attached-to-one-of-your-daughters,' I said. Just as I made this avowal we came suddenly round the corner upon a gardener cutting a hedge. I feared he had heard my confession, but I was much relieved by being assured that he was deaf. Mr Thomas said I had done quite right in coming to him, though he seemed a good deal taken aback.

He said also a great many complimentary things about my 'honourable high-minded conduct', asked what my prospects were and shook his head over them. He could not allow an engagement under the circumstances, he said, and I must not destroy his daughter's peace of mind by speaking to her or showing her in any way that I was attached to her. 'You have behaved so well that I don't know which of them it is, unless it is Mary.' 'No, it is your youngest daughter.' 'Poor little girl, she is so young.' 'She is nineteen.' 'Yes, but a mere child, and so guileless and innocent. She would be so fond of you. If I were a young man I should have done just what you have done and chosen her out of the rest. When you were here on Friday I saw she liked you. I said to my wife after you were gone, "That little Fanny likes Mr Kilvert." Long engagements are dreadful things. I cannot allow you to be engaged but I won't say "Don't think of it." Go on coming here as usual, if you can put constraint on your feelings and not show her that you like her more than the others. It is a cruel thing for you, I know, but it would be a still more cruel thing to tell her and destroy her peace of mind.'

Well, I thought to myself, whatever I suffer she shall not suffer if I can help it.

We had been walking along the path between the house and the garden and down the middle garden walk. The place is inextricably entwined in my remembrance with the conversation and the circumstances. I felt deeply humiliated, low in spirit and sick at heart. But it was a great deal to learn from her father that he had observed her liking for me. I believed she liked me before. Now I am sure of it. But it was hard to know this and yet not to be able to tell her or show her that I loved her. I was comforted by remembering that when my father proposed for my mother he was ordered out of the house, and yet it all came right. I wonder if this will ever come right. The course of true love never does run smooth. What has happened only makes me long for her more and cling more closely to her, and feel more determined to win her.

On this day when I proposed for the girl who will I trust one day be my wife I had only one sovereign in the world, and I owed that.

I went back across the brook with a sorrowful heart. At Clyro Vicarage every one was out. I left a note for Mrs Venables. 'He was very kind but gave no encouragement.' At Cae Mawr I found my sisters and Tom Williams playing croquet and just driven into the verandah by the rain. The afternoon had been grey, dull and dismal with an E. dark wind. Everything seemed gloomy and cold and the evening was irksome. I could not feel able to join in the Bezique at Cae Mawr.

The Reverend Francis Kilvert

14 September

1773 At supper, Lady MacLeod mentioned Dr Cadogan's book on the gout. Mr Johnson said, ''Tis a good book in general, but a foolish one as to particulars. 'Tis good in general, as recommending temperance and exercise and cheerfulness. 'Tis only Dr Cheyne's book told in a new way. And there should come out such a book every thirty years, dressed in the mode of the times. 'Tis foolish, as it says the gout is not hereditary, and one fit of the gout when gone is like a fever when gone.' 'But,' said Lady MacLeod, 'he does not practise what he teaches.' JOHNSON: 'I cannot help that, madam. That does not make his book the worse. People are influenced more by what a man says, if his practice is suitable to it, because they are blockheads. The more intellectual people are, the readier will they attend to what a man tells them. If it is just, they will follow it, be his practice what it will. No man practises so well as he writes. I have, all my life long, been lying till noon. Yet I tell all young men, and tell them with great sincerity, that nobody who does not rise early will ever do any good. Only consider! You read a book; you are convinced by it; you do not know the author. Suppose you afterwards know him, and find that he does not practise what he teaches; are you to give up your former conviction? At this rate you would be kept in a state of *equilibrio* when reading every book, till you knew how the author practised.' 'But,' said Lady MacLeod, 'you would think better of Dr Cadogan if he acted according to his principles.' JOHNSON: 'Why, madam, to be sure, a man who acts in the face of light is worse than a man who does not know so much. But I think there is something noble in publishing truth, though it condemns one's self.' I spoke of Cadogan's recommending good-humour. Mr Johnson said, 'A man grows better-humoured as he grows older, by experience. He learns to think himself of no consequence and little things of little importance; and so he becomes more patient, and better pleased. All good-humour and complaisance is acquired. Naturally a child seizes directly what it sees, and thinks of pleasing itself only. By degrees, it is taught to please others, and to prefer others; and that this will ultimately produce the greatest happiness. If a man is not convinced of that, he never will practise it. (Common language speaks the truth as to this. We say, a person is well-*bred*; as it is said that all material motion is in a right line, and is never *per circuitum*, in another form, unless by some particular cause; so it may be said intellectual motion is.') Lady MacLeod asked if no man was naturally good. JOHNSON: 'No, madam, no more than a wolf.' BOSWELL: 'Nor no woman, sir?' JOHNSON: 'No, sir.' Lady MacLeod started, saying low, 'This is worse than Swift.'

James Boswell

---

15 September

1657   Going to London with some company, we stept in to see a famous Rope-dauncer call'd *The Turk*. I saw even to astonishment the agilitie with which he perform'd; he walk'd barefooted taking hold by his toes only of a rope almost perpendicular, and without so much as touching it with his hands; he daunc'd blindfold on the high rope and with a boy of 12 yeares old tied to one of his feete about 20 foote beneath him, dangling as he daunc'd, yet he mov'd as nimbly as if it had ben but a feather. Lastly he stood on his head on the tope of a very high mast, daunc'd on a small rope that was very slack, and finally flew downe the perpendicular, on his breast, his head foremost, his legs and arms extended, with divers other activities. I saw the hairy woman, 20 years old, whom I had before seen when a child. She was borne at Augsburg in Germany. Her very eye-browes were comb'd upwards, and all her forehead as thick and even as growes on any woman's head, neatly dress'd; a very long lock of haire out of each eare; she had also a most prolix beard, and mustachios, with long locks growing on the middle of her nose, like an Iceland dog exactly, the colour of a bright browne, fine as well-dress'd flax. She was now married, and told me she had one child that was not hairy, nor were any of her parents or relations. She was very well shap'd, and plaied well on the harpsichord, &c.

John Evelyn

1822   I preached this morning on the Resurrection, in allusion to the funeral of Cottle's daughter which took place after the service was concluded. A considerable number of people attended the remains. Old Cottle and his family had a post chaise. Surely they would have judged more properly to have made less of an exhibition, as it calls forth the animadversion of their equals, and stirs up envy.

The Reverend John Skinner

1943   Clare Sheridan dined with me at La Belle Meunière. Clare is older, but still beautiful in her big, rumbustious way. She is affectionate and sympathetic. But she has become very spooky and talks a great deal about her psychic experiences. She says she lives more in the 'other world' now than in this. She told me that the whole of her youth had been in pursuit of adventure, or rather pursuit of love. She had had affairs with [1st] Lord Birkenhead, who notwithstanding his intellect and beauty was fundamentally coarse, with Lenin, with Mustapha Kemal and with Mussolini. Throughout the last affair Mussolini behaved like a musical comedy joke figure. He was so portentous and self-opinionated that she could not prevent herself laughing at him out loud. Mussolini was a bounder as well as a cad. Clare said she had come to realize that breeding was what mattered ultimately in men and women. Yet she is still red at heart. She disapproves of her cousin Winston in spite of her admiration for him. Earlier this year she spent fifteen hours sculpturing his head while he lay in bed in the mornings, as he does till midday, surrounded by telephones. She was surprised how off-hand Anthony Eden appeared to be with the Premier, in making lame excuses not to lunch or dine with him. One day an admiral was bidden to lunch with Mr and Mrs Churchill and Sir Stafford Cripps. The admiral sent a message that he had forgotten, when accepting the invitation, that he had an official luncheon elsewhere which he could not get out of. Churchill sent him back a message that unless his engagement was with the King, no other took precedence over his invitation. The admiral came to luncheon.

James Lees-Milne

16 September

1685 His Majesty was discoursing with the Bishops concerning miracles, and what strange things the Saludadors would do in Spaine, as by creeping into heated ovens without hurt, and that they had a black crosse in the roofe of their mouthes, but yet were commonly notorious and profane wretches; upon which his Majesty further said, that he was so extreamly difficult of miracles, for feare of being impos'd upon, that if he should chance to see one himselfe, without some other witness, he should apprehend it a delusion of his senses. Then they spake of the boy who was pretended to have a wanting leg restor'd him, so confidently asserted by Fr de Sta Clara and others. To all which the Bishop added a greate miracle happening in Westminster to his certaine knowledge, of a poor miserably sick and decrepit child (as I remember long kept unbaptiz'd), who immediately on his baptism recover'd; as also of the salutary effect of K. Charles his Majesty's father's blood, in healing one that was blind.

There was something said of the second sight happening to some persons, especially Scotch; upon which his Majesty, and I think Lord Arran, told us that Mons. — a French nobleman, lately here in England, seeing the late Duke of Monmouth come into the play-house at London, suddenly cried out to somebody sitting in the same box, *Voilà Monsieur comme il entre sans tête.* Afterwards his Majesty spoke of some reliques that had effected strange cures, particularly a piece of our Bl. Saviour's Crosse, and heal'd a gentleman's rotten nose by onely touching.

John Evelyn

1939 Tea with Rowena who was looking extremely glamorous in a powder-blue coat and skirt, with cyclamen lipstick. She has cut her hair short with a fringe, and looks totally different to those good old Holy Sepulchre days when we were both in love with Marion Gilmore (apparently M. is now a nun at Mayfield).

We went to Lyon's Corner House and ate buttered toast while the band played the 'Indian Love Lyrics' and Rowena told me she has got a sugar daddy whom she calls 'Uncle'. She says she is about to 'take the plunge' – which will make her the first of my convent friends to go over the edge. I'm longing to hear all the gory details.

After tea we went to my first wartime concert, Henry Wood conducting Beethoven's Ninth, and Moisevitch playing the 'Emperor'. What more could one ask?

Joan Wyndham

1940 This morning Sid and I nearly got bombed in the bus on our way to the first-aid post. Two dropped very close and we saw the smoke. Dovehouse Street first-aid post was short of clerks so we stayed till the all-clear at eleven. Lots of casualties streaming blood, very messy. There was a nice little doctor in gum boots who looked like Nero.

Came back to the studio to find Prudey in Madame A.'s room. *So* happy to see her again! She has been staying with the Baron in Oxford. We all drank tea and told our various experiences. Then Prudey and I went off to try and salvage some more of her stuff. I went too, hoping to find my *Apes of God*, which Leonard had borrowed.

When we got there it looked very dangerous, and Prudey said, 'Don't go in, you can't die a virgin!'

'But I'm *not* a virgin,' I announced proudly. Prudey did a double take.

'Oh really? Well that's fine, I expect you feel much better for it, don't you?'

'Well yes, I suppose I do.'
'I'm so pleased – did you use Volpar Gels?'
'No, but I'm going to.'
'You were lucky to have Rupert, of course. He's very sweet, isn't he? It's terribly important to be poked by someone nice the first time. Most girls get awful men, and it puts them off poking for good.'

Joan Wyndham

---

17 September

1580 The Quene's Majestie cam from Rychemond in her coach, the higher way of Mortlak felde, and whan she cam right against the church she turned down toward my howse: and when she was against my garden in the felde she stode there a good while, and than came ynto the street at the great gate of the felde, where she espyed me at my doore making obeysains to her Majestie; she beckend her hand for me; I cam to her coach side, she very speedily pulled off her glove and gave me her hand to kiss; and to be short, asked me to resort to her court, and to give her to wete when I cam ther.

John Dee

1916 [France] A tedious morning in the trenches prompts me to write down experiences and trivial little events which ordinarily I would not value enough to record, simply to pass the time. The trenches I am in are near G., were originally German, and have been recently captured by the British. I have not been really in the trenches for a long time, and I find the renewal of the experience particularly trying.

We got up here about 2.20 a.m. Sunday morning – a terribly long relief, for we started out for this line from G. Ridge at 8.30 p.m. Saturday night . . .

It was a smelly trench. A dead German – a big man – lay on his stomach as if he were crawling over the parades down into the trench; he had lain there some days, and that corner of the trench reeked even when someone took him by the legs and pulled him away out of sight, though not out of smell, into a shell-hole. We sat down and fell into a comatose state, so tired we were . . .

The men lay about torpidly until 4.30 a.m., when B. ordered a stand-to. We tried to keep awake merely for form's sake while the light very slowly grew. Stand-down went at 5.30, and B. made us tea, and added rum for the others; but the very smell of rum made me sick, because it is connected with the trenches last winter.

One always feels better with daylight – of this kind of life alone is the psalmist's saying true – in ordinary modern life, where unhappiness consists so much in *mental* agitation, it is startlingly false.

Arthur Graeme West

1944 What shall I write about? Shall I write about the bright morning with the sharp bird notes and the delicious spongy cooings of the pigeons on the roof of this house? Shall I write about the noises of the aeroplanes, the last flower on the wisteria that I can see mauve and pitiable out of my window? Shall I write about the war ending? Or my breakfast of porridge, toast and marmalade and coffee? Or just about autumn. Waking up cold in the morning; coming back cold through the low blanket of mist by the waterfall last night – from the pub on Shipbourne Common, where Eric bought me a thimbleful of cherry brandy for three shillings, and we heard the loud-mouthed woman holding forth on cubbing before breakfast.

In this house now – in the big part which Eric and I are sleeping in because Mrs Sloman is away, I have an eighteenth-century wooden mantel in my room, taken from an old house – then there is a china green basin and brass locks with drop handles to the doors. The furniture 'limed oak', ugly, and a chinchilla Persian cat is sleeping and grunting and dribbling on my bed. Outside the window a tractor is humming. Eric is having a cold bath, so that the water pipes sing.

Denton Welch

18 September

1804   I was all misery; the day was wretched. We had a fire in the drawing-room by which I sat all day without stirring. We had a good dinner of venison and a fig. We were all cross, Betsey on account of receiving a stupid letter from the husband, Justine unwell and I all thinking. I was delighted when it was bed time. I read Mde de Sévigné until I was quite tired. Rubbed mercury.

Harriet Wynne

1837   In looking back on the beginning of my illness, I feel sure that one of the principal causes of it was overworking my mind with too hard study, which is no uncommon cause of consumption. For many months before I was actually ill, I tasked my intellectual powers to the utmost. My mind never relaxed, never unbent; even in those hours meant for relaxation, I was still engaged in acquiring knowledge and storing my memory. While dressing, I learnt by heart chapters of the Bible, and repeated them when I walked out, and when I lay in bed; I read Gibbon when I curled my hair at night; at meals my mind was still bent on its improvement, and turned to arithmetic, history, and geography. This system I pursued voluntarily with the most unwearied assiduity, disregarding the increasing delicacy of my health, and the symptoms that it was giving way.

Emily Shore

1873   I had a nightmare that night. I thought something or someone leapt on to me and held me quite fast: this I think woke me, so that after this I shall have had the use of reason. This first start is, I think, a nervous collapse of the same sort as when one is very tired and holding oneself at stress not to sleep yet suddenly goes slack and seems to fall and wakes, only on a greater scale and with a loss of muscular control reaching more or less deep; this one to the chest and not further, so that I could speak, whispering at first, then louder – for the chest is the first and greatest centre of motion and action, the seat of θυμός. I had lost all muscular stress elsewhere but not sensitive, feeling where each limb lay and thinking that I could recover myself if I could move my finger, I said, and then the arm and so the whole body. The feeling is terrible: the body no longer swayed as a piece by the nervous and muscular instress seems to fall in and hang like a dead weight on the chest. I cried on the holy name and by degrees recovered myself as I thought to do. It made me think that this was how the souls in hell would be imprisoned in their bodies as in prisons and of what St Theresa says of the 'little press in the wall' where she felt herself to be in her vision.

Gerard Manley Hopkins

19 September

1915   I really meant to sit up and do some writing tonight but I am so tired & have such a headache from the day's anxiety and suspense that I feel I cannot – before I hear.

Sunday is a dreadful day; no possibility of getting news, but one has to wait and work all the same. It is extraordinary that one can go about one's business with apparent cheerfulness, knowing that all that counts in life may be gone *in aeternum*. I should lie awake at night thinking of it too, if it weren't that I get so tired that I sleep in spite of myself. But now – only to end each day of waiting, to bring the next with some possibility of definite news – is all that matters.

Vera Brittain

1944   Yesterday Eric and I went to the dentist in Sevenoaks, and while I was sitting in the waiting-room with him, I idly turned the pages of *Vogue* and suddenly came on my own face there in the March issue. Then I went out and bought hair stuff and when I came back Eric was waiting with his tooth pulled out and looking a little strained. We sat in the public gardens – Eric spitting blood a little into the flower beds, then we walked up to Aplin's and Eric had only green salad while I had Welsh rarebit and tomatoes and cake, with imitation cream and coffee.

Afterwards we looked at the church, into which I walked

all unawares with a lighted cigarette in my mouth. And on into Knole Park, between the two little lodges, towards four dappled fawn-coloured deer with delicate branching antlers. We climbed up towards the wonderful house and it began to rain, so we hid ourselves in a cavity under a fallen tree and lay there snugly with our feet out in the wet. The large beeches dripping round us, our cigarette smoke rising like tiny autumn bonfires.

Afterwards on towards the house where we saw that some windows had been blown in by a bomb and that a few tiles were off, but nothing serious. I wondered if Eddy Sackville-West might be lurking about somewhere, but we saw no one except an old man in pepper-and-salt with a fat spaniel. We walked right round the house, saw the little Gothic cottage and the sham ruins. I felt suddenly I knew it all so well that I longed to live there.

I thought again of our snug place in the leaves under the fallen tree, looking out on to the rising hill with the smoky curtain of rain falling into the stiff still green bracken, and the curious high squeaking of some solitary wood pigeons and then their gurgling coo. An eternal moment always dissolving which will yet re-occur a thousand thousand times to a thousand thousand other people when we are dead, who will look out in the same way through the windows in their heads and see the falling rain, the bracken, the pattern of the oak bark, and wonder, and go on wondering for years.

Denton Welch

---

20 September

1815   The next morning I set out for Lodgings. I knocked at a door; out came a pretty, lovely girl in a clean frilled bed gown, which hung over her bosom & shelved off at the bottom (which was frilled also), into the contour of her lovely shape. I was soon in a fluster & as she shewed me the rooms, was burning to touch her ripe lip, but her manner was so retired & proper, I dared not, had not courage to approach. I promised to call again, but on second thoughts, as I came down to be quiet I thought I had better go further on. At the next door out came a little, deformed, horrid creature, who spoke almost unintelligibly. I liked her rooms and took them, thinking highly of my own sagacity in thus preferring age & ugliness, being quite sure of no interruption but to be peaceable, retired, & comfortable. I passed the evening in musing on the happiness of that period of life, when the passions are cool & one's reason predominates. Ugly as the little creature was, I was convinced she was amiable & innocent, & tho I had two or three pangs of sensation as I caught her form & figure, I quieted my feelings by thinking habit would deaden my perceptions. I went to bed in a true, philosophic quiescence, thought I had escaped disturbance, dissipation, & extravagance by escaping from the frilled bed gown, & resolved through life to act on such principles of self command. I put this resolve in practice immediately by abstaining from eating a luscious pear, which I was dying to eat, which lay on a plate under my nose, but which I determined not to eat, as it would be more prudent to keep it till the next day after dinner; and as he who would regulate his passions in great things must begin by regulating his appetites in small, I fell asleep astonished at my progress in my new code of conduct, & felt my heart sympathize towards my hump backed little landlady, as she cannot excite my feelings of propriety & prudence. Alas, how soon was I convinced that tho Nature makes beauty dangerous, she generally renders deformity cunning.

About three the next morning, I was roused by the whole house shaking and soon after heard the tremendous bump & the well-known ring of a black smith's anvil & hammer. I buried my ears, nose, & eyes & head in pillows & blankets. Still the sound searched every nerve. I got up in a nervous ake, rolled my bed across the room, but all was useless, & totally unable to sleep or lie, I dressed & sallied forth. It was surely odd, I thought, I was not informed of the probability of this interruption round the corner & close under the back of my bed room. I saw these brown heroes thumping away with all their fury & totally unconscious how dreadfully they had irritated me. I called my little hostess in at Breakfast, & told her I was sorry I must leave her, as this noise was dreadful. I saw a sort of malicious pretence at astonishment on her features, & then expressing great sorrow at losing so nice a Gentleman, said I must pay for a week. To this I consented, & she seemed quite pleased. I have no doubt she got all her money by getting people in & then making them pay to get out again. There seemed a sort of consciousness in the maid-servant as I came in, as if to say 'ah, he's found it out.' If I was a cynic might I not say, 'alas! what security is there in this World,' for if one endeavours to avoid the allurements of beauty, one is sure to fall a victim to the cunning of age! I determined in future to prefer Beauty & frilled bed gowns with all their temptations to deformity however secure or age however experienced!

B. R. Haydon

21 September

1836 The devastation amongst the turnips still continuing; the like never remembered by any person with whom I have conversed on the subject. The common turnips mostly suffer. Myriads of insects appear on the under part of the leaves. They work to the heart of the plant and destroy the roots. Many acres that looked most promising are attacked; the leaf becomes yellow, and the turnips disappear altogether. There has been a miraculous dearth of wasps this year. I have scarce seen one in the garden.

William Dyott

1921 This book was originally intended to be a record of my developments through successive stages of muddle-headedness and midnight maunderings. I must try to pull it together again.

Walking along South Audley Street this afternoon, the streets half-filled with soft autumnal sunshine, I got a glimpse of the reality of my recent life; the meaning of it permeated my mind in the same way as the sunshine that was making the quiet purlieus of Mayfair so pleasant and so discreetly enchanted. Yes; I soberly accepted the fact that I have spent the rainless months since April in ruminating the final flavours of my prolonged youthfulness. This is a stilted way of saying that I am, beyond all doubt, less silly than I was six months ago. But the improvement may be only temporary. The question can be decided by future pages of this volume.

Turner informed me, late last night, that I had been 'discovering myself' in the past twelve months. He may be right; anyhow I have 'discovered' the futility of a great many things which once seemed important; and that is a valuable discovery; although it makes the composition of poetry increasingly difficult.

Siegfried Sassoon

1932   We talked a lot – or rather Rupert did and I listened – about his father and Trinity and lots of things. Before we went out he had made the suggestion that we should go to bed – we had much fun and a fight over that. It was a very cold evening and I felt very tired, but we went down Weston Lane and looked at the stars. I said that the happiness one got out of love was worth any unhappiness it might (and generally does) bring. I can't remember what Rupert said but he wasn't so sure about it not having had the experience I suppose.

Barbara Pym

22 September

1739   I began expounding, a second time, our Lord's sermon on the mount. In the morning, Sunday, 22, as I was explaining, 'Blessed are the poor in spirit,' to about three thousand people, we had a fair opportunity of showing all men, what manner of spirit we were of: for in the middle of the sermon the press-gang came, and seized on one of the hearers (ye learned in the law, what becomes of Magna Charta, and of English liberty and property? Are not these mere sounds, while, on any pretence, there is such a thing as a press-gang suffered in the land?), all the rest standing still and none opening his mouth or lifting up his hand to resist them.

John Wesley

1938   No sober silent weeks of work alone all day as we'd planned, when the Bells went. I suppose one enjoys it. Yet I was just getting into the old, very old, rhythm of regular reading, first this book then that; Roger all the morning; walk from 2 to 4; bowls 5 to 6.30: then Madame de Sevigné; get dinner 7.30; read Roger; listen to music; bind Eddie's *Candide*; read Siegfried Sassoon; & so bed at 11.30 or so. A very good rhythm; but I can only manage it for a few days it seems. Next week all broken. A minor treat today: solicitor in Lewes; then walk . . .

Virginia Woolf

1974   Catch a train to Blackburn, leaving Ted to bring up Janet and packing cases by car. I read up my background briefing on the way and do two meetings on my arrival. Am on the top of my form. This pleases me immensely, because I am determined to make this my last election if the results will let me – I want to go out on the peak, not in the trough, of my ability. I hate people who hang on, keeping the young ones out.

Barbara Castle

23 September

1795   A miserable night indeed. Alas! Alas! What a Fool to drink Coffee!

The Reverend William Bagshaw Stevens

1806   We had a man named Dovey in the evening who has been three years a prisoner in France, and is lately returned. He made a plan of the Tuilleries in artificial stones which is ingenious enough and he likewise did some very clever Tricks with Cards. Harriet bought a little Dog of him for two Guineas, the Beast is not worth five shillings – he is called Monsieur.

Elizabeth Fremantle

1896   Today is the day on which I have reigned longer, by a day, than any English sovereign, and the people wished to make all sorts of demonstrations, which I asked them not to do until I had completed the sixty years next June. But notwithstanding that this was made public in the papers, people of all kinds and ranks, from every part of the kingdom, sent congratulatory telegrams, and they kept coming in all day.

Queen Victoria

1905 People at home think God knows what I have been up to owing to my pimples – whilst I think I am more pure than most chaps, having with God's help avoided the worst pitfalls.

Sydney Moseley

1907 I must pay heed to the religion I have been brought up in . . . Everybody comments on my complexion. Is this the reward for keeping pure? If so, I will change, and be as the others.

Sydney Moseley

1949 Wrote leader on Russia having the atomic bomb which has created a great sensation. Find it quite impossible to get excited about the atomic bomb as such, can't see that it really alters anything.

Malcolm Muggeridge

24 September

1551 Agreed that the stamp of the shilling and sixpence should be: of on one side a king painted to the shoulders, in Parliament robes, and with a chain of the Order; five shillings, of silver, and half-five shillings, should be a king on horseback armed, with a naked sword hard to his breast. Also that York's mint, and Throckmorton's mint in the Tower, should go and work the fine standard. In the city of York and Canterbury should the small money be wrought of a baser state. Officers for the same were appointed.

King Edward VI

1789 Walked in the stubble fields near the Mill. The Country heavenly, and people with happy busy industrious beings, every hand employed about their Harvest. This delicious day is worth a million.

Lady Eleanor Butler

1796   The well we went to. Dr Jenner dined and drank tea with us this evening . . .

Lord Fauconburgh is afflicted by a Leprosic complaint. He told Dr Jenner that His shirt sometimes sticks to his back. Cheltenham Waters relieve him.

Dr Jenner has found that in *insane* patients He has moderated their violence by keeping them sick with tartar emetic.

He observed that a person is more liable to take cold who suddenly removes from *cold* to *heat* than from *heat* to *cold*.

Camphor water is an excellent medicine for nervous complaints . . .

Observing on eating too much Dr Jenner said let a person who has provided 4 mutton chops only eat two of them. In a quarter of an hour He will feel no want of more . . . Dr Jenner remarking on unfounded alarms for our constitution and health, said that last summer he was one day much agitated on perceiving a numbness in one of his legs, and many instances of paralytic complaints having lately happened, He concluded the numbness He felt to be a fit approaching, till happening to touch his Knee buckle, He found it pressed on a nerve, and was the sole cause of his fright.

Joseph Farington

1827   Workd in the morning as usual and sent off the proofs and copy. Some things of the black dog still hanging about me but I will shake him off. I generally affect good spirits in company of my family whether I am enjoying them or not. It is too severe to sadden the harmless mirth of others by suffering your own causeless melancholy to be seen. And this species of exertion is like virtue its own reward for the good spirits which are at first simulated become at length real.

Walter Scott

25 September

1756 Dinner on bread, water, and a little spirits, for stomach's sake: truly ate and drank to live.

I hope the kingdom of darkness totters.

Dr John Rutty

1940 By this morning I had worked myself up into such a state of passion over the absent Rupert – I hadn't seen him for a week – that I didn't know what to do with myself. All morning at the post I was thinking about him and wondering how much longer I could bear life without him.

On the way home I saw seventeen German planes in arrow formation cutting through the blue sky, with hundreds of shells bursting around them. The guns were so loud I took shelter in the door of the Servite church. As I was cowering there I heard a yell – 'Woo hoo! Joanie!' – and there was old R. lurching down the street with a cheery smile on his face, completely ignoring the guns.

'Lunch?' he said happily, pushing me ahead of him just as if nothing was happening. He was all brown and glowing, his thin cheeks flushed like pomegranates, talking about *Heloïse and Abelard*, which he had been reading at his ma's – that is, he read all the sexy bits and skipped the rest. We brewed coffee on the oil stove, while I sat on the edge of his chair with my arms round his neck. He looked around the studio appreciatively. 'Gosh, you have cleaned the place up – you know this studio's quite classy now. It used to be a howling wilderness where Jo and his cronies painted – now he'd damn well have to take his boots off before coming in! Would you say your artistic career has come to a grinding halt? I don't seem to see the usual dreadful paintings around.'

I explained that what with the bombs and working at the first-aid post I really didn't have time for art any more.

'All the more time for looking after Rooples,' he chortled with satisfaction. I choked down my happiness and got lunch ready. Rupert had bought minute steak – it took the whole of his meat ration. I hadn't had any for weeks. He set about frying the onions and I sat watching him, marvelling more and more at his extraordinary physical charm. Why the handsomest man in Chelsea and Fulham should want to sit around my dump frying onions is more than I can fathom.

Old Madame Arcana has got her eye on him too; every time I go to the lavatory she comes up in her yellow-striped Arabian coat with the dove on her shoulder, and makes passes at him until I pull the chain – then she shoots into the centre of the room and pretends she came up to borrow a smoke.

Boy, what a steak! And what onions!

After we had eaten he wanted to lie down with me but I resisted, and we crashed down together on to the sofa, most undignified.

'Now this here Heloïse,' Rupert said reprovingly, sitting on my stomach, 'she used to *glide* down to Abelard's couch – in fact she spent most of her time doing it, clad only in a loose-bodied gown and carrying a lamp. Now let's see *you* glide down to me, Joanie, ten stone or no ten stone.' Looking v. intense, I glided. 'You know I think I almost missed you,' R. said.

After that we quit being funny and made love very seriously, and I was filled with peace and delight. You can't write about sensuality mingled with tenderness and pity, it just becomes maudlin or goes bad on you in some way – so call it love and leave it at that, one of the few transcendent and satisfying things left in this bloody awful life.

Joan Wyndham

26 September

1818   Had a thorn taken out of the middle of that part of the body which Derham calls a large cushion of flesh by my wife last night.

The Reverend Benjamin Newton

1875   In the public footroad by Holland Park, I had accustomed the sparrows to come down pretty close to me for crumbs or pellets of bread, as I carried a piece with me when walking there every morning regularly before breakfast. Though I had been out of town nearly 4 weeks, they came down as usual this morning the moment they caught sight of me. A proof how well they know and remember individuals – I have frequently ascertained this in the same way since living in Kensington. Moreover, whatever change I made in dress, with a cloak or without one, in a black hat or white one, seemed to make no difference in their readiness of recognition. I believe they keep as a rule to the localities they were hatched in during lifetime – and not only when pairing, incubation &c. is going on.

Alfred Domett

1920   Eliot [T. S. Eliot] coming on the heel of a long stretch of writing fiction (2 months without a break) made me listless; cast shade upon me; & the mind when engaged upon fiction wants all its boldness & self-confidence. He said nothing – but I reflected how what I'm doing is probably being better done by Mr Joyce. Then I began to wonder what it is that I am doing: to suspect, as is usual in such cases, that I have not thought my plan out plainly enough – so to dwindle, niggle, hesitate – which means that one's lost. But I think my 2 months of work are the cause of it, seeing that I now find myself veering round to [John] Evelyn, & even making up a paper upon Women, as a counterblast to Mr Bennett's adverse views reported in the papers. Two weeks ago I made up Jacob [*Jacob's Room*] incessantly on my walks. An odd thing the human mind! so capricious, faithless, infinitely shying at shadows.

Virginia Woolf

1922   A great many things have happened, unrecorded. This has been the most sociable summer we've ever had. Sometimes I feel as if, instead of sleeping through the months in a dark room, I'd been up in the light all night. Clive & Mary came; Mary in grey silk stockings; couldn't jump a ditch; was very affable; said she liked long walks; sat on the floor; praised Clive; & half invited me to Wittering. Morgan came on Friday; Tom on Saturday. My talk with Tom deserves writing down, but won't get it for the light is fading; & one cannot write talk down either, as was agreed at Charleston the other day.

Virginia Woolf

27 September

1872   Maria told us the story of Anna Kilvert and the cat, and the Epiphany Star. It seems that when Aunt Sophia was dying Anna thought some mutton would do her good and went to fetch some. When she came back the nurse said, 'She can't eat mutton. She's dying.' Anna put the mutton down on the floor and rushed to the bed. At that moment Aunt Sophia died and Anna turned round to see the cat running away with the mutton and the Epiphany Star shining in through the window.

The Reverend Francis Kilvert

1919   Tonight we had the service of Installation of Prefects and House-captains. It seems rather a farce now, but I suppose it is really a good thing to keep it up. We shall soon lose all touch with the old Lancing, and it served as a connecting link. Last night, waiting for a bath, I had to endure seven solid minutes of the Head's conversation. He is a bore, though rather an old dear, I'm beginning to think.

Evelyn Waugh

1945   Talk turned naturally to the war – a tube tunnel, seen from the lighted platform. One was at no time aware of actually coming out; it is just that now *out* we certainly are and there is a curious silence embracing us – not an altogether pleasant silence either.

Frances Partridge

28 September

1777   My father died wanting about 22 days of compleating his 66th year. I want more than 4 months of compleating my 66th year which I think it utterly impossible I should ever do, for I grow daily weaker. The sea-bath, sea-air, or any air, has no effect to make me better, but all are flat and useless and I have neither pleasure nor emendment from them, or any of the means taken to restore me – 'tis a vain struggle and by no means worth the while, even to attempt to lengthen this poor *remnant* of life I yet keep possession of. Even could it be prolonged, which I think it cannot, it is not worth enjoying or holding, and I should be perfectly satisfied with the assurance the idle contest finished tomorrow – in short, I have no business above ground – I consume hourly, and both my feelings and my countenance make me look on myself rather as a dead than a living man. Ate a pretty smart dinner: soupe, mackrell, skate and a little bit of roast pork – ate with some relish and pretty well after dinner.

John Baker

1837 An escape took place from the Stow Workhouse last night: a blind sailor having eloped with a female pauper who has left behind her two bastard children. In the present unfinished state of the new workhouse the parties had found an opportunity of communicating with each other. But these are daily lessening so that in a day or two their project would have been baffled by additional locks and bars. In the course of the night each stole from their respective dormitories . . . and both escaped. I gave instructions to the police to look out for the runaways. The woman has left her two children chargeable and has therefore committed a felony and an act of vagrancy.

The Reverend Francis Witts

1926 Intense depression: I have to confess that this has overcome me several times since September 6th. (I think that, or thereabouts was the date.) It is so strange to me that I cannot get it right – the depression, I mean, which does not come from something definite, but from nothing. 'Where there is nothing' the phrase came [back] to me, as I sat at the table in the drawing-room. Of course I was interested; & discovered that, for the first time for many years, I had been idle without being ill. We had been walking, expeditioning, in the hot fine weather. I was writing the last pages of *To the Lighthouse* (finished, provisionally, Sept. 16th). Somehow, my reading had lapsed. I was hunting no hares. One night I got hold of Geoffrey Scott's book on Architecture, & a little spark of motive power awoke in me. This is a warning then; never to cease the use of the brain. So I used my brain. Then, owing to mismanagement, no one came to stay, & I got very few letters; & the high pure hot days went on & on; & this blankness persisted, & I began to suspect my book of the same thing; & there was Nessa humming & booming & flourishing over the hill; & one night we had a long long argument. Vita started it, by coming over with Plank, & L. (I say) spoilt the visit by glooming because I said he had been angry. He shut up, & was caustic. He denied this, but admitted that my habits of describing him, & others, had this effect often. I saw myself, my brilliancy, genius, charm, beauty (&c. &c. – the attendants who float me through so many years) diminish & disappear. One is in truth rather an elderly dowdy fussy ugly incompetent woman vain, chattering & futile. I saw this vividly, impressively.

Virginia Woolf

29 September

1590 Nurse Anne Frank most miserably did cut her owne throte, afternone abowt four of the clok, pretending to be in prayer before her keeper, and suddenly and very quickly rising from prayer, and going toward her chamber, as the mayden her keper thowght, but indede straight way down the stayrs into the hall of the other howse, behinde the doore, did that horrible act; and the mayden who wayted on her at the stayr-fote followed her, and missed to fynde her in three or fowr places, tyll at length she hard her rattle in her owne blud.

John Dee

1661 *Lords day*. At dinner and supper, I drank, I know not how, of my owne accord, so much wine, that I was even almost foxed and my head aked all night. So home, and to bed without prayers, which I never did yet since I came to the house of a

Sonday night: I being now so out of order that I durst not read prayers, for fear of being perceived by my servants in what case I was. So to bed.

Samuel Pepys

1826   They say the march of intellect is wonderful these days. Men navigate by steam, tram carts travel by steam; but this is nothing to the present fashion of travelling by paper kites. Today we witnessed the experiment made at Gloucester. For some days I had noticed two large paper kites hovering over the town. They were hoisted by a school master who amused himself with mechanical pursuits, letting off balloons etc. The wind being westerly, was favourable for an excursion to Cheltenham so he orders out his gig, or rather I think it was a four wheeled chair, attaches it to two paper kites, mounts with two or three companies and away they go, not very rapidly, not at a very regular pace, but progressing. The corners are turned cleverly by the charioteer sitting on a kind of dickey, beneath which the string of his kites is wound round a cylinder acted on by a winch. As for the kites they are careering steadily, one considerably in advance of the other, and at a much greater height. The cord attached to the further passes through the centre of the nearer, so one cord is attached to both, and both work in the same direction, thus double power is gained. The drive to Cheltenham was no doubt safely accomplished as we set out soon after and did not overtake them.

The Reverend Francis Witts

30 September

1830   I cannot omit a circumstance which occurred when I was walking through the village of South Brent which was gratifying to my feelings. The Bishop had been enquiring of a couple of old men respecting the present Curate of the Parish, and whether the Church was well attended, etc., etc. After he had done, I asked whether they remembered a curate of the name of Skinner some thirty years ago. They both replied in the affirmative, and said they never had one they liked so well when with them, and felt so much for when he went away: that they had talked of him and his kindness was to the poor. When I made myself known to them, they both shook me by the hand, and one of them said he hoped I should preach to them next Sunday as he wished to hear me again before he died.

This was not acting in the men, for they did not know me or the Bishop in the first instance, but entered into conversation with us as strangers passing through the parish, for the Bishop had left his carriage at the Vicarage.

After all the bitter almonds I am constrained to swallow, a sweet nut now and then is grateful.

The Reverend John Skinner

1863   Dined at the Athenæum, and was complimented on my good looks, but found my loss of memory of a very alarming kind. Having dined, and my spectacle-case being brought me, I took a nap in the drawing-room. Thought it some room belonging to magistrates and quarter sessions, and took the book-racks at a distance for the court. Everything seemed bigger and older. I at length was spoken to by some one, and asked him where I was. This is worse than anything that ever occurred. There is no doctoring for a case like this; nor can the patient minister to himself.

Henry Crabb Robinson

1918   I hope this pen works. Yes, it does.

The last day in September – *immensely* cold, a kind of solid cold outside the windows. My fire has played traitor nearly all day, and I have been, in the good, old-fashioned way, feeling my skin *curl*.

Katherine Mansfield

1794   Lady Inchiquin this morning described to me the death of Young Burke. Two days only before his death he was removed to Brompton, and it was not till then that his Father was sensible of his danger. On the day He died, He heard His Father so loud in his expressions of grief in the next room, as himself to be much moved by it. He ordered his servant to dress him & make him appear as well as He could. He then walked in to the next room to his Father & adressed him on his allowing his grief to overcome him. 'You unman me, Sir, by it – recollect yourself – come into me, and talk to me of religion, or some other subject'. They returned together and being seated the Young Man said, my heart flutters. Hearing a noise like rain He said does it rain? His Father replied No, it is the wind – Again hearing it He said surely it is rain, No said the Father it is the wind among the trees. The son then began to repeat that part of the morning Hymn from Milton – beginning with –

> *His praise ye winds! that from four quarters blow,*
> *Breathe soft, or loud; and wave your tops, ye pines!*
> *With ev'ry plant, in sign of worship wave.*
> *Fountains! and ye that warble, as ye flow,*
> *Melodious murmurs! Warbling tunes his praise.*

While proceeding in repeating the Hymn, He sunk forward into his fathers arms and expired. Mrs Burke came in at this distressing moment.

Lady Inchiquin says Mrs Burke is as well as can be expected, but that Mr Burke seems as far from recovery as ever. He scarcely speaks on any other subject than that of his Son, and when publick affairs are touched on says, Had Richard been living He wd. have been able to have suggested something for the publick good. That whenever He adopted any measure that gained him credit His Son instigated him to it. Thus far does He carry his fondness.

Joseph Farington

1916   [France] A fine morning . . . We built a kind of shelter during the day, and had a pleasant day altogether; good meals, but never quite enough. Peace came near tonight in several ways and filled us with a happy contentment as we went to bed in our shelter with plenty of candles. Warmth, and a misty autumn night; fairly quiet, too, for the Front! . . .

S., an officer here from Oxford, Nonconformist and, I think, religious, came back from a machine-gun course and remarked, half-ashamedly, that he had really come to the conclusion since he had been away that the war was really very silly, and we all ought to go home.

Nobody took any notice of what he said, or else treated it laughingly; but I saw he meant it, and really had seen something new. It had come to him as a definite vision, and he was a bit disquieted. This is as it should be, and I must get talking to him.

Arthur Graeme West

1935 Our wedding day 22 years ago. I got out early and tie up for V. a little bouquet of rosemary. She has no idea what it is all about. Now this ought to have offended me. But it doesn't in the least. Our love for each other is a thing which does not depend upon incidents or Annie Versaries. But how like her to be completely unaware of a thing which brings me back to Park Lodge when I dressed so carefully to go up to Knole! I would not have her different one single inch.

Harold Nicolson

2 October

1784 Rowed up the river as far as the lock, the longest row I ever took. Reflection on the folly of supposing oneself incapable of that which one has never properly attempted.

William Windham

1797 Counted in two miles, seventy-eight carriages, which, supposing me to go twice as fast as they, would give me in that space half the number more than the carriages that were in it at the commencement of the time, which would give 286 for the whole number of carriages upon the road, or that had been upon the road during the time that I was riding that two miles, viz. $78 \times \frac{2}{3} = 52 \times 5.5 = 286$.

William Windham

1938 Yesterday would have been the first day of the proclamation of war. It might be amusing to scribble down pall mall some higgledy piggledy of incidents: as they remain over; & will soon be forgotten.

The BBC in a measured trained voice: how the public was to go with warm clothing: no glasses: post cards: this interrupted by the ArchB's prayers: then cold menace: a spaced dictated message from the Admiralty to ships. Obviously we'd sunk mines. Then the afternoon (Wednesday) when all foreign stations were jammed. War broken out already L. thought. Then the statement that all poisonous snakes at the Zoo would be killed, & dangerous animals shot – Vision of London ravaged by cobras & tigers. Sense of preparation to the last hair. Some complacency on the part of organizers. How Mrs Nicholls was refused the key of the Square: trenches only available to residents. All this mixture of minute detail; with invocations to God; with Hitler baying & the Germans howling; then the composed & cultured voice breaking in, say about not taking pets. Then over all a feeling of the senselessness, futility, so that there was a dilution of emotion. A childs game. Yet extreme physical relief when peace seemed 24 hours longer.

Virginia Woolf

1967 Another conference is launched! My best hat, the one I've had for two years, rose to the occasion triumphantly, and I was amused to read in the press that I had been out specially to buy it. It is fantastic how the yearly ritual is perpetuated. Conference routine, and the press comments, are as traditional as Hallowe'en or Christmas time.

Barbara Castle

3 October

1800   NB When William and I returned from accompanying Jones, we met an old man almost double. He had on a coat, thrown over his shoulders, above his waistcoat and coat. Under this he carried a bundle, and had an apron on and a night-cap. His face was interesting. He had dark eyes and a long nose. John, who afterwards met him at Wytheburn, took him for a Jew. He was of Scotch parents, but had been born in the army. He had had a wife, and 'a good woman, and it pleased God to bless us with ten children'. All these were dead but one, of whom he had not heard for many years, a sailor. His trade was to gather leeches, but now leeches are scarce, and he had not strength for it. He lived by begging, and was making his way to Carlisle, where he should buy a few godly books to sell. He said leeches were very scarce, partly owing to this dry season, but many years they have been scarce – he supposed it owing to their being much sought after, that they did not breed fast, and were of slow growth. Leeches were formerly 2s 6d per 100; they are now 30s. He had been hurt in driving a cart, his leg broke, his body driven over, his skull fractured. He felt no pain till he recovered from his first insensibility. It was then late in the evening, when the light was just going away.

Dorothy Wordsworth

1888   Tired and nervous. Drove to the theatre at 8 to meet Gilbert and settle one or two points – arr. to cut down 2nd verse of couplet in Finale; to leave in Temple's song for the first night. Crammed house – usual enthusiastic reception. I was awfully nervous and continued so until the duet 'Heighday' which settled the fate of the Opera. Its success was tremendous; 3 times *encored*! After that everything went on wheels, and I think its success is even greater than the *Mikado*. 9 encores.

Arthur Sullivan

1944   I could not make up my mind whether or not I was still ill. After luncheon I took my temperature. It was just under 100. I decided that I was still ill, and had nowhere to go to be ill in, except my kind Aunt Deenie's. So in despair I put through a trunk call to her at Stow-on-the-Wold. There was no answer. I thought again, and took my temperature again. It was sub-normal. This, I decided, was absurd, and to take it out of myself, I would bicycle to Attingham. This I did, ten miles there, up and down precipitous hills, in a piercing east wind. I felt very much better for it.

James Lees-Milne

4 October

1788   That little Dirty village quack sent in his Bill. Never paid money with more reluctance.

Lady Eleanor Butler

1802   On Monday, 4th October 1802, my brother William was married to Mary Hutchinson. I slept a good deal of the night, and rose fresh and well in the morning. At a little after 8 o'clock I saw them go down the avenue towards the church. William had parted from me upstairs. When they were absent my dear little Sara prepared the breakfast. I kept myself as quiet as I could, but when I saw the two men running up the walk, coming to tell us it was over, I could stand it no longer, and threw myself on the bed, where I lay in stillness, neither hearing or seeing anything till Sara came upstairs to me, and said, 'They are coming.' This forced me from the bed where I lay, and I moved, I knew not how, straight forward, faster than my strength could carry me, till I met my beloved William, and fell upon his bosom. He and John Hutchinson led me to the house, and there I stayed to welcome my dear Mary. As soon as we had breakfasted, we departed. It rained when we set off. Poor Mary was much agitated, when she parted from her brothers and sisters, and her home. Nothing particular occurred till we reached Kirby. We had sunshine and showers, pleasant talk, love and chearfulness.

Dorothy Wordsworth

1934   A violent rain storm on the pond. The pond is covered with little white thorns; springing up and down: the pond is bristling with leaping white thorns, like the thorns on a small porcupine; bristles; then black waves; cross it; black shudders; and the little water thorns are white; a helter skelter rain and the elms tossing it up and down; the pond overflowing on one side; lily leaves tugging; the red flower swimming about; one leaf flapping; then completely smooth for a moment; then prickled; thorns like glass; but leaping up and down incessantly; a rapid smirch of shadow. Now light from the sun; green and red; shiny; the pond a sage green; the grass brilliant green; red berries on the hedges; the cows very white; purple over Asheham.

Virginia Woolf

5 October

1861   I am twenty-one today, the end and goal I have so often thought of. Up to this point I have been struggling, saying, 'When I am a man I shall do this, understand this, be great; now I am a boy, and from a boy little is expected.' The sum of intellectual progress I hoped for has been obtained, but how much below my hopes. My character has developed, but in what puny proportions, below my meanest anticipations. I do not feel a man. This book is an evidence of the yearnings without power, and the brooding self-analysis without creation that afflict me. I am not a man.

J. A. Symonds

1895   Weather bad. Attacked by inflammation of the testicles, and groaned all day.

George Gissing

1916   [France] Dull. I observed several more features in the common opinions concerning the war. G. said: 'Fancy all this trouble being brought on us by the Germans.' Universal assent.

Then B., the captain, remarked that it was really very silly to throw pieces of lead at one another, and from this someone developed the idea that our civilization was only a surface thing, and we were savages beneath the slightest scratch.

What no one seems to see is that our country may be at any rate partially responsible, or that those who, like conscientious objectors, refuse to debase themselves to the level of savages are worthy of any respect, intellectually, if not morally.

One observes again the 'It had to be!' attitude, which Hardy notes about the D'Urberville family.

So it is. People will not really move a finger to mould even their own lives outside the rules of the majority or public opinion. No one sits down to consider the rightness of his every action, and his judgements on political action he takes from the papers.

Independent judgement in private or public affairs is the rarest thing in the world.

Arthur Graeme West

6 October

1761   Peter Patterson was hanged yesterday, at Morpeth on account of the riot which happened there about eight months ago. Peter Patterson was a leader of the mob. In this riot Mr Fenwick of Bywell got his head broke. Nichol Waugh who came from Morpeth this morning gives the following account about Peter Patterson, viz.:

That he was with him on Sunday evening last when he was chearful. That yesterday morning he took his leave of Peter. That Peter died very penitent. That when he was hung up, the rope either slipt or broke and so he fell. That after he was recovered he was hung up a second time; then cut down; his head cut off; his heart taken out and thrown into the fire; then his four quarters were cut across but not cut off. He is supposed to have died worth between three and four thousand pounds. That excepting an annuity to his wife, he has left all his fortune to his mistress. Mr Brown of Kirkharle is trustee for the woman and children. Nichol Waugh gave me the above account at my own door at Brunton. Peter Patterson was about 74 years of age.

John Dawson

1786 Afterwards I happened to be alone with this charming Princess and her sister Elizabeth, in the Queen's dressing-room. She then came up to me, and said,

'Now will you excuse me, Miss Burney, if I ask you the truth of something I have heard about you?'

'Certainly, ma'am.'

'It's such an odd thing, I don't know how to mention it; but I have wished to ask you about it this great while. Pray is it really true that, in your illness last year, you coughed so violently that you broke the whalebone of your stays in two?'

'As nearly true as possible, ma'am; it actually split with the force of the almost convulsive motion of a cough that seemed loud and powerful enough for a giant. I could hardly myself believe it was little I that made so formidable a noise.'

'Well, I could not have given credit to it if I had not heard it from yourself! I wanted so much to know the truth, that I determined, at last, to take courage to ask you.'

'And pray, Miss Burney,' cried the Princess Elizabeth, 'had you not a blister that gave you great torture?'

'Yes, ma'am – in another illness.'

'O! I know how to pity you! I have one on at this moment!'

'And pray, Miss Burney,' cried the Princess Royal, 'were not you carried out of town, when you were in such a weak condition that you could not walk?'

'Where could your Royal Highness hear all this?'

'And were you not almost starved by Sir Richard Jebb?' cried Princess Elizabeth.

'And did not you receive great benefit from asses' milk?' exclaimed the Princess Royal.

Again I begged to know their means of hearing all this; but the Queen's entrance silenced us all.

Fanny Burney

1895 No sun, and much rain. In bed all day, groaning.

George Gissing

7 October

1660 To my Lord's and dined with him; he all dinner time talking French to me and telling me the story how the Duke of Yorke hath got my Lord Chancellors daughter with child, and that she doth lay it to him. Discoursing concerning what if the Duke should marry her, my Lord told me that among his father's many old sayings that he had writ in a book of his, this is one: that he that doth get a wench with child and marries her afterward it is as if a man should shit in his hat and then clap it upon his head.

Samuel Pepys

1663 I did keep my bed; and my pain continued on me mightily, that I keeped within all day in great pain, and could break no wind nor have any stool after my physic had done working. So in the evening I took coach and to Mr Hollyards, but he was not at home; and so home again. And whether the coach did me good or no I know not, but having a good fire in my chamber, I begun to break six or seven small and great farts; and so to bed and lay in good ease all night, and pissed pretty well in the morning, but no more wind came as it used to do plentifully, after it once begun, nor any inclination to stool.

Samuel Pepys

1758 Oh, how happy must that man be whose more than happy lot it is to whom an agreeable company for life doth fall – one in whom he sees and enjoys all that this world can give; to whom he can open the inmost recesses of his soul, and receive mutual and pleasing comfort to sooth those anxious and tumultuous thoughts that must arise in the breast of any man in trade! On the contrary, and I can speak from woful experience – how miserable must they be, where there is nothing else but matrimonial discord and domestic dis-quietude! How does these thoughts wrack my tumultuous breast, and chill the purple current in my viens! Oh, how are these delusive hopes and prospects of happiness before marriage turned into briers and thorns! But, as happiness is debarred me in this affair, I sincerely wish it to all those that shall ever tye the Gordian knot. Oh woman, ungrateful woman! thou that wast the last and most compleatest of the creation, and designed by Almighty God for a comfort and companion to mankind, to smooth and make even the rough and uneven paths of life, art often, oh too, too often, the very bane and destroyer of our felicity! Thou not only takest away our happiness, but givest us, in lieu thereof, trouble and vexation of spirit.

Thomas Turner

1895   A very bad night and much suffering. To-day sent for Dr Beaumont, who came and prescribed.

George Gissing

8 October

1767   The most shocking rainy Day I ever remember. Pray God send us better Weather. Rained all Day long without Intermission, & sometimes pouring.

The Reverend William Cole

1895   Dull weather. My ailment improved. Find that Dr Beaumont a decent fellow. Knows my books.

George Gissing

1898   *Leeds*. Last day of Festival. After last performance, the Chorus cheered me so tremendously, that I suddenly broke down, and ran off the orchestra crying like a child. When I came out of my room again, *all* the Chorus was waiting for me, and I shook hands with all! Then went and had a light supper at Albani's, and at 11.10 saw the Band off in their Special. Red and blue fire, and cheering as usual. When at supper was surprised by a serenade (by about 30 of the male chorus). I invited them in, gave them champagne and cigars, and they sang half a dozen pieces, retiring at 1 a.m. Went to bed tired – rather a trying day.

Arthur Sullivan

1946 In the church, the great gold pendulum swung slowly and threateningly, as if it were a giant's club foot, swinging to and fro idly in the dusk, while he waited, planning some treachery and death.

Just at the door was a lame woman behind a table heaped with apples, marrows, chrysanthemums, wheat and roses. I could see her surgical boot under the heap of fruits and flowers. She wore glasses too, and perhaps these gave me the notion that she was playing at being a schoolmistress who had ordered all her unruly charges up to the desk for punishment. I imagined her beating the fat bare bottoms of the marrows, pulling the shaggy gypsy hair of the chrysanthemums, slapping the already tingling cheeks of the apples. But what she said when she really opened her mouth was, 'Thanks, Vera' (or some such name as that), 'they'll be an enormous help.' Great stress on the 'enormous'.

Now as I write, I wonder if many of us ever think that, while we are talking, moving about our daily business, some stranger may be near us, listening, watching, melting away to write our words down in his little book at home, there to fix them as long as the ink and paper last, or longer still if they are found, printed and scattered broadcast all over the land.

Denton Welch

9 October

1775 My wife having been seized with her pains in the night, I got up about three o'clock, and between four and five Dr Young came. He and I sat upstairs mostly till between three and four, when, after we had dined, her labour became violent. I was full of expectation, and meditated curiously on the thought that it was already certain of what sex the child was, but that I could not have the least guess on which side the probability was. Miss Preston attended my wife close. Lady Preston came several times to inquire, but did not go into the room. I did not feel so much anxiety about my wife now as on former occasions, being better used to an inlying. Yet the danger was as great now as ever. I was easier from the same deception which affects a soldier who has escaped in several battles. She was very ill. Between seven and eight I went into the room. She was just delivered. I heard her say, 'God be thanked for whatever he sends.' I supposed then the child was a daughter. But she herself had not then seen it. Miss Preston said, 'Is it a daughter?' 'No,' said Mrs Forrest, the nurse-keeper, 'It's a son.' When I had seen the little man I said that I should now be so anxious that probably I should never again have an easy hour. I said to Dr Young with great seriousness, 'Doctor, Doctor, let no man set his heart upon anything in this world but land or heritable bonds; for he has no security that anything else will last as long as himself.' My anxiety subdued a flutter of joy which was in my breast. I wrote several letters to announce my son's birth. I indulged some imaginations that he might perhaps be a great man. Worthy Grange came and cordially congratulated me. He and Dr Young and Lady Preston and Miss Preston supped with me.

I have resolved to keep a journal of my life every day from this important era in my family, and I shall never omit putting down something of each day's history. To record fully and minutely how every hour was employed would be an intolerable labour, or would prevent action in the great measure. If I can look back and see how my life has been passed, by having so many marks of each day preserved, it is enough. I shall try to register the state of my mind, and although I am now writing this journal from short notes on the 24 of October, I am resolved for the future to put down the marks of each day before I sleep, or at latest the day after. I may at times make a review of a period and try to form something general out of a number of various ideas, and I think it would be agreeable to have my life drawn out in tables: by months or years, by my progress in knowledge, or by any other plans. I was this night most devoutly grateful to God.

James Boswell

10 October

1664 This day by the blessing of God, my wife and I have been married nine years – but my head being full of business, I did not think of it, to keep it in any extraordinary manner. But bless God for our long lives and loves and health together, which the same God long continue, I wish from my very heart.

Samuel Pepys

1839 After dinner my Cousins came in, in spite of their *négligé*, and I presented them to Lord Melbourne. I sat on the sofa with Lady Clanricarde, Lord Melbourne sitting near me, and Ernest near us and Albert opposite – (*he* is so handsome and pleasing), and several of the ladies and gentlemen round the sofa. I asked Lord M. if he thought Albert like me, which he is thought (and which is an immense compliment to me). 'Oh! yes, he is,' said Lord M., 'it struck me at once.'

Queen Victoria

1894 As examples of the kind of torment I am silently bearing all these days and years, I will set down two stories, of recent date.
1. In coming to live in the house, which I have furnished with special view to E.'s wishes and vanities, I made it my one request that she would keep out of the kitchen and not quarrel with the servant. After the servant's arrival (and she is very hard-working) I hear tumult from the kitchen. There stands E. cleaning a pair of boots, and railing at the servant in her wonted way. I had to put a stop to that by an outbreak of fury; nothing else would have availed; and this will only be effectual for a week.
2. To-day, the little boy has not been very well, owing to wet weather. At eight o'clock to-night, as E. did not come down to supper, I went quietly to the bedroom door, to listen, as I often do, whether the boy was asleep. To my amazement I heard E. call out 'Stop your noise, you little beast!' This to the poor little chap, because he could not get to sleep. And why not? Because the flaring light of a lamp was in the room. I have begged – begged – again and again that she will *never* take a lamp into the bedroom, but she is too lazy to light a candle, and then uses such language as I have written.

But for my poor little boy, I would not, and could not, live with her for another day. I have no words for the misery I daily endure from her selfish and coarse nature.

George Gissing

1919   This morning I tore out and destroyed all the first part of this diary about the holidays. There was little worth preserving and a very great deal that could not possibly be read and was really too dangerous without being funny, so all this book, now reduced to a very meagre pamphlet, must be this term and I shall have to be wiser next holidays in what I record.

Evelyn Waugh

11 October

1831   My love of solitude is growing with my growth. I am inclined to shun the acquaintance of those whom I do not like & love; on account of the *ennui*; & the acquaintance of those whom I might like & love – on account of the *pain*! – Oh the pain attendant on liking & loving, may seem a little cloud – but it blots from us all the light of the sun!! –

Elizabeth Barrett

1839   Got up at ½ p. 9 and breakfasted at 10. Wrote to Lord Melbourne. Signed. My dear Cousins came to my room and Albert gave me letters from Vecto, Louise, Uncle Ernest, and Uncle Ferdinand. They remained some little time in my room and really are charming young men; Albert really is quite charming, and so excessively handsome, such beautiful blue eyes, an exquisite nose, and such a pretty mouth with delicate moustachios and slight but very slight whiskers; a beautiful figure, broad in the shoulders and a fine waist. At about ½ p. 10 dancing began. I danced 5 quadrilles; 1. with Ernest; 2. with dearest Albert, who dances so beautifully; 3. with Lord Alfred; 4. with Ernest; and 5. with dearest Albert again.

Queen Victoria

1950   'Are you lost or eternally saved?' This was on a sandwich board being carried out in Regent Street by a young man. I frowned at it, because it isn't really right to ask such intimate questions in public. The young man smiled.
'It's all right,' he said. 'It ain't meant for you.'

J. R. Ackerley

12 October

1660 This morning I showed the King the young children which Dr Warner had preserved. The one was a male infant about 4 months, who was cut out of a woman's belly in Covent Garden (she dying of a consumption) and had been (now four years past) luted up in a glass, and preserved by a liquor of his preparation from putrefaccon, the flesh not so much as rumpled, but plump as it was when taken out of ye wombe. The other was 2 girls joyned together by the breast and belly (which monster was borne about the king's coming in), they were dryed, and preserved with spices.

Elias Ashmole

1796 Johnson the Watchmaker I called on this morning. I asked him how he preserved his health being so constantly employed in a sedentary business. He said by abstemiousness. That He never eats so much as He could, and when He finds himself a little indisposed He reduces the quantity of his usual allowance. He never takes Physick. He eats water gruel for breakfast – drinks half a pint at night. He scarcely knows what it is now to feel very hungry. Sometimes He is low and faint with a sinking of the stomach: but rest from business for a day restores him. He drinks a glass of cold water every morning when He gets up. Dr Fothergill of Bath told him that would carry of accumulating bile.

Joseph Farington

1905 Still resolving to be an author.
Toynbee Hall. Heard Sir John Gorst on Free Medical Aid. Met Loretta going to business, but hardly a second's stop, I think it is indeed goodbye. My love is dead – a natural death, as a writer in *Smith's Weekly* replies to an 'infatuated youth' of 17. Farewell, Goddess of my boyhood! Act 2 has indeed commenced.

Vegetarian dinner. Three courses for sixpence: soup, lentil fritter, apple tart.

Sydney Moseley

13 October

1663   *Rules for my health.* 1. To begin to keep myself warm as I can. 2. Strain as little as ever I can backwards, remembering that my pain will come by and by, though in the very straining I do not feel it. 3. Either by physic forward or by clyster backward, or both ways, to get an easy and plentiful going to stool and breaking of wind. 4. To begin to suspect my health immediately when I begin to become costive and bound, and by all means to keep my body loose, and that to obtain presently after I find myself going to the contrary.

Samuel Pepys

1777   There is such a sameness in my life at present it is not worth while to keep a Journal. I am afraid it is likely to continue longer than I could wish it, as no proposals have been yet made to me concerning my future way of life. I imagine my Father expects I stall stay at home in my present dependent situation. I cannot bear it. Though at present his behaviour is very kind and in some respects indulgent, but that moroseness he observes to some of the family is very disagreeable to me. I expect something of the same sort as soon as the first gust of paternal affection subsides, but I am determined to stay with seeming patience till April next, and behave in such a manner as not to give any just offence. I call this waiting the Chapter of Accidents, something fortunate may happen. (Mem. Never to have anything to do with my Relations, I know their dispositions only too well. Some of them begin to hint at my poverty already. I must be patient and if possible, Silent.)

Nicholas Cresswell

1975   Spent all morning rehearsing the first scene of *Hamlet* – four hours – and it was a wonderful experience. It's really why I do this job. Not for performances – not for plays – not for money – but for the satisfaction of having a really good rehearsal where the excitement of discovery spreads from actor to actor.

Peter Hall

14 October

1663   After dinner my wife and I, by Mr Rawlinsons conduct, to the Jewish Synagogue – where the men and boys in their Vayles, and the women behind a lettice out of sight; and some things stand up, which I believe is their Law, in a press, to which all coming in do bow; and at the putting on their veils do say something, to which others that hear them do cry Amen, and the party doth kiss his veil. Their service all in a singing way, and in Hebrew. And anon their Laws, that they take out of the press, is carried by several men, four or five, several burthens in all, and they do relieve one another, or whether it is that everyone desires to have the carrying of it, I cannot tell. Thus they carried it round, round about the room while such a service is singing. And in the end they had a prayer for the King, which they pronounced his name in Portugall; but the prayer, like the rest, in Hebrew. But Lord, to see the disorder, laughing, sporting, and no attention, but confusion in all their service, more like Brutes then people knowing the true God, would make a man forswear ever seeing them more; and endeed, I never did see so much, or could have imagined there had been any religion in the whole world so absurdly performed as this.

Samuel Pepys

1900   Have been here just a fortnight, and what have I done? Little more than nothing, first from illness and physical incapability, secondly from *brooding* and nervous terror about myself. Practically I have done nothing *for a month*. Have now finished and framed 1st Act, and they are rehearsing it.

Arthur Sullivan

1922   As for my views about the success of Jacob [*Jacob's Room*], what are they? I think we shall sell 500: it will then go on slowly, & reach 800 by June. It will be highly praised in some places for 'beauty'; will be crabbed by people who want human character. The only review I am anxious about is the one in the Supt.: not that it will be the most intelligent, but it will be the most read & I cant bear people to see me downed in public. The W[*estminster*] G[*azette*] will be hostile; so, very likely, the *Nation*. But I am perfectly serious in saying that nothing budges me from my determination to go on, or alters my pleasure, so whatever happens, though the surface may be agitated, the centre is secure.

Virginia Woolf

1943 Yesterday Italy declared war on Germany. What a strange mad war. A pity they didn't choose our side three years ago.

I am a wretched melancholy creature when I would like to be noble and strong and very intelligent. I lie in a hot bath brooding about G. (yes I still do in spite of putting him right out of my life) when I ought to be thinking about the Metaphysicals in a scholarly way or planning a great comic novel.

Barbara Pym

15 October

1756 This is the day on which I was married and it is now three years since. Doubtless many have been the disputes which have happened between my wife and myself during the time, and many have been the afflictions which it has pleased God to lay upon us, and which we may have justly deserved by the many anemosityes and desentions which have been continually fermented between us and our friends, from allmost the very day of our marriage; but I may now say with the holy Psalmist, 'It is good for us that we have been afflicted'; for, thanks be to God, we now begin to live happy; and I am thoroughly persuaded, if I know my own mind, that if I was single again, and at liberty to make another choice, I should do the same – I mean make her my wife who is so now.

Thomas Turner

1839 At about ½ p. 12 I sent for Albert; he came to the Closet where I was alone, and after a few minutes I said to him, that I thought he must be aware *why* I wished them to come here – and that it would make me *too happy* if he would consent to what I wished (to marry me). We embraced each other, and he was *so* kind, *so* affectionate. I told him I was quite unworthy of him – he said he would be very happy '*das Leben mit dir zu zubringen*', and was so kind, and seemed so happy, that I really felt it was the happiest brightest moment in my life. I told him it was a great sacrifice – which he wouldn't allow; I then told him of the necessity of keeping it a secret, except to his father and Uncle Leopold and Stockmar, to whom he said he would send a Courier next day – and also that it was to be as early as the beginning of February. I then told him to fetch Ernest, which he did and he congratulated us both and seemed very happy. I feel the happiest of human beings.

Queen Victoria

1900   *Lovely day* . . . I am sorry to leave such a lovely day.

Arthur Sullivan
[Final Entry]

1932   Today I must always remember I suppose. I went to tea with Rupert (and ate a pretty colossal one) – and he with all his charm, eloquence and masculine wiles, persuaded . . . [Here several pages have been torn out.]

Barbara Pym

16 October

1665   Thence I walked to the Tower. But Lord, how empty the streets are, and melancholy, so many poor sick people in the streets, full of sores, and so many sad stories overheard as I walk, everybody talking of this dead, and that man sick, and so many in this place, and so many in that. And they tell me that in Westminster there is never a physitian, and but one apothecary left, all being dead – but that there are great hopes of a great decrease this week: God send it.

Samuel Pepys

1834   Good God! I am just returned from the terrific burning of the Houses of Lords and Commons. Mary & I went in a cab and drove over the Bridge. From the bridge it was sublime. We alighted & went into the room of a public house, which was full. To witness the feeling among the people was extraordinary – the jokes and radicalism were universal. If Ministers had heard the shrewd sense & intelligence of these drunken remarks! I hurried Mary away. Good God, and are that throne & tapestry gone – with all their associations!

The comfort is there is now a better prospect of painting a House of Lords. Lord Grey said there was no intention of taking the tapestry down – little did he think how soon it would be.

It is really awful & omenous – one does not like to think. 'There is no House of Lords,' said one of the half-drunken fellows; 'they are extinguished, Sir.'

B. R. Haydon

1940 When we emerged into the Fulham Road this morning there didn't seem to be much of it left – they'd certainly buggered it up! The whole place was a shambles like the last days of Pompeii, with shop windows shattered and their goods destroyed, the road thick with glass and the air with dust. Tulley's has been burnt out and there are two houses down in Limerston Street. People still digging for bodies. Huge crater outside the tobacconist with a burst water main spouting in it. Poor old Redcliffe Road has lost another two houses, three bodies in the wreckage and my skylight broken.

As I approached number 48 there was a huge explosion and the time bomb finally went off behind 37; black smoke hung in the air and everyone ran as big bits of masonry hurtled towards us. The studio looked very dirty with bits of glass everywhere.

Went off to see if Rupert had been hurt but met him halfway – all that was wrong with him was a chill in his stomach, which he'd caught last week from leaping naked out of bed and putting out a fire bomb in his mother's garden by peeing on it. He was wearing his famous black overcoat that he used to impress clients with when he was in advertising. It hangs down to the pavement like a box all round him and has such huge padded shoulders that old ladies in buses turn pale when they lean up against him and half of him collapses.

While he was rather unwillingly patching up my skylight, Madame Arcana came up, pale and ghastly after the night's terrors, and said she hadn't been able to sleep because she had gone to bed in her stays, and when she had finally dozed off she dreamt that Aleister Crowley was trying to rape her, and woke up in a cold sweat just as the time bomb went off.

Joan Wyndham

17 October

1671 Next morning I went to see Sir Tho. Browne (with whom I had some time corresponded by letter, tho' I had never seen him before). His whole house and garden being a paradise and cabinet of rarities, and that of the best collection, especially medails, books, plants, and natural things. Amongst other curiosities Sir Thomas had a collection of the eggs of all the foule and birds he could procure, that country (especially the promontary of Norfolck) being frequented, as he said, by severall kinds which seldome or never go farther into the land, as cranes, storkes, eagles, and variety of water-foule. He led me to see all the remarkable places of this ancient Citty, being one of the largest, and certainly, after London, one of the noblest of England, for its venerable Cathedrall, number of stately churches, cleanesse of the streetes, and buildings of flints so exquisitely headed and squared as I was much astonish'd at; but he told me they had lost the art of squaring the flints, in which they once so much excell'd, and of which the churches, best houses, and walls, are built. The Castle is an antique extent of ground, which now they called Marsfield, and would have ben a fitting area to have plac'd the Ducal palace in. The suburbs are large, the prospects sweete, with other amenities, not omitting the flower gardens, in which all the inhabitants excel. The fabric of stuffs brings a vast trade to this populous towne.

I observed that most of the Church-yards (tho' some of them large enough) were filled up with earth, or rather the congestion of dead bodies one upon another, for want of earth, even to the very top of the walls, and some above the walls, so as the Churches seemed to be built in pitts.

John Evelyn

1793 Rose at ½ past 7 – morning hazy – much concerned at an acct. in the newspaper of the death of John Hunter, the excellent surgeon, to whom I was greatly obliged in the course of last summer for his advice &c on acct. on an incested Tumour on my Back, which He removed. Mr Hunter was in the Council room at St Georges Hospital and was suddenly taken ill and carried home in a close chair, expired about two o'clock. He mentioned to me once, that He had some obstruction or complaint abt. his Heart which He was well assured would cause his death *suddenly*, at some period.

Joseph Farington

1834 London. Went to see the ruins of the Houses of Lords and Commons, burnt down last night and still burning.

Colonel Peter Hawker

1908 It is one o'clock in the morning, but I cannot retire 'ere I write to relieve a full heart. I have just returned from seeing Goethe's *Faust* at His Majesty's, and I was much moved by it. I have seen my ideal love tonight. It is in the character of Margaret, so admirably acted by Miss Marie Lohr.

Sydney Moseley

---

18 October

1818 Sheridan once told Rogers of a scene that occurred in a French theatre in 1772, where two French officers stared a good deal at his wife, and S., not knowing a word of French, could do nothing but put his arms a-kimbo and look bluff and defying at them, which they, not knowing a word of English, could only reply to by the very same attitude and look. He once mentioned to Rogers that he was aware he ought to have made a love scene between Charles and Maria in the *School* *for Scandal*; and *would* have done it, but that the actors who played the parts were not able to do such a scene justice.

Thomas Moore

1834   Accounts arrived of the total destruction of the two Houses of Parliament by fire; it broke out on the evening of the 16th, but how occasioned, not yet discovered. May it not be an indication of Divine Providence to the reformers of the lower House to reform themselves instead of reforming the habits of the people by the encouragement given to insubordination and the neglect of the religious principles of their forefathers.

William Dyott

1924   Last night I had a letter from a solicitor and notary at Ayr telling me that Professor Grierson of Edinburgh University had awarded me the Tait Black Novel Prize for 1923 for *Riceyman Steps*. Money: £141, and asking me if I would accept it! I replied that I would. This is the first prize for a book I ever had.

Arnold Bennett

1944   Today I had a letter from Doubleday & Doran asking me to submit my new book to them for publication in America, the New York directors admiring my stories in *Horizon*. Eric and I were sitting up in bed, having breakfast, and we made jokes about earning the rent and ending up with silver-plated Rolls-Royces. The myth of American riches will last for ever in Europe.

Denton Welch

---

19 October

1827   Got hold of Mr Millet, another of the persons I came to look after; walked with him to his house; his wife, who is dead, was intimate with Miss Chaworth, and saw a good deal of Byron when he was a boy: said that Miss C. did not like Byron, nor did his wife, nor any of the girls. Showed me a poem in Byron's handwriting, written apparently soon after he left Harrow: doubted at first whether it was really Byron's handwriting, but on further examination concluded that it was: took a copy of it, preserving all its bad spelling. A note at my hotel directed 'To the immortal Thomas Moore, Esq.'; only think of an immortal *esquire*; expected to hear the chambermaids cry out, 'Some hot water for the immortal gentleman in No. 18.'

Thomas Moore

1827   Again to the sessions, upwards of a hundred prisoners for trial; how melancholy the increase of crime; when my brother was sheriff in the year 1798, at the spring sessions there was not one prisoner for trial. I observed what I considered a curiosity at Teddesley; green peas in as high perfection as in July.

William Dyott

1838   Put leeches on my throat, and whilst they were adhering read the romantic play translated by Mrs Sloman, which promises very well.

William Macready

1881   Gilbert came and sketched out an idea of a new piece [*Iolanthe*]. Lord Chancellor, Commander-in-Chief, Peers, Fairies, etc. Funny, but at present vague.

Arthur Sullivan

1937   Well: I will go to Maples about chaircovers; to Highgate to see Roger's house; & dream today, because I must unscrew my head & somehow freshen up if I am to write, to live, to go through the next lap with zest, not like old sea weed.

Virginia Woolf

20 October

1779   Last Tuesday, at the request of Lady S—, who patronized a poor actor, we all went to the play — which was Dryden's

Tempest – and a worse performance have I seldom seen. Shakspeare's *Tempest*, which for fancy, invention, and originality, is at the head of beautiful improbabilities, is rendered by the additions of Dryden a childish chaos of absurdity and obscenity; and the grossness and awkwardness of these poor unskilful actors rendered all that ought to have been obscure so shockingly glaring, that there was no attending to them without disgust. All that afforded me any entertainment was looking at Mr Thrale, who turned up his nose with an expression of contempt at the beginning of the performance, and never suffered it to return to its usual place till it was ended!

Fanny Burney

1788 That great worthless old Tyrant the Turkey Cock killed our beautiful Jersey spangled Cock who was the most perfect fowl for shape, size and plumage I ever beheld. A silver white with golden feathers.

Lady Eleanor Butler

1790 It is precisely a year this day since we received Mrs Barrett here. We have never had reason for a single instant's regret since we broke off with those false and perfidious Friends. *Au contraire – au contraire.*

Lady Eleanor Butler

1830 Staffordshire sessions. A remarkable warm day. I felt it quite uncomfortable as I rode Roany, who was ever a rough goer. A very full bench of magistrates, and a full bar of prisoners. No crimes of great magnitude, and crime will certainly increase from the effect of the new Beer Bill, which came into operation on the 18th. The state of the country is sufficiently demoralized without further incitement; and the effect of the Beer Bill must, to a certainty, add to the licentiousness of the populace, by affording them the means to be dissolute, from the readily obtaining sufficient to get drink at a cheap rate. Licensing Ale Shops in every village, which must become a rendezvous for vice in all its bearings!

William Dyott

21 October

1785   Bought Herrings and Oysters. Loud and violent altercation between Mary and the Fisherman. Mary Triumphant.

Lady Eleanor Butler

1855   I remember Charles Buller saying of the Duchess de Praslin's murder, 'What could a poor fellow do with a wife who kept a journal but murder her?' There was a certain truth hidden in this light remark. Your journal all about feelings aggravates whatever is factitious and morbid in you; that I have made experience of. And now the only sort of journal I would keep should have to do with what Mr Carlyle calls 'the facts of things'. It is very bleak and barren, this fact of things, as I now see it – very; and what good is to result from writing of it in a paper book is more than I can tell. But I have taken a notion to, and perhaps I shall blacken more paper this time, when I begin quite promiscuously without any moral end in view; but just as the Scotch professor drank whisky, because I like it, and because it's cheap.

Jane Welsh Carlyle

1919   This is Trafalgar day, & yesterday is memorable for the appearance of *Night and Day*. My six copies reached me in the morning, & five were despatched, so that I figure the beaks of five friends already imbedded. Am I nervous? Oddly little; more excited & pleased than nervous. In the first place, there it is, out & done with; then I read a bit & liked it; then I have a kind of confidence, that the people whose judgment I value will probably think well of it, which is much reinforced by the knowledge that even if they dont, I shall pick up & start another story on my own. Of course, if Morgan & Lytton & the others should be enthusiastic, I should think the better of myself. The bore is meeting people who say the usual things. But on the whole, I see what I'm aiming at; what I feel is that this time I've had a fair chance & done my best; so that I can be philosophic & lay the blame on God. Lovely autumn days come one after another; the leaves hanging like rare gold coins on the trees . . .

O yes, I should like a good long review in *The Times*.

Virginia Woolf

22 October

1658 Saw the superb funerall of the Protector. He was carried from Somerset House in a velvet bed of state drawn by six horses, houss'd with the same; the pall held up by his new Lords; Oliver lying in effigie in royal robes, and crown'd with a crown, sceptre and globe, like a king: the pendants and guidons were carried by the officers of the army; and the imperial banners, achievements, &c. by the heraulds in their coates; a rich caparison'd horse, embroider'd all over with gold; a knight of honour arm'd cap-a-pie, and after all, his guards, souldiers, and innumerable mourners. In this equipage they proceeded to Westminster: but it was the joyfullest funerall I ever saw, for there were none that cried but dogs, which the soldiers hooted away with a barbarous noise, drinking and taking tobacco in the streets as they went.

John Evelyn

1818 Talked of the Scotch novels. When Wilkie the painter was taking his portraits of Scott's family, the eldest daughter said to him, 'We don't know what to think of those novels. We have access to all papa's papers. He has no particular study; writes everything in the midst of us all; and yet we never have seen a single scrap of the MS of any of these novels; but still we have *one* reason for thinking them his, and that is, that they are the only works published in Scotland of which copies are not presented to papa.' The reason *against* is stronger than the reason *for*: Scott gave his honour to the Prince Regent they were not his; and Rogers *heard* him do the same to Sheridan, who asked him, with some degree of *brusquerie*, whether he was the author of them. All this rather confirms me in my first idea that they are *not* Scott's.

Thomas Moore

1937 I am basking my brains. No I didnt go to Paris. This is a note to make. Waking at 3 I decided I would spend the week end at

Paris. Got so far as looking up trains, consulting Nessa about hotel. Then L. said he wd. rather not. Then I was overcome with happiness. Then we walked round the square love making – after 25 years cant bear to be separate. Then I walked round the Lake in Regents Park. Then . . . you see it is an enormous pleasure, being wanted: a wife. And our marriage so complete.

Virginia Woolf

1943   The other night, as I was coming home in the dark, I saw a strange ungainly thing in front of me; then when I drew closer I saw that it was a man giving a piggy-back to a woman. They lurched a little. The woman said something. I looked at them quickly and saw that the man appeared very young with dark hair and eyes, a round face and short, stocky body. They laughed quietly together and said something more. I overtook them and left them quietly piggy-backing in the country lane at night. I wondered if they were just lovers, or whether the woman's legs were paralysed. They stuck out awkwardly on each side of his tough little body, like thin stiff chickens' legs.

Denton Welch

23 October

1818   Returned home to dinner at four; went to bed early, and was called up by Bessy at half-past eleven o'clock: sent for the midwife, who arrived between one and two, and at a quarter before four my darling Bessy was safely delivered of a son (and heir *in partibus*), to my unspeakable delight, for never had I felt half such anxiety about her. I walked about the parlour by myself, like one distracted; sometimes stopping to pray, sometimes opening the door to listen; and never with gratitude more fervent than that with which I knelt down to thank God for the dear girl's safety, when all was over – (the maid, by the by, very near catching me on my knees). Went to bed at six o'clock.

Thomas Moore

1855   A stormy day within doors, so I walked out early, and walked, walked, walked. If peace and quietness be not in one's own power, one can always give oneself at least bodily fatigue – no such bad succedaneum after all. Life gets to look for me like a sort of kaleidoscope – a few things of different colours – black predominating, which fate shakes into new and ever new combinations, but always the same things over again. Today has been so like a day I still remember out of ten years ago; the same still dreamy October weather, the same tumult of mind contrasting with the outer stillness; the same causes for that tumult. Then, as now, I had walked, walked, walked with no aim but to tire myself.

Jane Welsh Carlyle

1943 Patrick Kinross lunched. He was much more like his old self. He admitted that at first he found it difficult to reconcile himself to the un-war minded lives of his friends in London. They seemed unaware of and unconcerned with what was happening overseas. Furthermore, having accustomed himself to leading a picnic sort of life for so long he slightly disapproved of the conventional, pre-war way of living here. But he is already getting over these inhibitions. They are quite understandable. He still misses the mixture of seriousness and fun of his friends in the desert. He says that in spite of their deprivations they are happier than people here who have their comforts; and that in the 8th Army there is much wholesome buggery.

James Lees-Milne

24 October

1785 The Tooth-Ach so very bad all night and the same this Morn' that I sent for John Reeves the Farrier who lives at the Hart and often draws Teeth for People, to draw one for me. He returned with my Man about 11 o'clock this Morning and he pulled it out for me the first Pull, but it was a monstrous Crash and more so, it being one of the Eye Teeth, it had but one Fang but that was very long. I gave Johnny Reeves for drawing it 0. 2. 6. A great pain in the Jaw Bone continued all Day and Night but nothing so bad as the Tooth Ach.

The Reverend James Woodforde

1806 I have a horrid cold but the weather being fine I walked to Mursley to see an old Man who is a Hundred years old, his name is Peek, he married a few years ago a woman beyond seventy, who now takes care of him and her own Mother who is past a Hundred, manages a small Dairy and does everything, the two Centurions have lived too long and are almost returned to Childhood.

Elizabeth Fremantle

1914 This has been a bad day for me because my work overtook me instead of my keeping ahead of it, which always makes me feel depressed & unequal to being the exceptional & brilliant person I am determined to be. As a rule when I hear brilliant people like Miss Barton & Miss Rowe spoken of, I feel determined even to out-do them in glory, but on depressing days I feel I can never get to anything like their standard. But I can!

At 9.0 we had a fancy-dress dance which went on till 11.0. I went in my old Spanish peasant's dress; there really were some sights there. Miss Phillips as Plato was perhaps the most striking of anybody. I was fairly bored as it is very dull dancing with girls after having been to proper dances, & espec. as everyone danced so badly.

Vera Brittain

25 October

1668 *Lords day.* Up, and discoursing with my wife about our house and many new things we are doing of; and so to church I, and there find Jack Fen come, and his wife, a pretty black woman; I never saw her before, nor took notice of her now. So home and to dinner; and after dinner, all the afternoon got my wife and boy to read to me. And at night W. Batelier comes and sups with us; and after supper, to have my head combed by Deb, which occasioned the greatest sorrow to me that ever I knew in this world; for my wife, coming up suddenly, did find me imbracing the girl con my hand sub su coats; and endeed, I was with my main in her cunny. I was at a wonderful loss upon it, and the girl also; and I endeavoured to put it off, but my wife was struck mute and grew angry, and as her voice came to her, grew quite out of order; and I do say little, but to bed; and my wife said little also, but could not sleep all night; but about 2 in the morning waked me and cried, and fell to tell me as a great secret that she was a Roman Catholique and had received the Holy Sacrament; which troubled me but I took no notice of it, but she went on from one thing to another, till at last it appeared plainly her trouble was at what she saw; but yet I did not know how much she saw and therefore said nothing to her. But after her much crying and reproaching me with inconstancy and preferring a sorry girl before her, I did give her no provocations but did promise all fair usage to her, and love, and foreswore any hurt that I did with her – till at last she seemed to be at ease again; and so toward morning, a little sleep.

Samuel Pepys

1782 So much interrupted, find I shall be able to accomplish nothing, unless I build a study, and get all my books about me. Absolutely necessary for my tolerable enjoyment, and may be of use in improving my fortune. Decline even the little society within your reach and keep to yourself. That does not amuse you and serves only to waste your time. Grow more dissatisfied with myself every day and must take another course.

The Reverend W. J. Temple

1862 I have been doing a Latin Essay, 'Ut pictura poesis,' a nice enough subject had it been English. I noticed, when I was doing verses, that a little greenfinch had got into the hall and could not find its way out. The bird's feet were entangled with cobwebs from the ceiling, and it clung wildly to the wires of the oriel by the daïs. I found the poor thing tame and exhausted; I took it in my hands, and removed the cobwebs, and then I let it fly forth from the open window into the clear autumnal sky fresh with sunlight after rain. The creature sat dazed upon a battlement, and then hopped to another, and pecked a little moss. At last it felt its freedom, chirruped, and was away toward the woods. So would that some one might release me.

J. A. Symonds

26 October

1725 I turn'd off my Servant Charles Cook (whom I had warned away long before Michaelmass to get another Place at Our Lady-day next,) Because he was too much in favour with my Servant Hannah Beal, & was bolted into his Chamber with her Sunday Oct: 3 for a considerable time; At length Mr Bragg's Coach-Man (having a Mind to disturb them) pretended to go into the Chamber for Oates for his Horses: But the Door being fastend, he beat against it, & swore he would break it open; And was at last let in, where they both were. When I gave him 10s for 27 days since Michaelmass, he was not contented, & Swore often, 'till I threatend him to make him pay for Swearing 3 times, By God. He boasted on his good Service he had done; And I ask'd him whether it was in his making 16 Loads of Hay last my, sometimes 3, & never more than 4 Horses, at nights only Half a Year, or in Will Clark doing his Work for him at my Charge, or for looking after the Peck of Snails Mr Swarbrick saw together in the Garden, Or looking after the Grounds I had in Hand at Dulcot. He answer'd he did not know my Grounds at Dulcot . . . I don't remember any such thing nor You neither. I then said to him You Impudent Raskal do you give me the Lye? Get You out & never come hither again any more. He return'd no more, & went out of the Kitchin grumbling: But what he say'd I did not hear. Afterwards he sent Will Clark to my Study Door, for a Character of him. And I answer'd I would give none: For he had not behaved himself for me to give him a good one.

Dr Claver Morris

1947 Is there anything more pleasant than an autumnal weekend in London? I lazed in bed – revelled in the almost royal splendour of my bedroom, and rose late to arrange my dinner party for the Regent of Iraq and his Minister of Defence. It was a great success. The Regent brought me a coffee set of silver as a present – six cups and a huge salver with palm trees engraved on it. The coffee pot has a spout like a pelican – hideous.

'Chips' Channon

1981   Stepping across the gate into Sarah's arms. We embrace and kiss. So lovely to touch in legitimate time. We waste no time jumping in the car and heading into the distance.

Accumulated thoughts: I am wondering what it will be like to sleep together, having known each other for four years and been married almost two. Up the long winding roads the scenery was spectacular. Sitting there with Sarah at my side, the prison far behind and the wonders of the Scottish Highlands all around me I felt stunned with pleasure . . . How can I possibly explain this experience to anyone after fourteen years in prison? Every fibre was open and alert to this vast mountain scenery. Finally we reached our caravan situated high up on the hillside with a wide and full view of the valley. It was getting quite dark though still enough light for us to see our view from the caravan. Sheep were all around us. We looked down the valley to a spattering of cottages and farmhouses. The visual images were overwhelming. The night was spent in a small double bed with me always aware of Sarah next to me. I was restless. It will take some getting used to after fourteen years of sleeping alone . . . It's the first time in years I've slept on a mattress.

Jimmy Boyle

27 October

1784   In the evening, Fisher being expected, removed into the rooms which I had inhabited during my residence in the university, and to which I now return after an interval *of thirteen years*. Oh! that the intermediate time had been employed in the way in which it now appears to me that the perseverance of a month would always have enabled me to employ it. There is not a period of my past life that would not have been improved beyond all proportion by the very means that were necessary to secure happiness in future. How strange, then, the infatuation that could neglect such means! Other men, if they have been idle, have been happy; others, if they have sacrificed the hopes of future good, have sacrificed them to present enjoyment. To what have I sacrificed them?

William Windham

1943   We motored to Salcombe, having lost our way down lanes – all the signposts having been removed so that the German parachutists shall not know where they are – in the dark.

James Lees-Milne

1948   Bunny told me some long story tonight, recollected from her youth, about some performing dogs she had once seen acting a play. The husband (a terrier) goes off on a shooting trip, wearing a deerstalker hat, his gun on his shoulder; no sooner has he gone than his wife (another terrier) throws open her casement, to be serenaded by her lover (another dog). She invites him up, he clambers up the ivy, slips and she hauls him up to her balcony in her teeth. All are absurdly dressed. Bunny laughed as she recounted this until tears rolled down her cheeks, and I suppose I ought to have pretended to be amused too, but I couldn't, so she was disappointed and put out by my cold and I daresay priggish reception to her funny story. But I really hate such things. I even dislike seeing a dog 'begging', like the porter's dog, sitting up and working its arms up and down, or a dog 'offering its paw'.

J. R. Ackerley

28 October

1648   This day 8 yeare, my deare wife and I were married; this day shee was very ill and likely to swound away, the lord good in giving her strength and removing her distemper, the lord increase our grace, and make our lives more serviceable to him and one anothers good, but good is god to mee, in wife and children, and my comforts in them, oh sanctifie them thou god of grace, this day I felt my navill sore; I had left the stuffe lye in it, and whether that grated it or not I knowe not, but I found it at night, red, rawe, and moyst, wee applyed unguentum album to it; to which the lord in his mercy give a blessing that it may have a perfect recovery, I have reason to trust in god, because of his former goodnes, and I find him a god that answers prayer.

The Reverend Ralph Josselin

1814   I saw Kean's *Hamlet* last night, and totally disagree as to its being his worst part. The fact is we are ruined by the ranting habits of the stage. We are so used to noise, declamation, & fury, that was Nature herself to act it, she would appear tame. They complain Kean is insipid in his soliloquies! Absurd – what is the impression from his whole acting? Is it not of a heart afflicted youth, who silently 'wanders for hours in the lobby', in despairing desolation. At *these times* in *Nature* would he soliloquize, & how would he do it? Would he rant? Would he stamp? Would he thunder? Oh no, he would reason quietly; he would weep at his Father's name, & in half-suppressed sighs & bursting agony, lament his Mother's marriage. Was not this then the progress, the system, of Kean? It is impossible one who feels the parts of passion so justly should not feel as justly the parts of secret soliloquies. To me his whole conception & execution of Hamlet is perfect. You see him wander silently about, weary, in grief, disgusted; if he speaks, it is not to the audience; if he feels, it is not for applause. No, he speaks because impelled to utter his sensations by their excess. He weeps because his faculties can no longer retain themselves. The longer he acts, the more will he bring the World to his principles, and the time is not far distant when his purity, his truth, his energy, will triumph over all opposition.

B. R. Haydon

1942   My 39th birthday. A good year. I have begotten a fine daughter, published a successful book, drunk 300 bottles of wine and smoked 300 or more Havana cigars. I have got back to soldiering among friends. This time last year I was on my way to Hawick to join 5 RM. I get steadily worse as a soldier with the passage of time, but more patient and humble – as far as soldiering is concerned. I have about £900 in hand and no grave debts except to the Government; health excellent except when impaired by wine; a wife I love, agreeable work in surroundings of great beauty. Well that is as much as one can hope for.

Evelyn Waugh

---

29 October

1810   The dear little Angel expired at nine o'clock, on Monday morning the 29th Octr. She knew not Cole, on Saturday, and her agonies were great from that day to the moment of her death. My affliction almost overpowers me, at the loss of such a darling and lovely Child, but on account of my Baby I am obliged to exert myself in this severe trial.

Elizabeth Fremantle

1870   Today I found in a book a red silk handkerchief worked with the words 'Forget me not', and I am sorry to say that I have entirely forgotten who gave it to me. One of my many lovers no doubt. But which?

The Reverend Francis Kilvert

1922   Miss Mary Butts being gone, & my head too stupid for reading, I may as well write here, for my amusement later perhaps. I mean I'm too riddled with talk & harassed with the usual worry of people who like & people who don't like J.R. [*Jacob's Room*] to concentrate. There was the *Times* review on Thursday – long, a little tepid, I think; saying that one can't make characters in this way; flattering enough. Of course, I had a letter from Morgan in the opposite sense – the letter I've liked best of all. We have sold 650, I think; & have ordered a second edition. My sensations? – as usual – mixed. I shall never write a book that is an entire success. This time the reviews are against me, & the private people enthusiastic. Either I am a great writer or a nincompoop. 'An elderly sensualist' the *Daily News* called me. *Pall Mall* passes me over as negligible. I expect to be neglected & sneered at. And what will be the fate of our second thousand then? So far of course, the success is much more than we expected. I think I am better pleased so far than I have ever been.

Virginia Woolf

---

30 October

1826 Some of our friends in London had pretended that at Paris I might stand some chance of being encounterd by the same sort of tumultuary reception which I met in Ireland; but for this I see no ground.

It is a point on which I am totally indifferent – As a literary man I cannot affect to despize public applause – as a private gentleman I have always been embarassd and displeased with popular clamours even when in my favour. I know very well the breath of which such shouts are composed and am sensible those who applaud me today would be as ready to hiss me tomorrow and I would not have them think that I put such a value on their favour as would make me for an instant fear their displeasure. Now all this disclamation is sincere and yet it sounds affected. It puts me in mind of an old woman who when Carlisle was taken by the highlanders in 1745 chose to be particularly apprehensive of personal violence and shut herself up in the closet in order that she might escape ravishment. But no one came to disturb her solitude and she began to be sensible that poor Donald was looking out for victuals or seeking for some small plunder without bestowing a thought on the fair sex. She pop'd her head out of her place of refuge with the petty question 'Good folks, can you tell when the ravishing is going to begin?'

Walter Scott

1905 Never any more up West End – with its glaring temptations in the guise of handsome, graceful beauties. 'Tis easy, very easy to fall. Even now this morning comes the news of an infatuated Count's suicide in a leading Gaiety actress' boudoir. The actress is Gertie Millar.

Sydney Moseley

1947 An American girl in the train between Dover and Victoria, her first sight of England, said to me, 'My, what a number of chimneys! In our country we may have one chimney to each house; here it must be one chimney to each room.' That is one manifestation of England's cosiness before the war when every chimney would be smoking. Now the grates are empty, or nearly so.

James Lees-Milne

31 October

1702 Arriv'd now to the 82nd year of my age, having read over all that pass'd since this day twelvemonth in these notes, I render solemn thanks to the Lord, imploring the pardon of my past sins, and the assistance of His grace; making new resolutions, and imploring that He will continue His assistance, and prepare me for my blessed Saviour's coming, that I may obtain a comfortable departure, after so long a term as has ben hitherto indulg'd me. I find by many infirmities this yeare (especially nephritic pains) that I much decline; and yet of His infinite mercy retain my intellects and senses in greate measure above most of my age. I have this yeare repair'd much of the mansion-house and severall tenants' houses, and paid some of my debts and ingagements. My wife, children and family in health: for all which I most sincerely beseech Almighty God to accept of these my acknowledgements, and that if it he His holy will to continue me yet longer, it may be to the praise of His infinite grace, and salvation of my soul. Amen.

John Evelyn

1828 A nasty raw cutthroat gloomy day; birds walking about like fowls; came home without having had a shot. Shipped my boots and went to the river, to save my charter of never having a blank day. Got the first jack snipe I have seen this year, and one whole snipe (at 75 yards); all I saw, and all I shot at.

Colonel Peter Hawker

1940   Mummy is suspicious, because I haven't had the curse for two months. 'You're either anaemic or pregnant,' she said, 'and I mean to find out which.' So she's taking me to a doctor. She keeps on asking me if I'm still a virgin or whether there's any cause to believe I'm going to have a baby. She's really put the fear of God into me – it's not so much the thought of having a baby, it's the ghastly maternal fuss that would attend such an occurrence.

Joan Wyndham

1 November

1754   Choler reigned, and impelled into indecencies, not to say sins. Lord, pity and correct!

Dr John Rutty

1924   I must make some notes of work; for now I must buckle to. The question is how to get the 2 books done. I am going to skate rapidly over *Mrs D.* [*Mrs Dalloway*] but it will take time. No: I cannot say anything much to the point, for what I must do is to experiment next week; how much revision is needed, & how much time it takes. I am very set on getting my essays out before my novel. Yesterday I had tea in Mary's room & saw the red lighted tugs go past & heard the swish of the river: Mary in black with lotus leaves round her neck. If one could be friendly with women, what a pleasure – the relationship so secret & private compared with relations with men. Why not write about it? truthfully? As I think, this diary writing has greatly helped my style; loosened the ligatures.

Virginia Woolf

1933   What a bad sign it is to get the *Oxford Book of Victorian Verse* out of the library.

Barbara Pym

1980   Fiddly day. Take M. shopping locally. How difficult and time-consuming it is. By ill-luck we need a broom-head, some bananas, batteries, bulbs, bacon and Elastoplast – all from different shops. It takes ages and quickly ruffles the temper. How sheltered are the lives of most married men; and would shopping centres be different if we shopped more often?

Hugh Casson

2 November

1667   Up, and to the office, where busy all the morning. At noon home; and after dinner, my wife and Willett and I to the

King's House and there saw *Henry the Fourth*; and contrary to expectation, was pleased in nothing more then in Cartwright's speaking of Falstaffe's speech about *What is Honour?* The house full of Parliament-men, it being holiday with them. And it was observable how a gentleman of good habitt, sitting just before us eating of some fruit, in the midst of the play did drop down as dead, being choked; but with much ado, Orange Mall did thrust her finger down his throat and brought him back to life again. After the play, we home and I busy at the office late; and then home to supper and to bed.

Samuel Pepys

1698 This day I was with one Mr Fiddis, a minister at Holderness, who told me that, about six years ago, going to bed at a friend's house, some had out of roguery fixed a long band to the bedclose where he lay. About half an houer after he was got to bed they begun to pull, which, drawing the bedclose of by degrees put him into a suddain fright, and, looking up, he did really think and believe that he saw two or three spirits stirring and moveing about the bed, and says but that he discovered the string, and the partys confessing the fraud, he durst almost have sworn that he really saw strang things, which shews the effects of suddain frights.

Abraham De La Pryme

1743 The following advertisement was published:

FOR THE BENEFIT OF MR ESTE
By the Edinburgh Company of Comedians, on Friday,
November 4, will be acted a Comedy, called,
THE CONSCIOUS LOVERS;
To which will be added a Farce, called
TRICK UPON TRICK, or METHODISM DISPLAYED

On Friday, a vast multitude of spectators were assembled in the Moot Hall to see this. It was believed there could not be less than fifteen hundred people, some hundreds of whom sat on rows of seats built upon the stage. Soon after the comedians had begun the first act of the play, on a sudden all those seats fell down at once, the supporters of them breaking like a rotten stick. The people were thrown one upon another, about five foot forward, but not one of them hurt. After a short time the rest of the spectators were quiet, and the actors went on. In the middle of the second act, all the shilling seats gave a crack, and sunk several inches down. A great noise and shrieking followed; and as many as could readily get to the door, went out, and returned no more. Notwithstanding this, when the noise was over, the actors went on with the play.

In the beginning of the third act the entire stage suddenly sunk about six inches: the players retired with great precipitation; yet in a while they began again. At the latter end of the third act, all the sixpenny seats, without any kind of notice, fell to the ground. There was now a cry on every side; it being supposed that many were crushed in pieces: but, upon inquiry, not a single person (such was the mercy of God!) was either killed or dangerously hurt. Two or three hundred remaining still in the hall, Mr Este (who was to act the Methodist) came upon the stage and told them, for all this he was resolved the farce should be acted. While he was speaking, the stage sunk six inches more; on which he ran back in the utmost confusion, and the people as fast as they could out of the door, none staying to look behind him.

Which is most surprising – that those players acted this farce the next week – or that some hundreds of people came again to see it?

John Wesley

---

3 November

1916 [France] I sit on a high bank above a road at H. By my side stands a quarter of a bottle of red wine at 1.50 francs the bottle. The remaining three-quarters are in my veins. I am perfectly happy physically: so much so that only my physical being asserts itself. From my toes to the very hair of my head I am a close compact unit of pleasurable sensations. Now, indeed, it is good to live; a new power, a new sensibility to physical pleasure in all my members. The whistle blows for 'Fall in!' I lift the remnant of the wine to my lips and drain the dregs. All the length of the march it lasts me, and the keenness, the compactness, the intensity of perpetual well-being doesn't even leave my remotest finger-tips.

The silver veil of gossamer webs are round my hair, the juice of the autumn grape gladdening all my veins. I am the child of Nature. I wish always to be so.

Arthur Graeme West

1935 Miss Bigge to lunch. She said the Prince of Wales's reply to people who spoke to him about his morals was that he did his job and that his private life was his own. This is not so and never can be. It is deplorable and wretched that he carries on as he does. It is common knowledge.

John Reith

1943 Margaret Jourdain, who lunched with me at the Istanbul restaurant, amazed me by saying that she and Ivy, in order to effect economies when they needed a change in the country, used to stay in convents. Their only embarrassment was caused by meeting the Host carried through the cloisters when they were in their Jaeger dressing-gowns, spongebags in hand, on the way to the bathroom. Should they then kneel, or merely genuflect as a matter of politeness?

James Lees-Milne

4 November

1774 I went home and saw my wife and Veronica, then dined with the Colonel at his lodgings, and, as he was to be busy, just drank half a bottle of port; then sallied forth between four and five with an avidity for drinking from the habit of some days before. I went to Fortune's; found nobody in the house but Captain James Gordon of Ellon. He and I drank five bottles of claret and were most profound politicians. He pressed me to take another; but my stomach was against it. I walked off very gravely though much intoxicated. Ranged through the streets till, having run hard down the Advocates' Close, which is very steep, I found myself on a sudden bouncing down an almost perpendicular stone stair. I could not stop, but when I came to the bottom of it, fell with a good deal of violence, which sobered me much. It was amazing that I was not killed or very much hurt; I only bruised my right heel severely. I supped at Sir George's. My wife was there, and George Webster.

James Boswell

1802 I scalded my foot with coffee after having been in bed in the afternoon – I was near fainting and then bad in my bowels. Mary waited upon me till 2 o'clock, then we went to bed, and with applications of vinegar I was lulled to sleep about 4.

Dorothy Wordsworth

1936 Take today, and a day is only a year or a life in little. I woke up fearful, as I sometimes do, with my heart beating fast. I got breakfast ready, looking askance at Kit when she came downstairs, dressing the children by the dining-room fire. After breakfast, Kit and I smiled at one another, and planned to drive up to London to go to a party at which all the guests are to wear Austrian peasant costume.

I came up to my room, lit a cigarette, and, watching the grey cold day, felt stirred, aware of what life was. This inadequately described the feeling I mean. It is a feeling that comes to me when I pause, a slight excitement, expectation, forgetfulness of Time and worries of Eternity. This description is also inadequate. I wrote for about an hour and a half, describing a visit to a psychoanalyst. Then I read the paper.

Before lunch I took a walk up to the village. I felt peaceful, bought a packet of cigarettes, thought how lovely autumn was. After lunch I came upstairs, sat and read a little, started to write a letter to Joseph Hone who has written nicely to me about my review of his *Life of George Moore*. Kit came and lay down on the settee. I resented her presence. My head began to ache. I must go away, I thought. I'll go to Germany. I'll borrow money. When Kit, feeling my resentment, went and sat downstairs, I asked her to come back. I insisted she should rest while I took the children out. They came with me, and I sawed logs, and cut some with an axe. As I wielded the axe I thought I might murder the two children. Then I'd be mad, I thought. Shall I, perhaps, go mad? I took the two children with me to fetch drinking water. Kit came out with her coat on. I told her to go back, and took the children up to the little church. Val cried, and I let her cry, and then harshly wiped her face. When I came in I went up to my room and lay down on the sofa, planning to get away, to borrow money and go to Germany.

Malcolm Muggeridge

5 November

1685 It being an extraordinary wett morning, and myself indisposed by a very greate rheume, I did not go to church, to my very greate sorrow, it being the first Gunpowder Conspiracy anniversary that had ben kept now these 80 yeares under a prince of the Roman religion. Bonfires were forbidden on this day; what does this portend!

John Evelyn

1804 We went to Mrs Sheldon's in the evening and then to the Ball. I did not dance I found it very stupid, I sat by Lady Kenmare the whole time. Mr Cotton seemed *tout à fait épris avec la beauté de la belle* Beresford and *ils eurent l'air bien tendres.* We went to supper at about twelve; it was excessively well contrived; I sat between Fanny and Louisa Sheldon and facing Mr Cotton and Miss Beresford. Mr West and two other Gentlemen sung the former has got a fine voice, they pressed Eugenia to follow their example, but she was too wise to acquiesce. They say that Mr Cotter gives a ball tomorrow. Lady Mary looked very pretty with a nice velvet corset. Eugenia danced with Mr Farquhar, who makes a good use of his legs and danced *à la* Deshayes. It was two before we got away, I was much tired and most happy to get to bed. It was so cold and so late that I felt cross and stupid.

Harriet Wynne

1854 'Gunpowder Treason' falling on a Sunday we used none of the 'State Services'.

The siege of Sebastopol continues. What a pandemonium must be created by the perpetual discharge of 3000 guns.

The Reverend Benjamin Armstrong

1946 I stayed in London for no other reason than that Laura was entertaining her mother at Piers Court.

Evelyn Waugh

---

6 November

1660 Home and fell a-reading of the tryalls of the late men that were hanged for the King's death; and found good satisfaccion in reading thereof. At night to bed; and my wife and I did fall out about the dog's being put down into the Sellar, which I have a mind to have done because of his fouling the house; and I would have my will. And so we went to bed and lay all night in a Quarrell. This night I was troubled all night with a dream that my wife was dead, which made me that I slept ill all night.

Samuel Pepys

1661 Several thgs I had on my spirit in ye morninge y^t were big en: to make mee restles in minde (it may be to mar dutys for y^m), & now they are all off mee and are scarce memorable to be thankfull for them; but surely I have cause to be thankfull for heart's ease in respect of ye least of y^m this eveninge.

W^t a deale of patience is requiste to beare any converse wth our little children. How peevish and foolish are they! & w^t fits doth our heavenly Father beare with us in!

The Reverend Henry Newcombe

1855 Mended Mr C.'s dressing-gown. Much movement under the free sky is needful for me to keep my heart from throbbing up into my head and maddening it. They must be comfortable people who have leisure to think about going to Heaven! My most constant and pressing anxiety is to keep out of Bedlam! that's all ... Ach! If there were no feelings 'what steady sailing craft we should be,' as the nautical gentleman of some novel says.

Jane Welsh Carlyle

---

7 November

1788   The Vicar's large Dog went mad last night and was shot this morning. There must be some mysterious cause of all these large dogs in the country going mad. I suspect it originates from Potions administered to them by the numerous Vagabonds with which the roads and Villages Swarm, under the appearance of maim'd Sailors, servants out of place, Pedlars, etc., who meditate an attack upon the house and thus remove the incorruptible guardians from them.

Lady Eleanor Butler

1815   Passed an acute & miserable morning in comparing myself with Raphael. At my age he had completed a Vatican Room.

B. R. Haydon

1830   One of our companions from Coventry was a person employed in surveying and taking levels of the line for the proposed railway from Birmingham to London. An undertaking that depended on the result of one from Liverpool to Manchester. It will be a work of great magnitude and extent, and if carried into effect will render highways, horses, and canals useless.

William Dyott

1908   Again my heart is full and I could, with Cassius, 'weep the spirit from mine eyes'. Loretta, to whom I wrote about these reflections, interprets them as a passion for her; actually the wild tuggings at my heart seem to seek relief in the direction of Alma – of the Alphabets – whom I saw this morning, but to whom I must have looked a fright in my shabby wretched attire. She is tall and striking – and so appealing in her talk . . .

Alma asks me to come to see Martin Harvey tonight – but Alec has neither time nor *cash*! So he pretends another engagement.

The Girl in Blue (of the Tennis Court) sends letter, and so instead of going to school (and being unable to borrow any money) I rush home (penny ride from sixpence leaves fivepence) get my Dent's French book, ride to Tottenham Court Road and get a shilling back for a good book – and meet *her*! But what is it all – waste of Health, Energy, Time and Money!

Sydney Moseley

---

8 November

1661 I got up about 7 and got forward for Stockport, w^{re} I preached. Was in a broken frame, had my minde a little disquieted about a busynes. It is not good to let Sathan have an hole in one's coat. He will disquiet & disturbe wth it in duty if no worse. I had a full audience, & was not so prepared as I might have beene.

The Reverend Henry Newcombe

1785 A Rumour in the kitchen that a Rat had been seen in the Fowl yard. John Thomas (the mason) sent for in haste to stop up the Holes and quiet the alarms of the quality.

Lady Eleanor Butler

1796 I have been for some days attending lectures on chemistry. Specious as the advantages of the new nomenclature appear, they seem counterbalanced by the reflection, that on any revolution in the system, which surely stands on ticklish ground, the denominations deduced from it, must undergo a correspondent disorganization.

Saw distinctly this evening, through a microscope, the circulation of the white and transparent globules of blood, in the pellucid body and members of a water newt – a spectacle which impressed me with a more awful sense of the mysterious operations going on in nature, than the revolution of the planets.

Thomas Green

1949   Tomorrow is my father's birthday. He would have been seventy-seven. I never think of him.

'Chips' Channon

---

9 November

1666   We got well home; and in the way I did con mi mano tocar la jambe de Mercer sa chair. Elle retirait sa jambe modestement, but I did tocar sa peau with my naked hand. And the truth is, la fille hath something that is assez jolie. Being come home, we to Cards till 2 in the morning; and drinking lamb's-wool, to bed.

Samuel Pepys

1757   Having procured an apparatus on purpose, I ordered several persons to be electrified, who were ill of various disorders; some of whom found an immediate, some a gradual cure. From this time I appointed, first some hours in every week, and afterward an hour in every day, wherein any that desired it might try the virtue of this surprising medicine. Two or three years after, our patients were so numerous that we were obliged to divide them: so part were electrified in Southwark, part at the Foundery, others near St Paul's, and the rest near the Seven Dials: the same method we have taken ever since; and to this day, while hundreds, perhaps thousands, have received unspeakable good, I have not known one man, woman, or child, who has received any hurt thereby: so that when I hear any talk of the danger of being electrified (especially if they are medical men who talk so), I cannot but impute it to great want either of sense or honesty.

John Wesley

1813   Was nearly tortured to death by a relay of three dentists, who failed in drawing a tremendous tooth, and finished with breaking my jawbone, and complimenting me for the *sang-froid* with which I braved their infernal operations.

Colonel Peter Hawker

1947   Read Arthur Bryant on Pepys. It is odd how the English love a man who is not a humbug like themselves. To my mind Pepys is a mean little man. Salacious in a grubby way; even in his peculations there is no magnificence. But he did stick to his office during the Plague which is more than most men did. It is some relief to reflect that to be a good diarist one must have a little snouty, sneaky mind.

Harold Nicolson

---

10 November

1719   I came away from Bath at half an hour after 3, and I returned home (by Polton) in five hours. In the Evening there were white Flashes of Light rising from near the Horizon in the North East and West flying up to the Zenith (like a swift Cloud) and quickly spending itself and reviving: and it came so near over my House that I feared it would have set on Fire my House.

Dr Claver Morris

1822   I have made my first probation in writing, and it has done me much good, and I get more calm; the stream begins to take to its new channel, insomuch as to make me fear change. But people must know little of me who think that, abstractedly, I am content with my present mode of life. Activity of spirit is my sphere. But we cannot be active of mind without an object; and I have none. I am allowed to have some talent — that is sufficient, methinks, to cause my irreparable misery; for, if one has genius, what a delight it is to be associated with a superior! Mine own Shelley! the sun knows of none to be likened to you — brave, wise, noble-hearted, full of learning, tolerance, and love. Love! what a word for me to write! yet, my miserable heart, permit me yet to love — to see him in beauty, to feel him in beauty, to be interpenetrated by the sense of his excellence; and thus to love singly, eternally, ardently, and not fruitlessly; for I am still his – still the chosen one of that blessed spirit – still vowed to him for ever and ever!

Mary Shelley

1831 I remember how proud I used to be of going to Lady Mount Edgecumbe's suppers (one or two at the most) after the Opera. It was at one of these, sitting between Mrs Siddons and Lady Castlereagh, I heard for the first time the voice of the former (never having met her before) transferred to the ordinary things of this world – and the solemn words in her tragic tone – 'I do love ale dearly.'

Thomas Moore

11 November

1718 Dan Burgess preaching, said, 'I have but one whore in my congregation, and I'll fell her' – and making an offer to throw the Bible, a great many bowed to shun the book – at which he said, 'I think I have nothing else but whores.' Of the Apostles leaving all and following Christ, he said, 'marry! what had they to leave but a few old fishing netts,' etc.

The Reverend John Thomlinson

1822 It is better to grieve than not to grieve. Grief at least tells me that I was not always what I am now. I was once selected for happiness; let the memory of that abide by me. You pass by an old ruined house in a desolate lane, and heed it not. But if you hear that that house is haunted by a wild and beautiful spirit, it acquires an interest and beauty of its own.

I shall be glad to be more alone again; one ought to see no one, or many; and, confined to one society, I shall lose all energy except that which I possess from my own resources; and I must be alone for those to be put in activity.

A cold heart! Have I a cold heart? God knows! But none need envy the icy region this heart encircles; and at least the tears are hot which the emotions of this cold heart forces me to shed. A cold heart! yes, it would be cold enough if all were as I wished it – cold, or burning in the flame for whose sake I forgive this, and would forgive every other imputation – that flame in which your heart, beloved, lay unconsumed. My heart is very full tonight.

I shall write this life, and thus occupy myself in the only manner from which I can derive consolation. That will be a task that may convey some balm. What though I weep? All is better than inaction and – not forgetfulness – that never is – but an inactivity of remembrance.

And you, my own boy! I am about to begin a task which, if you live, will be an invaluable treasure to you in after times. I must collect my materials, and then, in the commemoration of the divine virtues of your Father, I shall fulfil the only act of pleasure there remains for me, and be ready to follow you, if you leave me, my task being fulfilled. I have lived; rapture, exultation, content – all the varied changes of enjoyment – have been mine. It is all gone; but still, the airy paintings of what it has gone through float by, and distance shall not dim them. If I were alone, I had already begun what I had determined to do; but I must have patience, and for those events my memory is brass, my thoughts a never-tired engraver. France – Poverty – A few days of solitude, and some uneasiness – A tranquil residence in a beautiful spot – Switzerland – Bath – Marlow – Milan – the Baths of Lucca – Este – Venice – Rome – Naples – Rome and misery – Leghorn – Florence – Pisa – Solitude – The Williams' – The Baths – Pisa: these are the heads of chapters, and each containing a tale romantic beyond romance.

I no longer enjoy, but I love. Death cannot deprive me of that living spark which feeds on all given it, and which is now triumphant in sorrow. I love, and shall enjoy happiness again. I do not doubt that; but when?

Mary Shelley

---

12 November

1666   This afternoon, going toward Westminster, Creed and I did step in (the Duke of York being just going away from seeing of it) at Pauls, and in the Convocation house yard did there see the body of Robt. Braybrooke, Bishop of London, that died 1404. He fell down in his tomb out of the great church into St Fayths this late Fire, and is here seen his Skeleton with the flesh on; but all tough and dry like a spongy dry leather or Touchwood all upon his bones. His head turned aside. A great man in his time, and Lord Chancellor – and now exposed to be handled and derided by some, though admired for its duration by others. Many flocking to see it.

Samuel Pepys

1799   Our unfortunate mother's sufferings were put an end to this morning, she expired at seven o'clock. Eugenia was called to her but she could not speak one word and died in her arms. We left the house almost immediately and removed to a lodging only three doors from it. It is a great comfort to us all that we came to town. Though it is shocking to be present at this scene of distress. Still I feel much less the shock having been near her than if I had been away, as I should always have feared that she might have wished to see me in her last moments.

Elizabeth Fremantle

1801   A beautiful still sunshiny morning. We rose very late. I put the rag-boxes into order. We walked out while the goose was roasting – we walked to the top of the hill. M. and I followed Wm. – he was walking upon the turf between John's Grove and the lane. It was a most sweet noon. We did not go into John's Grove, but we walked among the rocks and there we sate. Mr Oliff passed Mary and me upon the road – Wm. still among the rocks. The lake beautiful from the orchard. Wm. and I walked out before tea – The crescent moon – we sate in the slate quarry – I sate there a long time alone. Wm. reached home before me – I found them at tea. There were a thousand stars in the sky.

Dorothy Wordsworth

1974   I was called out of the Chamber by Norman before I could hear Heath's speech. Ted [Castle], glued to the gallery, told me it was one of the most effective Heath has made. I am fascinated by the chemistry of politics, which apparently operates in other people as well as myself: the inevitability most times of falling flat when too much is expected of one, and then reviving defiantly just when everyone has written one off.

Barbara Castle

---

13 November

1860   At the end of three months since I last wrote anything in this book, I take my pen in hand to record my determination to bring this journal (which is no journal at all) to an end. I have long seen that it is useless to attempt to carry it on, for I am entirely out of the way of hearing anything of the slightest interest beyond what is known to all the world. I therefore close this record without any intention or expectation of renewing it, with a full consciousness of the smallness of its value or interest, and with great regret that I did not make better use of the opportunities I have had of recording something more worth reading.

Charles Greville
[Final Entry]

1921   [Switzerland]

It is time I started a new journal. Come, my unseen, my unknown, let us talk together. Yes, for the last two weeks I have written scarcely anything. I have been idle; I have *failed*. Why? Many reasons. There has been a kind of confusion in my consciousness. It has seemed as though there was no time to write. The mornings, if they are sunny, are taken up with sun-treatment; the post eats away the afternoon. And at night I am tired.

'But it all goes deeper.' Yes, you are right. I haven't been able to yield to the kind of contemplation that is necessary. I have not felt pure in heart, not humble, not good. There's been a stirring-up of sediment. I look at the mountains and I see nothing but mountains. Be frank! I read rubbish. I give way about writing letters. I mean I refuse to meet my obligations, and this of course weakens me in every way. Then I have broken my promise to review the books for *The Nation*. Another *bad spot*. Out of hand? Yes, that describes it – dissipated, vague, not *positive*, and above all, above everything, not working as I should be working – wasting time.

Wasting time. The old cry – the first and last cry – Why do ye tarry? Ah, why indeed? My deepest desire is to be a writer, to have 'a body of work' done. And there the work is, there the stories wait for me, *grow tired*, wilt, fade, because I will not come. And I hear and I *acknowledge* them, and still I go on sitting at the window, playing with the ball of wool. What is to be done?

I must make another effort – at once. I must begin all over again. I must try and write simply, fully, freely, from my heart. *Quietly*, caring nothing for success or failure, but just going on.

I must keep this book so that I have a record of what I do each week. (Here a word. As I re-read *At the Bay* in proof, it seemed to me flat, dull, and not a success at all. I was very much ashamed of it. I am.) But now to resolve! And especially to keep in touch with Life – with the sky and this moon, these stars, these cold, candid peaks.

Katherine Mansfield

---

14 November

1666   Then carried her home, and myself to the Popeshead, where all the Houblons were, and Dr Croone; and by and by to an exceeding pretty supper – excellent discourse of all sorts; and endeed, are a set of the finest gentlemen that ever I met withal in my life. Here Dr Croone told me that at the meeting at Gresham College tonight (which it seems they now have every Wednesday again) there was a pretty experiment, of the blood of one Dogg let out (till he died) into the body of another on one side, while all his own run out on the other side. The first died upon the place, and the other very well, and likely to do well. This did give occasion to many pretty wishes, as of the blood of a Quaker to be let into an Archbishop, and such like. But, as Dr Croone says, may if it takes be of mighty use to man's health, for the amending of bad blood by borrowing from a better body.

Samuel Pepys

1793   Josiah Boydell & Mr Coombes dined with me.

Coombes informed us of many particulars of the condition & behaviour of the Queen of France after Her condemnation. When she was carried back from the Tribunal where she had received sentence of death, she requested that she might see her Children, which was refused. From this moment she appeared to have lost her senses, and continued in a state of insanity till her death. In the cart in which she was carried to execution, she took the executioner for the Dauphin & spoke to him as such. She recognized the Thulieries, and wondered she did not see her Children at the windows . . .

Coombes says the Dauphin or rather infant King of France is now under the management of a man who was formerly a Shoemaker, who is directed to instruct him in everything vicious and immoral.

Joseph Farington

1813   If this had been begun ten years ago, and faithfully kept!!! – heigho! there are too many things I wish never to have remembered, as it is. Well – I have had my share of what are called the pleasures of this life, and have seen more of the European and Asiatic world than I have made a good use of. They say 'Virtue is its own reward' – it certainly should be paid well for its trouble. At five-and-twenty, when the better part of life is over, one should be *something*; – and what am I? nothing but five-and-twenty – and the odd months. What have I seen? the same man all over the world – ay, and woman too. Give *me* a Mussulman who never asks questions, and a she of the same race who saves one the trouble of putting them.

Lord Byron

15 November

1807   Guard spoke of the death of the Revd Mr Booth. He was abt. 42 years of age, & died of a Palsy, which was attributed to the effect which the coming into possession of His Father's large property had upon His mind. While His Father lived He had been kept in very limited circumstances. His Father left £30,000 as appeared by His accounts besides very considerable estates near Ludlow & it has lately been found that He had a considerable Sum in Long Annuities.

Joseph Farington

1823   Dined at Phipps's; though Bessy at first refused, this being her birthday, and it having long been a fancy of hers that she was to die at the age of thirty, which she completed today.

Thomas Moore

1830   Another story Taylor told (we were talking of the Negroes and savages) of a girl who had been brought up for the purpose of being eaten on the day her master's son was married or attained a certain age. She was proud of being the *plat* for the occasion, for when she was accosted by a missionary, who wanted to convert her to Christianity and withdraw her from her fate, she said she had no objection to be a Christian, but she must stay to be eaten, that she had been fattened for the purpose and must fulfil her destiny.

Charles Greville

1921   Really, really – this is disgraceful – 15 days of November spent & my diary none the wiser. But when nothing is written one may safely suppose that I have been stitching books; or we have had tea at 4 & I have taken my walk afterwards; or I have had to read something for next days writing, or I have been out late, & come home with stencilling materials, & sat down in excitement to try one. We went to Rodmell, & the gale blew at us all day; off arctic fields; so we spent our time attending to the fire. The day before this I wrote the last words of Jacob [*Jacob's Room*] – on Friday Nov. 4th to be precise, having begun it on April 16 1920: allowing for 6 months interval due to Monday or Tuesday & illness, this makes about a year. I have not yet looked at it.

Virginia Woolf

16 November

1813   Went last night with Lewis to see the first of *Antony and Cleopatra*. It was admirably got up, and well acted – a salad of Shakspeare and Dryden. Cleopatra strikes me as the epitome of her sex – fond, lively, sad, tender, teasing, humble, haughty, beautiful, the devil! – coquettish to the last, as well with the 'asp' as with Antony. After doing all she can to persuade him that – but why do they abuse him for cutting off poltroon Cicero's head? Did not Tully tell Brutus it was a pity to have spared Antony? and did he not speak the Philippics? and are not '*words things*'? and such '*words*' very pestilent '*things*' too? If he had had a hundred heads, they deserved (from Antony) a rostrum (his was stuck up there) apiece – though, after all he might as well have pardoned him, for the credit of the thing. But to resume – Cleopatra, after securing him, says 'yet go – it is your interest', etc – how like the sex! and the questions about Octavia – it is woman all over.

Lord Byron

1823   My dear girl, who acknowledged that the fancy about her dying at thirty had haunted her a good deal, gave me a letter which she had written to me in contemplation of this event; full of such things as, in spite of my efforts to laugh at her for her nonsense, made me cry.

Thomas Moore

1837   The Bishop of London told Amyot, that when the Bishops were first presented to the Queen, she received them with all possible dignity, and then retired. She passed through a glass door, and, forgetting its transparency, was seen to run off like a girl, as she is. Mr Quayle, in corroboration of this, told me that lately, asking a maid of honour how she liked her situation, and who of course expressed her delight, she said: 'I do think myself it is good fun playing Queen.' This is just as it should be. If she had not now the high spirits of a healthy girl of eighteen, we should have less reason to hope she would turn out a sound sensible woman at thirty.

Henry Crabb Robinson

1858 Wrote the last word of *Adam Bede* and sent it to Mr Langford. *Jubilate*.

George Eliot

17 November

1813 I wish I could settle to reading again – my life is monotonous, and yet desultory. I take up books, and fling them down again. I began a comedy, and burnt it because the scene ran into *reality* – a novel; – for the same reason. In rhyme, I can keep more away from the facts; but the thought always runs through, through . . . yes, yes, through . . .

Mr Murray has offered me one thousand guineas for *The Giaour* and *The Bride of Abydos*. I won't – it is too much, though I am strongly tempted, merely for the *say* of it. No bad price for a fortnight's (a week each) what? – the gods know – it was intended to be called poetry.

I have dined regularly today, for the first time since Sunday last – this being Sabbath, too. All the rest, tea and dry biscuits –six *per diem*. I wish to God I had not dined now! – It kills me with heaviness, stupor, and horrible dreams; and yet it was but a pint of Bucellas, and fish. Meat I never touch – nor much vegetable diet. I wish I were in the country, to take exercise – instead of being obliged to *cool* by abstinence, in lieu of it. I should not so much mind a little accession of flesh – my bones can well bear it. But the worst is, the devil always came with it – till I starved him out, and I will *not* be the slave of *any* appetite. If I do err, it shall be my heart, at least, that heralds the way. Oh, my head – how it aches? – the horrors of digestion! I wonder how Buonaparte's dinner agrees with him? . . . My head! I believe it was given me to ache with. Good even.

Lord Byron

1898   Dined at home and went to the Savoy to conduct the 21st anniversary of the production of the *Sorcerer* – originally produced at the Op. Comique 17th November, 1877. Tremendous house – ditto reception. Opera went very well. Call for Gilbert and self – we went on together, but did not speak to each other.

Arthur Sullivan

1947   Awful days and nights since I last wrote. High fever all the time. The first night of this new attack, I was in so much pain that Eric gave me a morphia injection. Then I floated off wonderfully because the wireless was playing Mendelssohn's violin concerto in E. I floated away on this lovely music. Every day after that I was just drowsy, aching in a high temperature for more than a week . . .

    I don't want to think of writing any more. It is a deadness and a worry.

Denton Welch

18 November

1803   Went to Buckingham, to see Doctor Williams, who found me better, and ordered me to wear flannel waistcoats. We walked out and it was so dirty that I went in to Mrs East who lent me one of her daughter's pairs of stockings which I put on rather unwillingly – we were very merry.

Harriet Wynne

1810   At Godwin's with Northcote, Coleridge, &c. Coleridge made himself very merry at the expense of Fuseli, whom he always called Fuzzle or Fuzly. He told a story of Fuseli's being on a visit at Liverpool at a time when unfortunately he had to divide the attention of the public with a Prussian soldier, who had excited a great deal of notice by his enormous powers of eating. And the annoyance was aggravated by persons persisting in considering the soldier as Fuseli's countryman. He spent his last evening at Dr Crompton's, when Roscoe (whose visitor Fuseli was) took an opportunity of giving a hint to the party that no one should mention the glutton. The admonition unfortunately was not heard by a lady, who, turning to the great Academician and lecturer, said, 'Well, sir, your countryman has been surpassing himself!' – 'Madam,' growled the irritated painter, 'the fellow is no countryman of mine.' – 'He is a foreigner! Have you heard what he has been doing? He has eaten a live cat!' – 'A live cat!' everyone exclaimed, except Fuseli, whose rage was excited by the suggestion of a lady famous for her blunders: 'Dear me, Mr Fuseli, that would be a fine subject for your pencil.' 'My pencil, madam?' – 'To be sure, sir, as the horrible is your forte.' – 'You mean the *terrible*, madam,' he replied with an assumed composure, muttering at the same time between his teeth, 'if a silly woman can mean anything.'

Henry Crabb Robinson

1851 We were visited by a severe snowstorm and the snow lay 18 inches deep even where it had not drifted. In addition to the rareness of snow so early in the winter was the circumstance of its being accompanied by thunder and lightning, and also the fact that the elm-trees were still in full foliage and in their greenest garb.

The Reverend Benjamin Armstrong

19 November

1654 The lord good to mee and mine in outward mercies. this weeke was cold and snowy and wett, and now cleare and frosty, and so very seasonable, this weeke a sad hand of god on John Church dying in a very nastie condicon, the lice running by 100ds on his face, and crawling into his mouth, oh that I could tremble before the lord. this day my heart lett out on behalfe of my sister, the lord revive her in mercy, god was good to mee in the word, my heart in some measure plain towards the interest of christ, but its but strait, and I find much unactiveness therein.

The Reverend Ralph Josselin

1825 Mr Green, the new Professor of Anatomy in the Academy, commenced last night. As usual he affirmed the Greek Artists did not know Muscular Anatomy because their medical Professors were so ignorant. There is no argument but for *the degree*; because the Medical men knew *little*, is that any proof that the artists knew *nothing*? Certainly not.

It is extraordinary how Professors established for the very purpose of instructing youth in the principles of Anatomy, should begin to deaden their enthusiasm by saying, 'You must know it, because I am established to teach it,' but yet the Greatest Artist the world ever saw *didn't* know it. What is the inference made by lazy youth? Why, if the greatest artists did not know it, what use can it be to us?

B. R. Haydon

1923 Dined with Schuster and went to a party at Lady Colefax's. Was introduced to Lady Sandwich, but got nothing to eat. Only stayed an hour. Why are high-class parties so dreary?

Siegfried Sassoon

1947 The snow has gone, but it is still so cold. I had presents of books from Peggy Kirkaldy, and food from Aunt Dolly, jelly, muscatel raisins, crystallized fruits, just what I want. When people are good to me I feel dead, not alive enough to thank them properly.

Denton Welch

---

20 November

1815 Dear Maria sat again today and tormented me as I painted, with her lovely archness & wicked, fascinating fun. After sitting some little time, she insisted with that sort of irresistible, insinuating 'now do', which makes resistance useless when from the mouth of a beauty, she insisted she could paint the hair better than mine, & taking the brushes out of my hand, with a delicate apprehension and graceful shrink as she touched the paint, for fear of her black silk, just put on for the first time, flounced four times to the knee, taking my brushes, she dabbled a lock over the forehead, & then laughed with a rich thrilling at her own lovely awkwardness. I looked at her as she leant over, my hair & cheek accidentally grazed the silk that covered her exquisite bosom – I could have eat her bit by bit – but her Father had trusted her to my honor, & I would have split with passion rather than ventured to have touched her hand. She sat for three hours, with perfect good humour, sometimes singing sweet airs with a honey voice, sometimes mimicking ballad singers, with a comic simplicity that was exquisite, & sometimes asking my opinions on different things, and wondering at a new idea put into her mind with a lovely smile. Her face & form & air & manner are perpetual exciters of 'lovely fancies & all heavenly things'. Sweet, sweet Girl. She found some pretence to go shopping in Bond Street, tho I taxed her that it was only to shew her new flounces to the Bows, which she denied with a blush. Peace & happiness for ever attend her.

B. R. Haydon

1825   I have all my life regretted that I did not keep a regular journal. I have myself lost recollection of much that was interesting and I have deprived my family and the public of some curious information by not carrying this resolution into effect.

I have bethought me on seeing lately some volumes of Byron's notes that he probably had hit upon the right way of keeping such a memorandum-book by throwing aside all pretence to regularity and order and marking down events just as they occurd to recollection. I will try this plan and behold I have a handsome lockd volume such as might serve for a Lady's Album. *Nota Bene* John Lockhart and Anne and I are to raise a society for the suppression of Albums. It is a most troublesome shape of mendicity – Sir, your autograph – a line of poetry – or a prose sentence among all the sprawling sonnets and blotted trumpery that dishonours these miscellanies – a man must have a good stomach that can swallow this botheration as a compliment.

Walter Scott

1873 Edward Humphries married a young woman when he was 83 and had a son within the year. 'Leastways his wife had,' said Mrs Hall.

The Reverend Francis Kilvert

---

21 November

1703 The wet and uncomfortable weather staying us from church this morning, our Dr officiated in my family, at which were present above 20 domestics. He made an excellent discourse on I Cor. 15, v. 55, 56, of the vanity of this world and uncertainty of life, and the inexpressible happiness and satisfaction of a holy life, with pertinent inferences to prepare us for death and a future state. I gave him thanks, and told him I tooke it kindly as my funeral sermon.

John Evelyn

1946 I reach the age of sixty. Until about five years ago I detected no decline at all in physical vigour and felt as young as I did at thirty. In the last five years, however, I am conscious that my physical powers are on the decline. I am getting slightly deaf and the passions of the flesh are spent. Intellectually, I observe no decline in vigour; I can write with the same facility, which is perhaps a fault. But I do not notice that my curiosity, my interest or my powers of enjoyment and amusement have declined at all. What is sad about becoming sixty is that one loses all sense of adventure. I am well aware, moreover, that I have not achieved either in the literary or political world that status which my talents and the hard work I have done and do might seem to justify.

Harold Nicolson

1962 Broadcasting House dinner, and this, I think, is the part of the celebrations which I most feared. All the governors were there except the chairman. Speeches about me and then the deputy chairman, Sir James Duff, made me a presentation of twenty-four volumes of the OED and a television set. I was sitting opposite my own portrait which was not very congenial, but

before the speeches began I got the lights turned off except
two in the centre which was a tremendous improvement. I
suppose I spoke for about ten minutes . . .

Of course, afterwards, I thought of many things I might
have said and how much I could have made them all laugh by
going round the room, commenting on each individual whom
I knew in turn. What an extraordinary evening it all was.

John Reith

22 November

1616   Being Friday at night, about eight of the clock, being a very
dark and misty night, the waves of the sea seemed to be flames
of fire near about the Cobbe of Lyme, which in the fall and
breaking thereof gave such a light that they might see the
coast all along as far as Charmouth, as if it had been
lightning. It was seen of an hundred people of Lyme, and
confidently affirmed by Larcome, an honest man who saw the
same. Among which a boy of the town being present went to
the sea side and took up some of the water in a frying pan,
and brought it to the Company, who pouring the same on the
ground in falling seemed like to sparks of fire.

Walter Yonge

1654   Dreamd I was familiar with the pope. wife dreamd wee were
so with the protector lord lead mee not into temptacon.

The Reverend Ralph Josselin

1790   A right true November Day, dark, wet, windy and cold.

The Reverend James Woodforde

1976   Forty-six today; fifty in sight. The good thing I suppose is that
I have reached a point most people reach in their fifties rather
than their forties, so I reckon I can sit out the swing of fashion
against me. But I am doing too much. If I can get this theatre
right and devolve it so that major directors are running
segments of the company then I will have done something.

> But that requires a lot of thought and a lot of steady progress.
> The main thing I need is time, and time is what the Board may
> not give me.
>
> **Peter Hall**

---

23 November

1790 Sent for the man of the Hand. Paid him. Then sent him to the
Village for the man with the Bear. The man brought it. A tame
huge animal, female I suppose by the Master calling it Nancy.
We fed it with Bread and Mutton. It drank Small Beer. It was
exhibited in the field before our Cottage.

Lady Eleanor Butler

1880 Finished *Jane Eyre*, which is really a wonderful book very
peculiar in parts, but so powerfully and admirably written,
such a fine tone in it, such fine religious feeling, and such
beautiful writing. The description of the mysterious maniac's
nightly appearances awfully thrilling, Mr Rochester's character a very remarkable one, and Jane Eyre's herself a beautiful
one. The end is very touching, when Jane Eyre returns to him
and finds him blind, with one hand gone from injuries during
the fire in his house, which was caused by his mad wife.

Queen Victoria

1916 [France] A grey, warmer day. The sun looked through only
for a minute or two in the afternoon. We went in the evening
to an estaminet on the left. After that Cl. and I walked down
the road under the moon, and talking to him then I grew more
convinced of the brutalizing process that was going on: how
impossible it was to read, even when we had leisure, how
supremely one was occupied with food and drink. Cl. himself
said he found the same on his first campaign; it took him three
weeks to get back into a state where he could read, and so it
is. All my dreams of the days after the war centre round bright
fires, arm-chairs, good beds, and abundant meals.

Arthur Graeme West

24 November

1582 I dremed that I was deade, and afterward my bowels wer taken out I walked and talked with diverse, and among other with the Lord Thresorer who was com to my howse to burn my bokes when I was dead, and thought he loked sourely on me.

John Dee

1645 I had sought to god for my wife (that was oppressed with feares that she should not doe well on this child,) that god would order all providences so as wee might rejoyce in his salvacion, I had prayd with confidence of good successe to her: about midnight on Monday: I rose called up some neighbours: the night was very light: goodman Potter willing to goe for the midwife, and up when I went: the horse out of the pasture, but presently found: the midwife up at Buers, expecting it had beene nearer day; the weather indifferent dry; midwife came, all things even gotten ready towards day. I called in the women by day light, almost all came; and about 11 or 12. of the clocke my wife was with very sharpe paynes deliverd. Nov: 25. of her daughter intended for a Jane, she was then 25 y of age her selfe; wee had made a good pasty for this houre, and that also was kept well, wife and child both well prais bee my good and mercifull father.

The Reverend Ralph Josselin

1813 No dreams last night of the dead, nor the living; so – I am 'firm as the marble, founded as the rock', till the next earthquake . . .

I am tremendously in arrear with my letters – except to — and to her my thoughts overpower me: my words never compass them. To Lady Melbourne I write with most pleasure – and her answers, so sensible, so *tactique* – I never met with half her talent. If she had been a few years younger, what a fool she would have made of me, had she thought it worth her while – and I should have lost a valuable and most agreeable *friend*. Mem. – a mistress never is nor can be a friend. While you agree, you are lovers; and, when it is over, any thing but friends . . .

Rogers thinks the *Quarterly* will attack me next. Let them. I have been 'peppered so highly' in my time, *both* ways, that it must be cayenne or aloes to make me taste. I can sincerely say, that I am not very much alive *now* to criticism. But – in tracing this – I rather believe that it proceeds from my not attaching that importance to authorship which many do, and which, when young, I did also. 'One gets tired of every thing, my angel', says Valmont. The 'angels' are the only things of which I am not a little sick – but I do think the preference of *writers* to *agents* – the mighty stir made about scribbling and scribes, by themselves and others – a sign of effeminacy, degeneracy, and weakness. Who would write, who had any thing better to do? 'Action – action – action' – said Demosthenes: 'Actions – actions', I say, and not writing – least of all, rhyme. Look at the querulous and monotonous lives of the 'genus'; – except Cervantes, Tasso, Dante, Ariosto, Kleist (who were brave and active citizens), Aeschylus, Sophocles, and some other of the antiques also – what a worthless, idle brood it is!

Lord Byron

---

25 November

1699   There happen'd this weeke so thick a mist and fog that people lost their way in the streetes, it being so intense that no light of candles or torches yielded any (or but very little) direction. I was in it and in danger. Robberies were committed between the very lights which were fix'd between London and Kensington on both sides, and whilst coaches and travellers were passing. It began about four in the afternoone, and was quite gon by eight, without any wind to disperse it. At the Thames they beat drums to direct the watermen to make the shore.

John Evelyn

1882   First performance of *Iolanthe* at the Savoy Theatre. House crammed. Awfully nervous; more so than usual on going into Orchestra. Tremendous reception. First Act went splendidly.

The second dragged, and I was afraid it must be compressed. However it finished well, and Gilbert and myself were called and heartily cheered. Very low afterwards. Came home.

Arthur Sullivan

1945 So nothing – blank in me tonight after sickness and 'flu. All day touching at the drawing with my black pen, turning away from the writing always, because drawing soothes and lulls, and should do so, else there will be no good picture. It must all be built up of little cat pats, love pats; although many people will not believe this and think painters should be half-drunk louts who paint with their large loo-loos. But writing ought to be love pats, that tickle the patter with warmth as he pats; but it only is sometimes for perhaps five seconds.

It is lazier to be a painter than a writer, but only if you are both. If you are only a writer, then you are lazier, because you waste your hands. Only if you copied out your books most exquisitely you would be better.

Black man on the wireless sings, 'Don't want to be a Judas in my heart, Lord'. Gas fire roars so dryly. Maurice Cranston has been to tea. He can't think one thought out of the middle of his own head, but only out of someone's else's, and the heads he chooses are always secondhand too. It is a puppy biting its tail of hollowness. He reviews books for the *Church Times* and he saw my last one on a Charing Cross bookstall labelled boldly and badly 'Of Interest to Students of Abnormal Psychology'. He thinks I should tell Routledge to object, but I don't think it matters at all.

Writing is everything but the reality. Heavy as mud, powdery as meringue, silvered all over with clouding slime, everything true escaping underneath the words, like insects scuttling away – like the cars and bicycles in Trafalgar Square beetling, skidding away when the huge hand in the sky, God's hand, is only just put down to pluck them.

When your life has nothing left in it but your writing, then it grows so dear that even the badness is loved and groomed and cared for. But if real love comes into your life, it cuts away from your work, so that if you laugh at it, almost despite it for what it is worth, yet long for it too, brood on the time when you had nothing else, when all you had to live on was what you made, when your thoughts were hotted up and sharp, for you dared not let them cool.

Denton Welch

---

26 November

1775   A little after five I stole gently to —'s room, which I found to be neat and cosy. I sat about an hour. She indulged me in amorous dalliances of much familiarity, but though I preached from the Old Testament, could not think of allowing me ingress. I was much pleased with her unaffected goodness and being for the time calmed, I thought we might do more afterwards. There was nothing of art or feverishness on either side. I was clear that I was doing no ill. Such was my sensation or immediate impression.

James Boswell

1878   Chevalier, who allowed Whistler's talent, as every one would who has seen some of his pictures of the Thames at night with the magnificent array of lamplights on bridges, embankments &c obscured partially or reddened by fog or darkness or halfquenched in blue moonlight – gave us an anecdote of Whistler on his first arrival in England, which he said he had from an eyewitness. Whistler had invited a number of artists to see his works, on a Sunday morning. Those who went were ushered into his bedroom where they found him in bed! a great four-poster with curtains painted by himself. He jumped out immediately just as he was, in his nightshirt, and without stopping to put on even slippers, as he supposed they were anxious to see his productions, rushed to some portfolio and began to examine them, talking aloud to himself and commenting upon their contents, as he turned them over, one by one: 'Whistler, that's one of the best things you ever did,' or 'You must not part with that, Whistler, whatever you do!' &c. All this acting to give the impression of an eccentric genius and create a sensation. Chevalier said he had met him 'in society', dressed in a long coat, very tightly tied in at the waist, with an enormous collar spread out in front, of fur or some showy material.

Alfred Domett

1917   I dont like Sunday; the best thing is to make it a work day, & to unravel Brooke's mind to the sound of church bells was suitable enough. Such a wind in the night, by the way, that the milkman reported much damage down the road this morning, & raised our hopes, which were dashed on going out to see nothing smashed – not a stain of blood, or ever the remnant of a hat. It was fine & wet by turns, with a high cold wind continuously. We went to Kew, & saw a blazing bush, as red as cherry blossom, but more intense – frostily red – also gulls rising & falling for pieces of meat, their crowd waved aside suddenly by three very elegant light grey cranes. We also went into the orchid house where these sinister reptiles live in a tropical heat, so that they come out in all their spotted & streaked flesh even now in the cold. They always make me anxious to bring them into a novel.

Virginia Woolf

27 November

1703   The effects of the hurricane and tempest of wind, rain and lightning thro' all the nation, especialy London were very dismal. Many houses demolish'd and people kill'd. As to my own losses, the subversion of woods and timber, both ornamental and valuable, through my whole estate, and about my house the woods crowning the garden mount, and growing along the park meadow, the damage to my own dwelling, farms and outhouses, is almost tragical, not to be parallel'd with any thing happening in our age. I am not able to describe it, but submit to the pleasure of Almighty God

John Evelyn

1807   Universal deep snow. Such weather never remembered by the oldest person.

Lady Eleanor Butler

1872 Great fall of stars, identified with Biela's comet. They radiated from Perseus or Andromeda and in falling, at least I noticed it of those falling at all southwards, took a pitch to the left halfway through their flight. The kitchen boys came running with a great todo to say something redhot had struck the meatsafe over the scullery door with a great noise and falling into the yard gone into several pieces. No authentic fragment was found but Br Hostage saw marks of burning on the safe and the slightest of dints as if made by a soft body, so that if anything fell it was probably a body of gas, Fr Perry thought. It did not appear easy to give any other explanation than a meteoric one.

Gerard Manley Hopkins

1964 Lunched at the Golden Egg. Oh, the horror – the cold stuffiness, claustrophobic placing of tables, garish lights and mass produced food in steel dishes. And the egg-shaped menu! But perhaps one could get something out of it. The setting for a breaking-off, or some terrible news or an unwanted declaration of love.

Barbara Pym

28 November

1857 A glorious day, still autumnal and not wintry. We have had a delicious walk in the Park, and I think the colouring of the scenery is more beautiful than ever. Many of the oaks are still thickly covered with leaves of a rich yellow-brown; the elms, golden sometimes, still with lingering patches of green. On our way to the Park the view from Richmond Hill had a delicate blue mist over it, that seemed to hang like a veil before the sober brownish-yellow of the distant elms. As we came home, the sun was setting on a fog-bank, and we saw him sink into that purple ocean – the orange and gold passing into green above the fog-bank, the gold and orange reflected in the river in more sombre tints. The other day, as we were coming home through the Park, after having walked under a sombre, heavily-clouded sky, the western sun shone out from under the curtain, and lit up the trees and grass, thrown into relief on a background of dark-purple cloud. Then as we advanced towards the Richmond end of the Park, the level reddening rays shone on the dry fern and the distant oaks, and threw a crimson light on them. I have especially enjoyed this autumn, the delicious greenness of the turf, in contrast with the red and yellow of the dying leaves.

George Eliot

1860 Since I last wrote in this Journal, I have suffered much from physical weakness, accompanied with mental depression. The loss of the country has seemed very bitter to me, and my want of health and strength has prevented me from working much – still worse, has made me despair of ever working well again. I am getting better now by the help of tonics, and shall be better still if I could gather more bravery, resignation, and simplicity of striving. In the meantime my cup is full of blessings: my home is bright and warm with love and tenderness, and in more material vulgar matters we are very fortunate.

George Eliot

1923 Am still trying to make the most of (and prepare for the shattering of) my solitude. No doubt I shall soon get used to the old conditions, but at present I genuinely shudder at the thought of turning out of this room and not being able to play the piano in peace. Lately I have, not for the first time, actually thought, rather cravingly, of having a house of my own.

Siegfried Sassoon

29 November

1663 *Lords day.* This morning I put on my best black cloth-suit trimmed with Scarlett ribbon, very neat, with my cloak lined with Velvett and a new Beaver, which altogether is very noble, with my black silk knit canons I bought a month ago. I to church alone, my wife not going; and there I find my Lady

Batten in a velvet gowne, which vexed me that she should be in it before my wife, or that I am able to put her into one; but what cannot be, cannot be. However, when I came home I told my wife of it; and to see my weakness, I could on the sudden have found my heart to have offered her one, but second thoughts put it by; and endeed, it would undo me to think of doing as Sir W. Batten and his Lady do, who hath a good estate beside his office. A good dinner we had of *bœuf à la mode*, but not dressed so well as my wife used to do it. So after dinner I to the French church; but that being too far begun, I came home to St Dunstans by us, and heard a good sermon and so home.

Samuel Pepys

1694 I visited the Marquiss of Normanby and had much discourse concerning K. Cha. II. being poison'd. Also concerning the *Quinquina* which the physicians would not give to the King, at a time when in a dangerous ague it was the only thing that could cure him (out of envy because it had ben brought into vogue by Mr Tudor an apothecary), till Dr Short, to whom the King sent to know his opinion of it privately, he being reputed a Papist, (but who was in truth a very honest good Christian) sent word to the King that it was the only thing which could save his life, and then the King injoin'd his physicians to give it to him, which they did, and he recover'd. Being asked by this Lord why they would not prescribe it, Dr Lower said it would spoil their practice, or some such expression, and at last confessed it was a remedy fit only for Kings.

John Evelyn

1948 Degrees of affection: I said to Bunny [his aunt] – perhaps thoughtlessly – the other day when I was preparing Queenie's [his dog] meal, 'Thank God for this weather, it keeps Queenie's meat for me.'

'It's certainly an ill-wind,' coughed Bunny: the cold and fog get on her chest. 'However, so long as the dog's all right, that's the great thing.'

I suppose she was in a bad mood, poor old girl, for it is rare for her to make sarcastic remarks like this. Silly, too – for it is true. I am much fonder of the dog than of her. Degrees of affection, yes. I remember Nancy saying to me, 'I believe you'd sacrifice us any time to the dog.' I said, 'Yes, of course.' Being a woman, so vain, I suppose she thought I didn't mean it, but I did. I love my dog far more dearly than her. Some days later she remarked something about 'Joe puts his dog before people' – but there, of course, she was wrong. Only certain people. Only her, in that particular context.

J. R. Ackerley

---

30 November

1794 Mem. a Primrose in my Garden in full bloom, seen by myself and my Niece.

The Reverend James Woodforde

1825 Last day.

> 30 days,
> 22 hard at work
> —
> 8 lost.

The four last days have been uselessly (but unavoidably so) spent in musing, thinking, & strolling. The backs of the balls of my eyes were irritable, a sign I always dread. I left off directly, and am recovered.

22 days I have worked very hard, and though the Painting of my Picture is not completed, it is all so settled, that it soon will be with God's blessing.

B. R. Haydon

1937 Yes, its actually the last day of November; & theyve passed like a streak of hounds after a fox because I've been re-writing *3 Guineas* with such intentness, indeed absorption, that several times 5 minutes past one has shown on the clock & I still at it. So I've never even looked at this stout volume.

Virginia Woolf

1944 Collins sent me *English Story*, with my own story in it, mixed up with Elizabeth Bowen, Rex Warner, Henry Treece. I

suddenly began to read it with great interest, liking some bits
– other bits not. Usually I am overcome with shame when I
see something of mine in print, and never dare look at it. Even
someone else reading something of mine in my presence fills
me with horror.

I had an air letter from an Aircraftman Parker in India, who
apparently read *Maiden Voyage* and then started to track all
my other work, writing and painting, just as Symons tracked
Corvo in his book *The Quest for Corvo*.

This Parker has been amazingly persevering and has almost
found out everything there is to know about my published
things, even down to little poems in queer magazines!

He has been undertaking the search with another friend.
And everything they found about me, they put into a book
labelled 'Denton Welch – His Book'.

Now he wants to buy a picture to round off his search! He
wrote to the Leger, the Leicester, the Redfern. And the
Redfern forwarded his letter to me.

Isn't it crazy! I wonder if he will have the determination to
do anything like it again! He might do some quite interesting
research on a dead and gone obscure author.

It made me feel, when I heard of it, as if I had been
preserving myself on a top shelf for years, waiting to be
discovered. As if I were dead and done with, and watching
some future person ferreting me out.

Denton Welch

1 December

1813 I shall soon be six-and-twenty (January 22nd, 1814). Is there any thing in the future that can possibly console us for not being always *twenty-five*?

Lord Byron

1825 I think this Journal will suit me well; if I can coax myself into an idea that is purely voluntary it may go on – *Nulla dies sine linea*. But never a being from my infancy upwards hated task-work as I hate it – And yet I have done a great deal in my day. It is not that I am idle in my nature either. But propose to me to do one thing and it is inconceivable the desire I have to do something else, not that it is more easy or more pleasant but just because it is escaping from an imposed task. I cannot trace this love of contradiction to any distinct source but it has haunted me all my life. I could almost suppose it was mechanical and that the imposition of a piece of duty-labour operated on me like the mace of a bad billiard player, which gives an impulse to the ball indeed but sends it off at a tangent different from the course designed by the player. Now if I expend such eccentrick movements on this journal it will be turning this wretched propensity to some tolerable account. If I had thus employ'd the hours and half hours which I have while'd away in putting off something that must needs be done at last, My Conscience, I should have had a journal with a witness.

Walter Scott

1832 We were reading the evening papers, wherein it was mentioned that a British sailor, who had served in many engagements abroad, had been carried before Mr Justice Conant, charged with being drunk in the streets, with having abused the ministers, and with swearing aloud, that the British flag was disgraced by sailing in company with the French tricolour. The poor wretch, having no respondents, was fined by Mr Conant thirty shillings, or, in default, to two months' imprisonment in Coldbath Fields. On hearing his doom, he only replied, 'Sir, you may send me to prison, but the British flag is not the less disgraced.'

Our natural impulse was immediately to subscribe the trifling fine to liberate him, which Sir H. Cooke transmitted the next morning; but even this early interference was too late, the committee of Lloyd's Coffee-house had already anticipated our feelings, and rescued the poor drunken patriot. I need not add, that this coffee-house is the resort of all the great underwriters, and the donation was merely an act of strong public feeling.

Thomas Raikes

---

2 December

1775 When I came home, I found that my wife had been reading this journal and, though I had used Greek letters, had understood my visits to —. She spoke to me of it with so much reason and spirit that, as I candidly owned my folly, so I was impressed with proper feelings; and, without more argument than that it was disagreeable to so excellent a spouse, resolved firmly to keep clear. And when I reflected calmly, I thought it lucky that my journal had been read, as it gave an opportunity to check in the beginning what might have produced much mischief. I wondered at my temporary dissipation of thought when I saw the effects of my conduct. I valued and loved my wife with renewed fervour.

James Boswell

1808 Felt at breakfast something of weakness in right arm, which, combined with sensation in leg on same side, not quite pleasant; from a short time after rheumatism had left back and descended into leg and thigh, a sort of tingling and pricking there, as when limb has been asleep.

William Windham

1818 Conversation at breakfast about late hours. The porter of the late Lord Jersey came to someone and complained he could not stay with the Jerseys, 'because my lady was the very latest woman in London'. 'Well, but what then? All women of fashion are late, you can sleep afterwards.' 'Ah no, sir, that's not all, for my Lord is the earliest gentleman in London; and, between the two, I get no sleep at all.' I mentioned the circumstance of a man from the country visiting his friend in town, and both sleeping in the same bed without ever meeting for a fortnight.

Thomas Moore

1889 1st band rehearsal (*all* the music) of the New Opera at the Prince's Hall. Very few errors. Beautiful effect. Home to dine. After dinner wrote, arranged and scored the Overture, finishing at 3 a.m. Gilbert came down after rehearsal at Savoy at 11:15. Finally settled title *The Gondoliers or The King of Barataria*. Good title I think.

Arthur Sullivan

3 December

1803 Doctor Williams called and made me undergo a *blushing* operation. He finds me much about the same and I had to rub my side with Mercury which was very nasty work. I took an immense dose of Calomal. Played at cards.

Harriet Wynne

1908 The Climax again. Leave out from Day Book a figure of £2,000. The Bosses – Sir Philip and Edgar Waterlow – have to be told. Ashamed! The vultures waiting to pounce. . . . To add to this, although I fill my mind with all things pure, have bad dreams. Must go away and start afresh.

Destroying correspondence, which I had kept for years and wasted days, spending pounds on it. The folly of youth! NO QUARTER! Let my diary end with this repeated cry.

Sydney Moseley

1921 I dined with the Sangers last night, & enjoyed society. I wore my new black dress, & looked, I daresay, rather nice. That's a feeling I very seldom have; & I rather intend to enjoy it oftener. I like clothes, if I can design them. So Bertie Russell was attentive, & we struck out like swimmers who knew their waters. One is old enough to cut the trimmings & get to the point. Bertie is a fervid egoist – which helps matters. And then, what a pleasure – this mind on springs. I got as much out of him as I could carry.

Virginia Woolf

1977 The absurd but painful struggle against smoking. I first 'gave up' about twenty years ago, and once achieved an unbroken abstinence of nearly six months. Usually, now, the cycle is five or six weeks off; a week or two on. And usually too, the relapse is excused by some family mishap; or simply by too many people being around.

What is so strange is that I deeply hate the wretched little poisonous tubes, and positively look forward, on smoking days, to the day I've set myself for renouncing them again.

Philip Toynbee

4 December

1823 I received a bill of £8 15s od from Cruttwell, the lawyer, absolutely for doing nothing. This is the second time I have paid him the same amount for merely writing letters to the tithepayers, without taking any further trouble. I certainly shall freely express my sentiments.

The Reverend John Skinner

1855 I hardly ever begin to write here that I am not tempted to break out into Jobisms about my bad nights. How I keep on my legs and in my senses with such little snatches of sleep is a wonder to myself. Oh, to cure anyone of a terror of annihilation, just put him on my allowance of sleep, and see if he don't get to long for sleep, sleep, unfathomable and everlasting sleep as the only conceivable heaven.

Jane Welsh Carlyle

1893 Dull, warmer. In the afternoon went to see Shorter, and had rather a brusque conversation with him. However, he asked me to undertake a serial for the *Illustd London News*, to commence in a year's time or so. Got from him no cheques, but forms of account to fill up and send . . .

Thinking I had anything but pleased Shorter, I was astonished to receive by last post a note from him, which must have been written immediately after my departure. He will be 'exceedingly glad' to have 6 stories from me for the *Eng. Illustrated*, at 12 guineas each, I to keep the American rights. Moreover, he hopes I shall be able to dine with him shortly, and would like to 'see more of' me. Evidently he thinks me of some commercial value.

George Gissing

1940 Rowena rings to say, in a dead sort of voice. 'The worst has happened, Billy Bolitho says I'm definitely pregnant. Can you lend me fifteen quid till Saturday?' I said I could give her six, which was all I had, because I know just how she feels, and if she doesn't have the abortion before Saturday it will be too late. I met her in Dean Street and we wandered down to Durand's in the icy cold for a *delicious* lunch. Christ, their pastries are good! Poor Rowena couldn't eat anything.

She says that her only other chance is to put lots of ether soap up her bottom for ten days. Billy Bolitho says it's tough but infallible, but R says, 'How will I keep it from my Mum if I go around smelling like an operating theatre?'

Joan Wyndham

5 December

1792 My nights grow very restless – the Palms of my hands parched. *Nec nisi febre calet sanguis.*

He that is uneasy in one Posture fancies relief in a change. I cannot but believe that were I master of Time and Place I could heal or mitigate my Nervous Sorrow. Now like Regulus in his Tub of Nails which ever way I turn me or rather am turned I fall against the point of some Sharp Affliction.

The Reverend William Bagshaw Stevens

1920   Then – what? Gerald Duckworth engaged to Miss Chad – does that count as news? dinner at the Toynbees, but I cant go into that. What do I want to go into? How hard we work – thats what impresses me this winter: every compartment stuffed tight, chiefly owing to the press. Whether we can keep it up, I don't know. Then, both so popular, so well known, so much respected – & Leonard 40, & I nearing it, so there's not much to boast of. In my heart, too, I prefer the nondescript anonymous days of youth. I like youthful minds; & the sense that no one's yet anybody. This refers, with shocking slovenliness – but what will you? I cant write 2,000 words an hour carefully – to tea with Miss Hussey at Clifford's Inn. I dont know why I saw my own youth there: she on her own, a journalist, poor, untidy, enthusiastic; & a younger brother coming in, to tea; not so clever, at least not launched; awkward; oh but so young! Both going off to the play, as Adrian & I did, years ago; but perhaps she's happier than I was. Figure a poverty stricken room; gas fire broken; margarine; one table; books, mostly cheap ones; writing table; no ornament or easy chair – (perhaps I had it) dark November day; up several staircases; bath, kitchen behind a dingy curtain, & another woman sharing. We talked about the need of education. 'Surely education must achieve something' the brother stammered. She would have none of it – clever, & paradoxical, & flighty – advanced; but I forgive all that for the sake of youth.

Virginia Woolf

1935   I do not really think the House of Commons 'My Cup of Tea', I am too much of an individualist, and also, too self-centred and set in my ways. Enough if I remain a mute, just adequate back-bencher, but frankly most of the problems that so excite 'the Hon. Members' leave me quite cold and indifferent.

'Chips' Channon

6 December

1796   Heaviside told me that the late Duke of Leeds had related to him that *Dr Mead* had mentioned to his Grace that He had been called to the Tower to attend the Marquis of Tullibardine who died there. That He found him in a dying state owing to a mortification caused by a *voluntary* suppression of Urine which with exquisite pain He had endured 4 days, to avoid a public execution. 'I know it is all over with me said the Marquiss to Dr Mead, but I send for you to preserve appearances.'

Medical practice said Heaviside is very different from what it was formerly. Dr Mead only recd. half guinea fees: and it was the custom at that time for Physicians to attend a Coffee House in the evenings where they met a number of Apothecarys who described Cases to them and the Physicians were paid what they called Council fees for the advice they gave.

Joseph Farington

1813 This journal is a relief. When I am tired – as I generally am – out comes this, and down goes every thing. But I can't read it over, and God knows what contradictions it may contain. If I am sincere with myself (but I fear one lies more to one's self than to any one else), every page should confute, refute, and utterly abjure its predecessor . . .

I am so far obliged to this Journal, that it preserves me from verse – at least from keeping it. I have just thrown a poem into the fire (which it has relighted to my great comfort), and have smoked out of my head the plan of another. I wish I could as easily get rid of thinking, or, at least, the confusion of thought.

Lord Byron

1826 A bad and disturbd night with fever, headache and some touch of cholera morbus which greatly disturbed my slumbers. But I fancy Nature was scouring the gun after her own fashion.

Walter Scott

1868 At night the most violent gale I ever heard. One of our elms snapped in half.

Gerard Manley Hopkins

7 December

1801   I was very indifferent & very unwell indeed today so blown up with gouty Wind & strange feelings. Dinner to day, boiled Beef &c. Towards the evening I got something better. Cow, Beauty had a Cow-Calf.

The Reverend James Woodforde

1813   Went to bed, and slept dreamlessly, but not refreshingly. Awoke, and up an hour before being called; but dawdled three hours in dressing. When one subtracts from life infancy (which is vegetation) – sleep, eating, and swilling – buttoning and unbuttoning – how much remains of downright existence? The summer of a dormouse.

Lord Byron

1947   Sunday is not the happy day it should be. There is no rest for me because I do not work. I get up earlier instead of later and for a man of middle age and set habits this is disturbing. There is a drive to church. An ugly suburban church, bare and comfortless. No letters, which are for me now, as for my deaf father, the link with the world. No papers until noon and then papers that fill me with gloom and disgust. A weekly joint seldom edible. For quite other reasons, and in quite another form, the Victorian Sunday has returned as a day of wrath.

Evelyn Waugh

8 December

1661   I had a very remarkeable escape yᵗ I had fallen down stairs at John Sawry. Sure it was a wonderfull mercy to mee to be preserved, & it was very narrowly done. Blessed be God that kept mee as he did.

The Reverend Henry Newcombe

1762   I sat in writing till one. I then strolled through the streets. I was somewhat dull and thought myself a poor sort of a being.

At night I went to Covent Garden and saw *Love in a Village*, a new comic opera, for the first night. I liked it much. I saw it from the gallery, but I was first in the pit. Just before the overture began to be played, two Highland officers came in. The mob in the upper gallery roared out, 'No Scots! No Scots! Out with them!' hissed and pelted them with apples. My heart warmed to my countrymen, my Scotch blood boiled with indignation. I jumped up on the benches, roared out, 'Damn you, you rascals!' hissed and was in the greatest rage. I am very sure at that time I should have been the most distinguished of heroes. I hated the English; I wished from my soul that the Union was broke and that we might give them another battle of Bannockburn. I went close to the officers and asked them of what regiment they were of. They told me Lord John Murray's, and that they were just come from the Havana. 'And this,' said they, 'is the thanks that we get – to be hissed when we come home. If it was French, what could they do worse?' 'But,' said one, 'if I had a *grup o yin or twa o the tamd rascals I sud let them ken what they're about.*' The rudeness of the English vulgar is terrible. This indeed is the liberty which they have: the liberty of bullying and being abusive with their blackguard tongues. They soon gave over. I then went to the gallery and was really well entertained with the opera.

James Boswell

1861   G. had a headache, so we walked out in the morning sunshine. I told him my conception of my story, and he expressed great delight. Shall I ever be able to carry out my ideas? Flashes of hope are succeeded by long intervals of dim distrust.

George Eliot

1936   The Simpson crisis has been a great delight to everyone. At Maidie's nursing home they report a pronounced turn for the better in all adult patients. There can seldom have been an event that has caused so much general delight and so little pain. Reading the papers and even listening to announcements that there was no news on the wireless took up most of the week.

Evelyn Waugh

9 December

1661 I found my spirit much out of order. O my soule w^{re} have I beene all this while. So dead in dutys. So endles in my studdys. So unprofitable in company. So unedefying in my family. So negligent of meditation. So formall in preachinge. O my soule w^{re} hast thou beene? The L^d put some life into mee. After supp: wee went to see M^{ris} Wollen y^t hath not beene well. S. Woolmore was wth mee at my returne, and I desired to be humbled before God for my sin & g^t wickednesses. *I am more bruitish y^n any man.* My minde is still runinge before mee & it is after noth: but hath no heart to tarry at home wth mee.

The Reverend Henry Newcombe

1775 At supper my wife and I had a dispute about some trifle. She did not yield readily enough, and my passion rose to a pitch that I could not quite command. I started up and threw an egg in the fire and some beer after it. My inclination was to break and destroy everything. But I checked it. How curious is it that the thinking principle can speculate in the very instant of anger. My wife soon made up our difference. But I begged of her to be more attentive again.

James Boswell

1868 Honeysuckle out and catkins hanging in the thickets.

Gerard Manley Hopkins

1905 Oh, Lord! Millie has no one to guard, guide or protect her. Found a book called *The Decameron* which I learned she has been reading in bed until one in the morning. This is a climax. Up to the present I have been tendering advice and *begging* for its acceptance. *Now* my advice *must* be accepted. For the sake of our dear Mother in Heaven I feel that I am entrusted with her keep. I may be the youngest in the family, but someone has got to take the lead.

Sydney Moseley

10 December

1813 I am *ennuyé* beyond my usual tense of that yawning verb, which I am always conjugating; and I don't find that society much mends the matter. I am too lazy to shoot myself – and it would annoy Augusta, and perhaps – ; but it would be a good thing for George, on the other side, and no bad one for me; but I won't be tempted.

Lord Byron

1891 4.15 a.m. Have been up all night. A furious gale blowing. E. in long miserable pain; the Doctor has just given her chloroform, and says that the blackguard business draws to an end.

5.15. Went to the study door, and heard the cry of the child. Nurse, speedily coming down, tells me it is a boy. Wind howling savagely. So, the poor girl's misery is over, and she has what she earnestly desired.

Send notes to E.'s people in London, and one to Mother. Got through day without going to bed. Corrected some proofs. The wind, after lulling at mid-day, grew furious again towards night.

The baby has a very ugly dark patch over right eye. Don't know the meaning of it.

George Gissing

1892 Cold, rainy. *Little Grobby's birthday*. Present from Wakefield. He can just stand by himself, but not walk. Speaks no syllable, but understands a few words, such as 'window', 'fire'. Only two teeth. On the whole in very good health, feeding exclusively on Allen & Hanbury's Malted Food. First thing in the morning, I crowned him with a wreath of ivy.

George Gissing

1935 Most of the day at the House of Commons. Today for the first time I really liked it; boredom passed and a glow of pleasure filtered through me. But I wish I sometimes *understood* what I was voting for, and what against.

'Chips' Channon

11 December

1754 A poor, dull, sickly day: indigestion and choler.

Dr John Rutty

1866 Ill ever since I came home, so that the days seem to have made a muddy flood, sweeping away all labour and all growth.

George Eliot

1936 On Saturday I drove with the children to Croydon. Dad was out when we got there. When he came back, he looked unhappy and restless, and began to shout, as he always does when he's unhappy, about how he hated the Monarchy, but how there had to be humbug. I could see that his conscience was troubled. He told me how, on one occasion when Baldwin went to see the King, he had found him quite drunk, and how he picked up a glass to throw, and greeted him with: 'Well, you fornicating old son of a bitch, what do you want now?' I said my only regret was that he didn't throw the glass.

My father is one of the most tragic human beings I know, and in his way, one of the most loveable. He's obsessed with the idea that he lacks dignity, but his lack of dignity is due to a kind of raw sincerity, which has kept him from ever throwing in his lot with the Establishment. He finds life bitter just now, because he's out of things, and haunted by the idea that, being 73, he may soon find his faculties decaying, and become an object of pity. My mother worries him, too. Age makes her comatose. After his outburst, he puts his arms round Val, and said something like: 'Well she's all right, anyway.'

Malcolm Muggeridge

1948 I look towards almost everything I do as a series of ordered movements to achieve my object as quickly and unexhaustingly as possible. Returning from a walk with Queenie [his dog], for instance, on a weekday afternoon, my mind thinks out the steps ahead; put on a pan of water for her vegetables, the first move, and turn on the bath, if I need one. While these two long-term things are happening, dry Queenie before she gets all wet and muddy on my bed. Then scrape a carrot or two for her, ready to put in the water when it boils. Begin then to cut up her meat and mix her gravy. If time, prepare our own dinner – the parts Bunny can't do, such as peeling potatoes. When carrot water is boiling, pop them in. Finish Queenie's meat cutting. Or dash round to off-licence if I have to, for a bottle of booze for ourselves. Bath ready by then – have it. By the time I've done so, the carrots will be cooked and I can mix and give Q. her meal. Then I can sit down and relax with no more fidgets and enjoy my cocktail and book. It is only by seeing my life always as a sequence of arranged steps or moves that I am able to get through the quantity of things I have to do.

J. R. Ackerley

12 December

1807   Mr Clerkson the Chaplin was here by Nine o'Clock and celebrated the Catholick Marriage Ceremony before breakfast in the School room, the Miss Pouletts came in time for it, Harriet looked modest for the first time in her Life, in a long french lace Veil and behaved very well. After breakfast we all adjourned to the Church in the Carriage, where Mr Cathcart tied the second Knot, a great multitude was assembled to witness the gay wedding. On our return to the House, Harriet exchanged her Bridal apparel for her riding habit and at two o'Clock the new married Couple sett out in a new Chariot for Stoke Farm. The Horses were taken from the Carriage at the door, and they were drove by the *Swanbournians* all down the Village in the midst of great acclamations and huzzahing. Mr Cathcart stayed to dine quietly with us, we were all exhausted and tired, but very glad every thing is over.

Elizabeth Fremantle

1825   Impenetrably dark. Could not paint. Went out. Called on Hazlitt, as being all in character with the day, & had a regular groan!

B. R. Haydon

1827 Reconsiderd the probable downfall of my literary reputation. I am so constitutionally indifferent to the censure or praise of the world that never having abandond myself to the feelings of selfconceit which my great success was calculated to inspire I can look with the most unshaken firmness upon the event as far as my own feelings are concernd. If there be any great advantage in literary fame I have had it and I certainly do not care at losing it.

They cannot say but what I *had* the *crown*.

Walter Scott

1955 For a creative artist, someone who carries his factory about with him, to have domicile in England is no longer sensible. It is impossible to live there and keep your head above financial water. I have paid God knows how many hundreds of thousands of pounds to the British Government during my life and the privileges I have received in return are actually negligible. I love England with my roots and I would never become an alien citizen and renounce my allegiance to it, but I'll be god-damned if I'm going to allow myself to be rooked any more. Bermuda is a British crown colony and I am and shall remain a Britisher and, I hope, a bloody sight richer one.

Noël Coward

13 December

1559 The xiij day of Desember in the mornyng was by mysefortune in sant Dunstones in est a nold man on master Cottelle a talow-chandler, he fell downe in a trape dore and pechyd hys hed a-pone a pesse of tymbur, and brust owtt ys braynes, for he was beldyng, so the trape dore was left opyn.

Henry Machyn

1829 I took Lady Webster to Lady Aldboro's, where we staid till one o'clock. Three hours of *double entendre* is fatiguing. However she generally spares one any trouble in discovering the hidden meaning of her words, for she makes them plain enough.

Henry Edward Fox

1861 Found him very quiet and comfortably warm, and so dear and kind, called me '*gutes Fräuchen*' and kissed me so affectionately and so completely like himself, and I held his dear hands between mine ... They gave him brandy every half-hour.

Queen Victoria

1943 A Proustian incident. In a Bond Street jewellers, I saw an extraordinary marionette of a woman – or was it a man? It wore grey flannel trousers, a wide leather belt, masculine overcoat, and a man's brown felt hat, and had a really frightening appearance; but the hair was golden dyed and long: what is wrongly known as platinum; the mouth was a scarlet scar. Bundi began to growl, and as I secretly examined this terrifying apparition, I recognized Gladys Marlborough, once the world's most beautiful woman ... the toast of Paris, the love of Proust, the *belle amie* of Anatole France. I hadn't seen her since my wedding, but there seemed no reason to cut her, and I went up to her, and smiled, and put out my hand which she took shrinkingly and then, breaking into French (as she always did) said, '*Est-ce que je vous connais, Monsieur?*' 'Yes,' I said, 'I am Chips.' She looked at me, stared vacantly with those famous turquoise eyes that once drove men insane with desire, and muttered: '*Je n'ai jamais entendu ce nom là,*' she flung down a ruby clip she was examining, and bolted from the shop ... and I remembered how we had been allies for twenty years or more; how she used to telephone to me every morning; how I used to give her sugar in the last war when she was still dazzlingly beautiful; and how we used to lunch with Proust; and of the story that D'Annunzio fainted when he saw her, such was her beauty, then of the Blenheim days ... *Le temps qui coule* ... What an adventure.

'Chips' Channon

---

14 December

1801 Wm. and Mary walked to Ambleside in the morning to buy mouse-traps. Mary fell and hurt her wrist. I accompanied them to the top of the hill – clear and frosty. I wrote to Coleridge a very long letter while they were absent. Sate by the fire in the evening reading.

Dorothy Wordsworth

1861   Went over at 7 as I usually did. It was a bright morning; the sun just rising and shining brightly ... Never can I forget how beautiful my darling looked lying there with his face lit up by the rising sun, his eyes unusually bright gazing as it were on unseen objects and not taking notice of me ... Sir James was very hopeful, so was Dr Jenner, and said it was a 'decided rally', but that they were all 'very, very, anxious' ... I asked if I might go out for a breath of fresh air. The doctors answered 'Yes, just close by, for half an hour!' ... I went out on the Terrace with Alice. The military band was playing at a distance and I burst out crying and came home again ... Sir James was very hopeful; he had seen much worse cases. But the breathing was the alarming thing – so rapid, I think 60 respirations in a minute ... I bent over him and said to him '*Es ist Kleines Fräuchen*' [it is your little wife] and he bowed his head; I asked him if he would give me '*ein Kuss*' [a kiss] and he did so. He seemed half dozing, quite quiet ... I left the room for a moment and sat down on the floor in utter despair. Attempts at consolation from others only made me worse ... Alice told me to come in ... and I took his dear left hand which was already cold, though the breathing was quite gentle and I knelt down by him ... Alice was on the other side, Bertie and Lenchen ... kneeling at the foot of the bed ... Two or three long but perfectly gentle breaths were drawn, the hand clasping mind and ... all, all, was over ... I stood up, kissed his dear heavenly forehead and called out in a bitter and agonizing cry, 'Oh! my dear Darling!'

Queen Victoria

1899   Already thirty-eight years since that dreadful catastrophe which crushed and changed my life, and deprived me of my guardian angel, the best of husbands and most noble of men!

Queen Victoria

15 December

1840   A day of trial and day of interest, may it prove a day of warning and profit. I received an invitation to a clerical meeting at Heigham and wrote an answer to say I would accept it for this day. On arriving, in a few minutes I asked what was his hour of meeting. He replied with an earnest look, ''Tis not today.' Feeling ashamed at my carelessness I pretended to think it was not and said, 'No! next Tuesday.' Though I had come with only a slight doubt that this was the day. I tried to get out of my difficulty, but an attempt to extricate yourself from an evident deviation from honesty commonly plunges you the deeper. Thus it was with me. Seeing my note on the table I looked and saw that I had written to say I should come as today. I was obliged then to confess that I thought perhaps the meeting might be today. Having rested about half an hour, I started through the deep snow, my feet muffled with snowboots; for as I had not anticipated a return till the evening, it was useless waiting for the gig which I had ordered to meet me. Being nearly eight miles from home I urged my way through the falling snow; weeping, not at the idea of a weary walk, but that shame had prevented me from at once saying I had made a mistake in the day. For surely my deception is discovered. I do henceforth determine by God's grace to speak in simplicity and godly sincerity. Proceeding with a heavy heart I met with a circumstance which seemed to put fresh strength into my weary frame. When about half-way home I saw a man felling a tree in a field. I called and said 'What are you felling that beautiful tree for?' Looking up, he said, ''Tis, sir, a pretty tree but I want to make this piece a garden and it brouses over so.' I replied, 'Yes, my good fellow, 'tis like some great man whose conduct is injurious to those under his influence and God in mercy cuts him down.' The man looked at me earnestly but said little. I then spoke to him about his soul and called him to receive some tracts. Approaching, he said, 'You preach at Ketteringham, sir, I used to come and hear you but I am so far off now.' The tears rolled rapidly down his cheeks whilst I spoke to him, and on leaving and taking him by the hand he wept much and said, 'O would you, sir, come and see me when you pass this way. I live in the cottage by the road side.' Who can tell but that my mistake about Heigham was to bring me in contact with this poor man! Proceeding on my journey, I visited the cottages at Intwood and heard of poor Mr Drake whom I have seen from the pulpit spit frequently into the reading desk whilst preaching, and the other Sunday being completely lost in reading the service, the clerk raising his hand said, 'Sir, you are wrong.' When in great anger he exclaimed 'Then you ought to put me right.' When will such teachers be removed or converted! When, Lord, wilt Thou arise and have mercy on our Zion!

The Reverend W. W. Andrew

16 December

1641 Arriving at Lichfield, I first heard of my wife's death. She was a virtuous, modest, careful, and loving wife, her affection was exceeding great toward me, as was mine to her, which caused us to live so happily together. Nor was I less beloved and esteemed both by her father and mother, insomuch as at her funeral, her mother sitting near the corpse, with tears, professed to the Baron of Kinderton's Lady (who after told it to me) and others present, that she knew not whether she loved me or her only son better.

Elias Ashmole

1836 I wish I had leisure to commit to paper a hundredth part of the tales, poems, and dramas with which my brain is crammed. I have such splendid visions in my head that the idea of never realizing them with the pen is quite mortifying.

Emily Shore

1965 Sixty-six years ago today I was propelled from the womb. There were no electric trains, and motor cars were exciting curiosities. There was not even the thought of an aeroplane in the winter skies, and horse-buses clopped through the London street. There were no buses at all in Teddington. I can hardly believe that so much has happened in sixty-six years, but it has, and now men are whizzing about in outer space and taking photographs of the remote stars. Which only goes to show that man is a very remarkable animal. So remarkable that his main instinct – over and above his incredible cleverness – is still to kill and be killed, to maim and torture and massacre other animals for sport. Capital punishment having been abolished by the woolly-minded humanitarians in England, there has now been disclosed a hideous and revolting series of murders on the Yorkshire Moors by a girl of twenty-three and a man of twenty-seven. They have so far betrayed neither feeling nor interest in the progress of their preliminary trial. They have killed several children, apparently for 'kicks', and lastly battered a boy of seventeen to death with a hatchet. While the man was doing this, the girl sat with her feet on the mantelpiece, smoking. They will get a life sentence, which means fifteen years. So they will be out again and ready for more outrages. I have never thought the abolition of capital punishment a good idea, and I think so less than ever now.

Noël Coward

17 December

1758   The nervous optick tremors came on in the evening, and a cup of beer helped, even on this my usual half-fast day.

Dr John Rutty

1862   At p. 22 only. I am extremely spiritless, dead, and hopeless about my writing. The long state of headache has left me in depression and incapacity. The constantly heavy-clouded, and often wet, weather tends to increase the depression. I am inwardly irritable, and unvisited by good thoughts. Reading the *Purgatorio* again, and the *Compendium Revelationum* of Savonarola. After this record, I read aloud what I had written of Part IX to George, and he, to my surprise, entirely approved of it.

George Eliot

1871   Rescued a little kitten that was perched in the sill of the round window at the sink over the gasjet and dared not jump down. I heard her mew a piteous long time till I could bear it no longer; but I make a note of it because of her gratitude after I had taken her down, which made her follow me about and at each turn of the stairs as I went down leading her to the kitchen ran back a few steps up and try to get up to lick me through the banisters from the flight above.

Gerard Manley Hopkins

1946   John Turner, whom I first remember as a small boy of fourteen watching the air battles of 1940 and whooping with excitement and delight, came the other day after being in prison for four months, at Birmingham and then Wormwood Scrubs, for refusing to wear the King's uniform. It appears that he went on parade with yellow tie and battle-green corduroys. He has now had his tribunal, and is discharged if he will do welfare work, so he is probably going to the Arctic – is it Finmark? – with the Friends Ambulance Unit.

He looks well and scruffy; only a little, a little wild, and as if he was made of India-rubber. He talks all the time about Anarchy; with Christianity poking its head through the folds every so often.

Everybody, so he says, behaved very well indeed to him, both in the army and in prison. The people who had not seen active service were the most inclined to be hostile, but I haven't heard that before and, perhaps, hasn't he.

He did not mind being locked up. He seems to mind nothing. I was both reassured about human nature and untrusting of John's receptiveness. The Anarchic Christianity seemed to have come between him and all his experiences.

Denton Welch

18 December

1798   Pouncy called and brought an etching of Chas. 2d under the Oak. He looked very ill & much altered. He said on the 18th Augst. last He passed a worm of 6 Inches long which He conceived to have lodged in the Scrotum. – The circumstance is so singular, that the Apothecaries He has spoken to can scarcely suppose it came through the Penis, but that he both felt and saw. On Sunday last he passed another worm in the same manner & also a piece of flesh which looked like liver. He thinks he passed in all not less than a pint of blood while the Symptoms were upon him. The only sensations he feels are a shooting pain through the Pelvis, and an irritation at the bottom of the Seminal passage. On the whole the case appears to me to be most singular and dangerous, and I cannot but suppose some of the internal parts must be decaying fast which will probably turn to mortification. His eyes strongly expressed the alarming state of his constitution. He had the worms in bottles & proposed going to Cruikshanks, the Surgeon, tomorrow to consult him.

Joseph Farington

1813   Redde some Italian, and wrote two Sonnets on — . I never wrote but one sonnet before, and that was not in earnest, and many years ago, as an exercise – and I will never write another. They are the most puling, petrifying, stupidly platonic compositions. I detest the Petrarch so much, that I would not be the man even to have obtained his Laura, which the metaphysical whining dotard never could.

Lord Byron

1825   What a life mine has been. Half educated, almost wholly neglected or left to myself – stuffing my head with most nonsensical trash and undervalued in society for a time by most of my companions – getting forward and held a bold and clever fellow, contrary to the opinion of all who thought me a mere dreamer – Broken-hearted for two years – My heart handsomely pieced again – but the crack will remain till my dying day – Rich and poor four or five times – Once at the verge of ruin yet opend new sources of wealth almost overflowing – now taken in my pitch of pride and nearly winged (unless the good news hold) because London chuses to be in an uproar and in the tumult of bulls and bears a poor inoffensive lion like myself is pushd to the wall – And what is to be the end of it? God knows and so ends the chatechism.

Walter Scott

---

19 December

1785   Some time afterwards, the King said he found by the newspapers that Mrs Clive was dead.

Do you read the newspapers? thought I. Oh, King! you must then have the most unvexing temper in the world not to run wild.

This led on to more players. He was sorry, he said, for Henderson, and the more as Mrs Siddons had wished to have him play at the same house with herself. Then Mrs Siddons took her turn, and with the warmest praise.

'I am an enthusiast for her,' cried the King, 'quite an enthusiast. I think there was never any player in my time so excellent – not Garrick himself; I own it!'

Then, coming close to me, who was silent, he said – 'What? What?' – meaning, what say you? But I still said nothing; I could not concur where I thought so differently, and to enter into an argument was quite impossible; for every little thing I said the King listened to with an eagerness that made me always ashamed of its insignificancy. And, indeed, but for that I should have talked to him with much greater fluency, as well as ease.

From players he went to plays, and complained of the great want of good modern comedies, and of the extreme immorality of most of the old ones.

'And they pretend,' cried he, 'to mend them; but it is not possible. Do you think it is? – What?'

'No, sir, not often, I believe. The fault, commonly, lies in the very foundation.'

'Yes, or they might mend the mere speeches; but the characters are all bad from the beginning to the end.'

Then he specified several; but I had read none of them, and, consequently, could say nothing about the matter; – till, at last he came to Shakespeare.

'Was there ever,' cried he, 'such stuff as great part of

Shakespeare? only one must not say so! But what think you? –
What? – Is there not sad stuff? – What? – What?'

'Yes, indeed, I think so, sir, though mixed with such
excellences, that – '

'Oh!' cried he, laughing good-humouredly, 'I know it is not
to be said! but it's true. Only it's Shakespeare, and nobody
dare abuse him.'

Then he enumerated many of the characters and parts of
plays that he objected to; and when he had run them over,
finished with again laughing and exclaiming – 'But one should
be stoned for saying so!'

Fanny Burney

20 December

1664   Up and walked to Deptford, where after doing something at
the yard, I walked, without being observed, with Bagwell
home to his house and there was very kindly used, and the
poor people did get a dinner for me in their fashion – of which
I also eat very well. After dinner I found occasion of sending
him abroad; and then alone avec elle je tentoy à faire ce que je
voudrais, et contre sa force je le faisoy, bien que pas à mon
contentment. By and by, he coming back again, I took leave
and walked home; and then there to dinner, where Dr
Fayrbrother came to see me, and Luellin; we dined, and I to
the office, leaving them – where we sat all the afternoon, and I
late at the office. To supper and to the office again very late;
then home to bed.

Samuel Pepys

1800   We were employed the greatest part of the day in seeing the
poor people eat a most excellent dinner. Dancing again in the
evening for the Servants, the Ladies danced a great deal with
them. Lord B. is as kind and attentive as ever and insists on his
God child's coming in after dinner. Lord Cobham is a very
fine boy, but rather too quiet, he will be 4 years old in
February. Lady Temple has very engaging gentle manners,
and I like her excessively as she is perfectly unaffected, but

Mrs Nugent is the most conceited little woman I ever saw, she is very pretty though shorter than myself, she has the smallest head that can be, very thin and little. She is an amazing dresser, never appears twice in the same gown.

Elizabeth Fremantle

1950 'How's your sister? All right?' asked the young lady (a fluffy, blonde, hardboiled little piece, I always think) in the tobacconist's the other day. Something in her tone of voice seemed to make this question sound like a serious inquiry.

'Yes, thank you. Did you think she wasn't?' I asked.

'Oh no. I didn't think so. But things seem to happen so quickly these days. One day you're all right, and the next you're . . .' she seemed to hesitate.

'Dead?' I supplied, but simultaneously she brought out, 'Not so well.'

The conversation seemed to me worth recording.

J. R. Ackerley

1969 Frost and snow. Ted and I nearly lost our fingers pulling snow-frozen ivy off the trees to decorate the cottage. The car broke down, we had great difficulty in collecting the Christmas trees from Jackson's farm and Ted got into quite a suicidal mood. But I said that it is always a good sign when things go wrong before the night.

Barbara Castle

21 December

1760 Dr Poole, coming to see a child of his, paid my wife a visit, and charged me 10s 6d: really a fine thing it is to be a physician, who can charge as they please, and not be culpable to any human law.

Thomas Turner

1788 Died at Alnwick, Mary Robertson, an old ginger bread dealer: children at school being great customers.

Nicholas Brown

1801 *Monday 21st*, being the shortest day. Mary walked to Ambleside for letters. It was a wearisome walk, for the snow lay deep upon the roads and it was beginning to thaw. I stayed at home and clapped the small linen. Wm. sate beside me, and read *The Pedlar*. He was in good spirits, and full of hope of what he should do with it. He went to meet Mary, and they brought 4 letters – 2 from Coleridge, one from Sara, and one from France. Coleridge's were melancholy letters, he had been very ill in his bowels. We were made very unhappy. Wm. wrote to him, and directed the letter into Somersetshire. I finished it after tea. In the afternoon Mary and I ironed, afterwards she packed her clothes up, and I mended Wm.'s stockings while he was reading *The Pedlar*.

Dorothy Wordsworth

1840 Deeply sympathizing with the inhabitants of Silfield, I sallied forth in the snow on Saturday and having obtained from a farmer the names of the more distressed, I have this day been supplying their wants. I tried to go as a stranger but there was scarcely a cottage in which I was not recognized. I gave to each about five shillings in clothing. O what a privilege to be the Lord's Almoner! Remember me, O God, for good! Enlarge my heart! Let not my left hand know what my right has done!

The Reverend W. W. Andrew

1849 Shortest day. Gloomy and dull! Alas for the merry days of Winter which I had dreamed of! My poor fellow! Very cold, with a slight fall of snow.

Edward Leeves

22 December

1825 I wrote six of my close pages yesterday which is about twenty-four pages in print. What is more I think it comes off twangingly. The story is so very interesting in itself that there is no fear of the book answering. Superficial it must be but I do not disown the charge. Better a superficial book which

brings well and strikingly together the known and acknowledged facts than a dull boring narrative pausing to see further
into a mill stone at every moment than the nature of the Mill
stone admits. Nothing is so tiresome as walking through some
beautiful scene with a minute philosopher, a botanist or
pebble gatherer who is eternally calling your attention from
the grand features of the natural scenery to look at grasses
and chucky stones. Yet in their way they give useful
information and so does the minute historian – Gad, I think
that will look well in the preface.

My bile is quite gone. I really believe it arose from mere
anxiety. What a wonderful connexion between the mind and
body.

Walter Scott

1952 The Movietone News this week had a Christmas feature. A
large number of flustered turkeys were driven towards the
camera, and the commentator remarked that the Christmas
rush was on, or words to that effect. Next they were seen
crowded about their feeding trough, making their gobbling
turkey fuss, and the commentator observed, with dry humour
(again I do not remember his exact words), that it was no use
their holding a protest meeting, for they were for it in the
morning. Similar facetious jokes followed them wherever they
went, hurrying and trampling about in their silly way; for to
make them look as silly as possible was no doubt part of the
joke and easy to achieve: turkeys, like hens, like all animals,
are beautiful in themselves, and have even a kind of dignity
when they are leading their own lives, but the fowls, in
particular, look foolish when they are being frightened.

These jolly, lip-licking sallies, delivered in the rich, cultivated, self-confident voice of one who has no sort of doubt of
his own superiority to the animal kingdom, raised no laugh
from the considerable audience, I was pleased to note. I took
it from the silence that many other people besides myself
would have been glad to be spared jeers and jibes at these
creatures who, parting unwillingly with their lives, were to
afford us pleasure at our Christmas tables. It reminded me of
a shop window I noticed in Marylebone High Street, not
many weeks ago. A whole calf's head was displayed upon a

dish, and the tongue of the dead thing had been dragged out and twisted round into the side of its mouth so that it appeared, idiotically, to be licking its own lips over the taste of its own dead flesh. In order to make it more foolish still, a tomato had been balanced on top of its head. How arrogant people are in their behaviour to the domestic beasts at least. Indeed, yes, we feed upon them and enjoy their flesh; but does that permit us to make fun of them before they die or after they are dead? If it were possible, without disordering one's whole life, to be a vegetarian, I would be one; nothing could have been more disgusting and degrading than the insensitiveness displayed by these two exhibitions I have described.

J. R. Ackerley

23 December

1809   Mr Rutt, his nephew George Wedd, and myself walked to Royston. There was a remarkable gradation of age among us. We were on a visit to Mr Nash, who was fifteen years older than Mr Rutt, who was fifteen years older than myself, and I was in my thirty-fourth year, and fifteen years older than George Wedd. Mr Rutt and I were proud of our feat – a walk of thirty-eight miles! But old Mr Wedd, the father of George, was displeased with his son. He was a country gentleman, proud of his horses, and conscious of being a good rider. I was told that he disliked me, and would not invite me to his house. I offered a wager that I would gain his goodwill. After dinner we talked of books; Mr Wedd detested books and the quoters of books; but I persisted and praised Lord Herbert of Cherbury, and illustrated the beauty of his writing by citing that *wise and fine saying of his*, 'A fine man upon a fine horse is the noblest object on earth for God to look down upon.' Mr Wedd declared that he never thought Mr Robinson could make himself so agreeable, and I was invited to his house.

Henry Crabb Robinson

1945   After all I was able to get away to Battle for Christmas. Coming down in the train, I suddenly began to be alive again.

I've always noticed this – that the recovery of mental life, with me, is like suddenly recovering the use of a limb. There's a click, and lo! it's working again. Even the landscape, which had seemed dead, recovers its life, and faces come again into my consciousness, and ideas enliven what has been a stagnant mind. I kept thinking of all the lives I might have lived – a left-wing life, or a life of devotion to writing; all that I might have done, and understood that either life was so insignificant that it didn't matter, or so significant that it didn't matter. My play, the only thing I've succeeded in finishing since I left the Army, seems to be hurried and mediocre. All right, if I go to America, I'll settle down to a book; and if I don't go to America I will, too.

Malcolm Muggeridge

1969　At last we are on our way. With fourteen adults and six children to cater for over Christmas there is a hectic time ahead and I have a bilious reaction from the strain of the past weeks. But I have a hunch that this is going to be a great Christmas.

Barbara Castle

24 December

1841　Christmas eve festivities. We were amongst a select few invited by Sterling's little people to witness the unfolding of a mighty mystery which has occupied their small brains for the last week. The folding doors of the drawing-room being thrown open, the inner room appeared like a blaze of light & luxury. In the centre stood a fir tree reaching nearly to the ceiling, covered in all directions with lighted tapers & various gay & glittering symbols, while pendant from the lower branches were numerous presents for children and guests. Papa's ingenious irony had placed a foolscap on the top, immediately overshadowing the man in the moon & the Pope of Rome; crowns & helmets, paper flags & necklaces sparkled amongst the foliage & we all, old children and young, gave ourselves up to the enthusiasm of the moment. My present was a beautiful ivory pen tipped with silver & wreathed with laurel, a most elegant compliment. A.M. & C. were given some very fine engravings. The excitement having somewhat subsided I put off a volcano in the garden. The abandon of the children to their supreme delight was beautiful.

Barclay Fox

1903 (Christmas Eve) And now the great day arrives at work. I mean my rise. It is only 2s 6d. Not much, but good in comparison with the other rises. I started with 8s. Now I will get, with my new rise – the second I have had – 12s 6d. a week, and Mr Almond advised me to ask for another rise in middle of next year! He gave me Christmas present of 2s 6d. and encouragement, saying I must not think I am going backwards.

Sydney Moseley

1907 As the old year ebbs out the great question of morality again crops up. This lately has been the cause of my thinness (though people have different opinions about this). An 'immoral' boy, I am told, requires to appease his sex appetite about once in three months ... Nobody can help me solve this problem, which has oppressed me almost continuously. To do what W. suggested is of no use – I am terribly lacking in that sort of pluck. I feel a sense of uncleanliness about it all ... So I must put up with it.

Sydney Moseley

25 December

1837 And am I really eighteen years old? Am I no longer a child, and are so many of the years allotted to me for intellectual and spiritual improvement already past? How quickly they have flown! How appalling is the progress of time, and the approach of eternity! To me, that eternity is perhaps not far distant; let me improve life to the utmost while it is yet mine, and if my span on earth must indeed be short, may it yet be long enough to fit me for an endless existence in the presence of my God.

Emily Shore

1841 Whether this really was the day of Christ's birth is very doubtful yet I would not give up the annual festival for something. As my custom is I joined the Evanses at a good English roast-beef & plum pudding dinner at my cottage.

Barclay Fox

1866 Married a young parishioner of the name of Mahershalla-lashbaz Tuck. He accounted for the possession of so extraordinary a name thus: his father wished to call him by the shortest name in the Bible, and for that purpose selected Uz. But, the clergyman making some demur, the father said in pique, 'Well, if he cannot have the shortest he shall have the longest.'

The Reverend Benjamin Armstrong

1924 I have decided to try and grow a moustache because I cannot afford any new clothes for several years and I want to see some change in myself. Also if I am to be a schoolmaster it will help to impress the urchins with my age. I look so intolerably young now that I have had to give up regular excessive drinking. Christmas Day always makes me feel a little sad; for one reason because strangely enough my few romances have always culminated in Christmas week – Luned, Richard, Alastair. Now with Alastair a thousand miles away and my heart leaden and the future drearily uncertain things are not as they were. My only letter this morning was a notice of a vacancy from Truman & Knightley. There are coming to dinner tonight Stella Rhys and Audrey Lucas and Philippa Fleming. I should scarcely think that it will be a jovial evening.

Evelyn Waugh

1946 A peaceful Christmas Day spent in bed talking to people on the telephone. Sybil, Graham, Gladys and I had dinner. Delicious food, including caviare. Later, a party at Binkie's. Very enjoyable.

Noël Coward

26 December

1832 Captain — recounted a curious anecdote that had happened in his own family. He told it in the following words:

'It is now about fifteen months ago that Miss Manningham, a connection of my family, went with a party of friends to a concert at the Argyle Rooms. She appeared there to be suddenly seized with indisposition, and though she persisted for some time to struggle against what seemed a violent nervous affection, it became at last so oppressive, that they were obliged to send for their carriage and conduct her home. She was for a long time unwilling to say what was the cause of her indisposition; but, on being more earnestly questioned, she at length confessed that she had, immediately on arriving in the concert room, been terrified by a horrible vision, which unceasingly presented itself to her sight. It seemed to her as though a naked corpse was lying on the floor at her feet; the features of the face were partly covered by a cloth mantle, but enough was apparent to convince her that the body was that of Sir Joseph Yorke. Every effort was made by her friends at the time to tranquillize her mind by representing the folly of allowing such delusions to prey upon her spirits, and she thus retired to bed; but on the following day the family received the tidings of Sir Joseph Yorke having been drowned in Southampton River that very night by the oversetting of his boat, and the body was afterwards found entangled in a *boat cloak*. Here is an authenticated case of second sight, and of very recent date.'

Thomas Raikes

1915 Directly after breakfast I went down to Brighton, sent on my way with many good wishes from the others. I walked along the promenade, and looked at the grey sea tossing rough with white surf-crested waves, and felt a little anxiety at the kind of crossing he had had. But at any rate he should be safely in England by this time, though he probably has not been able to send me any message today owing to the difficulties of telephones and telegrams on Sunday and Christmas Day combined & the inaccessibility of Hassocks. So I only have to wait for the morrow with such patience as I can manage. Being a little tired with the energies of the night, I spent a good deal of the rest of the day in sleeping, thinking of the sweet anticipation of the morning and of the face and voice dearest of all to me on earth.

Vera Brittain

1939   On Boxing Day we did our panto – huge success! I played Aladdin, and had to run on, crying, 'I am that naughty boy Aladdin whose trousers always need some paddin'!' chased by Alfred as the Widow Twankey in a long curly wig, mob-cap and apron, waving a cane! His friend Bertie was divine as the Princess Zadubadour, in a transparent black evening dress, swooning on the floor and murmuring hoarsely, 'Leave me, leave me!' Alfred and Bertie had a great fight over a roll of cotton-wool for their busts. 'Give me my bust, you swine. You can't have it all, damn you!'

Everybody paid sixpence, and we raised 18/– for the Loaves and Fishes

Joan Wyndham

27 December

1817   Dined at Mr Allanson's. The party Mr and Mrs Walker, Mr Charnock, Miss and Miss A. Allanson, Capt Horn, BN, AFN, CEN. The most remarkable occurrence was Walker's eating, 1st a plate of haddock, 2nd a plate of fillet of veal and being twice helped to tongue, 3rd three slices of a saddle of mutton, 4th a large wing of a large duck, 5th two plates of roasting pig, 6th half the tail of a large lobster, 7th cheese and then dessert. NB He had no wager on his eating.

The Reverend Benjamin Newton

1870   After dinner drove into Chippenham with Perch and bought 2 pair of skates at Benk's for 17/6. Across the fields to the Draycot water and the young Awdry ladies chaffed me about my new skates. I had not been on skates since I was here last, 5 years ago, and was very awkward for the first ten minutes, but the knack soon came again. There was a distinguished company on the ice, Lady Dangan, Lord and Lady Royston and Lord George Paget all skating. Also Lord and Lady Sydney and a Mr Calcroft, whom they all of course called the Hangman. I had the honour of being knocked down by Lord Royston, who was coming round suddenly on the outside edge. A large fire of logs burning within an enclosure of wattled hurdles. Harriet Awdry skated beautifully and jumped over a half-sunken punt. Arthur Law skating jumped over a chair on its legs.

The Reverend Francis Kilvert

1915 I had just finished dressing when a message came to say that there was a telephone message for me. I sprang up joyfully, thinking to hear in a moment the dear dreamed-of tones of the beloved voice.

But the telephone message was not from Roland but from Clare; it was not to say that Roland had arrived, but that instead had come this telegram, sent on to the Leightons by Mr Burgin, to whom for some time all correspondence sent to Lowestoft had been readdressed:

T 233. Regret to inform you that Lieut. R. A. Leighton 7th Worcesters died of wounds December 23rd. Lord Kitchener sends his sympathy.

Colonel of Territorial Force, Records, Warwick.

Vera Brittain

28 December

1849 Violent storm this morning early, & the ground covered with snow when I got up. My poor Boy was always longing for the winter & saying how well He should be when the cold came. His bed is cold indeed! The cold overcomes me, & I got up with a presentiment of Ill, & lo! I have broken the crystal of my ring, which fell out. Luckily I found the Hair, which fell likewise. They work so universally ill nowadays, as it seems to me, in England! I would not have lost it for much! My poor,

poor boy! I am so weary – so incapable of interesting, or even amusing myself, with anything! If it were not the intense cold I think that I should make an escapade, & try to drown thought & grief in a *vero Baccanale*! There would be found scope enough for even my appetite, I believe.

Edward Leeves

1914   The year is nearly over. Snow has fallen, and everything is white. It is very cold. I have changed the position of my desk into a corner. Perhaps I shall be able to write far more easily here. Yes, this is a good place for the desk, because I cannot see out of the stupid window. I am quite private. The lamp stands on one corner and *in* the corner. Its rays fall on the yellow and green Indian curtain and on the strip of red embroidery. The forlorn wind scarcely breathes. I love to close my eyes a moment and think of the land outside, white under the mingled snow and moonlight – white trees, white fields – the heaps of stones by the roadside white – snow in the furrows. *Mon Dieu*! How quiet and how patient! If he were to come I could not even hear his footsteps.

Katherine Mansfield

1935   Its all very well to write that date in a nice clear hand, because it begins this new book, but I cannot disguise the fact that I'm almost extinct; like a charwomans duster; that is my brain: what with the last revision of the last pages of *The Years*. And is it the last revision? And why should I lead the dance of the days with this tipsy little spin? But in fact I must stretch my cramped muscles: its only half past eleven on a damp grey morning, & I want a quiet occupation for an hour. That reminds me – I must devise some let down for myself that wont be too sudden when the end is reached. An article on Gray I think. But how the whole prospect will take different proportions, once I've relaxed this effort. Shall I ever write a long book again – a long novel that has to be held in the brain, at full stretch – for close on 3 years? Nor do I even attempt to ask if its worth while.

Virginia Woolf

29 December

1786 My dear father was the principal object to all, and he seemed to enjoy himself, and to be enjoyed throughout.

We returned to my own apartment to our coffee, and the two governess ladies retired; and then came the King for Mrs Delany; and not for that solely, though ostensibly, for his behaviour to my father proved his desire to see and converse with him.

He began immediately upon musical matters, and entered into a discourse upon them with the most animated wish of both hearing and communicating his sentiments; and my dear father was perfectly ready to meet his advances. No one, at all used to the court etiquettes, could have seen him without smiling; he was so totally unacquainted with the forms usually observed in the royal presence, and so regardless or thoughtless of acquiring them, that he moved, spoke, acted, and debated, precisely with the same ease and freedom that he would have used to any other gentleman whom he had accidentally met.

A certain flutter of spirits, which always accompanies these interviews, even with those who are least awed by them, put my dear father off the guard which is the customary assistant upon these occasions, of watching what is done by those already initiated in these royal ceremonies: highly gratified by the openness and good-humour of the King, he was all energy and spirit, and pursued every topic that was started, till he had satisfied himself upon it, and started every topic that occurred to him, whether the King was ready for another or not.

While the rest, retreating towards the wainscot, formed a distant and respectful circle, in which the King alone moves, this dear father came forward into it himself, and, wholly bent upon pursuing whatever theme was begun, followed the King when he moved away, and came forward to meet his steps when he moved back; and while the rest waited his immediate address ere they ventured to speak a word, he began and finished, sustained or dropped, renewed or declined, every theme that he pleased, without consulting anything but his feelings and understanding.

This vivacity and this nature evidently pleased the King, whose good sense instantly distinguishes what is unconscious from what is disrespectful; and his stay in the room, which I believe was an hour, and the perfect good-humour with which he received as well as returned the sprightly and informal sallies of my father were proofs the most convincing of his approbation.

Fanny Burney

1914 To-day was my 21st birthday. There is nothing whatever to say about it. To be of age according to the law & to be one's own mistress does not impress me at all, nor does it fill me with grave & sober reflections. It is having nothing definite to do that makes another year seem a burden; when one is at least on the way towards achieving one's object, & things are happening, one's life is made up by events & not increasing years.

Vera Brittain

1978 Suddenly yesterday morning I observed that there was bright blood in my pee. Cancer of the bladder, naturally! But I was amazed to find that this assumption hardly seemed to bother me – though I've suffered so cravenly from Timor Mortis all my born days.

But when S. consulted one of her medical books it became quite obvious that the culprit was the beetroot we'd had for supper the night before. So my heroic composure was wasted, in a sense, but it's nice to know that I achieved it, however briefly.

Philip Toynbee

30 December

1800 The snow is deep but it was a beautiful clear day and we went to Buckingham in the coach with Lady Temple. Mrs Nugent bought a great deal of lace, she seems not to care how much money she spends in dress, but she truly improves upon acquaintance and is a pleasant, even-tempered little woman.

We called on Mrs Bennett and heard the ball tonight at Buckingham was not expected to be a good one, which made us not regret the not being able to go to it. This being Ld George's birthday, who is now 12 years old, he gave a potatoes feast to the poor children, with a shilling apiece, the Servants had a gay ball, and I was obliged to join in the dance.

Elizabeth Fremantle

1857 Mr Barwell showed me a sham bird of prey, flown as a kite, over fields where partridges are supposed to be. Terrified at the sight, the poor birds are completely scared, flying one at a time, and almost in face of the sportsman. The device is used when birds are hopelessly wild.

The Reverend Benjamin Armstrong

1936 There in front of me lie the proofs – the galleys – to go off today . . . a sort of stinging nettle that I cover over. Nor do I wish even to write about it here.

A divine relief has possessed me these last days – at being quit of it – good or bad. And, for the first time since February I shd. say my mind has sprung up like a tree shaking off a load. And I've plunged into Gibbon & read & read, for the first time since Feb. I think. Now for action & pleasure again & going about. I cd. make some interesting perhaps valuable notes, on the absolute necessity for me of work. Always to be after something. I'm not sure that the intensiveness & exclusiveness of writing a long book is a possible state: I mean, if even in future I do such a thing – & I doubt it – I will force myself to vary it with little articles. Anyhow, now I am not going to think can I write? I am going to sink into unselfconsciousness & work: at Gibbon first: then a few little articles for America; then $\left\{ \begin{array}{l} Roger \\ 3\ Guineas \end{array} \right\}$ Which of the 2 comes first, how to dovetail, I dont know. Anyhow even if *The Years* is a failure, I've thought considerably; & collected a little hoard of ideas. Perhaps I'm now again on one of those peaks where I shall write 2 or 3 little books quickly: & then have another break. At least I feel myself possessed of skill enough to go on with. No emptiness.

& in proof of this will go in, get my Gibbon notes & begin a careful sketch of the article.

Virginia Woolf

1968   Reluctantly back to work. Why does one always feel so muzzy after a holiday?

Barbara Castle

31 December

1666   Thus ends this year of public wonder and mischief to this nation – and therefore generally wished by all people to have an end. Myself and family well, having four maids and one clerk, Tom, in my house; and my brother now with me, to spend time in order to his preferment. Our healths all well; only, my eyes, with overworking them, are sore as soon as candlelight comes to them, and not else. Public matters in a most sad condition. Seamen discouraged for want of pay, and are become not to be governed. Nor, as matters are now, can any fleet go out next year. Our enemies, French and Duch, great, and grow more, by our poverty. The Parliament backward in raising, because jealous of the spending, of the money. The City less and less likely to be built again, everybody settling elsewhere, and nobody encouraged to trade. A sad, vicious, negligent Court, and all sober men there fearful of the ruin of the whole Kingdom this next year – from which, good God deliver us. One thing I reckon remarkable in my own condition is that I am come to abound in good plate, so as at all entertainments to be served wholly with silver plates, having two dozen and a half.

Samuel Pepys

1809   This is the last night of the year 1809 – a year perhaps of greater Idleness & folly, disappointment and anxiety I have not experienced since I commenced my Studies – such is my irregularity, & folly, that I dare not, O God, conclude it with one hope of amendment, in trembling awe, I trust in thee through Jesus Christ my Saviour, my mind is pregnant with hopes, & wishes, plans and schemes of virtue & industry & ambition. O God I humbly ask thee to pardon my past wickedness, on condition of future virtue – on this condition only I ask it thro Jesus Christ – my Blessed Saviour – O God listen to me, listen to my last prayer, uttered in the sincerity of pungent repentence. Amen – Amen – Amen –

B. R. Haydon

1823 A year to me of great enjoyment, but not of prosperity. My fees amounted to 445 guineas. As to myself, I have become more and more desirous to be religious, but seem to be further off than ever. Whenever I draw near, the negative side of the magnet works, and I am pushed back by an invisible power.

Henry Crabb Robinson

1844 Here ends the best & brightest & most blessed year of my life. It is as tho' I had reached the goal of my boy-existence & found it but the starting post of a new one. The mountain tops before me show higher than ever & life is become a more earnest business with a larger sphere & higher pleasures & deeper responsibilities – no longer alone but blest with the companionship of a noble & pure spirit, with the possession of a deeply loving heart; how abundantly grateful ought mine to be!

Barclay Fox

1857 The dear old year is gone, with all its *Weben* and *Streben*. Yet not gone either: for what I have suffered and enjoyed in it remains to me an everlasting possession while my soul's life remains.

George Eliot

1859 The old year is fled, never to come back again through all Eternity. All its opportunities for love and service gone, past recall. What a terrible thought!

Caroline Fox

1899 This year I have written 335,340 words, grand total. 228 articles and stories (including 4 instalments of a serial of 30,000–37,500 words each) have actually been published.

Also my book of plays – *Polite Farces.*

I have written six or eight short stories not yet published or sold.

Also the greater part of 55,000 word serial – *Love and Life* – for Tillotsons, which begins publication about April next year.

Also the whole draft (80,000 words) of my Staffordshire novel *Anna Tellwright.*

My total earnings were £592 3s 1d, of which sum I have yet to receive £72 10s.

Arnold Bennett

1915 *New Year's Eve 11.55*
This time last year He was seeing me off on Charing Cross Station after *David Copperfield* – and I had just begun to realize I loved Him. Today He is lying in the military cemetery at Louvencourt – because a week ago He was wounded in action, and had just 24 hours of consciousness more and then went 'to sleep in France'. And I, who in impatience felt a fortnight ago that I could not wait another minute to see Him, must wait till all Eternity. All has been given me, and all taken away again – in one year.

So I wonder where we shall be – what we shall all be doing – if we all still *shall* be – this time next year.

Vera Brittain

1969 I perceive, now, 31 December, that there has been no entry since 7 September. With my usual watchful eye on posterity, I can only suggest to any wretched future biographer that he gets my daily engagement book and from that fills in anything he can find and good luck to him, poor bugger. Personally I have neither the will nor the strength to attempt the task.

Noël Coward

Biographical notes on the diarists

Ackerley, J. R. (1896–1967) Served in the trenches of the Western Front during the First World War, was captured, became a prisoner-of-war in Germany, then an internee in Switzerland. In 1919 (incidentally, the year in which his parents married) he went up to Cambridge. Three years later he met E. M. Forster who helped him get the job of companion-secretary to the Maharajah of Chhatarpur. From 1935 to 1959 Ackerley was literary editor of the *Listener*. The diaries cover a period from 1948 to 1956 and describe both Ackerley's homosexual affairs and his relationships with three females: his aunt Bunny, his unstable sister Nancy, and his Alsatian bitch, Queenie. At Ackerley's death, the diaries were bequeathed to Francis King, who edited them for publication under the title *My Sister And Myself*.

Andrew, The Reverend William Wayte (1805–89) Educated at St Mary's Hall, Oxford, Wayte was married in 1834. After curacies at Cromer, Gimingham and Witchingham, in 1835 he took the living of Ketteringham in Norfolk. He was a vigorous preacher, frequently in conflict with the local squire, Sir John Boileau. He kept a diary intermittently from his ordination till his death; the fullest years are from 1839 to 1847.

Armstrong, The Reverend Benjamin (1817–90) After graduating from Cambridge, Armstrong was ordained deacon in 1841 and priest the next year. In 1850 he became vicar of East Dereham in Norfolk and held the living until his retirement on health grounds in 1888.

Ashmole, Elias (1617–92) He was a Royalist antiquarian, astrologist, solicitor, Commissioner of Excise, Comptroller of the Ordnance and Windsor Herald. He studied physics and mathematics at Brasenose College, Oxford, and was married three times. One of the earliest English Freemasons, he was initiated around 1646. The alchemist Backhouse is said to have told him the secret of the philosopher's stone. His collection of curiosities was the starting point for Oxford's Ashmolean Museum. Ashmole's diary is retrospective up until 1641, and then continues with irregular entries till 9 October 1687.

Bailey, John (1864–1931) Born in Norwich and educated at Haileybury and New College, Oxford, Bailey was called to the Bar in 1892, but never intended to practise, preferring to concentrate on literature. He became known as a lecturer, critic and author of books on poetry. He was also a great lover of the English countryside and from 1923 to 1931 was chairman of the executive of the National Trust.

Baker, John (1712–77) A barrister of the Inner Temple, he married an heiress, Miss Ryan, and lived in Horsham, Sussex. From 1771, he kept a daily diary of local and family events, including details of his minor ailments and an elaborate weather chart. The diary passed to Cardinal Manning and then to Wilfred Scawen Blunt before being published in 1909.

Barrett, Elizabeth (1806–61) Precociously learned, she was widely acclaimed as a poet in her lifetime. She was an invalid recluse from the age of fifteen until she eloped from her Wimpole Street home with the poet Robert Browning in 1846. Thereafter, the couple lived mostly in Italy. She had a son in 1849. The diary covers a brief period of her early life after the death of her mother.

Bee, Jacob (1636–1711) Bee was a Durham tradesman, whose diary, kept from 5 September 1681 to 27 February 1706, recorded local events such as deaths, marriages, election results, accidents and weather phenomena.

Bennett, Arnold (1867–1931) Born in the Staffordshire Potteries, where he set his most famous novels, Bennett was a journalist, critic and editor of *Woman* before devoting himself to literature. His first novel, *A Man from the North*, was published in 1898. From 1902, he lived at Fontainebleau in France for ten years, and married a Frenchwoman, from whom he later separated. He subsequently had a child by the actress Dorothy Cheston. He kept his *Journal* every day, with only brief gaps, from 1896 till 1931.

Benson, A. C. (1862–1925) Eldest surviving son of the Archbishop of Canterbury, E. W. Benson, brother of E. F. and R. H. Benson, he won scholarships to Eton and King's College, Cambridge, where he gained a first in classics. He taught at Eton but later, in 1903, returned to Cambridge to write. In 1904 he was elected a fellow of Magdalene and became master of the College in 1915. He published voluminous works, essays, criticisms, novels, biographies and poetry (he was the author of 'Land of Hope and Glory'), and kept a diary from 1897 to 1925, though only extracts have been published.

Birchall, Dearman (1828–97) Born in Leeds and educated at private schools in York and Croydon, he went into the cloth trade in Leeds. He started his own business in 1853, but was only a sleeping partner after he moved to Gloucestershire in 1869. His firm won prizes for cloth at various International Exhibitions. His first wife died two years after their marriage in 1861 and he remarried in 1873. He was then living at Bowden Hall, near Gloucester, where he housed his collections of china, fabrics and paintings.

Blunt, Wilfred Scawen (1840–1922) Educated at Stonyhurst and Oscott, he joined the diplomatic service at eighteen and served in legations in European capitals and Buenos Aires. In 1869 he left the service and married Byron's granddaughter, Annabella King-Noel, with whom he travelled extensively in the Middle East and India. He opposed British imperialism and was briefly imprisoned in Ireland. His diaries were published in 1919–20.

Boswell, James (1740–95) The son of Lord Auchinleck, he studied law with some reluctance in Edinburgh, Glasgow and Utrecht. Though he became an advocate in Scotland in 1766 and a barrister in England in 1786, he preferred writing and meeting the famous to practising his profession. He met Rousseau, Voltaire, Paoli and, in 1763, Dr Johnson, whose *Life* he wrote. In 1769 he married his cousin by whom he had seven children. On his father's death in 1782 he inherited a wealthy estate and made unsuccessful attempts at a political career. His wife died in 1789 after which Boswell's drinking and dissipation increased. He kept extensive journals for much of his life, though many of them were not published until this century.

Boyle, Jimmy (1944–) Born in the Gorbals district of Glasgow, Boyle was in and out of remand homes and Borstals from the age of thirteen until he was sentenced to life imprisonment for murder in 1967. His life changed from the brutality of normal prison existence with the setting up of the special unit at Barlinnie Prison in 1972. There he developed his skills as a sculptor. Finally released in 1982, Boyle, with his wife Sarah, became involved in social work, particularly the problems of heroin abuse and homeless teenagers.

Brittain, Vera (1893–1970) Born at Newcastle-under-Lyme, she spent her childhood in Cheshire where her father owned paper mills. She went up to Somerville College, Oxford as an exhibitioner in 1914, but her studies were interrupted by the First World War, which killed her brother, her fiancé Roland Leighton and other close friends. She served during the war as a VAD nurse, and recorded her wartime experiences in *Testament of Youth*. In 1919 she returned to Oxford, and in 1922 settled in London to work as a freelance journalist. In 1925 she married George Catlin. She was famous as a writer, lecturer, pacifist, feminist and socialist.

Brown, Ford Madox (1821–93) Brown was an English painter, born in Calais, and educated at the academies of Bruges, Ghent and Antwerp. He settled in England in 1845 and associated with the Pre-Raphaelites (Dante Gabriel Rossetti was for a time one of his pupils). From 1837 Brown exhibited mostly historical and biblical paintings and frescoes, his best-known work probably being *The Last of England*. He quarrelled with the Royal Academy in 1851, and helped to found the Hogarth Club and the Working Men's College.

Brown, Nicholas (*c.* 1722–97) Brown was an attorney at Alnwick and coroner for the county of Northumberland. He married a rich wife in 1749, and three years later inherited an estate at Alndyke from his grandmother. However, it was heavily encumbered, and had to be sold in 1762. Brown, who had a passion for cockfighting, kept a diary of local interest from 1767 to 1796.

Burney, Fanny (1752–1840) Daughter of the musician and author, Dr Charles Burney, she started writing at the age of ten, but burnt all her juvenilia when she was fifteen. Her first novel, *Evelina*, was published anonymously in 1778, though its author was quickly identified and showered with praise by such figures as Johnson, Reynolds and Burke. In 1786 she became second keeper of the robes in the royal household, a tedious post she retained until 1791. Two years later, she married General D'Arblay, a French refugee, and from 1802 to 1812 lived with him at Passy, near Paris. She then returned to England, nursing her father until his death in 1814. Afterwards she went back to Paris, and was in Brussels at the time of Waterloo. She returned to England with her husband, who died in 1818. She kept a full diary from the age of fifteen.

Butler, Lady Eleanor (1739?–1829) Sister of the Earl of Ormonde, Lady Eleanor, against strong family opposition, 'eloped' with Miss Sarah Ponsonby from Ireland and the two set up home together at Plas Newydd. They stayed there for over fifty years, and became known as the 'Ladies of Llangollen'. Their house with its Gothic decorations was visited by many distinguished guests, including Wordsworth, de Quincey, Walter Scott and Madame de Genlis. Only fragments of what was probably a daily diary remain.

Byrom, John (1692–1763) He was educated at Merchant Taylors' School and Trinity College, Cambridge, studied medicine abroad, wrote poetry and was interested in mystical theology. His invention and teaching of a system of shorthand or 'tychygraphy' introduced him to many distinguished contemporaries. He married his cousin Elizabeth in 1721, was a member of the Royal Society and a Jacobite sympathizer. His diary ends in 1744.

Byron, George Gordon (6th Baron) (1788–1824) He was born in London, brought up in Scotland, inherited his title in 1798, and was educated at Harrow and Cambridge. His first collection of poems, *Hours of Idleness*, appeared in 1807, but it was the publication of the first two cantos of *Childe Harold's Pilgrimage* in 1812 which brought him instant fame. Mounting debts, together with the break-up of his marriage and rumours of incest with his half-sister, led him to leave England in 1816. He then lived chiefly in Italy, espoused the cause of Greek independence and died of fever at Missolonghi before seeing any real military action. He wrote an enormous number of letters and intermittent journals, which, according to Thomas Moore (*q.v.*), were written with an eye to publication.

Carlyle, Jane Welsh (1801–66) Daughter of a Scottish doctor, she wrote poetry from the age of fourteen, and in 1821 was introduced to Thomas Carlyle. He took on first the role of her tutor, then of her lover, and they were married in 1826. Thereafter much of her energy was devoted to managing her temperamental husband, living in financial hardship in Edinburgh, the isolated farm of Craigenputtock, and London. She was one of the best letter-writers in the English language, but only kept a diary for brief periods. She was frequently ill, and never fully recovered from being knocked down by a cab in 1863.

Casson, Sir Hugh (1910–   ) Educated at St John's College, Cambridge, the Bartlett School of Architecture, University College, London. During the Second World War he was a camouflage officer. From 1944 to 1946 he became a technical officer at the Ministry of Town and Country Planning. He was director of architecture for the 1951 Festival of Britain, and professor of environmental design from 1953 to 1975.

President of the Royal Academy of Arts, he holds several honorary degrees.

Castle, Barbara (1910–   ) Educated at Bradford Grammar School and St Hugh's College, Oxford, she worked in the Ministry of Food during the Second World War, at the end of which she was a correspondent for the *Daily Mirror*. A Labour MP from 1945 to 1979, she was chairman of the Labour Party from 1958 to 59, and held the offices of Minister of Overseas Development, Minister of Transport, Secretary of State for the Environment, Productivity and Social Services. Since 1979 she has been MEP for Greater Manchester North.

Chalmers, Anne (1813?–?) She was the daughter of the Scottish divine and professor Dr Thomas Chalmers, and kept a diary for only one year, when she visited England in 1830. In 1836 she married Dr William Hanna, later to be her father's biographer.

Channon, Sir Henry, 'Chips' (1897–1958) Educated at Christ Church, Oxford, he was Conservative MP for Southend-on-Sea from 1935. From 1938 to 1941, he was Parliamentary Private Secretary to the Under-Secretary of State for Foreign Affairs. He was the father of Paul Channon, and his marriage to Lady Honor Guinness ended in divorce in 1945.

Cole, The Reverend William (1714–82) Cole was educated in Clare Hall and then King's College, Cambridge. He took holy orders in 1745 and subsequently became parish priest of Blechley (now spelt Bletchley) in Buckinghamshire. He kept a journal of a visit to Paris, and his Blechley diary covers the period from 29 December 1765 to 31 December 1767.

Coward, Noël (1899–1973) Educated privately, he made his first stage appearance in 1911. From his early twenties onwards, he was enormously successful on both sides of the Atlantic as a playwright, actor, singer, composer, revue and film writer. In his later years he lived in Jamaica, and found new success performing cabaret for American audiences. He also lived long enough to witness the successful revival of some of his earlier plays. He was knighted in 1970.

Cresswell, Nicholas (1750–1804) Born in the Derbyshire Peak District, he helped his father on his estate at Edale until, in 1774, he decided to go to America. He returned in 1777, and kept a diary all the time he was away. Cresswell married in 1781.

Dawson, John (c. 1727–69) A captain of the Northumberland militia, Dawson kept a diary from 8 March to 31 December 1761. It is concerned mostly with the activities of the militia, together with some notes on his son's education and other thoughts.

Dee, John (1527–1604) A mathematician, alchemist and Fellow of Trinity College, Cambridge, he was imprisoned by Mary I in 1555 on suspicion of compassing her death by magic. He was treated with more favour by Edward VI and Elizabeth I, both of whom consulted him on astrological matters. During one of his many trips abroad, a mob, considering him a necromancer, ransacked his Mortlake home. He was made Warden of Manchester College, married twice and died in great poverty. He kept a diary from 1577 to 1600.

De La Pryme, Abraham (1671–1704) Educated at St John's College, Cambridge, where he met Sir Isaac Newton and became interested in the occult. As a curate in Hull, he compiled local histories. He was given the living of Thorne and elected a fellow of the Royal Society in 1701. His diary chiefly records public events, anecdotes and notes on archaeological and topographical subjects.

Domett, Alfred (1811–87) Born in Surrey, he went up to St John's College, Cambridge, though he left without a degree. He wrote poetry and was an intimate friend of Robert Browning. In 1841 he was called to the bar, but the next year emigrated to New Zealand, where he held nearly all the chief administrative posts including Colonial Secretary and Prime Minister. In 1871 he returned to England to write.

Dyott, General William (1761–1846) He served as a soldier in Ireland, Nova Scotia, the West Indies, Egypt and on the Walcheren expedition. He travelled widely in Europe, was a friend of Prince William (later William IV) and aide-de-camp to George III. He was a Tory, and staunchly opposed to reforms. His wife left him in 1814. He kept a factual diary from 1781 to 1845.

Edward VI (1537–53) The Son of Henry VIII by Jane Seymour, he succeeded to the throne at the age of ten in 1547. Precociously learned, and of delicate health, he undertook full official duties, though the Government was controlled first by the Duke of Somerset (until his execution in 1552) and then the Duke of Northumberland. The latter persuaded the dying boy to nominate Lady Jane Grey as his successor. Edward kept a diary between the ages of eleven and fourteen.

Eliot, George (pseudonym of Mary Anne or Marion Evans) (1819–80) Born in Warwickshire, her early literary work included translating German religious and philosophical works, and contributing to the *Westminster Review*. While assistant editor of this periodical, she met George Henry Lewes, with whom she lived from 1854 until his death in 1878. He encouraged her to write fiction and her first major success came with the publication of *Adam Bede* in 1859. In 1880, seven months before her death, she married J. W. Cross. She kept an intermittent diary from 1849 to 1877.

Evelyn, John (1620–1706) Educated at Balliol College, Oxford, Evelyn was a wealthy Royalist, who spent four years in Europe during the Interregnum, and held several minor public offices after the Restoration. A member of the Royal Society, he published a manual of arboriculture and thirty-four other works, but his fame rests chiefly on the diary which he kept from 1641 to 1706, and which was first published in 1818, having been discovered the year before in an old clothes basket at Wotton, the house where he died.

Farington, Joseph (1747–1821) A landscape painter and topographical draughtsman, Farington entered the Royal Academy schools in 1768; in 1783 he became ARA and in 1785 RA. From 1776 to 1780 he lived in Keswick, Cumberland, but thereafter in London. His engravings of the English Lakes were published in 1789 and 1816. He died following a fall down some stairs at Didsbury church. He kept copious diaries from 1793 to 1821, and they were first published in serial form in 1922 in the *Morning Post*.

Fox, Caroline (1819–71) The daughter of a wealthy Quaker scientist, Robert Were Fox, and younger sister of Barclay Fox (*q.v.*), she was born and lived at Falmouth. She knew John Stuart Mill, Carlyle and Wordsworth and other eminent people who went to Cornwall for their health. She travelled abroad several times and, with her sister, translated English religious works into Italian. She began to keep a diary when she was sixteen, and continued throughout her life. Extracts from it were first published in 1882.

Fox, Robert Barclay (1817–55) Also born in Falmouth, he was the elder brother of Caroline Fox (*q.v.*). He married Jane Backhouse in 1844. He started writing a journal in 1832, when he was fourteen, and continued till 1854, but did not keep a regular daily record after his marriage. The journal was first published in 1979.

Fox, Henry Edward, 4th and last Lord Holland (1802–59) The third son of Henry Richard Vassall Holland, 3rd Lord Holland, he was a delicate child. He was educated privately and then at Christ Church, Oxford. In 1833 he married the daughter of the Earl of Coventry. Disliking politics, he went into diplomacy and in 1835 was chargé d'affaires in Vienna, subsequently working in Frankfurt and Florence. He returned to England in 1846, but still travelled a great deal and died in Naples. He edited his father's *Foreign Reminiscences*, published in 1850, and *Memoirs of the Whig Party during my Time*, published in 1852. His journal was published in 1923.

Fremantle, Elizabeth (1779–1857) The daughter of Richard Wynne of Falkingham, Lincolnshire, and sister of Eugenia (*q.v.*) and Harriet Wynne (*q.v.*). The family left England in 1788 and lived in Italy and Switzerland. She married Sir Thomas Fremantle in Naples, a vice-admiral who sailed with Lord Hood, associated with Lord Nelson and took part in many engagements including Trafalgar. Elizabeth nursed both her husband and Nelson on their return journey from Tenerife in 1797. Her husband, to whom she bore a numerous family, died in 1819. She kept a diary from 1789 to 1857, and her husband's death was the first event that caused her to miss a day.

Gissing, George (1857–1903) Born in Wakefield, he was educated at Owen's College, Manchester, from which he was expelled for stealing, a crime that earned him a month in prison. In 1876 he spent a year wandering round America; he then settled in London, subsidizing his writing ambitions by coaching in Latin and Greek. He married twice, both times unhappily, to girls of socially inferior origins. His novels, notably *New Grub Street*, published in 1891, deal with the degrading effects of poverty.

Green, Thomas (1769–1825) He was born and lived in Ipswich. Illness prevented him from taking up his place at Cambridge. He entered the Middle Temple, but, on coming into his father's property, gave up law for reading and travel. His diary covers the period from 1796 to 1811, and is much concerned with his reading.

Greville, Charles (1794–1865) Educated at Eton and Christ Church, Oxford, he was a page to George III. He left Oxford early to become private secretary to Lord Bathurst. He held the sinecure secretaryship of Jamaica, and was Clerk to the Privy Council from 1821 to 1859, serving under five monarchs. He kept a record of mainly public events from 1814 to 1860.

Hall, Sir Peter (1930–) Born in Suffolk, he went to St Catharine's College, Cambridge, and was artistic director of several theatres before forming the International Playwrights' Theatre in 1957. From 1960 to 1968 he was managing director of the Royal Shakespeare Theatre. With Lord Olivier he was co-director of the National Theatre from April to November 1973, since when he has been director. He has been married three times.

Hawker, Colonel Peter (1786–1853) Starting in the army as a cornet in 1801, he was a captain of the 14th Light Dragoons during the Peninsular War. He was badly wounded at Talavera, and retired from the army in 1813. He became lieutenant-colonel of the North Hampshire militia. He patented an improvement to the pianoforte and devised alterations for firearms, which were demonstrated at the 1851 Exhibition. He was a keen sportsman and author of the much-acclaimed *Instructions to Young Sportsmen*.

Haydon, Benjamin Robert (1786–1846) Haydon was a self-taught artist of historical painting, who failed entry to the Royal Academy. Dogged by continual debt and a manic personality which frequently bordered on insanity, he painted portraits of the famous, knew Leigh Hunt, Reynolds, Keats and Wordsworth, promoted schemes for the decoration of public buildings, established new schools of art and lectured. In 1821 he married Mary Hymans, but five of their children died. On 22 June 1846 he committed suicide, and the coroner's jury brought in a verdict of insanity. Selections from his twenty-seven volumes of intensely personal journals were edited by Tom Taylor and published in 1853.

Hearne, Thomas (1678–1735) His parents' poor circumstances sent Hearne first into day labour, but his exceptional academic skills were recognized and he was sent to school and subsequently to St Edmund Hall, Oxford. He became an assistant keeper at the Bodleian Library and remained there, refusing offers of other posts until 23 January 1716, when he was shut out for refusing to take the oath to the Hanoverian dynasty. He spent the rest of his life in St Edmund Hall, continuing his work as an antiquary. His diary, kept from 1705 until his death, was frequently dangerously outspoken and finally filled 145 volumes.

Hopkins, Gerard Manley (1844–89) The eldest child of nine from a very religious High Anglican family, Hopkins was educated at Balliol College at the time of the Oxford Movement. In 1866 he was received into the Roman Catholic Church under the sponsorship of Cardinal Newman. In 1868, having decided to become a Jesuit, he symbolically burnt his early poems (though copies of some were sent to Robert Bridges). Nine years later he was ordained a Jesuit priest. He preached in Liverpool, taught at Stonyhurst and was professor of Greek at Dublin University from 1884 to 1889. His *Poems*, with their distinctive use of 'sprung rhythm' were not released for publication by Bridges until 1918.

Horsley, The Reverend J. W. (fl. 1886) The chaplain of Clerkenwell prison, he kept a diary of his work in the prison for the month of August 1886.

Josselin, The Reverend Ralph (1617–83) Educated at Jesus College, Cambridge, he spent some time as a schoolteacher before his ordination in 1640, the year in which he married. He became vicar of Earls Colne, Essex, in 1641 and stayed there until his death. He was also school-master there from 1650 to 1658. His diary starts with a summary of his life up to 1644; the period from 1646 to 1653 is the most detailed.

Kilvert, The Reverend Francis (1840–79) One of the six children of the Reverend Robert Kilvert, a Wiltshire rector, Francis was educated privately until he went up to Oxford. After his ordination, he worked for a time as curate to his father. From 1865 to 1872 he served as curate to the Reverend Richard Lister Venables, vicar of Clyro in Radnorshire, then returned for another four years as curate to his father. In 1876 he received the living of St Harmon in North Radnor-shire, and the next year that of Bredwardine, in Herefordshire. In August 1879 he married Elizabeth Anne Rowland, but died suddenly of peritonitis a month after his wedding. His widow inherited the *Diary*, but is said to have destroyed two large sections of it for personal reasons; of the twenty-two remaining notebooks, all but three were destroyed by an elderly niece of Kilvert's. The three volumes were first published in 1938–40.

Lees-Milne, James (1908–   ) Educated at Eton and Magdalen College, Oxford, from 1931 to 1935 he was private secretary to the 1st Baron Lloyd. From 1935 to 1936 he worked for Reuters, and from then until 1966 was on the staff of the National Trust, acting as its adviser on historic buildings from 1951. He has published many books on history and historic buildings.

Leeves, Edward (c.1795–c.1871) Brought up at Tortington, near Arundel in Sussex, Leeves moved as a young man to Venice, where he spent most of his life. In 1849 the threat of an Austrian invasion made him return to England. In London he met and fell in love with Jack Brand, a trooper in the Royal Horse Guards, who died of cholera shortly afterwards. Leeves returned heartbroken to Venice.

Longford, Francis Angier Pakenham, (7th Earl of) (1905–   ) Educated at Eton and New College, Oxford. From 1932 to 1946 he lectured in politics at Oxford, and was a prospective parliamentary Labour candidate in 1938. He held many Government positions, Parliamentary Under-Secretary to the War Office from 1946 to 1947, Minister of Civil Aviation from 1948 to 1951, First Lord of the Admiralty 1951, Lord Privy Seal and Leader of the House of Lords from 1964 to 1968, Secretary of State for the Colonies from 1965 to 1966. Lord Longford has published several religious and historical biographies.

Lowe, Roger (?–1679) An apprentice to a South Lancashire mercer in Aston-in-Makerfield, he was a zealous Presbyterian and unofficial notary of Aston. He kept a diary between 1663 and 1674.

Lowndes, Marie Belloc (1868–1947) Born in France, she was the daughter of Louis Belloc, a French barrister, and sister of Hilaire Belloc. She was brought to London after her father's death in 1872, and by 1887 was working on the *Pall Mall Gazette*. She married Frederick Lowndes, and became a well-known writer of novels and plays.

Machyn, Henry (1498?–1563?) A merchant taylor and funeral furnisher, Machyn lived in the London parish of Trinity the Little. A fervent Catholic, he lived through the reigns of Edward VI, Mary and Elizabeth. His diary records details of funerals, pageants, revels and executions. There were plenty of the last during Mary's reign – in one 1554 entry he records the hanging and quartering of fifty-seven people in different parts of London. Machyn kept his diary from 1550 to 1563. He makes few personal references; when he does he refers to himself in the third person. He mentions his own birthday twice, but gives two different dates for it. His diary is much used by literary scholars to establish London speech of the time (for example, Machyn writes 'welwet' and 'wacabond', rather in the style of Sam Weller).

Macready, William (1793–1873) The son of an Irish actor-manager, Macready was educated at Rugby and intended for a legal career. But following his father's financial difficulties, the young Macready started acting in the family company. He played Romeo at Birmingham in 1810, and Hamlet in Newcastle the next year. In 1816 he first appeared at Covent Garden, and by 1819 was established as Kean's rival, particularly in the major tragic roles. In 1837 he successfully took over the management of Covent Garden, and from 1841 to 1843 managed Drury Lane. He continued to act in the provinces, France and America. At his last appearance in the States in 1849, there were riots, fomented by his jealous American rival, Edwin Forrest. Macready retired from the stage in 1851, and died at Cheltenham. His diaries were first published in 1875.

Manningham, John (*c.*1580–1622) Manningham entered the Middle Temple as a student in 1597, and was called to the degree of utter barrister in 1605. He lived at Bradbourne in Kent. His diary, kept from March 1601 to April 1603, records anecdotes and observations, as well as making famous references to Shakespeare.

Mansfield, Katherine (pseudonym of Kathleen Mansfield Beauchamp) (1888–1923) Born in New Zealand, she was educated at Queen's College, London, from 1903 to 1906. She returned to New Zealand to study music, but came back to London in 1908. She married in 1909, but left her husband soon after and gave birth to a stillborn baby by another man. In 1911 she met John Middleton Murry, whom she married in 1918. Only three collections of her short stories were published in her lifetime, but they attracted attention for their originality and Chekhovian influences. From 1916 she knew she had tuberculosis, and subsequently travelled much for her health. She died at an institute run by Gurdjieff at Fontainebleau.

Moore, Thomas (1779–1852) Born in Dublin, Moore was educated there at Trinity College, and then entered the Middle Temple. In 1803 he was appointed admiralty registrar in Bermuda, but soon relinquished the post to a deputy. In 1811 he married the actress Bessy Dyke. His musical talent brought him an entrée to society, and from 1801 to 1834 Moore continued to produce his *Irish Melodies*, and in 1817 his *Lalla Rookh* was published. Two years later his deputy in Bermuda defaulted, leaving Moore with a debt of £6,000, and the poet had to leave England to escape arrest. He lived in Italy and France until the debt was repaid, returning to England in 1822. In 1824 he sanctioned the burning of the *Memoirs* of Byron (*q.v.*), which had been entrusted to him, but he later wrote a *Life* of the poet, who had been a great friend. In 1835 he was awarded a literary pension, but his later years were overshadowed by the loss of his two sons and mental decay.

Mordaunt, Viscountess (*c.*1630–79) Granddaughter of the 1st Earl of Monmouth, Elizabeth Carey married John, Viscount Mordaunt during the Interregnum. She helped her husband support the Royalist cause, and in June 1658 successfully bribed the jury trying him for high treason. She bore him five sons and two daughters. She was a devout high churchwoman, and much of her journal takes the form of prayers.

Morris, Dr Claver (1659–1727) Born at Caundle Bishop in Dorset where his father was rector, Morris was educated at New Hall, Oxford. He took his BA in 1679 and MD in 1691. In 1683 he became an extra licenciate of the Royal College of Physicians. He was married three times. In 1685, after his first marriage, he set up as a physician in Wells, and continued to practise in that area for the rest of his life.

Moseley, Sydney (1888–1961) He joined the *Daily Express* in 1910, and subsequently went to Cairo, where he edited English newspapers and was correspondent for the *New York Times*. He founded the *Southend Times*, and contested the parliamentary seat of Southend-on-Sea in 1924. The author of many publications, he was influential as a writer about the early days of television.

Muggeridge, Malcolm (1903–) Educated at Selwyn College, Cambridge. In 1927 he married Katherine Dobbs. From 1927 to 1930, he lectured at the Egyptian University in Cairo. Thereafter he held a variety of journalistic posts: from 1930 to 1932 he was on the editorial staff of the *Manchester Guardian* and its Moscow correspondent from 1932 to 1933; from 1934 to 1935 assistant editor of the *Calcutta Statesman*; from 1935 to 1936 on the editorial staff of the *Evening Standard*; from 1946 to 1947 Washington correspondent for the *Daily Telegraph* and its deputy editor from 1950 to 1952; from 1953 to 1957 editor of *Punch*. He served as a major in the intelligence corps during the Second World War. He gained fame both as a writer and television personality.

Newcombe, The Reverend Henry (1627–95) Educated at Cambridge, Newcombe was ordained a Presbyterian minister in 1648. He became rector of Gawsworth in 1650, subsequently living in Manchester. He kept a diary for most of his life, recording his duties and spiritual feelings, but only the section from 30 September 1661 till 29 September 1663 has survived.

Newton, The Reverend Benjamin (1761–1830) Educated at Cambridge, Newton received his MA in 1786. He held various livings, first as vicar of Devynnock, Brecknockshire, then in 1799 of Bedwyn, Wiltshire, and in 1800 of Norton St Philip in Somerset. From 1814 till 1840 he was rector of Wath, near Ripon in Yorkshire. He was chaplain to the Duke of Portland and magistrate for the North Riding of Yorkshire.

Nicolson, Harold (1886–1968) Born in Tehran, he was educated at Wellington and Balliol College, Oxford. He married Vita Sackville-West, with whom he created the gardens at Sissinghurst. After a controversial diplomatic career, he became a journalist in 1929. He was an MP from 1935 to 1945, a junior minister in Churchill's wartime Government, and was well known as a writer, critic, journalist and broadcaster. His complete diary, kept from 1930 to 1964, runs to three million words.

Orton, Joe (1933–67) Born in Leicester, Orton left school at sixteen and went to the Royal Academy of Dramatic Art two years later. There he met Kenneth Halliwell, with whom he lived for the rest of his life. In 1962 they were both jailed for six months for defacing library books. In 1964 Orton's first play *The Ruffian on the Stair* was broadcast, and *Entertaining Mr Sloane* appeared in the West End. Orton's reputation increased with other plays until he was battered to death by Halliwell, who afterwards committed suicide.

Partridge, Frances (1900–) Educated at Bedales and Newnham College, Cambridge, she worked in David Garnett's and Francis Birrell's London bookshop, which was a centre for the Bloomsbury Group. In 1933 she married Ralph Partridge, a friend of Lytton Strachey. She lived at Ham Spray – the house in Wiltshire bought in 1924 by Ralph and

Strachey where Strachey had died – for thirty years. Her husband died in 1960.

Pepys, Samuel (1633–1703) The son of a London tailor, Pepys was educated at St Paul's School and Magdalene College, Cambridge. In 1655 he married Elizabeth St Michel, daughter of a French Huguenot exile. They had no children and she died in 1669. Pepys was a naval administrator who became Secretary to the Admiralty in 1686. In 1679 he became MP for Harwich and in 1684 President of the Royal Society. The revolution of 1688 put an end to his career. His diary was kept in shorthand from 1 January 1660 till 29 May 1669, and was discontinued because Pepys feared for his eyesight. It was first deciphered by the Reverend John Smith in 1825 and edited for publication by Lord Braybrooke. The full, unbowdlerized text did not appear until the edition by R. Latham and W. Matthews (1970–1983).

Pym, Barbara (1913–80) Born in Oswestry, she was educated at Liverpool College, Huyton, and St Hilda's College, Oxford. During the Second World War joined the WRNS and worked in naval censorship. Later she was employed at the International African Institute as an editorial assistant and worked there for many years. In 1950 her first novel to be published, *Some Tame Gazelle*, came out, to be followed by five more, until the changing attitudes of the 1960s led to rejection of her subsequent work. She remained unpublished until 1977, when a *Times Literary Supplement* list, in which Philip Larkin and Lord David Cecil both named Barbara Pym as one of the most underrated novelists of the century, led to a revival of interest in her work, publication of a new book and reissues of her old ones. She kept diaries, with occasional breaks, from 1931.

Raikes, Thomas (1777–1848) Educated at Eton, Raikes entered his father's merchant business, but later became a socialite, gambler, dandy and friend of Beau Brummell. He visited the German courts, The Hague, Paris, Russia and Ireland, living abroad from 1833 to 1841 because of financial troubles. He kept a diary from 1831 to 1847 in Paris and London.

Reith, John (created Baron 1940) (1889–1971) Educated at the Royal Technical College, Glasgow, Reith spent five years in an engineering apprenticeship. He served during the First World War, rising to the rank of major. In 1922 he became the first general manager of the BBC, its managing director in 1923, and director-general from 1927 to 1938. From 1940 to 1942 he was Minister of Information, Transport, Works and Planning. He was involved in Commonwealth Telecommunications from 1945 to 1950, and worked in various development corporations from 1946 till 1964.

Ritchie, Charles (1906–   ) Born in Halifax, Nova Scotia, he went to university in Canada and Oxford. In 1934 he joined the Canadian Department of External Affairs, and in 1939 was posted to London as second secretary. In 1954 he was Canadian ambassador to Germany; from 1958 to 1962 permanent representative to the United Nations; from 1962 to 1966 ambassador to Washington; and high commissioner to London from 1967 to 1971, when he retired from the foreign service.

Robinson, Henry Crabb (1775–1867) Born at Bury St Edmunds, the son of a tanner, Robinson was articled to a Colchester attorney. From 1800 to 1805 he studied in Germany, where he met Goethe and Schiller. He was in Spain from 1807 to 1809, as a war correspondent for *The Times*. He was called to the bar in 1813 and practised until 1828. He was one of the founders of London University and an early member of the Athenaeum Club. His diary, which he kept from the end of the eighteenth century, was first published in 1869.

Rutty, Dr John (1698–1774) Born in Wiltshire of Quaker parents and educated at Leyden, Rutty took a medical degree in 1723, and from 1724 practised in Dublin. His diary, which he kept from 1753 till the end of his life, was chiefly concerned with his spiritual life.

Sassoon, Siegfried (1886–1967) Educated at Marlborough and Clare College, Cambridge, he left the latter without taking a degree, although he later became an honorary fellow. He was brought up by his mother as a country gentleman and encouraged to write poetry. He fought in the trenches with distinction during the First World War, though he later threw away the MC he was awarded. His disapproval of the war was expressed in some of his finest poems. His reputation as a poet and prose writer grew through the 1920s and 1930s, and his writing reflected his interest in hunting and the countryside. His poetry grew increasingly religious and in 1957 he became a Roman Catholic.

Scott, Sir Walter (1771–1832) Born and educated in Edinburgh, Scott turned from the bar to literature when collecting Border country ballads.

His first writings were translations from the German, then he moved to poetry, and finally to novels. *The Lay of the Last Minstrel*, published in 1805, made him famous. In 1813 he turned down the offer of the laureateship, and from then on concentrated on writing novels, which were published anonymously to huge acclaim. He was created a baronet in 1820, but in 1826 he was faced with financial ruin when the publishing partnership he had entered into with John Ballantyne in 1809 collapsed. Scott worked even harder to pay off the huge accumulation of debts, shortening his own life in the process. He started his *Journal* in 1825, and it was first published in 1890.

Shelley, Mary Wollstonecraft (1797–1851) The daughter of William Godwin and Mary Wollstonecraft, she eloped with Shelley in 1814, travelling with him to Switzerland and later Italy. She married him in 1816 after the suicide of his first wife. All their children except one, Percy, died in infancy. Mary returned to England in 1823 after her husband's death. She is remembered as the author of *Frankenstein*, published in 1818, but wrote other novels, biographies and short stories, as well as editing her husband's works.

Shore, Emily (1819–39) Born at Bury St Edmunds, Emily was the eldest daughter of a free-thinking curate. She was precociously learned, writing poetry, fiction and treatises on ancient and natural history. She was twenty when she died of consumption in Madeira on 7 July 1839. Her sisters, also of literary bent, edited a selection from her *Journal*, which was published in 1891.

Skinner, The Reverend John (1772–1839?) Educated at Trinity College, Cambridge, Skinner was ordained deacon in 1797 and priest in 1799. In 1800 his uncle bought him the living of Camerton, near the Somerset coalfield. Skinner's wife and other members of his family died of consumption. He was a keen antiquarian.

Slingsby, Sir Henry (1601–58) MP for Knaresborough, Slingsby was one of the fifty-nine who voted against the Bill of Attainder against Lord Strafford. He fought for the King against Parliament at York, Marston Moor, Naseby and Newark. In 1655 he was implicated in the Royalist plot at Hull. He was condemned to be hanged, drawn and quartered, but was actually beheaded on Tower Hill. His diary covers the period from 1638 to 1648.

Stevens, The Reverend William Bagshaw (1756–1800) The son of an apothecary and surgeon, Stevens was brought up in Abingdon and educated at Magdalen College, Oxford. He published a book of poems in 1775. Round that time he was appointed as usher to Repton School. When he was ordained deacon in 1778 he was promoted to assistant master and became domestic chaplain to Sir Robert Burdett at Foremark. Stevens was unlucky in love, being twice rejected in favour of richer suitors. He became master of Repton and died of a stroke after a 'fit of immoderate laughter' at the antics of an Italian and his monkey. He started his journal on 15 March 1792 and continued it until 1799.

Strother (1763–?) At the age of fifteen he went from Hull to York, where he was a draper's assistant for six years. His diary was kept from 8 August 1784 to 17 July 1785. He gave it up through modesty and lack of time.

Sullivan, Sir Arthur Seymour (1842–1900) The son of a military musician, Sullivan was a chorister and won the Mendelssohn Scholarship, which enabled him to study at the Royal Academy of Music and the Leipzig Conservatory. He was a conductor, composer and organist, who wrote an enormous variety of music, but is best remembered for his collaborations with W. S. Gilbert on their famous run of comic operas which continued for nearly thirty years (with a break from 1890 to 1893 when they quarrelled, reputedly over a carpet at the Savoy Theatre). Sullivan was knighted in 1883. Frequently ill, he died suddenly and was buried in St Paul's Cathedral.

Symonds, John Addington (1840–93) Educated at Harrow and then Balliol College, Oxford, he took a double first in classics. Tuberculosis frequently forced him to live abroad, in Italy and Switzerland. In 1864 he married Janet North, but increasingly recognized his homosexuality. He wrote works on art, poets and travel, and translated much Greek and Italian poetry. He kept an intermittent diary from the age of eighteen, and a more continuous one from 1860 till his death.

Temple, The Reverend William Johnstone (1739–96) Educated at Edinburgh University and Trinity Hall, Cambridge, he abandoned law for the church after the bankruptcy of his father. An essayist and lifelong friend and correspondent of Boswell, he also knew Johnson and Gray. In 1766 he was ordained deacon and priest, and became rector of Mamhead, Exeter. The next year he married a rich wife, but continued to experience financial difficulties. In 1775 he was chaplain to Bishop Keppel, and from 1776 until his death was vicar of the wealthy living of Gluvias in Cornwall. He fathered eleven children.

Thomlinson, The Reverend John (1692–1762) Educated at St John's College, Cambridge, he became curate of Rothbury and then rector of Glenfield in Leicestershire. He unashamedly sought a rich wife, eventually marrying his patron's daughter. His diary is in three parts: the first being extracts from an earlier one; the second, from 1717 to 1719, complete; and the third, from 1721 to 1722, less consecutive.

Toynbee, Philip (1916–81) Educated at Rugby and Christ Church, Oxford, he was editor of the *Birmingham Town Crier* from 1938 to 1939. During the Second World War he was in the intelligence corps, the Ministry of Economic Warfare, and on the staff of SHAEF France and Belgium. He was literary editor with Contact Publications and, from 1950, a foreign correspondent on the staff of the *Observer*. Also a novelist, he married twice and had five children.

Turner, Thomas (1729–93) Born at Groombridge in Kent. By 1754 he was living in East Hoathly in Sussex, working as a schoolmaster, but gave this up to open a general store. He was twice married. His diary was kept from 2 February 1754 until 3 July 1765.

Victoria, Queen (1819–1901) The daughter of George III's son, the Duke of Kent, she succeeded her uncle William IV in 1837. In 1840 she married her cousin Prince Albert of Saxe-Coburg and Gotha, and bore him nine children. After his death in 1861 she went into near-seclusion for some years. She was the longest reigning English monarch and kept a detailed, almost daily diary from the age of thirteen.

Waugh, Evelyn (1903–66) Born in Hampstead, Waugh was educated at Lancing College and Hertford College, Oxford. After some unhappy years as a schoolteacher, he published his first hugely successful novel, *Decline and Fall*, in 1928. As well as being a novelist, he established himself as a journalist and travel writer. During the Second World War he served in the Royal Marines and his experiences in Crete and Yugoslavia provided the background for his trilogy, *Sword of Honour*. He was twice married, and in 1930 became a Roman Catholic. After his second marriage in 1937, he lived in the west country. His diaries were first published in 1976.

Welch, (Maurice) Denton (1915–48) Born in Shanghai, he spent some of his childhood in China before being educated at Repton and Goldsmith's School of Art. His first ambition was to become a painter, but a bicycle accident in 1935 left him severely crippled and an invalid for the rest of his life. He published an autobiographical work, *Maiden Voyage*, in 1943, and also wrote a novel and short stories.

Wesley, Charles (1707–88) At Christ Church, Oxford, his earnest system of religious study earned the description 'Methodist'. He was ordained priest in 1735 before a mission to Georgia, but dated his conversion from Whit Sunday, 21 May 1738. He preached in London, but then became an itinerant preacher and lieutenant to his brother, John (*q.v.*). Charles married in 1749, and thereafter his wife accompanied him on his travels. He retired through ill health in 1761. He is said to have written 6,500 hymns. His diary was begun in January 1729, kept regularly for twenty years, and then irregularly till 1756.

Wesley, John (1703–91) Educated at Christ Church, Oxford, he was ordained deacon in 1725 and priest in 1728. From 1727 to 1729 he assisted his father, also a clergyman, and then returned to Oxford as a tutor. In 1735 he went on the mission to Georgia, still at that time a high churchman, and returned in 1738. Three days after his brother Charles (*q.v.*), on 24 May 1738, he underwent conversion and Methodism was born. His new ideas were rejected by the established clergy, so Wesley began his travels, preaching in the open air to huge crowds of the poorest members of society. This he continued throughout his life, covering 250,000 miles and preaching over 40,000 sermons. In 1749 his brother Charles prevented him from making an unwise marriage, but he eventually married in 1751, though his wife left him twenty years later. His diaries, which record the founding of the Holy Club (Methodism) at Oxford, were begun in 1725, but kept more fully from 1735 to 1790.

West, Arthur Graeme (1891–1917) Educated at Highgate School, Blundells and Balliol College, Oxford, West enlisted as a private in the Public Schools Battalion in 1915 and was sent to France. He was commissioned as an officer, and was killed by a sniper's bullet.

Windham, William (1750–1810) Educated at Eton, Glasgow and University College, Oxford, he became MP for Norwich in 1784. He left the Whigs to become Secretary of War under Pitt in 1794. In 1801 he went out with Pitt and lost his Norwich seat, but was soon elected for St

Mawes in Cornwall. In 1806 he became Secretary of State for War and the Colonies. He was a member of the famous Literary Club, and knew Burke and Johnson, standing by the latter's deathbed. He married in 1798 and died after a tumour operation. His diary, kept from 1784 to 1810, was published in 1866, revealing a surprisingly vacillating personality in a man who had had so much public success.

Witts, The Reverend Francis Edward (1783–1854) He was rector of Upper Slaughter in Gloucestershire from 1808 to 1854 and vicar of Stanway from 1814 to 1854.

Woodforde, The Reverend James (1740–1803) Born at Ansford in Somerset, he was educated at Winchester and New College, Oxford, of which he was elected a fellow in 1761. From 1763 to 1773 he took various curacies in Somerset, before returning to New College, of which he became sub-warden. In 1774 he was presented with the living of Weston Longville in Norfolk, but did not take up residence there until 1776. His niece Nancy lived with him from 1779 till his death. In 1774 he proposed to a girl who jilted him for someone richer, and never married. His diary, under the title *The Diary of a Country Parson*, was published in five volumes between 1924 and 1931.

Woolf, Virginia (1882–1941) The daughter of Sir Leslie Stephen, she was educated at home. After her father's death in 1904, Virginia, with her sister Vanessa and her brothers, moved to Bloomsbury, where they formed the focus of the Bloomsbury Group. In 1912 she married Leonard Woolf and in 1915 published her first novel, *The Voyage Out*. In 1917 Leonard and Virginia founded the Hogarth Press. Her novels grew increasingly innovative and influential, and she also wrote essays and criticism. Throughout her life she was plagued by recurrent mental illness and finally drowned herself in the River Ouse near her home at Rodmell in Sussex. She was an indefatigable letter-writer and diarist. Her diaries, published in five volumes between 1977 and 1984, vividly demonstrate the changing moods of the creative process.

Wordsworth, Dorothy (1771–1855) The sister of William Wordsworth, she lived with various relatives after her mother's death in 1777 until in 1795 she joined William at Racedown in Dorset. They continued living together, through his marriage, until his death. They moved to Alfoxden in Somerset to be near Coleridge, but in 1799 settled in Dove Cottage, Grasmere. In April 1829 Dorothy became ill and in 1835 suffered a severe mental breakdown, from which she never fully recovered. Her journals of life with William and various travels and expeditions have made her a literary figure in her own right, and it seems very likely that her brother made use of them for his work.

Wyndham, Joan (1922–   ) She studied art in London during the Second World War, and then joined the WAAF. After the war she became involved in a variety of ventures, including opening Oxford's first espresso bar, catering for pop festivals and actors at the Royal Court Theatre, and working in Fleet Street on women's magazines. She is married with two daughters.

Wynne, Eugenia (1780–?) The sister of Elizabeth Fremantle (*q.v.*) and Harriet Wynne (*q.v.*), she travelled in Europe with the rest of the family. In 1806 she met and married Robert Campbell of Skipness. They had numerous children and lived in Scotland until his death. Her diary is less full than that of her sister, Elizabeth. They both started them on the same day, but Eugenia's peters out after her marriage.

Wynne, Harriet (1784–?) She married James Hamilton of Kames. Her diary was started while she was a girl at a Catholic boarding school.

Yonge, Walter (1581?–1649) A Puritan, the son of a merchant, he was educated at Magdalen College, Oxford and in 1600 entered the Middle Temple. He became a JP for Devonshire, and in 1628 sheriff. He was MP for Honiton and, during the Civil War, victualler for the navy. His diary is in two parts, from 1604 to 1627 and 1642 to 1645.

Index of diarists